Praise for Jo Ann Brown

"An amazing story of unfolding love while the past comes back to haunt you. The question is will love prevail in this Amish setting where community and family are involved in all the important decisions of life."
—Jerry Eicher, author of The St. Lawrence County Amish series

"From the moment I met Jo Ann Brown's characters in A Hope for Healing, I was invested. Then riveted. Spend a little time with them in Bliss Valley. You won't want to leave."
—Adina Senft, USA TODAY bestselling author of the Whinburg Township Amish series

"A Hope for Healing is heartfelt and heartwarming. Jo Ann Brown never fails to deliver the perfect Amish tale."
—Pamela Desmond Wright, author of The Amish Bachelor's Bride

"Jo Ann Brown writes a tightly researched, authentic Amish novel. A Hope for Healing...will make you gasp, jump, and keep turning the pages, as Brown turns the Amish novel expectations upside down. You'll yearn for Gideon and Rosemary to finally find healing in each other's arms, and you'll be anxiously looking for any more books by this bestselling author—guaranteed!"
—Patricia Johns, Publishers Weekly bestselling author of Their Amish Secret

"A beautiful and emotional journey of love and faith by a gifted author."
—Samantha Price, USA TODAY bestselling author

"Master storyteller...Jo Ann Brown crafted a warm and emotionally satisfying story! Reading it is like escaping to Amish country deep in Bliss Valley."
—Tracy Fredrychowski, USA TODAY bestselling author of the Women of Lawrence County series

"Jo Ann Brown's masterful writing and compelling characters capture your heart while leaving a lingering reminder of what faith, hope and love are truly all about."
—Cathy Liggett, Publishers Weekly bestselling author

Also available from Jo Ann Brown
and Love Inspired

Secrets of Bliss Valley

A Wish for Home
A Promise of Forgiveness
A Search for Redemption

Visit the Author Profile page at LoveInspired.com for more titles.

A HOPE
FOR HEALING

Jo Ann Brown

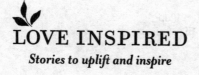

LOVE INSPIRED
Stories to uplift and inspire

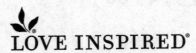

LOVE INSPIRED®

Stories to uplift and inspire

Recycling programs for this product may not exist in your area.

ISBN-13: 978-1-335-66258-3

A Hope for Healing

Love Inspired
22 Adelaide St. West, 41st Floor
Toronto, Ontario M5H 4E3, Canada
www.LoveInspired.com

Printed in U.S.A.

For Sunnie and her feline friend Shadow,
who inspired so much of this story.

A
HOPE
FOR HEALING

Chapter One

Whoever had first said that silence was golden must have been a genius.

As he drove his wagon along the road rising and falling among the undulating hills covered with January snow, Gideon Wingard felt his shoulders loosen from the tension that had been laid, day by day, upon them. That heaviness had eased with each mile between him and Smoketown.

Now in the heart of Bliss Valley as far south of Route 30 as Smoketown was north, the only sounds were birdsong and the clip-clop of Domino's hooves on the asphalt. No questions were being fired at him by a loving *mamm*, two doting *grossmammis* and four maiden *aentis* each time he walked into the farmhouse where they lived in different wings. No queries were buzzing around him from his five older sisters. Each time they visited, with or without their husbands and families, questions were aimed in his direction.

"Have you found someone to marry yet?" was usually the first question followed by "Gideon, if you don't find a wife soon, all the *gut* choices will be gone. Do you want to have to settle for the last apple on the tree?"

No one gave him a chance to answer before the inevitable comment followed: "I know a nice girl who's looking for a husband. *Komm* over to supper on Saturday, and I'll introduce you."

He always gave the noncommittal answer his sisters had learned meant he wasn't interested. Why couldn't they get it through their heads—and their hearts—that a man needed to be able to provide for a wife and family before he decided to have them? It had to be *his* choice.

Silence *was* golden. Or near silence, he corrected himself with a smile.

The only voice was his thoughts. It was filled with a mixture of excitement at the possible adventure ahead of him... and a wagonload of guilt. He knew the latter was silly. His five sisters were married, and they and their husbands and *kinder* would keep an eye on *Mamm* and the others at home.

One of his sisters had drawn him aside before he left and asked him in a whisper, "If you hear of a farm for sale in Bliss Valley, will you let me know straightaway? We've heard *gut* things about the bishop there."

Gideon had nodded. He wasn't the only one unhappy with the changes their local bishop was trying to institute. There were rumblings about the district splitting or families deciding to leave. Their bishop was trying to insist young people be baptized a year after they finished school at fourteen so there would be no running around time before they became members of the *Leit*. That wasn't the tradition in Lancaster County, and people weren't happy with the abrupt change.

Property wasn't easy to come by in the county where more *Englisch* development seemed to get underway every day. Gideon looked across the snow-draped fields on either side of the road. The meadows followed the hills before dropping toward a covered bridge across a sleepy creek. Were any of the farms for sale? Unlikely. Most plain families had probably lived on the land since their ancestors arrived three hundred years ago.

Picking up a piece of paper with an address written on it, he glanced at the mailbox he was passing. 577 Bliss Valley Road. Not too far now.

His hands tightened on the reins, and he felt Domino's reaction.

"Sorry, old friend," he called, then laughed. If anyone overheard him chatting to the black-and-white horse as if Domino were human, they might think he'd lost his mind.

Gideon couldn't submerge his eager anticipation to reach his destination. The *Englischer* who'd come to their farm in Smoketown to fix the stationary engine that ran the lift carrying the chopped corn to the top of the silo, had told him about a widow in Bliss Valley who was looking to supplement her farm income by renting a building close to the road. The man had been able to describe the exterior of the building and give him a name and an address, but no more.

"You'll see Mrs. Mishler's place about a mile past that new quilt store," the man had said. "It's right on the road that bisects Bliss Valley a mile or two south of Strasburg. You can't miss it."

Gideon gave a disgusted chuckle as he steered Domino around an ice-covered pothole at the edge of the road. His first clue should have been when the man reassured him it was impossible to miss the building. That might be true, but Gideon had had to stop twice to get directions after he'd left Strasburg and driven south. Road signs were down at a couple of intersections, and road names sometimes disappeared and then reappeared in a mile or so without explanation. He was accustomed to the familiar roads around Smoketown, but he'd never been to Bliss Valley.

Seeing a sign set in front of a small cottage by the road, he guessed it must be the quilt shop the *Englischer* had spoken of. "Quilts Are Bliss" stated the hand-painted board leaning against the porch railing. The white building looked as if it could use paint, but the wooden steps were clean as were the pair of rockers on the porch. A cat was wrapped around itself with its tail against its nose, sleeping in the sun and ignoring the cold.

On the other side of the road, he noticed what looked like a shop in what must have been the barn that once belonged to the small house. The building retained hints of its former red, but most of the boards had weathered to gray. Its sign announced "Bulk Grocery Store." He'd need to visit the store for food.

If the building for rent wasn't available… No, he wasn't going to let negative thoughts pierce his brain. He was about to grab on to the future he wanted.

When the front passenger-side wheel bounced over a heave in the road, Gideon focused on driving. Another difference. At home, he could trust Domino to find his way.

If all worked out as he hoped, he'd soon be considered a neighbor in Bliss Valley. The residents along the crisscrossing country roads would come to his shop when they needed to have work done on harnesses, tack and saddles. He hoped to make new ones as well, but to begin with, he'd concentrate on repairs.

A mailbox ahead on the right was simple, black with white numerals painted on it. 623 Bliss Valley Road.

The address he'd been given.

Drawing back on the reins, he slowed the horse as they approached a farm lane heading up a hill toward a white farmhouse that in the summer would be hidden behind a trio of maple trees. Now their branches were bare silhouettes against the blue sky. He paid no attention to the house or the barn and silos beyond it. Instead, his eyes focused on the fieldstone building across the farm lane from the mailbox.

That must be the space for rent. It was a simple box with a slate roof. A pair of windows shared a wall with a door. None offered a clue to what was inside. It was tempting to jump out and peek in the windows, but he couldn't act like a giddy boy if he wanted the widow to take him seriously.

Driving along the gentle rise of the farm lane edged by snowbanks, he stopped the wagon holding his supplies and tools under an oak tree that had a few yellow leaves clinging to it. One drifted down to hang on the brim of his black hat as he stepped out.

He brushed it away as he appraised the house. White clapboard covered half of it. The other half had been covered with the same fieldstone as the building by the road. Chimneys topped the roof at both ends, and simple windows glittered in the sunshine. However, it was the collection of porches that made the house unique. Two, on the narrower sides of the building, must be accessed from the second floor while the one on the front and smaller ones on the side and back were at ground level. A *dawdi haus* at the far side of the house was connected by a breezeway.

The whole place had an empty feeling. No clothes hung on the pulley line between the house and the main barn. He saw a single horse in the nearby meadow, but no other stock. The cows must be inside. There was too much snow for them to graze outside. A couple of men worked among trees farther up the hill beyond some other buildings, but he wasn't sure if the orchard belonged to this farm.

Gideon sighed. He'd been told the farm was owned by a

widow, so maybe that was why the place seemed forsaken and deserted. Even so, he'd expected to see signs of *kinder* and work around the outbuildings.

Standing under the tree wasn't getting him anywhere. After telling Domino he wouldn't be long, he strode toward the house. He didn't consider going to the front door. If Bliss Valley was anything like the district where he'd been raised, nobody came to the front door except *Englischers* and funeral directors.

There was a single step up to the small back porch. A snow shovel leaned against a storage cupboard built into one corner. It was ruffled on the bottom as if it had struck too many stones. Like everything on this farm, it appeared to be barely holding on.

He looked at the closed door in front of him. A window beside it was covered by a dark green shade, surprising him. Why wasn't the widow welcoming sunshine into the house on such a chilly day?

"It's none of your business," he muttered, reminding himself he wasn't there to get to know the widow. He was there to see if her building by the road would work for his shop.

He rapped his knuckles on the door. He wasn't used to knocking. In Smoketown, he knew his neighbors and they knew him. Nobody bothered with knocking. They opened the back door and called out to discover if anyone was inside the house. If there was, an invitation to enter came back.

But he didn't know anyone in Bliss Valley.

When nobody answered, he knocked again, harder and longer this time. Was the widow hard of hearing? Or was the house empty? He glanced over his shoulder at the barn. Maybe someone was out there. As he was about to go and find out, the door opened.

"*Ja?*" asked a distracted woman.

He took in the sight of her. She was tall, almost as tall as he was. Her light brown hair had escaped from her bun and heart-shaped *kapp* to curl in tight spirals along her jaw. Nobody would call her pretty because her nose was a bit long and dark crescents shadowed her wide-spaced gray eyes that emphasized her round face. She looked exhausted and drained. Yet, he couldn't pull his gaze away. There was something intriguing about her features, even when her delicately curved lips were tilted in a frown.

An impatient frown, he realized when she repeated, *"Ja? Can I help you?"* Her grimace deepened as she tried to clean her hands with a dish towel. They were covered with some sort of sticky dough she didn't want to get on the black dress she wore beneath an apron of the same color.

Bread, he guessed.

"I'm looking for Mrs. Mishler," he hurried to reply when her eyes narrowed as if she wondered why he'd knocked on the door and then stood there saying nothing.

"You've found her. I'm Rosemary Mishler." She continued to wipe her hands on the towel, but bits of bread dough clung to her slender fingers. "Can I help you?"

She was the widow who was looking to rent one of her outbuildings? He'd envisioned an older woman, not a woman in her twenties. Most especially not this woman whose face fascinated him with its strong lines and assertive chin. If he had an ounce of sense, he'd apologize for interrupting her and turn on his heel and go...

Go where? Back to Smoketown and the misguided match-makers in his family? He'd be *dumm* to return to that life. Wouldn't he always regret not giving himself a chance to chase his dream?

"Ja, you can help me," he said to answer the questions in his head. He needed a break from family machinations, no matter how well-intentioned they were. "My name is Gideon Wingard. I've been told you've got a place I can rent."

"For what?" Not a hint of a smile eased her expression.

"I want to open a tack shop."

She evaluated him with her cool stare as if trying to determine if he was being honest. Her gray eyes were assessing him without apology, and he wondered what she hoped to see—or not see. He could have assured her he always said what he meant, but why would she take a stranger's word?

Uncomfortable under her scrutiny, which seemed to find him lacking, he filled the silence by saying, "I saw the building by the road when I turned up the lane. I've been told that's the space you're renting."

He fought not to wince. He sounded like a *kind* begging for a treat. He was at the Mishler farm to do business. It was past time to put aside his amazement at how young and attractive Rosemary Mishler was and focus on making his dream come true.

"I don't know you," she replied, but she stopped trying to clean her hands. "Who sent you here?"

"Nobody sent me. Word moves quickly along the Amish grapevine, ain't so?"

"*Ja.*"

"If the building still is unrented, can I look at it?"

She glanced past him to where Domino was standing by the wagon. "I guess so. Give me a moment."

The door shut in his face. He took an instinctive step back. What a change from his chatty family! Rosemary Mishler was a woman of few words, and she acted as if she hated wasting a single one on him.

Not wanting to duck his head to try to peer past the shade on the window by the door to see if she was going to return, he stepped off the porch and walked to his wagon. He sighed. This wasn't an auspicious beginning to what he'd hoped would become a long-term business arrangement.

The door reopened as he reached the wagon. Looking over

his shoulder, he watched Rosemary cross the yard. She'd put on a heavy black coat and her bonnet. She walked with an easy elegance, but her posture made it clear she wished he'd go away.

"What did you say your name was?" she asked.

"Gideon. Gideon Wingard."

"Related to the Neal Wingards on the other side of the Bliss Valley Covered Bridge?"

"Most likely." The everyday practice of making connections through family and common friends was the beginning of any relationship among the plain people. It might be a *gut* sign she was thawing enough to consider him as a possible tenant. "All the Wingards are linked one way or another. However, I don't know any of the Wingard families in Bliss Valley."

Her eyes widened. "You aren't from Bliss Valley?"

"No. I'm from Smoketown." He took Domino by the reins and walked him and the wagon with them toward the road. "I assume if you rent me the building, I can put Domino in the field beside it."

"*Ja.* He'll keep my horse company." For the first time, a faint smile tugged at her lips. "I've noticed Misty watching the cows as if he'd like to join them. I figure he's lonely." The smile grew a bit wider, and he had to wonder what she'd look like without the darkness beneath her eyes. "Guess I should mention Misty's my buggy horse."

"I figured that." He gave her a grin.

Big mistake, because she lowered her eyes and strode past him toward the building as if looking at him was painful.

Don't be melodramatic, he warned himself. He'd said that often to his oldest sister who liked to make something out of nothing. He'd caught Rosemary Mishler in the midst of making bread, and she'd need to get back to it. It wasn't anything other than that.

"Aren't you coming?" she called back over her shoulder. For a moment, she sounded so much like his *mamm* that a flush of homesickness washed over him.

Gideon hadn't realized that he'd stopped in the middle of the road as his thoughts took off as fast as Domino liked to. Tugging on the horse, he murmured, "Guess she's not very patient, ain't so?"

The horse bobbed his head as if he understood, and Gideon had to smother his chuckle. If she noticed, Rosemary would think he was laughing at her, and in a way he was. She was so serious.

She's a widow, his brain whispered. *She may be sad rather than serious.*

The thought swept away his yearning to find humor in the situation. He'd seen his *mamm*'s grief in the years after his *daed* died. Did Rosemary have *kinder*? He'd seen no sign of that, so she might be alone in that big farmhouse. More alone than his *mamm* had been in the grim days after his *daed*'s fatal heart attack.

But he needed to find out if Rosemary had *kinder*. Youngsters could become a problem for his work. He had tools that could be very dangerous in a *kind*'s hands. His middle sister's youngest had nearly put out her eye with a sharp awl. That incident had been the final persuasion he'd needed to find a place of his own, far from the curious fingers of his nieces and nephews and their friends. If Rosemary had youngsters running around the farm, this arrangement would have to be temporary. He'd stay long enough to find another place to set up shop. He wasn't going to chance a *kind* being injured.

Sobered, Gideon drew the horse and wagon to a stop beside the small building. Knowing Domino would wait for him, he walked to where Rosemary was standing by the door.

When she glanced higher along the hill, he turned to follow her gaze. When one of the men working there looked in their direction and waved, she waved back. He heard a soft sigh sifting past her lips.

Again, he wanted to ask why, and again he halted himself. This was going to be a business arrangement. Nothing more.

He followed her into the building, his nose wrinkling at the cool, damp and dusty smell. He ignored the odor as he looked around. The space was what he'd been looking for. When Rosemary lifted the dark green shades, the windows offered views over the hills and fields. There would be room for his tools, his machinery and his worktables. One table already sat in the middle of the space. It was covered with papers, which he didn't disturb. If he rented the place, he would return them to Rosemary to dispose of as she wished.

Cupboards and two large closets could provide storage for his supplies of leather. A door opening at the rear of the space led to a small room with a metal bed on one side and a kitchen with a small stove, refrigerator and a sink with running water on the other. A chair and a table with a propane lamp on it were crammed in a corner. Seeing a roll-top tub through a half-opened door, he craned his neck to see a showerhead hung over one end of the tub. He doubted it was tall enough for him, but he'd make do.

Now sure he wanted to rent the building, he took time to look in the cupboards. He had long hours ahead of him to get his shop set up and find work. He didn't want to get too excited before he discovered what she expected him to pay for the space. If it was beyond what he could afford, he'd have to find another place.

Gideon hid his astonishment when Rosemary told him the rent was fifty dollars less than he'd assumed. He held out his hand. She hesitated a moment, then shook it.

A shimmer of something that reminded him of how the

air trembled when lightning cut through it flickered from her soft skin to his palm. He held her hand a moment too long, or maybe she held his.

Either way, they both jumped when a throat was cleared beyond the outer door. He saw two men standing there, two men who couldn't look less like each other. One was tall and thin; the other was shorter and as round as a millstone. The tall man had thick dark hair, and the squat man's head was almost bald. Neither man wore a beard, and their clothing bore signs of sweat and dirt.

The pair must have come down the hill at a near run. Why had they dropped what they were doing and rushed here?

Heat climbed Rosemary Mishler's cheeks. Calvin and LaVern couldn't have picked a worse time to snoop. She submerged the guilt at her uncharitable thoughts. No doubt, the two men had seen her hand in Gideon's. She didn't need their gossiping to create more rumors about her. The two of them had been Eddie's best friends. In fact, both had been hunting with Eddie the day he died. They'd offered consolation during the days leading to the funeral, and she'd appreciated their thoughtfulness until Calvin had tried to monopolize her time at the meal after Eddie was buried and LaVern had come calling the following day.

Forcing her gaze to her tenant, she saw he wasn't smiling, and she appreciated he didn't ply her with fake grins as LaVern did. Since Eddie's death, LaVern had made it clear, in his opinion, she should remarry as soon as possible, and her best choice for a husband would be LaVern Spaeger. Calvin had hinted he'd be interested in walking out with her as well, but she'd pretended not to notice. She had no interest in remarrying. How could she find another man who suited her as perfectly as Eddie had? He was—and would always be—the one and only love of her life.

She sighed. Maybe Calvin and LaVern saw preventing her from being alone as a kindness. Had Eddie asked them to take care of her if something happened to him? Both men had hinted that he had, but she wasn't sure whether to believe them. Her usual *gut* insight into other people was as foggy as a morning along the creek.

Before the shocked silence could go on too long, she locked her hands behind her back and squared her shoulders. "Gideon, these are two of my neighbors." She gestured toward the thinner man. "Calvin Hertzler. And that's LaVern Spaeger. This is Gideon Wingard. He's renting this building. On a trial basis." She saw Gideon's surprise at her statement, but she hurried on. "He will have three months to see if this is a *gut* location for him. A fair arrangement, ain't so?"

Gideon's brows lowered, but he didn't contradict her. She wanted to tell him she'd intended to suggest that probationary period, but had gotten interrupted by Calvin and LaVern's arrival.

"I think so," Gideon said, and she released the breath she'd been holding.

She drew in another quick breath as LaVern pushed inside, shoving her out of the way. She sensed Gideon tensing. From how eagerly he'd looked over the space when they came in, she guessed he was already thinking of it as *his* shop. She glanced over her shoulder.

A mistake, because her gaze was caught by Gideon's brown eyes. He was a *gut*-looking man, taller than she was. That wasn't common. Eddie had been tall, too. His height might have been the first thing that had attracted her to him. She was glad she'd accepted his invitation that first evening to take her home in his buggy because, otherwise, she might never have had the chance to discover he was the perfect match for her. He'd been a true gift from God, sharing her dreams of having their own farm and filling it with *kinder* who would work side by side with them and praise the Lord for the blessings He'd bestowed upon them.

Gideon cleared his throat, bursting her treasured memories like fragile soap bubbles. She wanted to gather them to her heart because they'd seldom emerged into the light during the four months since Eddie's death.

"What type of business?" demanded LaVern.

"Repairing harnesses and other tack." No hint of acrimony tainted Gideon's voice, and Rosemary guessed he'd met other people like LaVern, people who didn't hesitate to stick their noses into everyone else's business.

Looking around, the dark-haired man sniffed. "Smells like critters have been using this place for an outhouse."

Rosemary started to reply, but Gideon said, "A few open windows will air it out. Happens to places that have been closed for a while."

"This one has been shut since Eddie tripped over his own feet and shot himself." LaVern lifted papers off the table and glanced at them.

Rosemary heard gasps. One was hers and the other belonged to Gideon. In the doorway, Calvin looked ashen, his expression raw.

"LaVern…" Calvin's voice was taut.

"*Ja, ja.* Back to work." Striding to the door as if he owned the farm, he tossed over his shoulder, "See you around, Rosemary."

How dare LaVern be so heartless! Eddie had been his friend. She wanted to order LaVern off the farm and tell him never to come back, but her late husband would have cautioned her to turn the other cheek. Eddie had been a *gut* man, and she'd tried harder to emulate his ways since his death.

"Tell me he's one of a kind around here," Gideon said. "His words were trivial, but sounded like a threat."

Though she wanted to agree, because she'd told LaVern—multiple times—she wasn't interested in him courting her, she forced a fake smile. "LaVern doesn't always think before he speaks."

"But you let him help you on the farm?"

Wanting to ask him how *he* would deal with a man who wouldn't take no for an answer, she said, "The *Leit* has been helpful."

"*Ye shall not afflict any widow, or fatherless child. If thou afflict them in any wise, and they cry at all unto Me, I will surely hear their cry.* Did they preach those two verses from the twenty-second chapter of Exodus at your husband's funeral?"

She nodded.

"I heard them at my *daed*'s funeral, too. God expects His *kinder* to watch out for one another, but they're not an excuse to interfere with a mourning family. Does he—"

Not wanting to hear what he was about to ask, because she feared he'd seen the truth in her neighbors' motives, she cut him off with a stiff smile. "I think we're set, then. The rent is due the first day of each month. Of course, if the first falls on a Sunday, it's due the next day." She glanced out the window to make sure both LaVern and Calvin had already walked past the largest barn and were on their way toward the orchard. "If you don't have food for tonight, you're welcome to *komm* to the house."

"I'll be fine, but *danki*."

"*Gut.*" It was *gut*, because she needed some time alone after the surprising changes in her life in the past few minutes. "If you need anything as you settle in, let me know." She faltered, then said, "I hope the three months will give you enough time to decide if this site works for you."

"It should. Can I ask you another question?"

"Ask all you want. I'll give you what answers I have."

"Are there any *kinder* on the farm?"

"No. Why?"

"The tools I use are sharp. Very sharp."

"There's a hasp on the outer door. You'll need to get a padlock to put on it."

"*Gut.* Is it okay if I come to the house if I've got more questions?"

She appreciated that he didn't want to interfere more than he already had. "There or at the quilt shop."

"Which quilt shop?"

"The one about a mile up the road." She hooked a thumb toward the west. "Quilts Are Bliss. A friend of mine runs it, and there are about a half dozen of us who help there."

"To sell the quilts?"

"To sell *our* quilts. It's a consignment shop. If there's anything else you need..."

"I think I'll be fine. Tonight I'm going to unpack and settle in."

"Once word gets around you're here, I'm sure you'll have plenty of people stopping by to welcome you to our district." She glanced at the fly-splattered walls. "If you want to repaint, there's some paint in the shed next to the dairy barn."

"You mentioned you had cows. Who milks them for you?"

"Nobody. I do the milking. It's just two now." She raised her chin at the surprise on his face. "Since Eddie died, the farm has been my responsibility, and I didn't want to sell the herd." Without another word, she walked out. She couldn't stay when tears burned at the back of her eyes. Each time someone asked that question, she had to accept Eddie was gone.

Everything was gone. Her marriage, her dreams, her happiness, her steadfast faith...all gone.

Chapter Two

How many more times did she need to tell her well-meaning friends she wasn't interested in a match?

Rosemary was glad she wasn't at the quilt shop today. Yesterday, when she'd stopped by, the other quilters had debated how long it would take for Rosemary's new tenant to ask her to walk out with him. Though the owner, Grace, had cautioned them to keep speculation to themselves, Rosemary had sensed sparkling eyes on her the whole time she'd been at the shop.

Lord, danki *for giving me the excuse to stay home and bake today.* She drew a cookie sheet out of the oven and put another in. She set the cookies pocked with chocolate and butterscotch chips on a cooling rack. When she'd woken before dawn, fighting off the remnants of the flu that seemed unwilling to leave her alone, she'd mixed a batch of cookies before she went out to milk the cows.

She loved her time in the barn. The odors and the aromas of animals and hay and dust from the old building's corners combined to make a tantalizing, homey scent. It reminded her of happier times when she and Eddie had worked together as they reached for their goals of creating a home, which they would share with their family.

The twinge that came whenever she thought of those precious days was no longer a surprise. However, that didn't lessen the pointed barb cutting into her heart, stripping away her breath as she ached for what she'd lost.

Yet, when she was alone in the barn, she could pretend nothing had changed. She milked the cows as she'd done when Eddie had to be away. She took the time to talk to each one as if the cow could understand. The music of the *millich* falling into the pail and the skittering of the barn cats when they came to beg for a bowl were a comfort. As was the first light of dawn, gray and hesitant when it pushed aside the darkness.

Most important, she could keep her hands so busy her mind had to focus on what she was doing instead of random, painful thoughts of continuing her life without Eddie.

Eddie had been perfect.

Perfect for her, perfect for them and perfect in every possible way. While other men had looked past her to her two younger, much prettier sisters, Eddie had said he'd seen only her the first time he'd walked into the Sunday service after he'd moved to Bliss Valley from the northwest corner of Pennsylvania. He'd sought her out after the communal lunch, and within minutes they were sharing everything about their lives. She'd told him things she'd never spoken of with anyone else, not even her sisters. He'd been as forthcoming with her, speaking of his life in western Pennsylvania and how a disagreement with his own *daed* had set him on the road to find a life of his own in Lancaster County. After a single attempt to urge him to reconcile with his parents, she'd never spoken of it again because she'd seen how deeply the idea pained him.

Eddie had always enjoyed hunting, and sometimes he'd gone off for several days with friends. She'd never begrudged him that time away, because she knew how important it was to have time with others. He hadn't complained once about how often she spent time with her elderly neighbor, Iva, and her family. That was, Rosemary had been certain, the secret to the success of their marriage. They were open with one another, accepting that while they had so much in common, there were a few things they didn't. Celebrating the differences as much as the times together had strengthened their bond.

But then one night Eddie hadn't come home. It hadn't been the first time she'd gone to bed alone, but on each occasion he'd told her ahead of time he'd be late because he'd gone into Lancaster City or somewhere else in the county to deliver apples or to sell some of their beef calves. She'd listened with half an ear for him to return and always slept better once she welcomed him home.

But that night, there hadn't been any rattle of buggy wheels or the clatter of the wagon returning. The back door had remained closed rather than squeaking open on hinges neither of them remembered to oil. No footfalls coming up the stairs.

That night, there had been silence.

As the timer sounded again, jarring her from her memories, Rosemary pulled out another sheet of cookies. She reached to slip another into the oven, then realized she hadn't spooned out any cookie dough while she'd been lost in her reverie. Losing track of time and tasks had happened a lot right after the funeral, but she'd thought she'd gotten past having her thoughts drift away from the pain-filled present.

Apparently not.

Finishing the batch of cookies, she cleaned the counters and washed the dishes. She left the baking dishes dripping in the drainer while she filled a plate with warm cookies. Realizing she'd made a double batch out of habit, she decided she'd drop off some at Gideon's shop later.

He must be settling in well, though she hadn't spoken to him since his arrival the day before yesterday. Would he be able to make a go of his business in her old dairy shed? There were other small businesses along the road. They were long-established, and she had no idea how a new business would do, though Grace's quilt shop was flourishing and had opened a few weeks ago. However, Grace had customers who'd followed her from the quilt shop where she used to work in Strasburg.

Telling herself that growing the business was Gideon's concern, not hers, she put the cookies into the inverted cake container and sealed the plastic top, so they didn't go stale. Not something she'd had to worry about when Eddie was alive. He'd gobbled up her cookies almost as fast as she could take them out of the oven. More than once, she'd teased him about burning his fingers on hot cookies in his impatience.

Now...

Shaking those thoughts out of her head as she'd done so many times before, Rosemary pulled her black wool cloak over her shoulders, but didn't bother with her bonnet. She picked up the plate and went out the back door to visit Iva Chupp.

Iva was listed in the Lancaster County directory of plain families and districts as Rosemary's next-door neighbor. In Rosemary's estimation, the elderly woman was far more than that simple description. Rosemary had known Iva her whole life, and when Eddie had suggested they look at the farm next door to Iva's small house, she'd been thrilled.

In the days following Eddie's death, Iva had provided a bulwark for Rosemary to lean against without having to hide her feelings. The elderly woman had lost her own husband more than twenty years before, so she seemed to comprehend each emotion, some contradictory, Rosemary was experiencing.

Not once had Iva urged her to be strong or grateful for the time she'd had with Eddie or to look to the future.

"God never promised us we wouldn't suffer grief," she'd said the week after Eddie's funeral, "but according to the forty-sixth Psalm, He vowed to be our refuge and our strength during our troubles. Let Him hold you in His hands, Rosemary. He knows your grief, for He has endured grief on behalf of the whole universe from the moment He created it and us."

Rosemary had tried to live by those wise words, but it hadn't been easy. Especially when the world was quiet at a winter's day's end and she couldn't avoid facing how alone she was. Last night, it'd been comforting, when she looked out the window, to see lights on in Gideon's workroom.

Snow crunched beneath Rosemary's feet as she crossed the field. The trees were bare and the breeze cold. Hearing raucous cries, she looked up to see starlings circling in their amazing patterns through the sky. She wished they were robins because she couldn't remember the last time she'd heard a robin's sweet chirp. The fields were stripped of their crops and lying in wait for the plow's return once the snow was gone. She had to believe that spring would come soon, and she'd be able to get rid of her thick socks and boots. But, for today, when the air was fresh, she breathed in the crisp scents of winter.

The farmhouse on the far side of the field might once have been a twin to her own. During the more than one hundred years since the two houses had been built, additions and alterations had changed them. The *dawdi haus* on Rosemary's house was little more than a pair of rooms connected to the kitchen while someone had attached a full house onto Iva's home. One or another of Iva's *kins-kinder* had lived in the extension through the years, but it was empty now.

That was one of the reasons Rosemary tried to stop by the house at least every other day. Iva's daughter checked on her *mamm*, but also had responsibility for her husband's *daed*, who was in poor health. Efforts Iva's family had made to urge her to leave the huge house and move in with one of them had been futile.

Rosemary opened the door to the laundry. Poking her head in, she called as she did each time before she entered the kitchen, "Are you home, Iva?"

"Where else would I be?" Though the words were sharp, the old woman's voice was cheerful.

Iva was no fragile octogenarian, bent and wizened. Though the top of her head barely reached Rosemary's shoulder, her presence made itself felt. In the last year, Iva had relented and allowed a chair to be brought in for her use during the three-hour-long church services every other week. Until then, she'd sat on a backless bench as she had throughout her long life. Her eyes remained sharp, and her tongue did as well, though she never spoke cruelly. Just with an honesty some people found off-putting.

After years of being pulled into a bun under her *kapp*, her white hair had thinned so the center part in her hair was as wide as Rosemary's index finger. But Rosemary had never seen Iva with her *kapp* askew or her apron pinned wrong as some women did when they began to have trouble taking care of themselves.

This morning, Iva sat in her rocker by the kitchen window, which gave her an excellent view of the road. As always, she held a quilt on her lap. She motioned for Rosemary to come over.

"Did you bring me cookies?" Iva asked.

"Of course."

"What flavor?"

"Chocolate butterscotch chip."

"My favorite!"

Rosemary smiled as she set the cookies on the table near Iva, then poured herself a cup of the old woman's strong *kaffi* before refilling Iva's cup. Sitting at the table near the rocker, she asked, "Would you like more *millich*?"

"It's fine the way it is." She focused her pale blue eyes on Rosemary. "Almost as fine as that young man who's been hanging around your dairy house by the road." Her snowy brows lowered. "I assume you know he's there."

"Of course, I know he's there." She spooned some sugar into her cup, knowing if she didn't the bitter flavor would linger in her mouth. "His name is Gideon Wingard, and he's renting the building. He works on harnesses and tack."

"*Gut* for him. Lying in bed dreaming never got the work done, ain't so?"

"We'll see how it works out."

Iva frowned as she reached for the biggest cookie on the plate. "Is he a troublesome man?"

"Not at all. He seems quite kind."

"Is he?"

Rosemary wagged a finger at her friend. "Don't read anything into my words. He's my tenant. Nothing more."

Iva chewed the cookie before saying, "Perhaps then, if he's so considerate, we shall be *gut* neighbors. You could use a *gut* neighbor who can help you if something on the farm is too much for you. Someone other than Calvin Hertzler and La-Vern Spaeger." She took another bite. "Not once have they done anything for someone without expecting something in return." Her eyes narrowed. "I know what they want from you, Rosemary."

"So do I," she replied, trying to keep her voice light, "but they're going to realize I mean what I say when I tell them I'm not interested in remarrying."

"Now."

Though Iva didn't turn every conversation to Rosemary choosing another husband as *Mamm* did, it was a subject she didn't want to discuss. She didn't want to lie by suggesting that someday, if she found a second man as perfect for her as Eddie had been, she'd marry again.

"What are you working on?" Rosemary asked, looking at the quilt in Iva's lap. The fabric was well-worn and faded.

"A quilt I found among my *mamm's* old things." She patted it. "I'd forgotten about it."

"It's old."

"*Ja,* older than I am." She chuckled. "And it's well-traveled. It's been to Europe and back."

"How did that happen?" Rosemary was delighted at the change of subject.

"My *daed* was drafted at the end of World War II, and his alternative service was with a program we now call the Heifer Project. He joined other plain men and *Englischers* on ships across the Atlantic. They took care of the livestock, cows, pigs, sheep and chickens bound for farms over there. Most of the animals in Europe had been killed during the war, either by the bombing or for food, and the farmers needed stock to rebuild. While my *daed* was across the ocean, my *mamm,* who was a young bride, sent him a quilt because she worried he wasn't warm enough. He gave it to a family living in a bombed-out house while he and some of the other men rebuilt the house."

"But it's here in Bliss Valley now."

"On the fiftieth anniversary of the war's end, the *kinder* who'd found comfort under the quilt brought it back here so they could thank my *daed* and *mamm.* He'd passed away a few years before, but *Mamm* accepted it with their gratitude." She sighed. "Oh, it was a *wunderbaar* day. It goes to show that no matter where we travel, God brings us back to where we're meant to be." Another sigh slipped past her lips, but it sounded happy. "One of these days when you've got more time, Rosemary, I'd love to tell you the whole story because it's one that shouldn't be lost when I die."

She forced a smile. "I'd love to hear it." That wasn't true. Hearing how Iva's parents had been separated when they were newlyweds, but been reunited to share a long life together was a sharp reminder Eddie wasn't coming back.

"You look exhausted." Iva eyed Rosemary. "Have you been sleeping?"

"I have. Most nights." She sighed. "I have a touch of that bug that made the rounds a couple of weeks ago, but I'm feeling much better than last week."

"That's *gut* to hear. If the nausea returns, try some ginger. It'll ease the sickness."

She nodded. "I had a glass of ginger ale last night before bed."

"Do so each night for the next week, and your stomach should stay calm."

"I will."

Iva's eyes twinkled. "We've talked about your newcomer and my old quilt. What other news have you heard?"

The old woman finished her first cookie and two more while they talked. Rosemary didn't have much other news beyond Gideon's arrival, but she needn't have worried. Iva seemed to hear every bit of gossip throughout Lancaster County, though she seldom went beyond her own front yard except for church services.

"Can you believe that?" Iva asked after sharing a tale of a dog and a pig running away together and ending up stuck on an icy pond.

"I always listen with a skeptical ear," Rosemary said.

"I'm glad to hear that." She looked out the window toward the road. "Bliss Valley may look idyllic. However, appearances can be deceiving. Don't assume everything is as it looks."

"Is something wrong, Iva?"

She waved aside the question. "Just an old woman's caution. After living so many years, I've seen more than I can remember." She laughed and reached for another cookie.

When Rosemary stood to leave, Iva held up her hand. "Wait a moment. I've got something for you."

"You do?"

She shifted in the rocker and pointed to the sewing machine behind her. On it were stacks of folded material. "I want you to take some fat quarters."

"Why?"

"I want you to use them to make a quilt."

"For you?"

Iva shook her head. "Not for me. For you."

"But I—"

"You make quilts to sell at Grace Coffman's shop, but I want you to use these to make a quilt for yourself." Stretching, she picked up a trio of the bundles from the sewing machine. She checked them, then put one back and selected another. "These are for you."

Rosemary took the bundles. With her experienced eye, she gauged there were enough pieces to make a large wall quilt or perhaps, if she was thrifty when she cut the pattern, enough for a quilt top for a twin bed. She ran her finger along the sides of the bundles, savoring the smooth texture of the cotton that had been dyed in a multitude of colors and designs. Since the first day her *mamm* had put a needle in her hand and began teaching her to make small, even stitches, Rosemary had loved the sensation of fabrics and threads sifting through her fingers.

"But why a bundle of fat quarters?" she asked.

Fat quarters were cut from a bolt in a specific way. First, the fabric was cut in half horizontally, then vertically. That left four pieces for each yard, each about twenty-two by eighteen inches. Many shops sold the fabric in bundles, and the larger the quilt, the more bundles one needed. Fat quarters were used by quilters with beginner skills or those who wanted to make a quilt in a hurry.

"Why not?" Iva asked.

"I haven't used fat quarters since I was a teenager."

"Then there's the reason." Iva smiled. "Sometimes to go forward with our lives, we need to reconnect with what's behind us. I know you like making quilts that challenge your skills."

"You're right." Complex patterns in the piecing and the quilting kept her from being bored…or thinking too much.

And thinking too much was what she wanted to avoid right now. Did Iva realize that?

Rosemary wanted to ask, but didn't. She'd hesitated too long on thanking her neighbor for her kind gift. Not sure what she'd make from the fat quarters, she held them close as she bid the older woman goodbye and left. The quilt she'd been working on was almost done. Once it was complete and on display at Grace's shop, she'd figure out something to do with this fabric. She'd create a design that would show her gratitude for Iva's friendship and kindness.

She wasn't sure how right now, but for the first time in months, she was looking forward to something.

Late in the afternoon, when the sun aimed its brightest beams into his shop, Gideon traced a line on the strip of leather he needed to cut lengthwise before he attached it in place. When he straightened and looked at the material on the table, he scowled. The line that was supposed to be straight was as crooked as the roads leading through Bliss Valley. Such a sample of his work would send potential customers fleeing to find another leatherworker.

Looking at the tools he had hung on the pegboard along the wall opposite the door, he considered which one would help him salvage the piece of leather. He was reaching for an awl to punch holes in the leather in the hopes of making it into a thin belt, but paused and glanced over his shoulder as a car turned into the farm lane. Could it be an *Englischer* who'd heard about his shop opening?

He stretched to remove the uneven piece of leather before a customer could see it, then paused. The silver car continued along the lane toward the farmhouse.

Going to the table, he repositioned the piece of leather. This time, when he measured out the length he wanted, the line was straight. He selected a knife that would allow him to cut the leather in a single pass. He'd use a finer knife to rid the edges of any burrs so the length of leather would be smooth when he sewed an identical piece to it before connecting it to the metal rings that would be part of a harness.

Because he'd been concentrating on his work, he wasn't sure how much time had passed before the silver car came back toward the road. He glanced up as the door to his shop opened.

A tall, slender woman walked in. An *Englischer*, who wore her dark blond hair cropped short with a streak of pink that dropped over her large dark glasses. When she lifted them off, he saw her eyes were the same dark brown as her eyebrows. Faint pink dusted her cheeks, accenting her sharp cheekbones.

She didn't smile. "Do you know the people who live in the farmhouse?"

"*Ja.* She—"

Not giving him a chance to go on, she said, "This *is* the Mistle farm, isn't it?"

"Mistle?" He put the strip of leather on the table. "Do you mean Mishler?"

The woman's mouth twisted. "I do. Is this the Mishler farm?"

"*Ja.*"

"Are you part of the family?"

"No. I rent this building from Rosemary Mishler."

The woman glanced at the envelope she held. "Yes, Rosemary. That's her name."

"You probably can find her at the house."

"I looked there, and nobody was home."

"She might be in the barn. Did you check there?"

She gave him a shocked look as if he'd asked her to drive her car to the moon. When he noticed the suede boots that reached to her knees and were decorated with gold buckles and what he assumed were rhinestones, he understood her disbelief at his question.

"You can," he hurried to say, "stick your head past the barn door and call her name. You don't have to go in."

Her nose wrinkled. "No thanks. I don't have time to play hide-and-seek. Will you give her a message from me?"

"Sure." He pulled his marking pencil out of his pocket. "Let me see if I can find a piece of paper." He held the pencil out to her.

She shook her head. "Tell her I left something in her kitchen, and I don't want it back. Six months was long enough for me."

"Left it in the kitchen, and you don't want it back." He scribbled the words onto the back of the discarded piece of leather. What was she talking about? He was curious, but Rosemary's business wasn't his.

The *Englisch* woman handed him the envelope. It was sealed with the name Mishler and the farm's address written in block letters across the front. "And give her this. It'll explain."

"Explain what?"

"What *she* needs to know." Her voice was clipped, but strong emotions burned in her eyes. Her gaze darted around the room, lingering for a moment on the windows before moving on again.

She wanted to leave, but was she concerned someone would see her? If so, she shouldn't have worn a bright red coat and white denims tucked into her boots.

"Don't forget to give her the envelope as soon as you see her," the woman said as if he didn't know what to do with the stuff between his ears, "but tell her to check out the kitchen before she opens the envelope and reads what's inside. Got it?"

"*Ja.* Got it."

"Good." The *Englisch* woman eyed him up and down again, then walked toward the door. Pausing, she didn't look at him. "Do you know when she'll be back?"

"No, like I told you—"

"Yeah, I know. You just rent this place." She left, not quite slamming the door in her wake.

Gideon was tempted to hold up the envelope and see if he could discern something about the contents. He grabbed his straw hat and walked toward the door, hoping it wouldn't take too long to find Rosemary and deliver the letter.

As he opened the door, he heard the unmistakable rattle of buggy wheels on the asphalt farm lane. Rosemary's buggy! When had she driven away? It must have been when he was putting up the pegboard. His hammering would have drowned out the sound of her wheels. He rushed out the door and caught up with the buggy as Rosemary drew it to a halt near the house. Sliding the driver's-side door open, she peered out.

"Gideon? Is something wrong?" she asked.

"I don't think so. Some *Englisch* lady just stopped by and said she'd put something in your kitchen. Something she didn't want to be responsible for any longer. Something she'd had for about six months."

"What is it?"

"She didn't say."

"That's strange."

He nodded. "Very. I thought maybe she was interested in buying one of your quilts."

"I don't sell them here. Just at Grace's consignment shop."

"The *Englisch* woman was blond, and she drives a silver car."

Rosemary shrugged. "I meet plenty of *Englischers* at the shop, and tourists sometimes turn up the wrong farm lane."

"I don't think she was in the wrong place." He held out the envelope. "She asked me to deliver this to you as soon as I saw you."

"Deliver it to me?"

"She said you should check what she left in your kitchen before you read what's inside the envelope."

"How bizarre!"

"It is, ain't so?"

She reached into the buggy and pulled out two bags of groceries. Handing one to him, she dropped the envelope in the other one. "I figured you could use some flour and sugar and *kaffi*, too."

"*Danki.*" He was astonished by her thoughtfulness. "Tell me what I owe you, and—"

"Don't worry about it now. I think I should check what's in the kitchen." She walked toward her back door.

He followed after putting the bag of groceries back in the buggy, curious what an *Englischer* had left in Rosemary's kitchen.

When she opened the back door, she gasped. He looked over her head to see a *kind* standing on a chair by the counter. The little girl, her braided hair as black as the wood stove at the far end of the kitchen, wore a T-shirt with some sort of cartoon creature on it, bright pink jeans and sparkly sneakers. If he had to guess, he'd put her age at around five or six. She had a pudgy face and bright blue eyes, which were as wide as saucers as she looked from Rosemary to him.

She drew her hand out of an open container holding cookies. She jumped from the chair, slipping the hand holding the cookie behind her back. The chair wobbled. Her guilty expression said it all.

Or so he thought before she looked at Rosemary and asked, "Are you my mommy now?"

Chapter Three

Rosemary ran across the kitchen to right the chair before it could tumble on the *kind*. As she skirted two half-filled paper bags on the floor, she saw the shock on Gideon's face. It matched the dismay cramping inside her.

A *kind* by herself in Rosemary's kitchen? Why? How? And why was the little girl asking if Rosemary was her *mamm* now?

Where was the little girl's real *mamm*? It couldn't have been the woman who stopped at Gideon's shop...or could it?

Nothing made sense.

She glanced from the cute little girl to Gideon again. His wide eyes filled with astonishment told her he didn't have any more idea of what was going on than she did. Questions battered her lips, but she had spent time with enough *kinder* to know it was important to keep them from seeing an adult's true feelings in uncertain circumstances.

She'd learned that from her own *mamm* who always maintained a tight hold on her emotions when *Daed* had another explosive outburst about something that had annoyed him.

Mamm had remained calm through the tumultuous times after Rosemary's brother vanished into the *Englisch* world and now since Joel had come home. She knew he intended to stay because he'd fallen in love with Grace Coffman and was taking baptismal classes so they could marry within the next year.

Rosemary must show that serenity now when faced with an unknown *kind* who'd asked such an outrageous question. Her *mamm*...now? What did the little girl mean?

Because the youngster had spoken in English rather than *Deitsch*, Rosemary knew she should reply in the same language. If she only knew what to say first...

The *kind* was dressed in *Englisch* clothing, which was another question that needed to be answered. Why was an *Englisch kind* in her kitchen?

She set her bag of groceries on the table. Where were Gideon's? She shook her head, knowing she needed to focus on the immediate problem.

Picking up a torn winter coat and a pair of mittens, one with the thumb missing, from the floor, she put them on the table before she bent toward the *kind* and said in the most cheerful voice she could manage, "Hi there! Who are you?"

Instead of answering, the *kind* took a bite of the cookie, then another. She chewed with obvious pleasure, but didn't look at Rosemary.

"I'm Rosemary," she tried again. "What's your name?"

The little girl didn't answer as she finished the cookie. She looked past Rosemary to the chair, then toward the cookie container. Her silent message was unmistakable.

If bribery would get the *kind* talking, Rosemary was willing to do that. "Do you want another cookie?"

As if neither Rosemary nor Gideon stood in the kitchen, the little girl climbed up on the chair again and stretched her short arms across the counter to reach for the cookie container.

"Is she deaf?" Gideon asked, startling her.

She hadn't forgotten he was there. She doubted she could be unaware of him being in the same room. However, she had been intent on getting the *kind* to answer.

"She heard us come in." Rosemary glanced at the *kind* who was gravely selecting cookies from the ones stored in the container and stacking them on the counter in front of her.

"She could have felt the cold air when the door opened."

Rosemary went to the stove, picked up a ladle lying nearby and clanged it on one of the burners. Both Gideon and the little girl flinched.

"She can hear," she said, putting the ladle on the counter. She faltered. What was she going to do to convince the little girl to answer her? She didn't want to upset the *kind* who must have been distressed at being left in a strange house by herself. What had the *Englisch* woman...?

The envelope!

Rosemary searched her grocery bag, lifting out the items she'd bought. She left them on the table after she pulled out the envelope Gideon had given her. Though she wanted to tear into it, she could only stare at it.

Some instinct she couldn't name warned her that everything in her life was about to change again. She didn't like change, especially the change that came with loss and grief. That kind of change she'd endured already.

When her brother had vanished without telling her goodbye.

When Eddie had died without her being able to tell him goodbye.

Was this the prelude to another goodbye? Or was it something different?

Her gaze shifted and connected with the *kind*'s. As pain and dread and uncertainty roiled through her, she saw matching emotions in the little girl's eyes. Eyes that looked as old as

Iva's without any of the joy her neighbor brought to each day of her life. As if the *kind* had suffered in her few years more than any person should in their whole life.

An emptiness in Rosemary urged her to draw the little girl to her in an embrace that could help them both, but as she took a half step toward the chair, the *kind* turned away and reached for another cookie. The moment between the two of them was gone as if it'd never existed.

Had it been there? Maybe Rosemary was seeking something that didn't exist. No! She was sure there had been an ephemeral bridge between them.

"Do you think the answer is in there?" Gideon asked, edging toward her, but keeping his eyes on the little girl who was again helping herself to cookies.

"I hope so." Rosemary opened the envelope and pulled out several pieces of paper, including another envelope. Ignoring the small light brown envelope, she unfolded the pages and began to read.

She groped for another chair and dropped into it as she stared at the words in front of her.

Dear Mrs. Mishler,
I've done all I can, and I don't want to do any more. Who wants to be around a kid who won't talk to you? She's not my responsibility. She's yours.

In case she's being as stubborn as usual, her name is Braelynn. Sometimes she'll answer to it. Most of the time, she won't. Maybe you can get her to listen to you.

Rosemary looked up from the page. "Her name is Braelynn, according to the letter."

"Hey, Braelynn," Gideon called in English. "Want some *millich*—some milk to go with those cookies?"

The *kind* nodded, but didn't speak.

Arching his brows at Rosemary, he said, "I'm assuming there's *millich* in the fridge."

"*Ja.*" She started to rise, but he put a hand on her shoulder. "Let me."

Rosemary bit her lower lip as she watched Gideon walk over to the refrigerator. He looked back at her, and she pointed to a cabinet near the sink where the glasses were stored. Getting one, he filled it partway with *millich*. He went to the little girl and held out the glass.

She snatched it from him, almost spilling its contents. Gulping the *millich* without pausing, she looked into the empty glass.

"More?" he asked.

Again, she didn't respond, not even when he slipped the glass out of her hand and poured in more *millich*. She grabbed it again, but took no more than a sip before she put it on the counter and dipped her cookie in it.

Gideon walked back to where Rosemary sat. Motioning to her, he went into the living room. She hesitated, taking a glance at the *kind* who was enjoying a cookie coated with *millich*. Grabbing the contents of the envelope, she followed him. She'd have a *gut* view of Braelynn from the other room.

She caught up with him near her quilt frames that claimed half of the room. She turned her back on them, though she wished she could work on her quilt-in-progress. Sewing was her haven, a time when she had to slow down, focus on each stitch and clear her mind of anything but her gratitude that God had given her skill with a needle.

Gideon turned to face her, but she shifted so both of them could see into the kitchen.

"What's the rest of the letter say?" he asked. "Read it out loud. She's busy with her cookies, so she's not paying any attention to us."

"She wasn't paying attention to us in the kitchen, either." *Except when our eyes connected.*

He shook his head. "You're wrong. She was hyper-aware of everything we did and said." Rubbing his knuckles under his chin, he said, "I wonder why she didn't respond."

"Maybe the answer is in here." She picked up the letter and began to read it, stumbling over the hasty and scrawling handwriting. It was as if the woman couldn't write fast enough in her rush to get the *kind* out of her life.

"'If you can get her talking and keep her talking,'" Rosemary read aloud, "'you're doing better than I could. Maybe she's got autism or something. All I know is she's not normal. No normal kid refuses to look at you whenever you talk to her. Maybe you'll figure out a way to get it through her stubborn head there are other people in the world, and she should remember it's not all about her.'"

Tears welled into Rosemary's eyes. "That's so cruel to say about a *kind*."

Gideon's face hardened with his frown. "That *Englisch* woman was more worried about ruining her boots than she was leaving a young *kind* in an unfamiliar house by herself. That doesn't sound like someone who's thinking with her heart." His gaze dropped to the pages again. "What else does she have to say?"

Rosemary found the spot where she'd left off on the bottom of the second page and read, "'At least she'll get lots of fresh air in the country on your farm. I can't let her outside by herself here in Lancaster. She always finds trouble. Just like her mother did. Maybe that's why Madison died so young. She lived too fast. Anyhow, Madison's kid is your problem now. I'd say she's your husband's problem, but I hear he's also dead. Can't say I'm sorry. He never took responsibility for what he did, and Braelynn's better off without him. I don't know you, but you're probably better off without him, too.'"

She gasped at the hateful words. What type of person spoke so callously of a dead man?

A hand settled on her elbow, and she raised her eyes to Gideon's. Sympathy had replaced most of the anger on his face, startling her. He hadn't asked to be mixed up in whatever was going on. All he'd done was rent her outbuilding. Yet, he stood beside her, offering her silent solace in the midst of the mess her life had become. His kindness threatened to undo her, letting the tears dammed behind her eyes cascade out like a flood tide.

Wanting to thank him, wanting to lean against his broad chest and lose herself in a moment of self-pity, she squared her shoulders and raised her chin. She was missing Eddie. Her longing for a man's arms around her had nothing to do with Gideon and everything to do with her grief. If Eddie were here...

Eddie!

She scowled at the pages she held. "*He never took responsibility for what he did, and Braelynn's better off without him.* What can that mean? How did Eddie know Braelynn?"

"I was hoping you knew."

"I don't." She drew out the smaller envelope she'd held behind the written pages. Could whatever was in it give her the answers she sought?

She handed Gideon the pages and opened the envelope. A single sheet of paper and a photo were inside. The picture was of two people facing the camera, snuggling close. A Lancaster City street sign marked the corner where they stood, though she couldn't make out the names. The man looked like Eddie, but was wearing *Englisch* clothing, a black T-shirt with elaborate writing on it and a picture of a snake wrapped around a woman dressed in wisps of clothing. The other person in the photo was a young *Englisch* woman with ebony hair. She had on a flowing dress with garish flowers scattered across it. She was pregnant.

Turning it over, she saw someone had written *Eddie and Madison* on it in pencil. Was she the Madison mentioned in the letter, and was that Rosemary's Eddie? She tilted the photo toward the window to view it more easily. The man in the photo had Eddie's stubborn chin and brown eyes. Madison was *Englisch*, so why was Eddie with her, his arm around her shoulders and her hand over his heart? Was it a photo from his *rumspringa* before he had moved to Bliss Valley and Rosemary had met him? But what had he been doing in Lancaster? He'd told her he'd spent his life, until just before he met her, in a community near Lake Erie.

She hoped the paper from the envelope would explain. Unfolding it, she gasped. It was a birth certificate issued by the Commonwealth of Pennsylvania about five and a half years before. The name on it was Braelynn Mishler.

Mishler? No, it had to be a coincidence!

But she read on past where the *mamm*'s name was listed as Madison Nesbitt to where the *daed*'s name was typed.

Edward John Mishler.

Her late husband's name.

The night Eddie had asked her to marry him, he'd vowed there would never be any secrets between them. She'd believed him, vowing the same. She'd believed him that night, and she'd believed him every day since then.

Until today.

He hadn't told her everything. He'd lied about what might have been the most important thing in his life.

His daughter.

How could you, Eddie? her heart demanded. *How could you tell me you'd be honest with me and keep this part of your past a secret? What* else *didn't you tell me?*

She didn't get an answer, and she never would.

Gideon stepped forward when Rosemary rocked on her feet, then paused. Was he out of his mind? He'd left Smoketown because he wanted time away from the complications created by an overly loving family.

Not that anyone would describe Rosemary and this little girl as a family. Why had the *Englisch* woman left the *kind* in his landlady's kitchen?

"Oh, my!" Rosemary breathed as she stared at the paper she held.

He put his hand on her left elbow and guided her toward the light blue sofa that was covered with a quilt in shades of blue, green and purple. He wanted her to sit before she toppled over. She let him move her a single step, but refused to go beyond that. She continued to stare at the paper in her hand.

Curious, he stepped behind her and looked over her shoulder. He was used to being able to do that with the much shorter women in his family, but he had to angle his head to see past Rosemary's heart-shaped organdy *kapp*.

He inhaled sharply. A birth certificate! He looked into the kitchen at the *kind* who had a puddle of *millich* in the center of the counter and crumbs everywhere. Braelynn was smiling as she ran her fingers through the *millich*, spreading it farther. With her focus on the mess she was making, the little girl was oblivious to the tension weaving through the living room like a massive web.

"May I?" he asked as he reached around Rosemary for the birth certificate.

Not sure if she'd relinquish it or not, he was relieved when she handed it to him and turned to face him. She must not have realized how close he stood because her eyes widened and she backed away so they were an arm's length apart. He heard her breath puff out in astonishment. His would have done the same if he hadn't halted it. Standing face-to-face, his gaze level with hers, was such a heady sensation that he felt dizzy.

His head spun more when Rosemary pointed toward the bottom of the page. "My husband's name was Edward John Mishler."

The names of the *kind*'s parents were Edward John Mishler and Madison Nesbitt. Wanting to deny what he was seeing, he said, "Edward and John are pretty common names."

She gave him a scathing look, which he deserved. *Ja*, the names were common, but together with her husband's last name and the veiled information in the letter, there could be little doubt.

The *kind* had to be her late husband's. By the ashen shade of her face, he guessed she hadn't known about the little girl.

Only then did he notice the photograph in her other hand. He didn't ask her permission before he tilted the picture so he had a *gut* view of the people. He frowned at the image of two *Englischers*. A man and a woman. Neither looked much older than teenagers, though the woman was very pregnant.

"Who are they?" he asked.

"According to what's written on the back of the photo, that's Madison Nesbitt with Eddie." Her voice was as dull as if all life had sifted out of her.

"Your husband?"

She nodded, her face growing paler. Her voice became steady, however. "Was the woman who left the *kind* here the one in the picture?"

Turning it over, she pointed to the two names. "Madison. Like on the birth certificate and in the letter. Was she the woman you talked to?"

He scrutinized the picture, then shook his head. "The woman I talked to didn't look like the one in this picture. Not the same color hair and—"

"*Englischers* change their hair color."

"I know, but the face of the woman who came to the shop was very different. Her eyes might have been another color, too. I'm not sure about that." He compared his memory of the woman who'd given him the envelope to the one in the photo. "Could the woman who came here have been part of Eddie's family?"

"He had only one sibling, a brother who died when they were young." She faltered, then rallied to say, "Or so he told me."

Gideon wasn't surprised she was questioning everything her husband had told her. If Rosemary hadn't known about Braelynn—and he was sure she hadn't from her reactions—she must be wondering what other aspects of his past Eddie Mishler had failed to mention.

Hearing a wet slap, he looked toward the kitchen again to see Braelynn splashing *millich* everywhere. He almost pointed it out to Rosemary, but his curiosity of what and who had brought the *kind* to the farm today halted him.

"Did the woman," Rosemary asked, "mention anything about Eddie?"

He shook his head. "Pretty much all she said was that she'd left something for you in your kitchen. And she mentioned something about not wanting to be responsible any longer. That six months had been enough." He looked at the birth certificate again and Braelynn's *mamm*'s name. "Do you know Madison Nesbitt?"

"Why would you think I knew her?"

"She's with your husband in that photo. It is your Eddie, ain't so?"

She nodded before saying, "I understand why you're confused. Looking at what he's wearing… Until now, I've never seen Eddie in anything but plain clothing."

He exhaled with a hiss. Everything was adding up to an answer he didn't want to accept. There might be one way to find out the truth.

"May I?" He held out his hand toward the photo.

Without a word, she put the picture on his palm.

Gideon walked into the kitchen and right to where the little girl was slapping her hands in the *millich* to make it fly in every direction. Braelynn froze when she realized he was coming toward her.

A frightened kitten.

The description erupted into his mind. The little girl was skittish and set to flee the moment someone looked in her direction. At the same time, she was ready to bristle and lash out, hissing, if she was cornered. He didn't want to provoke either reaction. He wanted her to listen to what he had to say.

"Hi, Braelynn," he said in the tone he used to soothe his nieces and nephews when they were getting too boisterous.

Her face became blank.

Okay, she wasn't going to make it easy for him. He couldn't make it easy for her, either. Shocking her out of her tight control seemed cruel, but he had to get through to her somehow.

He thrust the photo toward the little girl. Aware of Rosemary coming to stand beside him, he asked, "Have you seen this, Braelynn?"

With a gut-deep cry, the little girl jumped to the floor where *millich* and cookie crumbs were spread out in a crazy-quilt pattern. Tears bubbled from the corners of her eyes. She hung her head and made a soft moaning sound as she rocked from one foot to the other.

He knelt so he could meet the *kind*'s eyes. "Braelynn, will you look at this?"

Again, she groaned, but didn't give him any other answer. He started to move to where Braelynn wouldn't be able to ignore the photo, but Rosemary's hand on his arm halted him.

No, not her hand, but the trill of something as sweet as the first robin's song in the spring. It lilted through his head and down to the soles of his feet. He yanked his hand back, shocked by the unexpected reaction to her fingers on him.

He thanked God none of the doting women in his family had witnessed his reaction. They would have been certain he'd found the perfect wife. Just as they had a half dozen times before when they thought they perceived some invisible connection between him and a woman with whom he was talking. They'd been wrong each time.

"Leave her be for now," Rosemary said. "Don't force her to look."

Sorting through his thoughts that were scattered around him like the crumbs on the floor, he didn't trust his voice enough to speak. He followed as Rosemary went to the kitchen table. When she had spoken, it was in *Deitsch*.

He nodded and handed her the photo. "You may need this for the police."

"Police?" Her eyes widened. "Why would the police be involved?"

"She was left here. Abandoned. That has to be some sort of crime."

"Maybe, but if she's Eddie's *kind*, I'm her step*mamm*."

"I didn't think of that." He'd been so shocked at finding the little girl in the kitchen he hadn't considered any relationship between Rosemary and Braelynn.

Her voice broke. "If she's Eddie's, how could he have kept

it a secret?" As if to herself, she added, "Did he think I'd love him less if I discovered he had a *kind*?"

He would have had to be a *dummkopf* to attempt to answer either question. Anything he said—either to defend her late husband or to accuse him—could have been the very worst thing he could say. She was in shock, horrified at the idea her husband had kept the important fact he had a *kind* from her. Even if Gideon had known Eddie Mishler and witnessed the short marriage he shared with Rosemary, Gideon still would have been an outsider.

"You've got your hands full with the *kind*," he said. "If you want, I can try to find out more about what's going on."

Why had he offered to do that? He didn't want to get more involved in this sticky situation.

"I'll talk to our ordained men. They'll guide me in what to do." She was calm once more.

On the other hand, he trembled like a newborn colt standing for the first time on its feet. "That sounds like a plan. Rosemary, as far as me being here…" He stopped, wanting to get his words right before he blurted out something to make her situation worse. "I told you when I first came that my tools are dangerous if a *kind* tries to use them, and—"

She cut him off by saying, "If you feel you must leave, then go. Right now, I've got to figure out what I'm going to do with a *kind* who won't talk to me."

Her words, spoken from her heart, were like a slap across the face. As he took one step, then another toward the back door, she didn't look in his direction. Apparently, the zing of sensation when he touched her arm hadn't been something she'd felt, too.

Stepping outside, he knew if he had a half ounce of *gut* sense, he'd go to the shop and start packing and leave for… where? He wasn't going to return to Smoketown where nothing would have changed. He had to find another place to set up shop. Until then…

He'd buy a padlock. That was all he needed to do to keep the little girl away from his tools. He'd stay away from the farmhouse while he grew his business and lived his own life. Rosemary had made it clear she didn't want him involved.

And he didn't need to get his life mired in someone else's problems. Yet, if that was so, then why couldn't he think of anything as he walked down the lane but about how he might help her and the little girl?

Chapter Four

Concentrating was impossible for Gideon. He should have been having the time of his life getting his tools arranged so he could start work as soon as he had customers. He'd made a sign out of a discarded pallet he found behind the shop. He'd painted it with his name, what service he provided and the days and hours he planned to be open. For now, it would be every day except Sunday. He couldn't let a possible customer stop by when the shop wasn't open.

The sign was done, but not much else.

He'd brought his sewing machine inside and set it near the window. It didn't look that different from his *mamm*'s ancient treadle sewing machine, but was made for far thicker materials like leather. Instead of a flat table, his machine had two levels with a sharp slope between them. That allowed the leather's weight to be supported while he sewed. A thick cast-iron bar ran along the top from the right side of the sewing machine to the left to lessen the impact of the needle hitting the leather. He'd found the old machine in a barn and refurbished it, scrubbing off the rust and replacing the belts and oiling the wheels. Once it had begun to move in the smooth, steady motion he needed, it had proved to be more efficient and sturdier than any modern machine.

But instead of finishing setting it up, Gideon found himself staring out the window at where snowflakes came down in the thick curtain. Not thick enough, because he could still make out the lines of Rosemary's farmhouse.

What must she think of him for leaving her alone with a *kind* who didn't want to cooperate? Rosemary had tried to hide she was overwhelmed, but he'd seen each of his sisters show the same "deer in the headlights" expression when they started taking care of their first *boppli*. They'd eventually become comfortable and competent.

Would Rosemary become as comfortable and competent? It wasn't as if Braelynn was a newborn. Except for her size, he would have labeled her a tiny adult. The few times she'd looked in his direction, he'd witnessed emotions too strong and painful for a *kind*.

He considered going to see if Rosemary needed help. The women in his family would have been scandalized at such an offer, because a man's place wasn't taking care of *kinder* unless he had no wife to help him. That was one of the reasons a bishop urged a widower to remarry. Nobody expected a man to know his way around a kitchen or a laundry room. His place was in the barn and the fields or at his business.

Would the local bishop insist Rosemary marry if she was going to continue taking care of Braelynn? The community would look for a man for her. Someone close to her age would be preferred, and someone nearby would be considered a better choice.

He gulped so loud the sound echoed through the shop. What

had he gotten himself into by moving to Bliss Valley? He'd come there to make sure he had a choice. Not to *be* the choice.

By the end of the day, Rosemary was so exhausted that crossing a room threatened to make her collapse. A day that had started so well with running errands had become as appalling as the one when she'd gotten the news that Eddie had been shot.

She wanted to argue that no day could ever be as bad as that one. Twenty-four hours ago, she would have said the day of Eddie's death was the nadir of her life. If so, today had been a close second.

She'd spent the rest of the day trying to gauge what Braelynn would do next. Rosemary waffled between being glad Gideon wasn't there to see what a mess she was making of everything and wishing he were there to give her a chance to catch her breath. Everything she tried with the *kind*, other than feeding her, had failed. Even then, the little girl wolfed the food down like someone who'd never sat at a table before.

Could that be true? Braelynn had refused to use a chair until Rosemary threatened to remove the food from the table. Grudgingly, the *kind* had relented.

But that had been the only time Rosemary had convinced Braelynn to do as she requested. The *kind* spoke rarely, and when she did, it was either in a whisper so low Rosemary strained to hear her or with a screech that seared Rosemary's ears. The little girl seemed to have two emotions: indifference and rage. Trying to anticipate which reaction would come next had Rosemary tiptoeing about as if picking her way through a minefield.

She'd believed if she and Braelynn had time alone, they'd get to know each other. It hadn't taken more than a half hour for Rosemary to discover the little girl had no interest in anything but eating. The *kind* never asked about her *daed*. Rosemary realized the little girl might not have any idea she was in the house where Eddie had lived. Or maybe she didn't care as she ate three peanut butter sandwiches and four more cookies before Rosemary insisted on a pause before Braelynn made herself sick.

The little girl had stared at her as if to ask, *What should I do now?* Remembering she'd bought picture books to give to Naomi King's twin boys, Rosemary had hoped Braelynn wouldn't think the books aimed at toddlers were boring. Rosemary had breathed a sigh of relief when the little girl sat in the rocking chair by the front window and paged through the books, looking at each picture.

As if she'd always been in the house.

The thought sent more grief through Rosemary. How long should she wait before asking the *kind* what she knew about her *daed*? She wondered if the little girl already knew the truth, that Eddie had been killed in that horrible hunting accident. Her own grief slammed into her so hard it almost knocked her sideways.

She walked stiffly to the sink and put the dishes Braelynn had used in the sink. Rosemary hadn't had anything for lunch or for supper, but she wasn't hungry. Her stomach was knotted like a macramé plant hanger. With glances toward the living room to make sure the little girl was in sight, she cleaned the kitchen. Trying to focus on the sticky job of washing the counter didn't halt the thoughts that sped through her head like lightning through a summer sky.

Why hadn't Eddie told her about his daughter? The photo of him and the woman identified as Madison lay on the kitchen table, taunting her. Her fingers itched to pick it up and examine every inch of it in the hopes of finding some sort of answer.

She couldn't solve this on her own. She needed to speak

with Jonas Gundy. The bishop would advise her on what to do and whom to contact. Did she need to alert the police as Gideon had suggested? Someone might be looking for Braelynn.

Some instinct that came from a place she couldn't name told her that she didn't need to worry about that. The woman who'd left her in Rosemary's kitchen had told Gideon she didn't want the little girl back.

By eight p.m., Rosemary was exhausted. She could tell the little girl was as well. How much effort did it take for the *kind* to feign indifference to everything Rosemary said or did?

Rosemary said, "It's time for bed, Braelynn."

She expected the *kind* to ignore her, but Braelynn closed the book she'd been looking at for the past half hour, put it on the table by where she sat and stood. When Rosemary started up the stairs, carrying the bags she'd found in the kitchen along with the little girl, Braelynn followed without a word.

Going into the small bedroom across the hall from where she'd slept alone for the past four months, Rosemary turned on the battery-powered light on the dresser. She'd bought it after she and Eddie exchanged vows, because it was a cute pastel, perfect for a *boppli*'s room. A *boppli* she and Eddie wouldn't ever share. She didn't dwell on the irony that Eddie's *kind* now would be sleeping in the room.

A set of twin beds, each covered by one of Rosemary's quilts, took up most of the room, but there was space for a tall dresser and an empty toy box. When Braelynn's eyes shifted toward the box that was decorated with trees and sheep and a single cow, Rosemary knew she must find things to entertain the youngster.

The couple who'd sold the farm to her and Eddie had had fourteen *kinder* and even more *kins-kinder*. Before they'd left, the wife had told them to check the attic if they needed anything for their own *kinder.* They'd left plenty of stuff in boxes and trunks up there. So many times, Rosemary had been going to climb the stairs and explore what had been left behind, but she'd never gotten around to it.

Tomorrow, she promised herself. No, tomorrow morning she needed to spend some time at Grace's new quilt shop. The quilters took turns helping Grace as she got the shop established and ready for the influx of tourists in spring.

"Early tomorrow," she murmured.

Braelynn's head turned toward her, then away. If Rosemary had needed proof the *kind* was paying attention to everything she did or said, there it was.

Could she persuade the little girl to speak to her if she kept talking? It was worth a try.

"I'm going to unpack your bags," Rosemary said. "All right?"

No answer.

Hoping she didn't sound silly, she continued her monologue. She commented on each item she pulled out of the bags that were half-full. She found some underwear and socks for Braelynn, a couple of shirts and another pair of pants. Nothing for her to sleep in or a second pair of sneakers. The ones she wore wouldn't be of any use in the snow. Most of the clothing was worn to threads. Two of the socks had holes in the heels.

The little girl needed clothes. Rosemary could sew some simple dresses for her, but wasn't sure if Braelynn would consent to wearing plain clothing. Underwear and socks might be available at LaVern's store, which was across the road from Grace's quilt shop, and there were several thrift and consignment clothing shops in the area where she might find shoes and boots in the *kind*'s size. If not, she could reach the outlets in Ronks in a half hour.

One last item was stuffed into the bottom of the second bag. Rosemary tugged out a matted and dirty stuffed toy. It was ugly. The color was somewhere between tan and a sickish yellow. What small tuffs of fluff remained looked as if they'd been dragged through a plowed field. A stubby tail might once have been longer. Turning it over in her hands, she realized what it was supposed to be.

A lion.

A lion whose mane had been sheared by someone wearing a blindfold. A single whisker was embroidered into one side of its face, and its missing eye had been replaced by an off-white plastic button. Its leather nose might once have been black, but it had faded to a dirty gray.

Rosemary looked from the battered toy to Braelynn. The little girl was watching her. Her tiny hands were clenched at her sides. Though Braelynn was silent, Rosemary knew the *kind* was anxious about a stranger holding her beloved toy.

"Does your friend have a name?" Rosemary asked as she held out the lion.

Braelynn snatched the toy and held it over her heart. She glared at Rosemary as if she'd kept the toy away from her.

"Cleo," Braelynn said, her voice rough.

"Cleo? What a nice name! Did you give it to her?"

The *kind* nodded.

"You and Cleo need to decide which bed you want to use tonight."

"Yellow." Braelynn pointed to the bed closer to the door. She tapped yellow fabric sewn into the pinwheel design of the broken dishes quilt. The other pieces were black, purple and green. Braelynn touched each one and called out the name of the color as she did.

"What a smart girl you are!" Rosemary smiled. "You know your colors already."

Braelynn began to smile, then wiped her face clean of any expression. She turned her back on Rosemary.

Keeping her sigh silent, Rosemary slipped out of the room. She got one of Eddie's shirts from the closet in the bedroom they'd once shared. Each time she'd decided she must go through his clothes, she'd found an excuse to postpone the task. She knew in her head that he wasn't coming home again, but her heart refused to give up its foolish hopes.

She took the light blue shirt into the room where Braelynn stood and spread it on the other bed. Stepping back, she watched as the little girl edged toward the shirt and ran her fingers along its front.

"I know it's too big," Rosemary said, "but it'll be more comfortable than what you're wearing." Maybe if she got Braelynn's clothing into the washer tonight and hung it up in the laundry room, the shirt and pants would be dry by morning. "Let's get you changed."

The little girl stepped aside and gave her a steady glare.

Rosemary didn't react...as Braelynn had done so many times today. She wasn't going to leave because the *kind* was shy. Or was there more to Braelynn's reluctance than modesty? Could the little girl be trying to hide something?

"Shirt first," Rosemary said. "Just toss it on the floor."

For a full minute, then another, Braelynn didn't move. When Rosemary was ready to give up, the *kind* put down her stuffed toy and pulled her shirt over her head.

A gasp exploded from Rosemary when she saw the bruises on the *kind*'s shoulders and upper arms. Someone had gripped the little girl so hard the imprint of fingers were visible.

Again, Rosemary had to resist the urge to hug Braelynn and say how sorry she was that the *kind* had suffered such cruelty. She didn't move. If she did, the little girl would scurry away or lash out. Doing either would erase any chance Rosemary had of helping Eddie's daughter.

Fury rushed through her when she realized the woman

who'd deserted Braelynn today had been—if the woman was honest, and Rosemary wasn't sure of anything—taking care of the *kind* for at least two months while Rosemary and Eddie were married. Had she bruised the little girl?

Other questions exploded in Rosemary's mind. Eddie often was away on business overnight when he had deliveries. Could he have been spending time with his daughter during that time? Why had Braelynn's *mamm* died? And how?

Too many questions that had no answers.

Rosemary noticed the *kind* was wearing a necklace. From its tarnished gold chain hung what looked like a round locket with a cross embossed on its front. She bent to look at it.

"No!" Braelynn clamped the necklace to her narrow chest with both hands.

"I just want to look at it. May I?"

The *kind* didn't move and continued to glare at Rosemary.

With a sigh, Rosemary acceded again. Was she making things worse by giving in to the little girl time after time?

"Let's get you ready for bed so you can get to sleep. If—" A cookie popped out of Braelynn's pants pocket and broke into pieces when it hit the floor. "Why do you have a cookie?"

"For later." The little girl paused, then added, "Tonight!"

She believed the little girl, because everything Braelynn did was furtive. Once, when she was much younger, Rosemary and her sisters had found an abused puppy by the side of the road. Scars had crisscrossed its body where bones showed through as if they'd been drawn on the brown and black fur. That dog, which they nursed back to health, never could keep from shying whenever anyone put a hand near it. After years of being spoiled by three little girls and following them everywhere, the dog had continued to act as if it couldn't trust them.

Will Braelynn be the same years from now just like PeeWee?

Rosemary started at the thought. She'd been so focused on

taking care of the little girl that she hadn't given any thought to what she should do with Braelynn. If she contacted the authorities, what would they do with the *kind*?

She tried to ignore that thought while she helped Braelynn into the shirt that was so large it pooled on the floor by her feet. The little girl refused to clean her teeth or have her hair brushed or say her prayers. Each time, Rosemary agreed because she could see the *kind* was weaving on her feet with exhaustion.

"Sleep well, Braelynn," she said as she reached to turn off the lantern.

The little girl turned her face into her pillow and clutched her filthy toy.

Gathering up the clothes, Rosemary went into the hall. She shut the door partway, waiting for a cry of protest. Should she have left the light on low for Braelynn?

She waited by the door, but didn't hear a sound from inside the room. *Be with her, Heavenly Father*, she prayed. *You know her heart and her needs. I could use all the help You can give to do what I can for her as long as she's here.*

Putting the clothes in the washing machine and starting it, Rosemary looked across the kitchen to her sewing machine. A large battery was on the floor beneath it, and a pile of quilt blocks sat on top of the fat quarters Iva had given her. Both teased her to come and immerse herself in piecing them together. Since Eddie's death, she'd lost herself so many nights at her sewing machine.

But tonight wasn't for quilts. She needed to make clothes for Braelynn. The small dresses wouldn't take her long to cut and stitch on the machine. Picking up a length of pale pink cloth she'd bought for a dress before she began wearing black to mourn Eddie's passing, she thought how cute it would look on Braelynn. She set it down and picked up the black polyester she had left from making her own clothes. As Eddie's daughter, Braelynn should wear black for a year in honor of her *daed*.

Pausing, she looked out the nearby window. Lights were on in the building where Gideon was setting up his shop. She didn't want to be alone. She could use someone else's advice about what was best for Eddie's daughter.

She turned away. She didn't know anything about Gideon Wingard, other than he was a leatherworker. Something must have caused him to leave Smoketown. Something like what had caused her brother to leave Bliss Valley? Gideon hadn't jumped the fence into the *Englisch* world, but she had no idea what would have compelled him to turn his back on his home. Whatever problems he had left behind there, she didn't want them to seep into her own life.

Rosemary spent the next two hours cutting fabric and sewing it together. By the time she couldn't keep her eyes open or stop the yawning that threatened to split her face in half, she had five dresses, only three of them black, and five aprons for Braelynn. She'd made them a bit larger than the shirt the little girl had been wearing and kept deep hems, so Braelynn could wear them through a growth spurt.

Tomorrow, while she was at the quilt shop, she'd pick up some buckram or other stiff fabric along with bright blue polyester and blue ribbon to make a bonnet for the little girl to wear to service, though Rosemary knew she wouldn't take the little girl on Sunday. She wasn't sure how Braelynn would react to so many strangers. Rosemary wasn't even sure if the *kind* would cooperate while she stitched it. Would the little girl agree to wear it?

Pushing herself to her feet, she yawned hard. She wasn't going to find any more answers tonight.

Rosemary didn't intend to, but after she'd turned off the propane lamp in the kitchen, she looked out the window again toward Gideon's shop. Snow was falling again, slower than earlier. She could see the building was as dark as it had been before Gideon moved in. He must have gone to sleep.

Something she'd be smart to do, too.

Climbing the stairs, she tiptoed to Braelynn's door and opened it. She bit her lower lip as sorrow rose in her like a flood when she saw Braelynn curled up on the bed like a lonely puppy, her hands clutching the mangy-looking stuffed lion. Trails of tears glistened on her cheeks, and a sob hiccupped from her, though she was asleep.

Rosemary longed to rush to the bed, to scoop up the *kind* and comfort her. Waking Braelynn who'd found escape in her sleep, though it was restless, would have made Rosemary almost as heartless as the person who'd left those marks on the *kind*'s skin.

The little girl had been left—dumped!—in a strange house with strangers who didn't have things she must have considered normal like a television and electric lights. Had anyone explained to Braelynn what was about to happen? If they had, had the *kind* comprehended it?

How could she when Rosemary couldn't understand why anyone would leave the little girl and race away without any explanation except convoluted hints in a hastily written letter? If someone had treated a puppy or a kitten like that, they would have been charged with animal cruelty, but for a *kind*...

Her own tears threatened to tumble out. She blinked them away as she tiptoed into the room. She drew the covers up over Braelynn, not wanting her to be roused by the chill settling on the house. Right now, the *kind* might be happiest in her dreams because her waking world had spun out of her control.

Wanting to bend and kiss the little girl's mussed hair, Rosemary didn't. She backed away and drew the door partially closed.

The enormity of what she faced loomed before her in the darkness. How could she help a *kind* who was weeping for what had been lost when Rosemary hadn't come to terms with her own loss? Shock riveted her as she realized she and Braelynn had two things in common.

They'd both lost Eddie, and neither of them knew what to do next.

Chapter Five

Rosemary was avoiding him.

Gideon was as sure of that as he was his own name.

During the past two days, he'd gone to the farmhouse at least a dozen times, but each time, nobody answered the door. He'd peered into the kitchen, wondering if Rosemary was too busy with Braelynn to come to the door. The kitchen had looked deserted, and he hadn't seen anyone come or go. Once, he'd detected a light in the barn, but by the time he pulled on his coat and went to the door, the light was out.

Knowing he couldn't put off talking with her any longer if he wanted to keep the electricity on in his shop so he could use his sewing machine, he recalled how she'd said she often spent time at the quilt shop. Was that where she'd been? He tried to imagine her working at the shop with a recalcitrant *kind*. Or had Braelynn become more cooperative?

Don't get more involved, he warned himself as he had since the *Englisch* woman had stopped to deliver that envelope.

But he couldn't let his reluctance to get his life tangled up with anyone else's keep him from working to make his business thrive in the three months he had before he and Rosemary decided if he was going to stay. That's all it was. Business. Rosemary had made it clear she didn't want him sticking his nose into her life, and he was fine with that.

Yet, if that were true, then why was his heart beating faster than his horse's hooves on the road as he drove toward the quilt shop?

"Don't be silly," he muttered. "Be glad your *aentis* and *grossmammis* and sisters aren't watching you obsess over a woman."

Gideon turned his wagon into the parking lot that wrapped around the small building. Two cars were parked next to the shop. A three-sided barn at the back had room for four buggies and horses. Only three were parked under it, so he took the last place. Getting out, he put two rubber chocks behind the rear wheels, which would keep the wagon from rolling if Domino shifted. That could injure his horse.

Taking a deep breath, Gideon walked around to the front. It was a blessing the women in his family couldn't see him opening the door to the Quilts Are Bliss shop and entering. His *grossmammis* would have been peering from behind the racks of quilts lining the large room, sure nobody would notice them. Though, he knew, if they'd been there, they might as well have had a sign over their heads pointing at them because their version of whispering was almost a shout. His *aentis* would be right beside them, speculating. Then there would have been his sisters focused on whatever he said or did. Their leader would have been Darlene, his oldest sister, who at ten years Gideon's senior was the most determined to see him wed and nearby where she could keep a close eye on him.

He loved the distaff side of his family, but wished he could convince them they were smothering him. He'd tried. So many times, but his pleas had failed to reach past their assumptions that what they were doing was right.

Or as *Grossmammi* Wingard would say, "In one ear and never hitting their brain before going out the other."

He smiled. His *daed*'s *mamm* had a saying for any occasion. Pithy and always to the point.

A wave of homesickness flooded him, startling him. How was that possible? He'd been eager to put the big farmhouse behind him and live his own life, so why was he missing the hustle and bustle of his extended family before he'd been gone a week?

Gideon heard a muffled conversation from the back as he closed the door. He guessed there was at least one more room tacked onto the rear of the building. Everywhere he looked, there were quilts. In fact, the shop was overflowing with quilts and quilted items and materials for making more quilts. It was as if a rainbow had exploded, splashing color everywhere. A few of the quilts were dark, traditional colors. Most, however, had been made in bright hues that glowed in the sunshine coming through the windows.

Scents of fresh *kaffi* and recently ironed cotton filled the space. He guessed the room at the back must have both a *kaffi* maker and an ironing board. The smells reminded him of home.

Another powerful wave of emotion passed through him. *Not homesickness*, he argued with himself. *Nostalgia*. It wasn't as if he'd closed a door forever. Just for now.

"Can I help you?" a woman asked.

Startled, Gideon broke away from his bothersome thoughts. He'd been so mired in them that he hadn't noticed the short woman coming toward him. She had the brightest red hair he'd ever seen beneath her heart-shaped *kapp*.

"Is Rosemary here?" he asked.

"Rosemary Mishler?"

"*Ja.*" He wondered how many women in the area shared her name, which wasn't common among plain women.

"You must be Gideon."

It wasn't easy to hide his annoyance that he'd traded his family chattering about him and his business for a female landlord who did the same. "*Ja.* I'm Gideon Wingard."

"Welcome to Bliss Valley and to Quilts Are Bliss!" The woman's face brightened with a smile. "I'm Grace Coffman."

"Do you own this shop?"

"*Ja,* and, as the sign out front says, I sell the quilts." Without a pause, she added, "Rosemary said you're renting that old dairy house from her. What type of business are you planning to have?"

Apparently, Rosemary hadn't shared the details. He was amazed how relieved he felt about that. Maybe he hadn't been wrong in his first impression that she was a woman who minded her own business and respected other people's.

After he'd explained again how he planned to repair harnesses and tack as well as make new pieces, Grace smiled. "We need someone with your skills here. I'm glad you've come. But you aren't here to chat. You're looking for Rosemary. I think she and Braelynn are still out back." Holding up one finger, she said, "Let me check."

He waited while she disappeared into the rear room. Hearing the sound of wheels, he looked out the bay window to see a pair of buggies going past. One was open-topped and contained a quartet of giggling teenage girls. The other was a family buggy, and he saw two little *kinder* sitting next to a woman on the front seat. In the back, shopping bags with a major retailer's logo were visible. Both sights were familiar, and he guessed in most ways Bliss Valley wouldn't be that different from Smoketown.

"Gideon!" came a soft voice. "I didn't expect to see you here."

Facing Rosemary, who had paused near the counter with its cash register, he let his eyes linger on her fascinating face for only a moment. He didn't want her to think he was staring. Too many of his thoughts since he'd arrived had been about her and wondering how she could act so normal. His *mamm* had taken to her bed for almost a year after *Daed* died when Gideon was starting school, and she hadn't wanted to speak to her *kinder* for half that time. Rosemary was handling her farm alone and working at the quilt shop and dealing with a new tenant and an abandoned *kind*.

Was Rosemary stronger than his *mamm*, or did she not regret the loss of her husband as much as *Mamm* had?

His gaze was caught by hers, and he knew she mourned her husband with each breath. The pain darkening her eyes was so powerful it nearly sucked away his own breath.

"You told me you could be found here," he said, needing to say something. Anything.

Her eyes widened, then she nodded. "That's true. I did."

"Where's Braelynn?"

"She's in the back. She's not talking to anyone or acting as if she hears when someone talks to her." She frowned. "You didn't think I'd left her alone, did you?"

"I thought maybe someone had returned to take her home."

"No."

A thousand words were included in that single one. He could almost hear them all. No, nobody had come to claim Braelynn. No, the *kind* hadn't opened up to share anything more about her past. No, the little girl was as uncooperative as she'd been when she arrived.

No.

No.

No.

The list could go on and on, but Rosemary wasn't complaining about the burdens on her slender shoulders. At least not to him.

"What do you need?" she asked.

He focused on her again. "I've contacted the electric company to have the bill for the building's electricity sent to me."

"Oh, I never thought about that. *Danki.*"

"They told me they needed your okay before they make the change."

"How do they want us to do that?"

"They suggested the easiest way would be for you and me to sign on their website and change it there."

Her eyes widened. "But—"

He chuckled. "That's not going to happen, I know. When I told the woman on the phone that, she suggested we call them together. They'll talk to you while you confirm your account number. Once you give the okay, they can bill me."

"That makes sense." She pointed to a counter that was almost hidden beneath a jumble of colorful quilts. "Grace has a phone there. Do you have the number with you?"

"*Ja.*" He hesitated, then said, "But you'll need your account number when we call. The lady was quite emphatic about that."

"I know it."

"You know your whole account number?"

She almost smiled as she said, "I'm *gut* with numbers, Gideon."

"You must be." He glanced toward the counter. "Is it okay if we call now?"

"*Ja.* I'm sure you're very busy, too."

He followed her behind the counter. Taking the phone, he punched the number in and waited while it rang. After responding to several prompts, he was put on hold with a message that his call was important and he was seventh in the queue.

"It's going to be ten minutes or so before a real person comes on the line," Gideon said. "Sorry."

"You don't need to apologize." She lifted the top quilt off the pile on the counter. "I'll work here until you need me on the phone."

He watched as she folded the quilt to show off its pattern and colors. As he listened to the tinny music in his ear, he admired her quick, deft motions. He should have guessed any woman who could run a farm on her own could master any task.

As he thought that, she picked up a quilt that looked big enough to cover his wagon. She struggled to hold it off the floor and find the opposite corners.

"Let me help," he said.

"You need to stay on the phone." Her words were ground out between gritted teeth, and he realized the quilt must be heavy.

Hitting another button, he smiled. "I put it on speaker. We'll hear when the music stops and a human being is on the other end."

Gideon came around the counter and grasped the bottom of the quilt. She breathed a sigh of relief when he eased the weight off her shoulders.

Looking at the vast array of colors between them, he recognized the amount of work put into the intricate hand-quilted stitches that bound the layers of the quilt together. "It's a fancy one with the reds and greens and whites. I don't know if I've seen this pattern before."

"It's common, though the pattern has a lot of names." She found the corner she sought and straightened. "Some people call it The Wanderer's Path. Others use the name Solomon's Puzzle."

"What do you call it?"

"The Drunkard's Path."

He chuckled. "That's the perfect name for a quilt where the pieces wander in any line but a straight one. Okay, what do we do now?"

"Fold it in thirds lengthwise."

"Huh?"

"Watch me." She brought both corners together underneath the quilt and motioned with her head for him to do the same.

He did, but not as adroitly. She waited without comment while he worked to make the folds even.

A voice came from the phone, but it was the same recorded voice asking him to remain on the line. He paid it no mind as he followed Rosemary's directions. He stepped toward her, and she handed him the edge she held. Bending, she lifted the opposite end and motioned for him to fold it in half in her direction. As he did, a sweet scent washed over him.

Lilacs.

The sweet smell of spring and perfect for her with its light and enticing aroma that urged him closer. His gaze locked with hers, and he couldn't help being delighted at how he could look straight into her eyes. Eyes that were a lush gray with speckles of silver that danced like stars on a winter night, but there was nothing cold about their fire. He took a half step toward her, then halted when she spoke.

"There," she said. "You can let go of it. I've got it."

"Tell me where you want it."

He thought—for a split second—she'd protest, then she nodded.

"Put it on top of the other large quilt on the table to the left of the door," she said.

Toting the thick bundle of quilt as if it were as fragile as a newborn bird, he wondered if she had any idea that he'd been desperate to get away from her and that delicious scent while he still could. He stepped aside and let her adjust the quilt to her satisfaction.

"Do you sell many quilts that big?" he asked.

"*Ja. Englischers* like the huge quilts either for king-sized beds or to hang on their walls."

"It must have taken months to finish this."

"About one hundred hours, so it's priced at a thousand dollars. We price our work for ten times the number of hours we take to quilt it."

A suspicion niggled in the back of his mind. "Did you make this?"

"My sisters and I did." Again, that wisp of a smile played along her lips. "The three of us have worked together from the first time Erma—who's the youngest—was able to stitch a straight seam. It's a *wunderbaar* excuse to spend time together."

He wished he could describe time spent with his sisters as *wunderbaar*. "You're very close to your family."

"I have been." Color splashed across her face as if someone had slapped her as she hurried to add, "Everything has changed since Eddie's death."

"I guessed that. If you don't mind me asking, how long has he been gone?"

"Four months."

Four months? She'd lost her husband only four months ago? And now she was dealing with a little girl who was her late husband's *kind*?

God, he prayed, *You know more than I do how much help she needs. Please send it. I can't…*

A discordant sound from the phone broke into Gideon's prayer. He crossed the store and picked it up. The call had been dropped. Redialing the number, he heard a rapid busy signal. Hanging up, he tried again and got the same result.

"There must be some trouble with phones at the electric

company," he said as he faced Rosemary, who was folding a smaller quilt, her face lowered so he couldn't see her expression. "I can come back later and try again."

"Why don't we wait for tomorrow?" She continued to look at the quilt instead of him. "We can use the phone I share with my neighbors, so we don't keep this one in use."

"*Ja, gut* idea. Tomorrow works better for me, too."

"*Gut.*" She held the quilt close as if it were a shield. The lush pinks and warm ivories sent a rich warmth over the unusual planes of her face. "I'll stop in at your shop sometime during the afternoon, if that works."

"*Danki*, Rosemary." Again, he felt he should say something else, but words vanished as he noticed how intriguing she looked as she stood with her arms around the quilt and a single strand of her light brown hair falling forward along her cheek.

Before he couldn't keep from moving closer to her and pushing that vagrant tress back over her ear, he strode toward the door. He opened it, hurrying out. As he turned to shut it behind him, he saw the door to the back room open and several female faces peer out, including Braelynn who stared at him blankly. Curiosity bloomed on the other faces as eyes turned toward Rosemary and then glanced toward the door.

Gideon felt like a coward for leaving her there while he rushed to his wagon. They were her friends, he reminded himself. She'd know how to handle them. He hadn't moved to Bliss Valley to exchange one set of matchmakers for another.

Rosemary sat in her favorite chair, rocking as she stitched the ruffle at the back on the bonnet she was making for Braelynn. The little girl had been obliging about Rosemary fitting the bonnet to her head after they'd returned home from Grace's shop. Fascinated by how Rosemary had cut the fabric, Braelynn had watched until it was time for her to go to bed.

The *kind* hadn't asked a single question, though Rosemary had seen them in her eyes. Rosemary had swallowed her own curiosity. A simple query like if Braelynn wanted more *millich* could cause the little girl to close up, so Rosemary hadn't risked it.

Their visit to the quilt shop hadn't brought any change in the little girl. She hadn't spoken a single word, not even to Grace. Most *kinder* responded to Grace's bright smile and brighter red hair. Not Braelynn. She'd given Grace the same inert expression she offered everyone else.

The only time Braelynn's face had shown any emotion was when she and Rosemary had come out of the shop to discover LaVern loading groceries into the buggy. Braelynn had been curious what was in them and smiled when she saw a bag of coconut marshmallows on top. That smile vanished when the little girl realized Rosemary was looking at her.

Swallowing her sigh, Rosemary had thanked LaVern for his kindness in realizing she'd need extra food with another mouth to feed, but had ignored his attempts to flirt with her. She hadn't guessed Braelynn's non-expressive expression might prove to be useful for her, too, but it had, and LaVern had left sooner than he usually did when he chanced upon her alone.

If Braelynn had been aware of the underlying meaning in LaVern's words as he talked about walking out with Rosemary, the little girl showed no sign then or later. For once, Rosemary was grateful for the *kind*'s lack of interest in everything around her. That allowed Rosemary to act as if the conversation with LaVern had never happened.

And the one with Gideon, though that conversation was much more difficult to dismiss from her thoughts. The image of his caramel brown eyes lingered as well as how his lips had tilted with an easy grin as they stood face-to-face with the quilt between them.

Rosemary shook those alluring memories aside as she helped

Braelynn get ready for bed. She opened the dresser and pulled out a nightgown she'd found in one of the trunks in the attic. Washing it out by hand before they went to Grace's shop, she was glad to have it for the little girl to wear tonight.

There had been half a dozen trunks and big boxes in the attic. Most were filled with clothes for *bopplin* and *kinder*. She would have to find someone who could use the clothing that was too small for Braelynn. Looking at it reminded her how she'd failed to give Eddie the *kind* they'd wanted. She stuffed the tiny garments back in and closed the trunk. Another trunk was locked, so she ignored it. In others, she'd found toys and books and some unused coloring books. She'd seen Braelynn eyeing them, but the little girl hadn't gone over to examine the items.

Though Rosemary wondered why, she knew better than to ask. She pulled the little girl's new nightgown over her head and said a prayer she'd learned as a *kind*. She tucked Braelynn in with Cleo and wished her sweet dreams. She didn't attempt to kiss the *kind*'s cheek. The one time she had, Braelynn had let out a screech that must have rattled the neighbors' windows.

Rosemary went back downstairs. She didn't return to her chair. She remained at the bottom of the steps and listened to the house settle into the cold night. Snow fell beyond the window beside her, and a chill clamped onto her.

She told herself to move from the window. Her quilt frame urged her to remember her friends would be coming to the house for a quilting frolic in a few days. They were planning to make a quilt to be auctioned off to benefit the Bliss Valley Volunteer Fire Department. She should make sure everything was ready to begin.

Yet, she didn't move.

How could her life change so much in only a few days? Last week, she hadn't met either Gideon or Braelynn. Now, every thought she had was wrapped up in one or the other. Was this the answer to the prayer she'd offered up since Eddie's death? She'd prayed for God to show her a reason to feel alive again.

The creak of her back door made Rosemary stiffen. Who was calling in the midst of a snowstorm on a weekday night? Was it Gideon? She was shocked how her heart jumped at the thought. She ignored it and rushed to the kitchen.

She almost burst into tears when she saw *Mamm*. Rosemary flung her arms around her before *Mamm* could unbutton her coat. Patting her back, *Mamm* stepped back to shrug off her outer clothes.

Rosemary bit her lower lip, struggling not to cry like a *kind* seeking comfort after a bad dream. She knew *Mamm* would offer it. Sharon Beachy was a small woman who often faded into the background, especially when *Daed* was in one of his tempers, but *Mamm* had a resilience anyone would be *dumm* to underestimate. More than once, *Mamm* had reassured Rosemary that nobody expected her to jump into another marriage.

"That wouldn't be proper," *Mamm* had said. "You need time to find someone with whom you can be as happy as you were with Eddie. But you must find a husband sooner than later."

Rosemary had refrained from replying every time *Mamm* turned to the need for a man to oversee the farm. *Mamm* thought Rosemary should devote herself to her home and her garden and the *kinder* they would share. She understood why *Mamm* said what she did.

Mamm's marriage had never been serene, but not once had she appeared unsettled by the chaos of events around her. She'd withstood many storms, including her son jumping the fence and then returning, as well as her son-in-law's death and her husband being put under the *bann* when it was discovered he'd lied about an affair he'd had while married. *Mamm* had been a rampart for the rest of the family, holding them up and making sure each of them had what they needed. She'd made meals and clothes and kept them and the house immaculate. She'd skirted the anger that blossomed between her oldest *kind*—her only son—and her husband. With all her heart, *Mamm* believed a woman's greatest glory was her home, and she had focused her energies on that. She couldn't imagine any other sort of life.

Not for herself, and not for her widowed daughter.

Mamm sat at the kitchen table and said, "A cup of tea would be *gut* to warm my old bones."

"You aren't old," Rosemary replied, "and a cup of tea sounds great."

As Rosemary put on the kettle and opened the cupboard to get cups and tea bags, the events of the past few days poured out of her. *Mamm* didn't ask many questions, and Rosemary wondered how much the older woman already knew. She didn't ask as she poured the tea and brought *millich* from the refrigerator. Setting everything on the table, she sat across the table and watched the water in her cup turn brown.

"It sounds like God sent Gideon here when you needed him," *Mamm* said.

"He's focused on his shop. I'm glad that the building is being used."

"I'm glad you have someone with you on this farm." *Mamm* went on stirring her tea, the spoon making tinkling sounds against the cup. "I've been worried about you being here by yourself."

"I've been fine." She forced a smile. "Braelynn is here, and Gideon is by the road. Plenty of folks around here."

"That's *gut*. Another example of how God doesn't make mistakes," *Mamm* said. "That *kind* is no mistake."

"I know that."

"Do you?"

"Mostly," she admitted, relieved the subject had turned from Gideon to Braelynn. Why? Because he had enticing eyes and he'd been kind enough to help her fold the large quilt shouldn't be any reason for him to loiter in her thoughts. *Focus.* "I wish I'd known about Braelynn before this."

"That was Eddie's decision, not God's. The next decision is yours. What will you do now?"

Rosemary lifted her bag out of her cup and put it on her spoon, giving herself a moment to consider her answer. "I don't see any decision I need to make. If I don't take Braelynn in, where would she go? She's my husband's *kind*, and the day we married, she became my *kind*."

She couldn't help thinking of how *Mamm* hadn't hesitated to welcome her adopted son's family to be part of theirs. Only now did Rosemary comprehend how much strength her *mamm* possessed. She prayed she had as much.

"But what if there is someone out there looking for Braelynn?" she asked. "Her *mamm* must have some family."

Mamm reached for the sugar bowl and took out a single spoonful to stir into her tea. Rosemary almost smiled, but knew her *mamm* would be bothered by Rosemary pointing out that *Mamm* was heeding her *doktor*'s admonition to limit sugar in her diet. When the *doktor* had first mentioned it, Rosemary had kept less sugar on the table until Eddie had complained there wasn't enough. She'd gone back to making sure the bowl was always at least half-filled.

"What if there *is* someone looking for her, Rosemary?" *Mamm* asked. "You need to speak with Jonas about this."

She nodded. Though the bishop was younger than *Mamm*, Jonas Gundy was a blessing for his two districts. He thought through each question posed to him before answering.

"Jonas," *Mamm* continued, "offered *gut* guidance to your brother after he came back to Bliss Valley."

Rosemary stiffened and saw her *mamm*'s frown. Though her adopted son had left home for almost a decade, *Mamm* had never lost her dream of having her family together again. Not just in the same room, but connected heart-to-heart. She'd forgiven Joel for leaving, and she expected her three daughters to do the same.

Telling her *mamm* that forgiveness wasn't easy was something she couldn't do. Yet, she wouldn't be hypocritical and act as if Joel's vanishing hadn't happened and hadn't changed their lives.

"I know you and Joel haven't spoken much since he came home," *Mamm* said into the silence.

Not more than a dozen words, she concurred. "Our paths haven't crossed often."

Mamm's face lost all expression. A sure sign, Rosemary knew, she was guarding her emotions because allowing them to show would cause more distress.

"You and Joel are family," *Mamm* said. "Your paths don't cross. Your paths should be side by side." She took a sip of her tea, then put the cup onto the table. "Braelynn is now a part of our family. When your brother first returned to Bliss Valley, he slept where he could. Under trees, in barns, on someone's back porch. He didn't expect to find any open doors here. Don't let Braelynn feel unwanted, Rosemary."

"I wouldn't!"

"No? You still haven't welcomed your brother home, ain't so?"

"I told you. Joel and I have talked, *Mamm*."

"Maybe so, but nothing has been resolved between you."

"We're working on it." That was a blatant lie, and guilt sliced through her. Other than on church Sundays, she'd seen her brother a few times. Four, maybe five. That was it. Each time, they'd exchanged greetings. Nothing else.

She'd wanted to say more.

Joel had wanted to say more.

Yet, she'd cut each conversation short. She wasn't sure how long she could speak to him before the anger that had been simmering for most of her life burst out. When Eddie had told Joel to stay away from their farm, she'd been almost relieved. His edict had allowed her to avoid the confrontation she didn't want to have.

"When are you going to forgive him?" *Mamm* asked, ripping Rosemary away from the quagmire of her thoughts.

"That's not an easy question to answer."

"How can it be? To be forgiven, we must forgive. It's as simple as that."

"Was it simple to forgive *Daed* when he betrayed you?"

Mamm compressed her lips together. "It wasn't simple to forgive and mean it with my heart, but what I had to do was simple."

"I don't understand."

Her *mamm*'s face softened along with her voice. "Rosemary, you do understand we must forgive others so we can be forgiven as well, ain't so?"

"*Ja.*"

"It's easy to know what to do, but not easy to do what we must."

Rosemary nodded. She could understand that, though she couldn't understand how *Mamm* had come to forgive *Daed* after she'd learned he'd had an affair.

"Sometimes," *Mamm* went on, "our best ally in forgiving is realizing that we don't have to forget as well. We can let time dull the edges of our pain. That helps when facing the question if it's worse not to forgive or to hand the remnants of that pain over to God. He forgives all, Rosemary, even the truth in our hearts. Don't close yourself off to your brother or to God. If you let them in, you may discover it's not as hard as you expected."

Rosemary wanted to believe her *mamm*. When *Mamm* changed the subject to Braelynn and bid Rosemary *gut nacht* once her tea was finished, Rosemary's thoughts didn't shift far. It wasn't easy to accept she was acting toward Joel as Braelynn was toward her. Shutting him out and not getting to know the decent man he was now instead of the reckless boy he'd been. The realization sent a thudding pain into her heart. She was angry because he'd left Bliss Valley for almost a decade. She couldn't change just because Joel was home now and was ready to forgive and ask for forgiveness. She couldn't offer forgiveness.

Braelynn couldn't forgive her for…

Sorrow ripped through Rosemary as she realized she had no idea what the root was of the *kind*'s fury. She knew nothing about Braelynn other than she was Eddie's.

"Why didn't you tell me the truth?" she whispered, though there was nobody in the house but a *kind* who didn't understand *Deitsch*. "Did you think I would turn my back on your daughter?"

There was no answer.

Just as there hadn't been any answer from Eddie whenever she'd spoken to him for the last four months. Other widows had spoken to her of being able to recall their late husband's voices years after they'd died.

Eddie's voice in her heart had been buried along with him. All that was left were questions she didn't know how to answer.

Chapter Six

Rosemary got up before the sun in order to do her barn chores as she had every morning for the past four months. Dizziness and a ripple of nausea almost sent her back to bed, but the work couldn't wait. She was only milking a couple of cows now. However, cleaning the barn took longer with the cows inside. She looked forward to when the weather warmed and the herd could graze in the meadow.

Dressing with hands that were clumsy with exhaustion, she wondered why she'd bothered to change for bed last night. She hadn't found sleep as she tossed and turned…as she'd done the night before and the night before that.

In the three days since she'd found Braelynn in her kitchen, her well-ordered life, the life she had depended on to keep from having to confront her grief, had fallen apart. It had been revealed to be a house of cards, though until Braelynn's arrival, she'd convinced herself everything was as solid as the foundation under her home.

What a *dummkopf* she'd been! Because everyone had seemed

to believe her facade of dealing well with Eddie's death, she'd begun to believe it, too. Whom had she thought she was fooling?

Not God. He could see into her troubled heart. Had He brought Braelynn into her life so she couldn't hide from the truth any longer?

"There must have been easier ways to get my attention," she mumbled into the gray-and-red scarf she'd wrapped around the turned-up collar of her black wool coat before she went out into the predawn twilight. In the spring, the larks would be waking the other birds, but now the world was silent beneath its covering of snow.

A snowflake landed on her nose, and she swallowed her groan. This was the third storm in the same number of days. Or it could have been a storm that had lingered in Lancaster County instead of continuing east. Either way, if snow continued to fall, she'd need to shovel out the walk to the house again. The farm lane was plowed by an *Englisch* neighbor who had a blade on the front of his pickup truck.

When a gust of wind scoured her face, Rosemary ducked her head. She raised it again and saw a light flickering in the barn.

Her heart lurched. She always left a light on overnight in the barn when the cows were in the barn, but it was an electrical light. It didn't flicker like...

Like a flame.

Paying no attention to the icy spots on the path getting dusty with fresh snow, she rushed into the barn.

Scents of animals and hay and fresh *millich* greeted her. She'd loved going into barns since the first time she'd toddled after her brother, Joel, when he went to do the chores *Daed* had ordered him to do. *Daed* never should have been a dairy farmer because he hated the barn work.

Go away, she ordered the memories. Now wasn't the time

to be distracted by thoughts of the bad relationship between her brother and their *daed*.

She slapped the switch on the wall. Unlike the house, the barn had electricity made by a diesel stationary engine. It ran the lights and the dairy cooling tank that she'd used when, before his death, she and Eddie had milked twenty cows twice a day. Now the *millich* she got from two cows fit in the fridge in the utility room.

Nothing happened.

Everything was in shadow except that flickering light. Or so she thought.

Suddenly, a darkened shape, taller than any of her cows, emerged from the darkness. The light moved along with it. Who—or what—was in her barn? She gave a frightened yip before she realized the shifting shadow belonged to Gideon.

Pressing her hand over her heart that hammered like a woodpecker against a tree, she stared at him. The strong planes of his face were emphasized by the lantern he carried. Though his black hair was tousled and showed the outline of the hat he wasn't wearing, his light brown eyes were bright and twinkling.

Her fingers started to go to her own hair to smooth it back, but she halted them. She'd made sure her hair was neat beneath her *kapp* before she put on her bonnet. Glad its brim hid her own eyes, which she guessed were neither bright nor twinkling but dull with her lack of sleep, she tried to steady her breath. It wasn't easy when Gideon's smile teased her to give him one in return.

When she remained silent, his smile wavered. "I'm sorry if I scared you."

"What are you doing in my barn?" She hated how her voice quavered.

"Your power's out," Gideon said, gesturing with his elbow toward a dark light bulb between the rafters. "When I saw the lights were off, I came to make certain everything was okay." He hooked a thumb over his shoulder in the direction of the outbuilding where her diesel engine was housed. "It looks as if you've run out of diesel. Don't you have automatic delivery set up?"

"*Ja...*" She shook her head. "We did have it on automatic delivery last year, but I had to change delivery companies a couple of months ago when the previous one went out of business. I must have overlooked making the same arrangements."

"I hope I didn't overstep, but I called the emergency number on the wall in the engine shed. They said they'd be out within an hour or two."

Rosemary blinked as she stared at him. *He* had called her diesel provider without speaking with her first? Was he trying to take over her farm? To take Eddie's place? With each question rushing through her head, her heart thudded harder against her ribs, making it impossible to catch her breath.

"I—I—" She clamped her lips closed before she said something that would cause her to embarrass herself. If one of her friends had made the call on her behalf, she would have been grateful. Gideon's actions when he did the same thing shouldn't annoy her.

But she wasn't annoyed. She was feeling *dumm*, and she hated that feeling. Eddie had assured her so often that he was impressed with her *gut* sense, but he'd also said at the same time she should leave business decisions to him. He hadn't said more; yet the implication was clear. She couldn't handle the farm without his help.

She had. For the past four months, she'd done what she had to, milking cows, taking care of the animals and getting equipment ready for spring planting in the fields she wasn't renting to her neighbors. Despite knowing *hochmut* was wrong, she'd been proud of her accomplishments.

Until this morning.

Gideon set the kerosene lamp on a window ledge and frowned when she didn't add anything more. "You don't need to look so worried. I think I got the fuel pump stopped in time. I checked, and I didn't see any dregs from the tank. Once you get the diesel here, I can get it restarted for you."

"*Danki.*" The word wasn't as bitter on her tongue as she'd expected. She thanked God for that. "*Danki* for all you've done, but I know how to start the stationary engine."

"I'm sure you do, but I thought you might want to focus on Braelynn this morning." He leaned one hand against the wall.

"That's kind of you." Why did she sound so stiff? He had done a *wunderbaar* thing to save her from what would have been expensive repairs on the diesel engine. "I mean... I should have said..."

He put a hand on her shoulder. If his intention had been to help her regain her composure, it had the opposite effect. A buzz she hadn't expected vibrated through her.

Rosemary stepped hastily back, so hastily Gideon's hand lingered in midair as if she'd vanished without a trace. He glanced from her to it before lowering it to his side.

"I should have said *danki* sooner." She squared her shoulders, then motioned past him. "I'd better get to the milking. Pansy gets testy if she's not milked on time."

He didn't move. "I'd be glad to do the chores until you and Braelynn are on firmer footing with one another."

"*Danki*, but I can't ask you to take care of a herd that's not yours."

"You didn't ask, and it's no different from when you got help after your husband's death."

"I didn't have help then," she blurted before she could halt herself.

"Not at all?"

"My brother, Joel, offered as did others, but I told them I could handle it myself." She allowed herself a half smile. "And I have…until now."

"*Ja*, a lot changed when Braelynn arrived, ain't so?"

She appreciated his attempts to understand. Yet, if he could understand how different her life was with the *kind* in it, why couldn't he see that accepting his help would mean having to accept—once and for all—that Eddie wouldn't come back?

And accepting Braelynn was here to stay?

She was flooded with guilt. Braelynn was Eddie's daughter, and Rosemary shouldn't be imagining the *kind* leaving. This had been Eddie's home. It should be Braelynn's, too.

"A lot has happened since *you* arrived," she said to cover her thoughts again.

He grinned. "That's true. I never thought my desire to open my own business would trigger changes in someone else's life. If you want to milk the cows, I can carry the milk cans out and set them in the snow until the diesel gets here."

"If you could take them to the back porch, it'd be better."

"You have room for the *millich* in the house?"

She nodded.

"Okay," he said. "To the house it is."

Letting her shoulders relax, she said, "*Danki.*"

"You don't have to keep saying that."

"But I'm grateful for your help."

"It's what friends do for each other."

He considered them friends? Why shouldn't he? They were neighbors now, so it made sense they were friends as well.

As she bent to clean the cow's udder so she could begin milking, she asked, "Are you getting settled in?"

"*Ja.*" *Millich* cans clanged together, and then one was set on the concrete floor next to her. "Now all I need are some customers."

"Word will get around that you're here," she said, pulling the portable milker closer, so she could hook it to the cow. "Once it does, you'll get more work than you can do."

"That would be great."

Rosemary straightened and listened to the pulsing sound of the battery-operated milker. Patting the cow on the rump, she asked, "Why did you choose to come to Bliss Valley?"

"I needed to get away from an overly well-meaning family."

She wanted to ask him what he meant, but said, "Being an hour from Smoketown should help. If you miss them too much, you can visit."

"That's what I was hoping when I heard you had a building for rent." Without a pause, he asked, "Have you decided what you're going to do about Braelynn?" As he spoke the *kind*'s name, he looked toward the house.

She did, too. There was no sign of lights or movement.

"I'm going to talk to Jonas," she answered. "Our bishop."

"A *gut* idea. He'll know which authorities to contact."

She flinched and hoped his eagle eyes hadn't noticed.

But they had. "What's wrong?"

"I hate the idea of abandoning a *kind* who's already been abandoned." She patted the haunch of the cow again to give herself something to do with her unsteady hands. "And why are we even talking about this? There's no reason for her to go. She's Eddie's daughter, and I'm her step*mamm*."

As she spoke the words she'd first said after discovering Braelynn in the kitchen, she knew they were true. The moment Rosemary had married Eddie, Braelynn had become a part of their family.

Rosemary completed the milking and thanked Gideon for his help. When she offered him breakfast, he declined. He was eager to finish setting up the machines he used. As he left, he urged her to visit his shop and see them when she had a spare moment. She told herself it was curiosity that made her heart beat a bit faster at the invitation.

It couldn't be anything else. She wouldn't let it be anything else.

But if that were so, why did she stand in the barn's doorway and watch him put the cans on the back porch? She couldn't take her eyes off his easy stride as he went down the lane to his shop, whistling a merry tune. She envied his lack of the anxiety that dogged every step she took.

The kitchen was empty when Rosemary walked in, her boots crunching on the snow she'd tracked in with her. She took off her boots and padded to the auxiliary refrigerator Eddie had put into the utility room for times like this. As she put the *millich* in it, she was grateful for his foresight. To throw out the *millich* would have been such a waste. If they couldn't use it all, she'd make custard pies. She could serve them when the other quilters came to work on the quilt for the upcoming mud sale.

For now, however, she was going to get breakfast started. She put *kaffi* in the percolator and set it on the stove. She turned her attention to making oatmeal. Braelynn had gobbled it for breakfast each day, so that was a battle Rosemary didn't have to face. Once the oatmeal was simmering, she took a cup out and filled it with *kaffi*. She added a splash of *millich* and a teaspoon of sugar, mixing it up. Giving the oatmeal another stir, she took a deep drink of the *kaffi*.

She spat it out, then wiped her apron and counter. What was wrong with the *kaffi*?

Dipping her finger in the sugar bowl, she raised it to her nose and then to her lips. A single taste revealed why her *kaffi* had been so disgusting.

The sugar bowl was filled with salt.

Rosemary set down the cup and looked at the trash basket. She didn't see any sign of the missing sugar there. Where could it be? She glanced at the sink, but no sugar was by the drain. Had it melted?

As she turned away, something crunched beneath her socks. Not snow, she realized. Sugar. She followed the trail of crystals to the back door. Opening it, she frowned. A pockmarked area beyond the steps caught her eye. She knew that sugar scattered on snow melted it just as salt did.

That explained the missing sugar from the bowl, and Rosemary had no doubts who'd played the prank on her. Had Braelynn done it as a childish joke or an intentional effort to ruin Rosemary's morning?

Closing the door, Rosemary dumped the salt in the bowl down the drain. It had sugar mixed in with it and was worthless. She rinsed out the sink. She didn't sweep the floor. Two could play at pranks. She cleaned the bowl before refilling it from the sugar canister in the pantry. She made sure it was at the same level the salt had been. Setting it on the table, she poured a fresh cup of *kaffi* and added sugar. She sipped as she stirred the oatmeal.

Footsteps on the stairs announced Braelynn's arrival. Rosemary greeted her with a *gute mariye*, but got no answer. She hadn't expected one. Sensing the little girl's eyes following her motions as she spooned out the oatmeal, poured some *millich* on it and brought the bowl to the table, Rosemary sat.

"My *kaffi* is delicious this morning," she said, watching the *kind* who hadn't moved.

No reaction. Nothing at all. The little girl could have been a statue in the doorway. Only her eyes moved, and no hint of her emotions was visible in them. The glint of the sunshine on the locket she wore around her neck seemed the most living part of her.

"Don't let your breakfast get cold," Rosemary said.

Braelynn edged forward like a kitten sneaking through a kennel. Climbing onto her chair, she stared at the bowl in front of her.

Rosemary waited for a reaction—any reaction—from the *kind*. When Rosemary spooned crystals from the sugar bowl onto the oatmeal, the little girl sat in silence.

"I hope you'll find this is delicious today, too," Rosemary said.

No answer.

Was the little girl trying to gain the upper hand by not responding? Or was she trying to hide her guilt?

Rosemary smothered a shudder as she couldn't help imagining why the *kind* acted as she did. What had Braelynn's *mamm* and previous guardians done to her to make her so unwilling to speak? Every little one Rosemary knew babbled with excitement about everything in their lives. Every little one Rosemary knew, she reminded herself, had grown up with loving parents, grandparents and a vast extended family so they never felt alone or lost.

How would those *kinder* have reacted if they'd been dropped off in an *Englisch* house? People around them would have been talking in a language they didn't know, and many of the things that were familiar to them would have been missing while things they'd never seen had been put in their place.

Braelynn picked up her spoon and dug into her bowl. She didn't hesitate as she took a big bite of the oatmeal. With her head down, her expression was invisible.

Rosemary was taken aback. Had she been wrong? Could *she* have been the one to put the salt into the sugar bowl? She'd been upset enough last evening to make such a *dumm* mistake. Maybe she shouldn't have jumped to conclusions that Braelynn had played a prank on her.

She cast her thoughts back through last evening. Hadn't

there been plenty of sugar in it when she offered it to *Mamm* for her tea?

Fatigue threatened to flatten her like a steamroller, and she gulped her *kaffi*, hoping the caffeine would kick in.

It was going to be a long day.

Again...

Gideon glowered at the small kitchen stove on one side of his living quarters. The burners worked fine, but the oven refused to light. The pilot light was out. He could get a strip of cardboard and use it to ignite the pilot light. That would work fine, if he had a piece. The cardboard boxes he'd brought from Smoketown had been knocked down and put out with the trash.

Turning off the oven and the burner, he left the door open so any fumes would dissipate. He could make a sandwich and warm up some soup as he'd done every other night since he'd gotten to Bliss Valley. His stomach growled, and he thought of the potato and beef casserole *Mamm* had made and frozen for him before he'd left Smoketown. All he needed was a working oven.

He pulled on his coat and grabbed his hat, which he kept on the deep windowsill. Lowering the flame in the lamp in his workspace, he buttoned his coat close to his chin as he walked up the lane to Rosemary's house. He had to wonder if he was using the need for some matches as an excuse to see how her day had gone with Braelynn. Since he'd helped Rosemary with morning chores, he hadn't seen her or the *kind*.

Noticing a buggy parked at the top of the lane, he faltered. He didn't want to intrude if she had company. His stomach rumbled again, a reminder that if he didn't cook up the casserole, it soon wouldn't be any *gut*.

Gideon stepped up onto the back porch. If Rosemary had

a guy calling… His eyes shifted toward the window, though he tried to halt them. He saw a man sitting at the table with his back to the door. Rosemary rose to come to the door. Wanting to wave her away and leave her to enjoy her company, he couldn't make his hand obey him any more than he had his eyes.

"You don't need to stand out in the cold," she said as she opened the door and smiled.

When he was caught in the glow of her smile, something inside him melted as the snow had that afternoon. He savored the sensation until a chair scraping across the floor intruded. A thin man with a huge black beard got up.

"I'm—I'm—I'm sorry to disturb you," Gideon stammered.

Her smile didn't fluctuate. "You haven't. What can I do for you?"

"I was wondering if you had some matches I could use." He stuck his hands into his pockets, praying he didn't look as uncomfortable as he felt. "I thought I'd brought everything I needed, but somehow I forgot matches, and the pilot light is out on the oven, and I should have checked before I got supper ready to cook. I—" He shut his mouth before more babbling fell out of it.

The man with the thick beard came to stand beside Rosemary. "You must be Gideon Wingard."

"*Ja.*" Had the man guessed his name because of his stupid blathering? He told himself not to be ridiculous.

Rosemary saved him from more embarrassment by saying, "Gideon, this is Jonas Gundy, our bishop."

"Nice to meet you," Gideon said, shocked by the relief racing through him that her visitor was the bishop. Had he lost his mind? It shouldn't matter to him who called at the farmhouse.

To cover his unsteady thoughts, Gideon appraised Jonas Gundy. He was about Gideon's height and without an ounce of fat anywhere on his lanky body. His beard looked more massive because his face was thin. It was daunting, but the bishop's smile dashed away any hints of a stern Old Testament patriarch.

"I'd heard you've moved here," Jonas said as Rosemary motioned for Gideon to join them at the kitchen table. The bishop took the cup Rosemary offered him. "From Smoketown, ain't so?"

"*Ja.*"

"Curtis Reel's districts or Linus Hiester's?"

"Linus's," he replied and nodded his thanks to Rosemary who put a steaming cup in front of him before she sat in her usual chair, which offered her a *gut* view of both men. Where was Braelynn?

Jonas nodded, but Gideon caught the flicker of curiosity in the bishop's eyes. It wouldn't be seemly for Jonas to speak of another bishop, whether negative or positive. The flash had been enough for Gideon to know Linus Hiester's reputation for changing long-held traditions had reached Jonas's ears and Jonas was wondering if Gideon had moved to Bliss Valley to get away from Linus's edicts.

Into the silence, Gideon asked, "Where's Braelynn?"

"In bed." Rosemary glanced at the ceiling. "Or at least I assume she is. She's proving to be more devious than I'd expected."

As she explained about the salt in the sugar bowl that morning, Gideon was glad his lips weren't the only ones twitching in a grin.

Jonas became serious as he said, "Tell me more about the *kind*, Rosemary."

Gideon picked up his cup and took a drink, surprised to discover it was hot chocolate instead of *kaffi*. He'd been so focused on Jonas he hadn't noticed the aroma of chocolate in the kitchen. While Rosemary gave a concise outline of what had happened since they'd discovered Braelynn in her kitchen, he sipped and listened. She might have been talking about events that had involved strangers rather than herself. Not a hint of emotion filled her voice, and he wondered if she had any idea how her face resembled the *kind*'s blank one.

Were they both hiding feelings too painful to put on public display?

When she finished, ending with how Braelynn seemed content to spend time by herself, she added, "I get the feeling she's been left alone far too much. When she seems to be enjoying something, like coloring, she brings it to a quick end."

"As if she expects happiness to be fleeting?" the bishop asked, impressing Gideon with his insight.

Rosemary folded her arms on the table and leaned toward them. "If you want my opinion—"

"We do," urged Jonas. "You know her better than anyone else in Bliss Valley."

"And I barely know her. The poor *kind*! Alone in the world and with no expectations of that changing. Jonas, she has deep bruises on her shoulders and arms."

"Abused?"

"*Ja.* No *kind* should have marks on them like that."

"Do you have any idea who did it to her?"

"They're recent, but I don't know. It could have been the woman who left her here, or it could have been someone else. I've asked her, but she refuses to answer."

"Scared?" asked the bishop.

"Less scared than resigned." She blinked a couple of times, but no hint of tears tainted her voice. "In my opinion, she's had hope fail her too often, so she doesn't dare to hope any longer."

"She reminds me," Gideon said, "of a cat we once had dropped off at our farm. It longed to be around people. You could see that, but it either didn't know how or didn't dare to get close to anyone because it'd been abandoned one time too many."

"That's it." Rosemary's face lit anew as she smiled at him. "*Danki*, Gideon."

Jonas sipped his hot chocolate, his gaze moving between Gideon and Rosemary. Gideon took a gulp from his cup. He almost choked on the hot liquid, but managed not to spew it over the table.

Rosemary gave him an odd look, but turned to Jonas as the bishop put his cup on the table.

"I will speak with Children's Services, Rosemary," Jonas said. "I know Naomi King... Have you met her, Gideon?"

He started to shake his head, then glanced at Rosemary. "She may have been at the quilt shop when I stopped in."

"She was," Rosemary replied. "She was the one with the twin boys." She rolled her eyes at her own words. "You might not have seen them. I think they were napping when you came in."

Jonas went on as if they hadn't spoken. "Naomi worked with Children's Services when she found a *boppli* on the steps of the family's *dawdi-haus* last year. She may have a name and number for me to contact. She's still a licensed foster parent, though she has enough to keep her busy with three very young ones." He smiled, easing his lean features.

"Foster parent?" she asked. "Why would we need one of those? I'm Braelynn's step*mamm*."

"If what was in the letter is true."

Rosemary's shoulders grew taut, and Gideon yearned to put his arm around them to ease her distress. "Why would anyone go to the trouble to make up a fake birth certificate?" she asked.

"It may not be fake." He raised his hands in a pose of surrender and smiled sadly. "Rosemary, Gideon, I'm not trying to look for trouble where there might not be any, but the truth is that we don't have any idea what the truth is."

She nodded, seeming to shrink into herself. Was she thinking of how her late husband had failed to tell her about his *kind*?

"What about Eddie's family?" the bishop asked.

"He doesn't have any immediate family," she said. "His parents died in an accident about five years ago."

"What about other relatives?"

"I don't know." A flush rose up her cheeks as if she were horrified to have to admit that.

"The social workers are going to want to know if any of his relatives are alive."

"Why?" asked Gideon, though he knew he should have kept his mouth shut. He didn't have any say in what happened to the *kind*.

Jonas sighed. "The authorities may want to make sure no blood relative wants to lay claim to Braelynn."

"But I'm her step*mamm*." Her hands clenched around her cup so hard that Gideon was amazed it didn't burst in a shower of shards. "Shouldn't she be with me?"

"Do you want her here?" Jonas's question was soft, but seemed to echo like a gunshot across an empty field.

When Gideon looked at Rosemary, he saw every bit of color drain from her face. The longing to pull her into his arms and comfort her was so strong his feet pressed against the floor, urging him to stand and go to her. He stayed where he was. She wouldn't appreciate him acting so boldly, especially when the bishop was sitting beside her.

"Jonas," she said, "I'm so short on sleep, I can't begin to tell you what I want. However, if she is Eddie's daughter, she's mine, too. I'm praying God will see me through each day and help me deal with every challenge Braelynn presents me."

"He is with you, even through this turbulent time." Jonas patted her arm. "He listens to your prayers. Don't doubt that."

"I don't," she replied.

Gideon had to admire her faith. If his was as strong, would he have been able to stand up to his family and ask them to let him walk the path God had set out for him before he was born? Whether it meant he married or not.

"Eddie told me he was from western Pennsylvania," Rosemary said. "We should start there."

"Which district?" asked Jonas.

"I don't know. Near Lake Erie."

It was impossible for Gideon not to gasp at her unexpected remark. She didn't know where her husband had lived before he came to Bliss Valley?

Rising, she went to the counter and opened a drawer beneath it. She brought a book back to the table and opened it. He leaned forward and saw it appeared to be a guest book. From hers and Eddie's wedding or from his funeral? He didn't ask as she ran her finger along one page of names and addresses and then turned it to the next pages.

"There were several guests from Erie County at our wedding," she said, pointing to the names.

Jonas pulled a piece of paper from his pocket and scribbled the names and addresses on it. "I can contact the bishops in that area, and they may be able to clear up the mystery."

Did the bishop notice how she shuddered when he said *mystery*? What else did she suspect Eddie had hidden?

Chapter Seven

All day the next day, Rosemary stayed close to home. She hoped Jonas would come to share whatever he'd found out with her. Though she knew it was likely to be a week or more before he had anything definitive, she couldn't keep from glancing out the windows that gave her a view of the farm lane. No buggies pulled up it.

She let the shade drop against the window after peeking out yet again. Locking her hands behind her, she crossed the living room and almost stepped on Braelynn who was stretched out, coloring in one of the books Rosemary had brought from the attic.

The book's pages, which had been kept out of the sun, were as creamy as the day it'd been bought. Braelynn dug into the tin box of crayons, many of them broken, to find the exact color she wanted for the barnyard scene with cows and goats and chickens.

Chickens!

"Ach!" Rosemary gasped. "I forgot to feed the chickens."

"Braelynn wanna help!" She jumped to her feet and ran to get her coat.

Rosemary froze, shocked by the sound of the *kind*'s enthusiastic voice. Braelynn hadn't said a single word today until now. Not even when Rosemary had given her a plain dress to wear. The little girl looked darling in the pale pink with its small black apron. After wearing nothing but black herself for the past few months, Rosemary hadn't had the heart to put out such a somber dress for the little girl. Did Braelynn even remember Eddie?

"All right," she replied, hoping her voice didn't sound as squeaky to the *kind* as it did to her. "*Komm* with me, and I'll show you how to feed them."

Amazement filled her when Braelynn nodded as she pulled on her coat. Rosemary helped her button it, making sure she didn't touch any of the places where Braelynn had been bruised, before getting her own coat and her bonnet. She pulled a stocking cap over the little girl's head because Braelynn's bonnet wasn't finished yet.

Did the bruises still hurt? Braelynn hadn't complained once, but Rosemary wondered what—who!—had caused those bruises.

Braelynn skipped out the door. Rosemary watched in amazement. The little girl was acting like a carefree *kind* as she trailed Rosemary to where the corn was stored.

Rosemary filled the small bucket and led the way to the coop. She paused and said, "Chicken coops can be stinky."

Pinching her nose, Braelynn didn't say anything.

Was the little girl going back to silence? Rosemary prayed that wouldn't be so.

The coop was a small shed with two openings into the run. A short door on the side was for entry into the coop where the chickens were safe from predators and had a quiet place to lay their eggs.

Braelynn ran forward as the rooster let out an enthusiastic crow. She halted in astonishment, her fingers laced through the chicken run's wire.

Rosemary wondered if Braelynn had seen chickens other than in storybooks. The *kind* stared at them as if they were the most wondrous creatures on earth.

"Is that the little red hen?" asked the little girl, confirming Rosemary's thoughts. She pointed to a rust-colored chicken.

It was the rooster, Rosemary knew, but didn't want anything to stop the conversation. *"Ja,"* she said as she held out the bucket to the *kind*. "It's a red chicken."

Braelynn scattered the corn within the run as Rosemary showed her. She gasped as the chickens came running to feast. "Where are Turkey Lurkey and Ducky Lucky?"

"Who?"

"Chicken Little's friends." Braelynn peered through the wire. "Which one is Chicken Little?"

"Which one do you think?"

"That one." She pointed to a hen coming out of the coop. Bits of straw clung to her feathers, a sure sign the chicken had been sitting on a nest. "He's little. Is that Chicken Little?"

Again, Rosemary cautioned herself. It wasn't the time to explain that any chickens sitting on a nest for more than a few minutes were hens, not roosters.

"Must be," she said, wanting to keep the *kind* talking. She dumped the last of the corn into the center of the run.

"So where are Turkey Lurky and Ducky Lucky?"

"Ducky Lucky has flown south until spring, and Turkey Lurkey is in his own coop at Calvin's farm." Her neighbor raised a few turkeys for *Englischers* to buy for Thanksgiving and Christmas.

The little girl looked up and gasped again as large flakes of snow drifted out of the low clouds. "The sky is falling!"

"Not the sky. Just snow." She held her hand up and lowered it to let the *kind* see the clump of snowflakes on her glove. "Chicken Little must have been mistaken."

"Snow!" Braelynn twirled away from the coop. "It's snow!"

"It is. See if you can catch some flakes, too."

Rosemary watched, a mixture of joy and sorrow seeping through her, as the *kind* zipped around the yard, holding up her hands and then lowering them to watch the snowflakes dissolve into her mittens. Joy that Braelynn was acting as a five-year-old should, but sadness that this seemed to be something new for the little girl. How was it possible she'd never played outside in falling snow before?

The little girl bounced back to the chicken coop and peered at the chickens again. "Braelynn hold them!"

Rosemary shook her head, hating to say no. "Hens can peck your fingers."

The *kind* looked at her, baffled.

Rosemary tapped her own finger. "Ouch!" she exclaimed.

Braelynn's eyes got big. "But chickens are nice. No ouch."

"*Ja*, they are nice, but they don't like to be picked up. They'll let you know that right away." She smiled. "In a few months, there will be chicks. You'll like holding them."

"Chick?"

"A *boppli*—a baby—chicken. They're little and soft and don't peck your fingers as long as you're careful with them."

"Braelynn wanna hold."

"You're going to have to wait. We don't have any chicks right now."

"Braelynn get chicks!" She stamped her foot.

"As soon as they're born, we'll visit them."

"Promise?"

Wondering how many promises had been made to the *kind* and how few had been kept, Rosemary hesitated. Would Braelynn be on the farm by the time the chicks emerged in the spring?

"I will let you know when we can start watching for chicks," she hedged.

As the little girl turned back to watch the chickens, Rosemary wished again for news about Braelynn. She must be patient. Or at least try to be. How many times had *Mamm* urged her daughters to follow the teachings of Romans 12:12? *Rejoicing in hope; patient in tribulation; continuing instant in prayer.*

It was *gut* advice, and like so much *gut* advice, easier to give than to do. She glanced at Iva's house across the field. How much she would appreciate her elderly friend's insight right now! If she went...

She negated that thought. She wasn't sure how Braelynn would act in another house or with another stranger. When they'd gone to Grace's shop, Braelynn had huddled in a corner, resisting every effort to get her to join the others. That might explain why nobody but *Mamm* and Jonas had come to see her in the wake of Braelynn's arrival. It wasn't like the community to stay away during such a momentous happening.

But it's been less than a week since she got here.

That seemed impossible. Time had slowed to a standstill while she spent each day hardly daring to breathe as she waited for Braelynn's next reaction. As the little girl tried to get the chickens to come closer, Rosemary's gaze shifted to Gideon's shop at the bottom of the lane.

She smiled. A visit there might give her a better idea of how Braelynn would act beyond the house and the yard. Gideon had offered to help, so maybe it was time for her to accept. Another puff of happiness flitted through her like petals on the wind. No, she wasn't going to think about how nice it would be to talk to him again. She must not think that way about another man when Eddie, her dearest Eddie, had been gone such a short time. She'd never forgive herself for being fickle and turning her back on the blessing God had given her when He brought Eddie into her life.

But I never thought it'd be this lonely to be all alone night after night.

The smooth motion of his strap cutter against leather was the only sound in Gideon's shop. He was slicing long, narrow strips of leather. When he'd put some of his belts on display at an inn near the Smoketown Airport, he'd had a lot of sales. The owners had guessed—quite rightly—that their customers who took both tourist and business tours of the farmlands would be interested in his craftsmanship.

He needed to make similar contacts in Bliss Valley to expand his business so he could reassure Rosemary that he'd be able to continue paying his rent. To grow his business, he had to find a place here to showcase his wares. That's what he'd come there to do: take control of his life and his business. He would make the decisions. It wouldn't be someone else's choice.

And he was doing that. A single trip to LaVern Spaeger's bulk grocery store had shown him it wasn't the location he sought. The store was poorly lit, and the wares looked as if they'd been run over by a semi. Jonas, on his way out last night, had suggested Gideon contact Colt Jackson who ran a booth at the Central Market in the city of Lancaster. The bishop also mentioned the Acorn Farm Inn not far from the Bliss Valley Covered Bridge, which was run by a Mennonite woman.

Gideon planned to do that, but the thought of the bishop sent his mind toward Rosemary again. She was taking up too many of his thoughts. What had happened to his intention not to get

involved with anything other than his business? Getting close
to Rosemary—and Braelynn—would be stupid. He didn't want
to be sucked into more drama, greater than what he'd left behind. He'd made his choice to step aside from others' turmoils.
He couldn't forget that.

A motion caught his eye. He groaned as his thoughts came
to life. Rosemary was coming down the lane along with Braelynn.

The little girl walked as far from Rosemary as she could,
but kept glancing at Rosemary. Were those wary looks? Or
something else altogether?

For her part, Rosemary was swinging a small covered basket as if her life was perfect. It was an illusion. It had to be.
Her life had been upended four months ago by her husband's
death and all over again by Braelynn's arrival.

Were they walking past his shop?

He hoped they were.

He hoped they weren't.

Again, he groaned. How could he expect to keep his life on
an even keel when his own mind was tormenting him with
indecision?

Gideon went to the door and made sure he was smiling
when it opened. "Where are you bound on such a cold day?"

"To bring you these." Rosemary opened the basket and
pulled out a plate of cookies.

Chocolate chip or oatmeal raisin, he guessed. Not that it
mattered. He liked both.

"*Komm* in," he urged. "It's freezing out there."

"January in Bliss Valley is either freezing or snowy."

"Or both this year."

"*Ja.* I don't know which I'd prefer, which is a *gut* reason for
God to oversee the weather and not me."

Setting the plate on the counter he'd set up to divide his work area from the entry, he watched Braelynn. She was intrigued by his sewing machine and the tools displayed on the pegboard along the walls. He stepped forward to halt her before she could get too close to either of them. He put his hand on the sewing machine. She backed up a step, and he wondered if he'd scared her. That hadn't been his intention. He'd wanted to move between her and the enticement of examining his tools. Too many of them would be dangerous in the hands of a young *kind*.

Rosemary asked, "Wouldn't you like a cookie?"

At the offer, the little girl rushed to Rosemary. Braelynn took two of the cookies and crouched on the floor as she relished them. Gideon followed and selected a cookie from the plate. Chocolate chip and warm. Yummy!

When Rosemary chose one, he found himself watching each graceful motion she made. Her most commonplace was as delicate as a bird swooping over a field. The black she wore wasn't a flattering color, but nothing could lessen the sweet rose warmth of her cheeks and the luscious tint of her lips. He'd be a fool to lose himself in their depths.

She raised her gaze toward him, and he was skewered by the fatigue in her eyes. A fatigue underlined her unremitting strength. Suddenly, he wanted nothing more than to pull her into his arms and help her push aside the burdens she carried in her heart.

Knowing he should say something, he searched his mind. "Oh, I should have let you know that the electric company sent me a confirmation I'll be getting the bill from now on."

"I'm glad that's taken care of."

"Me, too." What a stilted conversation! He didn't know what else to say, and he guessed she felt the same.

"If you have any other concerns, let me know." She held out her hand to Braelynn. "Let's get back to the house. Our sugar cookies should be ready to cut out and bake now."

He didn't dare take a breath as he waited to see what the *kind* would do. Would she acquiesce to Rosemary's request or act as if she hadn't heard a word said to her?

"Braelynn have a drink of water?" the little girl asked.

Hoping he didn't look stunned, he said, "Go ahead. The sink's in the back. Don't touch anything else. Okay?"

She gave a quick nod and raced around the corner and into his private room.

"You didn't need to do that," Rosemary said softly so her voice didn't reach the *kind*. "She could have waited until we got to the house."

"I know, but I'm amazed she's talking to you."

"Cookies."

"What about them?"

"Cookies are the best way I've found to get her to do what I need her to do. Cookies and chickens."

"Together?"

A smile tugged at her lips. "Not so far, but if that's what it takes, I'll set up a chicken coop in the summer kitchen."

"At least you've now got a couple of things that work."

"*Ja*, and I'm grateful to God for that. I know He has a reason for everything that happens, but I've got to admit I don't have the slightest idea what He wants me to do with her."

"Take care of her?"

"It can't be that simple."

He glanced into his small kitchen where the little girl was filling a glass and emptying it out before refilling it. "Maybe, in this case, Rosemary, having someone to take care of her is what's been lacking from her life."

"I keep wondering why Eddie didn't take her after her *mamm* died."

"Don't torture yourself with questions you'll never get answered while you walk the earth. I know Braelynn's life didn't begin the day she arrived at your house, but in many ways, it has."

Her brows rose. "I never thought of it that way."

"Maybe—"

A shriek rang through the shop.

Gideon whirled and saw his worst nightmare come to life. Braelynn stood by his worktable, blood dripping from her right hand. He'd taken his eyes off her for a moment, and one of his tools had hurt her.

He rounded the end of the counter. He wasn't quick enough. Rosemary brushed past him. She stopped in front of the *kind*, and he tried to do the same. His shoes skidded, then stuck. He nearly careened into them. Twisting, he hammered his shoulder into the doorframe.

"Gideon, do you have a first aid kit?" asked Rosemary, her attention on the little girl whose hand she cupped in her own.

Grateful that she hadn't seen his clumsy impact, he said, "It's under the counter."

"We need an antibiotic and a bandage."

"Do you have any with dinosaurs on them?" Braelynn asked.

"No." His answer came gruffer than he'd intended because he was surprised she'd spoken to him.

"Whatever you have will be fine." Rosemary led the *kind* to his stool and lifted her onto it.

Bringing the small box, he couldn't look away from Rosemary's face. It was gentle and filled with compassion that revealed the truth. She considered Braelynn more than a responsibility. She cared deeply about the difficult *kind*.

An ache to be part of the connection they were creating almost made him stumble again. Had he lost his mind? He'd left Smoketown to avoid getting caught up in a situation he couldn't control. He couldn't let loneliness betray him into forgetting his resolution. It was better that he said nothing as he handed the box to Rosemary. Even so, her soft thanks resonated through him as if it'd been as loud as a clap of thunder.

"Let's take care of that," Rosemary murmured.

Braelynn's sobs had softened to hiccups. "Braelynn hurts!"

"I know, *liebling*." She opened the box and took out a clear bandage and the tube of antiseptic. After applying both, she asked, "Better?"

Braelynn stared at her, then at Gideon, meeting his eyes for the first time.

Making sure he didn't shift his gaze away, he steeled himself for the little girl's answer when Rosemary asked, "How did you get cut?"

"The glass bit Braelynn."

What? He didn't have any tools made of glass. His shoulders eased when Braelynn admitted she'd hit the glass too hard against the tap. She'd cut her finger while trying to fish the shard out of the sink.

Rosemary reassured her she didn't need to feel bad about the broken glass. "Next time, call me. I'll take care of it, so you don't get hurt."

"You will? You won't get mad at Braelynn?"

"Nobody should get angry because of an accident."

"Really?" Distrust filled the *kind*'s eyes.

Gideon watched, wondering what had happened to this *kind* before she'd come into Rosemary's life. The bruises on her arms below the sleeves of her pink dress had turned a sickish shade of yellow-green.

Had Eddie Mishler known what his daughter was going through? How could he have and been the man Rosemary believed him to be?

Something didn't add up, and Gideon wasn't a guy who

wanted to leave questions unanswered. He needed to get to the truth, though he wasn't sure where to begin.

All he knew was that he had to do something. He wasn't sure how he could and stick to his plan to keep his life under his own control. There had to be a way. All he needed to do was figure it out.

Chapter Eight

Rosemary folded her hands on the table the next morning and began to talk to Braelynn about the chores they had ahead of them. She didn't ask the *kind* if she wanted to help. She simply said, "We will do…" and "After that, we'll…" She wanted the little girl to know Rosemary considered her an integral part of the household.

At least for now.

Jonas could have been right when he said that Braelynn might not be Eddie's daughter.

No, she wasn't going to think of that. She needed to be grateful Braelynn hadn't spent the whole morning in her room as she had previously. The little girl had slipped away for about a half hour before coming back as Rosemary finished washing the breakfast dishes.

"Lots of chores," Braelynn grumbled. "Braelynn wanna play with chickens."

"We'll find time to play, too. God wants us to be happy." When the little girl gave her a look filled with curiosity, she smiled. "It says so right in the one-hundredth and forty-fourth Psalm. *Happy is that people, whose God is the Lord.* We are His people, so we rejoice in that."

"Huh?"

She repeated the verse, but the little girl gave her the same blank stare.

"I guess," Rosemary said, "you've never heard that psalm."

"What's a some? Like some of this or some of that?"

"Not some. *Psalm.* It's a poem or a song a king wrote to praise God. There are one hundred and fifty of them."

The *kind* gasped. "Do you know all of them?"

"I know some."

"Some some-psalm?" The little girl giggled.

Rosemary chuckled, too, hoping the sound hid how floored she was. She'd begun to wonder if the *kind* knew how to giggle. What other surprises did the little girl have in store for her?

"Something like that," Rosemary said, which caused Braelynn to snort with laughter before dissolving into giggles again.

Glad Braelynn was in such a *gut* mood, Rosemary decided it was time to check the bandage on the little girl's hand. Braelynn had refused to let her do that before breakfast. Rosemary couldn't let her stubborn refusal lead to an infected finger. Even if she had to wrestle the little girl to the floor and sit on her while she tended to her index finger.

The image shocked Rosemary. When she'd imagined having *kinder*, she'd thought about feeding them and teaching them to do chores as well as reading them stories and saying a prayer and tucking the covers around them before tiptoeing out of the room at day's end. She'd envisioned laughter and tears and sharing special moments she'd treasure forever.

She hadn't conceived of a *kind* who refused to talk for days at a time or cooperate or to do something Braelynn didn't want to do...just to spite Rosemary. Leaving Braelynn by herself was something Rosemary couldn't do because she feared the little girl would run away. When she'd first arrived, Braelynn had spent hours staring out the front window. Was she plotting a way to escape? Or was the little girl waiting for someone to come for her? Someone who never came?

Rosemary's heart broke each time she thought that. She would have comforted the *kind* if Braelynn would let her near. For the past week, Braelynn had stood just beyond Rosemary's fingertips, almost as if daring her to try to touch the *kind*. A couple of times, Rosemary had taken a step toward her. Each time, Braelynn skittered back far enough to remain out of reach.

That morning, as she cleaned the kitchen with Braelynn helping by emptying the trash can and setting her boots together under their coats, Rosemary dared to believe things had changed. Braelynn didn't initiate a conversation, but she would respond—most of the time—when Rosemary spoke to her. They worked side by side in the house and tending to the animals, though Braelynn wasn't interested in any others but the chickens.

Coming into the house to prepare their midday meal, Rosemary paused as she was hanging up her bonnet. A buggy rolled to a stop in front of her barn, then another and another. She glanced at the calendar. Was today the day for the quilting frolic?

No, next week.

So why were there a half dozen buggies parked in her lane?

"Who's that?" asked Braelynn. Fear mixed with her curiosity.

Before Rosemary could reply, the kitchen door opened and a crowd of women and *kinder* poured into the house. Like a twig in a flood tide, she and Braelynn were swept toward the living room.

Greetings were called out and bowls and covered platters set on the table until it looked as if they were preparing for a barn raising. Each of the ten women coming in carried satchels, which they set by the door.

For once, Rosemary was as speechless as Braelynn.

Two toddlers rushed forward and threw their arms around Braelynn. The little girl stiffened for a second, then softened into their enthusiastic embrace.

"Boys," called Naomi King. The twins' *mamm* was much shorter than Rosemary. Her golden hair glistened in the sunshine coming through the windows. "Coats and boots off first."

Rosemary followed the twins toward Naomi whose *boppli*, May, was sitting between her feet. Naomi was taking May's coat off and untying the winter hat from under the *boppli*'s chubby chin. As the boys pulled off their knitted toques, Rosemary asked, "What's going on?"

"A 'happy you're here' shower."

"A what?"

"Braelynn is too big for a *boppli* shower, so we thought this was a way to let her know we're glad she's here. It was Laurene's idea, as you may have guessed." Naomi didn't look up as she undid the buttons on her twins' black wool coats. With obvious experience, she caught both coats as the three-year-olds tossed them at her in their excitement. "Jared, Jesse, remember what we talked about?"

"Be *gut*," said Jared.

"Be nice," Jesse added in the same deflated voice as his brother. "Fun?"

"*Ja*, we'll have fun." She ruffled their pale blond hair and then scooped up the wiggling *boppli* who chewed on her knuckles. Leaning May on one hip, she turned to answer a question from Rosemary's sister, Alta.

Making sure her face didn't lose its smile, Rosemary tried

to suppress the envy that flooded her. How much she wanted *kinder* of her own! She and Eddie had talked about a family. Not once had he given her any clue that he already had a *kind*. Now he was gone along with her chance for the *boppli* they'd hoped for.

But she had a *kind*. Because Braelynn was recalcitrant and only spoke when she wanted to didn't mean she wasn't part of Rosemary's life. More yearning rose through her as she imagined Braelynn being as spontaneous and loving as Naomi's twins were.

As if she'd said that aloud, Braelynn edged forward and looked around her. "Baby," the *kind* said in wonder. "Pretty baby."

"Ja." She drew the little girl forward to get a better view of May. "She is a very sweet *boppli*."

"Bubble?"

"Boppli," she said. "It's how we say baby."

"Why not say baby?"

Rosemary had no time to answer as a girl close to Braelynn's age pushed forward. Mary Beth Hershberger was the daughter of Laurene and Adam, their deacon. Her hair was a shade darker than the twins'. Today, it was twisted in a small bun and covered by a fine net to hold it in place. The way the little girl bounced around, Rosemary suspected the net's task would be overwhelming.

All four *kinder* started talking at once. Mary Beth grabbed Braelynn's hand and led her and the twins into the living room where they pulled out boxes with coloring books and crayons and toys from under the *kaffi* table. Sitting, they sorted through the collection until they found what they wanted.

Arms were flung around Rosemary, and she smiled at her younger sisters. Erma and Alta were so close in age they'd been almost like twins. They'd stuck together while Rosemary had spent time with their older brother, Joel.

Until he jumped the fence, leaving her with a hole in her heart that hadn't healed.

Sometimes, our best ally in forgiving is realizing that we don't have to forget as well. We can let time dull the edges of our pain. That helps when facing the question if it's worse not to forgive or to hand the remnants of that pain over to God. He forgives all, Rosemary, even the truth in our hearts. Don't close yourself off to your brother or to God. If you let them in, you may discover it's not as hard as you expected.

Her *mamm*'s words echoed with surprising clarity in her mind as Rosemary greeted her sisters and the other women from her quilting circle.

When a cup of warm cider was pressed into her hands, Rosemary took a sip and tried to catch her breath. She'd seen wrapped boxes in the satchels, and she guessed each one contained something that would be intended to make Braelynn feel at home. Looking around, she realized, other than Grace Coffman, every member of their quilting circle was present, even Lori Ann Hertzler and Teresa Spaeger whom she hadn't seen much since Eddie's death. Lori Ann was Calvin's sister, and Teresa was LaVern's, and Rosemary wondered if they'd felt odd visiting when their brothers had been Eddie's best friends.

Laurene came to give her a hug. Rosemary tried to thank her. Waving away her words, Laurene smiled. Her hair had grown enough to make a bun not much larger than her daughter's. She no longer looked like she was straddling the fence between the plain world and the *Englisch* one, and Rosemary knew she didn't have any regrets about leaving her marketing job behind to live plain.

"She's so cute," Laurene said, smiling. "How is she settling in?"

"It's slow." That was an understatement, but she didn't want to chance Braelynn hearing the conversation. "We'll get there."

"I'm sure you will."

Both of them turned to look at the *kinder*. Rosemary's heart threatened to break when she saw the twins and Mary Beth playing with some plastic ponies in impossible colors. Braelynn sat to one side, watching them. Her expression said it all. She wanted to be part of their game, but couldn't as they babbled and laughed and made the ponies prance and fly.

Rosemary realized what the problem was. The *kinder* couldn't understand each other. Naomi's twins and Mary Beth spoke *Deitsch* because they were too young to attend school, and Braelynn knew nothing but English.

"Oh, dear," Laurene said. "I didn't think of how they'd talk to each other."

"I know a way." Rosemary raised her voice and asked, "Who wants cookies?" in both English and *Deitsch*.

The kids jumped to their feet and rushed to her. Glad she'd made extra cookies yesterday, Rosemary gave every *kind* one cookie for each hand. She left them sitting by the cupboard in a small circle as they munched. When one of the twins held out his cookie and pointed to the chocolate chips, Braelynn tapped her own cookie.

"They'll figure it out," Laurene said. "Don't worry."

Naomi laughed. "The two most useless words of advice ever given to a *mamm*."

The back door opened, and Grace Coffman walked in, her bright red hair matching her wind-chafed cheeks. "Sorry I'm late." She lowered her voice when she saw Teresa across the kitchen. "Someone came over to chat about buying my building again, and I couldn't get him to take no for an answer and leave."

Rosemary sighed. LaVern could have a single-track mind and kept going forward at full speed until something—usually common sense—derailed him. She hoped he'd come to see reason soon because Grace wasn't going to sell after having dedicated so much time to getting her shop open.

Grace's arrival must have been a signal for the party to begin. Rosemary was herded into the living room. Someone tried to do the same for the *kinder*, but Braelynn refused to move until she saw the pretty boxes being set next to where Rosemary sat.

Creeping closer, Braelynn inspected every face in the room. Was she hoping to see someone familiar? Again, Rosemary's heart hurt as she realized Braelynn felt alone in the crowded room. Rosemary wished she could help the little girl, but knew any offer would be rebuffed.

She needn't have worried. When Braelynn realized the boxes held clothing and handmade toys and new coloring books, she sat on the floor beside Rosemary's chair and admired the contents as the others did when the gifts were passed around so everyone could see them. She nodded when Rosemary asked her if she wanted to open the next one.

Braelynn undid it with care and handed Rosemary the paper before lifting the lid to reveal two faceless dolls, a girl and a boy, dressed in plain clothing. She touched one face with a wistful expression on her own, then handed the box off to Lori Ann to pass around the circle.

Thanking everyone for their generosity, Rosemary put her hand over her stomach when it growled.

"Eat!" announced one twin.

"Fun!" shouted the other.

Everyone rose, and Braelynn came with Rosemary to join the others in the kitchen. The little girl paused and sighed as she looked back at the stack of gifts.

"Very nice, ain't so?" Rosemary asked.

Braelynn nodded.

"We need to thank everyone."

"Why?"

Every muscle in Rosemary's body froze, even her lungs, as she saw puzzlement in the *kind*'s eyes. The conversations flowing around them vanished into distant whispers as Rosemary leaned toward the little girl. She took Braelynn's hands in hers and didn't release them when the *kind* tried to pull away.

Braelynn halted when Rosemary said, "The gifts are for you, *liebling.*"

"For Braelynn?"

"*Ja.*"

"All of them?"

"*Ja.* My friends and my family brought them for you."

"Why?"

Rosemary was stumped. How could she explain to a five-year-old that everyone was trying to make up for what she'd experienced before she came to Bliss Valley? That they wished Braelynn could erase the bad memories that seemed to haunt her.

It was impossible, so she chose a far simpler answer. "They want you to be happy."

"All Braelynn's?"

"*Ja.*"

"Dolls with no smiles, too?"

"*Ja.*" Tears crowded her eyes as she heard Braelynn's description.

"Oh." The *kind* didn't say anything else. Was she afraid Rosemary was lying to her?

Rosemary feared that was so, and again she longed to hug the frightened *kind.* She was about to suggest Braelynn go and look at her gifts again when they were called to the table.

On the table were sandwiches and pickles and casseroles and a kettle of chicken corn noodle soup. Rosemary guessed it would be delicious, but doubted she'd be able to swallow a single bite when she ached for a *kind* who had been so hurt she couldn't believe someone would do something *wunderbaar* for her.

A collection of buggies were at the farmhouse when Gideon drove his wagon into the lane. He'd had a successful day meeting with both Colt Jackson and Samuel King. Colt hadn't wasted any time saying he'd like two dozen belts in various lengths for his booth at the Central Market. Samuel, who ran a buggy repair shop in the southern portion of the valley, had agreed to pass along the word Gideon was available for tack repair as well as new products.

Gideon had liked both men. Colt, an *Englischer,* wished he were a cowboy riding the western ranges, but hadn't ever left Bliss Valley. Samuel had, Gideon was surprised to learn, for a short time. It'd been long enough, however, for him to get into the car accident that had left him with a limp. Gideon guessed there was much more to the story, but hadn't pried.

He was grateful for both men's support. It was a small beginning, but a definite step forward to proving to himself that he could build a solid business in the small building.

Opening the door to his shop, he glanced at Rosemary's house. He was glad to see she had people visiting. Being in the house with an antagonistic *kind* had to be hard on her.

He took one step into his shop and stopped. It looked as if a storm had swept through his work area and the room behind it. Tools were scattered over the table holding his sewing machine and across the floor. He could see the blanket and sheet on his bed had been tossed into a heap beside his dresser. The few dishes he had on the shelves had been pulled out. A couple were broken on the counter. Flatware was strewn everywhere, mixing with his tools.

Who had done this? And why? He'd met only a handful of people. So why had someone trashed his shop?

"Is this a bad time?" asked a deep voice behind him.

A tall man walked into the shop. His hair was light brown, and his eyes were a pale blue ringed by a darker shade. There was something about him that looked familiar, but Gideon wasn't sure what.

"Wow," the man continued before Gideon could think of an answer. "You look like you need some help cleaning up."

"I need some help figuring out who did this."

"You should ask Rosemary." He took off his black hat and gestured in the direction of the farmhouse. "She or one of her guests might have seen something."

"I hope so." Remembering he was running a business, Gideon asked, "How can I help you?"

"I wanted to stop by and say hello. I'm Joel Beachy."

"Nice to meet you."

The man seemed taken aback by Gideon's smile.

Questions rushed through his head, but he didn't ask them. Instead, he fell back on a standard question he used with potential customers. "What can I do for you, Joel?"

"Tell me how Rosemary is doing."

The request startled him as much as if the other plain man had curled up his fists and struck him. "Why?"

"I'm her brother."

No wonder the man looked familiar. There was a similar curve to their faces, and lines edging Joel's eyes suggested they crinkled like Rosemary's did when she smiled. But he wasn't smiling now. He looked somber and uneasy and hopeful at the same time.

"So why are you asking *me* how she's doing? Why don't you ask her yourself?"

"Two reasons. One is that our relationship has been pretty rocky since I came back to Bliss Valley."

He wanted to find out where Joel had been but asked, "What's the other reason?"

"You've been here for over a week now." Joel's lips tilted in a wry smile. "When have you heard Rosemary open up about anything?" His smile vanished as he rubbed his hands together with what Gideon guessed was nervous energy. "Since Eddie's death, she seems determined to prove to the whole world that nothing's changed for her. She refuses help with the farm."

"I've noticed that."

"I'm sure you have." He pulled off his hat and set it on the deep windowsill. "I've offered several times to take over the milking. I thought when the little girl came to live with her, Rosemary might reconsider my offer. She hasn't."

"That might be my fault."

"Yours? How?"

"I've been doing her morning barn chores. It gives me a *gut* start on my day, and she spends the time with Braelynn."

Joel's eyebrows rose nearly to his hairline. "I can't believe my ears. Maybe she's beginning to realize she doesn't have to do it all on her own." His brows lowered again as he sighed. "Or maybe she didn't want *my* help."

"I don't understand. You're her brother."

"A brother who's made a lot of mistakes." He leaned one hand on the sill and scanned the shop as if he could find whatever answer he was seeking amid the mess. "She's not wrong to blame me for leaving without letting her know where I was going. I did, and I'm sorry for that. We once were close. I miss that. Do you have sisters?"

"Five of them."

Joel's brows shot up again. "Five? Me, too." He chuckled. "That's more than enough to keep me on my toes." His smile faded. "I'm trying to bridge the distance I put between me and Rosemary when I jumped the fence and got myself into trouble."

"I don't understand what you want from me." Getting involved in another messy family was the last thing he intended to do.

"Tell me. Do you think she's doing okay?"

"I think she's filled with grief and doesn't want anyone to know."

Joel nodded. "That sounds like my sister." He put his hat on. "Could you do me a favor, Gideon? If you see she needs something, will you let me know? I don't want her struggling when I can help."

"I'll let you know, though I'm not sure it'll make any difference."

"You do know her already." His smile was fleeting before he walked out and closed the door behind him.

Gideon sighed and muttered, "What a mess!" He wasn't sure if he meant the shop or the situation between Rosemary and her brother. There wasn't much he could do about the latter, but he needed to know why his business and his home had been trashed.

Grabbing his own hat, he set it on his head as he went outside and walked up the lane. Joel had been right. Someone at Rosemary's gathering might have seen something to identify who was responsible for the destruction.

When he entered the kitchen, nobody seemed to notice his arrival. Rosemary was talking to Grace. Braelynn stood to one side, watching the other *kinder* playing with a ball. The women chattered with the comfort of a lifetime of knowing one another. Did the little girl feel like an outsider?

He did. He scolded himself. He'd come to Bliss Valley in order to get away from his well-meaning but smothering family. It was past time for him to get to know his new neighbors. His life was revolving too much around Rosemary and Braelynn. Too often, when he was working, his mind drifted away to thoughts of them and wondering what the future held for them. He should be focusing on what he could control and let the rest go…just as he'd tried to convince his family to do.

He should act more like a tenant and less like a friend who wanted to help Rosemary with the troubles in her house.

And in her heart.

Hoping nobody heard his gulp at his own thought, Gideon eased back toward the door. He didn't reach it before a woman halted him.

"You're Rosemary's tenant, ain't so?" she asked. "We haven't met. I'm Lori Ann Hertzler. I think you've met my brother."

"I have." He didn't add that he hadn't liked Calvin. "I'm Gideon Wingard. I'm hoping you or someone else saw someone going into my shop earlier."

She shook her head. "It was closed up when Teresa and I drove by." She motioned to another woman who hurried over and introduced herself.

Both women examined him as if he had a sign that said Need a Wife around his neck.

So he wasn't surprised when Lori Ann said, "Rosemary has had it tough. It's bad enough, ain't so, for her husband to die, but to have that debacle with her brother…" She shook her head and sighed as she couldn't imagine anything worse.

Not wanting to gossip, he said, "It's *gut* Rosemary is strong."

"Too strong. She didn't cry at her husband's funeral."

"She probably was in so much shock she didn't comprehend what was happening."

Lori Ann sniffed her disagreement. "Maybe so, but you're living here now, so you should know the truth. Her brother was arrested right in the middle of church," she said with a superior arch of her brows. "If it'd been me who had to watch the police take my brother away, I'd be mortified."

"In the middle of church?" he couldn't help repeating. Was that arrest what Joel had been referring to when he said he'd ruined things between him and his sister?

"Not in the *middle*." Teresa frowned at her friend. "Lori Ann, you shouldn't exaggerate."

"It's no exaggeration he was taken away by the cops who wanted to talk to him about a man named Phillips—"

"Philbin," corrected Teresa. "His name was Philbin or Philburn or something like that."

Lori Ann waved her hand to dismiss the other woman's words. "His name isn't important. What's important is that he sells drugs and Joel Beachy was involved with him."

"Joel Beachy sold drugs?" He was stunned. Had his first impression of the man been so wrong?

"That's the rumor," Lori Ann said in an oddly triumphant tone.

"I don't listen to rumors." He walked away. No wonder Joel was worried about how to approach his sister. Rosemary must have heard the same stories, and whether they were true or not, it had to hurt her to hear her brother whispered about behind his back.

Though the women hadn't been whispering. They seemed to take odd delight in spreading rumors.

He moved closer to the door and spoke to each of Rosemary's guests as they left, asking if there had been anything out of the ordinary near his shop when they came up the drive. None of them had seen anything. It was disappointing, but it also told him the malicious damage had been done before they arrived around noon.

A thought niggled at him as he glanced at where Braelynn was standing by the stack of gifts. Could the *kind* have snuck into the shop and made the mess? That didn't seem possible. Many of the tools had been stored too high for her to reach, even using one of his chairs.

But who had wrecked his shop? And why?

"What's wrong?" Rosemary asked when Gideon closed the door behind Naomi and her three *kinder*.

He explained what he'd discovered in the shop. "I was hoping there would be a witness."

"I'm sorry," she said. "I can't help. Braelynn and I were here in the kitchen until we went out to feed the animals."

"Can I ask what was going on here?"

"Sort of a belated *boppli* shower." She turned to where Braelynn was staring at the opened boxes, but not touching anything. "A non-*boppli* shower as Laurene Hershberger called it. Friends and my sisters wanted to help."

"Lori Ann Hertlzer and Teresa Spaeger are your friends?"

"*Ja.*" She hesitated, then said, "They're members of our quilting circle. I don't know them that well, which is why I was surprised to see them here today."

"They told me about what happened to your brother at church."

Color exploded across her face as if she'd been slapped. Going to the sink, she rinsed her hands. "I don't want to talk about it, Gideon."

"They said he was selling drugs for someone named Philbin."

"I don't think that's the man's name, but I'm not sure what it really is. All I know is he's a horrible criminal who tried to ruin my brother's life." She wiped her hands and hung the towel over the handle on the oven door. "The police suspected Joel, but it turned out this Mr. Philbrick—I think that's his name—was trying to frame him."

"Why?"

"I've got no idea."

"You never asked your brother?"

"No."

"Why not?"

She edged past him to collect the sugar bowl and the creamer from the counter. Putting the latter in the refrigerator, she set the sugar bowl on the table. She glanced at him as if hoping he'd take the hint and leave. When he didn't move, her shoulders rose and fell with a deep sigh before she gestured toward the table.

He took a seat and waited for her to do the same. As she did, she asked, "Would you like some *kaffi*, Gideon?"

"I've had enough today to float a cruise ship, and if I drink any more I won't sleep tonight. And, no, I don't want another piece of pie or a cookie or anything else. I'd like you to answer my question, if you'd be so kind."

"Joel and I don't talk often." She gave a nonchalant shrug, which he guessed was feigned. "Don't make something out of nothing."

Gideon considered for a moment telling her about Joel coming to his shop, but before he could, she peppered him with questions about what had happened there with the mess. Braelynn eased into the room while he explained.

"It shouldn't take too long to clean it up," he said before turning to Braelynn who had come to stand in the doorway. "Did you have a fun party?"

For a second, she frowned. "Fun is the twins' word."

Rosemary explained, and he nodded. "It sounds as if you all had fun."

"Fun kids."

He wondered if Rosemary was as astonished as he was at Braelynn's pronouncement. After seeing her in the corner, watching as the others rolled a ball back and forth, he'd expected her—if she said anything at all—to complain about feeling left out.

"I'm glad you liked them," Rosemary said, recovering before he did.

"Braelynn likes kids, though they spoke Chinese."

His laugh refused to be silenced, but somehow he turned his head and made it sound like a sneeze. It was more difficult to withhold another chuckle when Braelynn asked Rosemary to teach her how to speak Chinese.

"We speak *Deitsch*," Rosemary said in the patient tone he admired.

"Dutch?" Braelynn shook her head. "Not Dutch, Chinese."

Gideon exchanged a quick grin with Rosemary before asking Braelynn to show him her gifts. The *kind* was most excited about a coloring book filled with pictures of chickens and ducks. He noticed she was ignoring the doll that wore a yellow dress like the little girl's.

"Isn't this a nice doll?" he asked.

"No face."

"Because," Rosemary said, "you can imagine the doll to be anyone you want her to be. You can look at the doll and see anyone you wish."

"Like Braelynn? Like Madison?"

He glanced at Rosemary. The other name on Braelynn's birth certificate had been Madison Nesbitt. He was startled to realize that, until this moment, he'd assumed the name wasn't a real one.

"Like your *mamm*?" Rosemary whispered.

Sorrow filled her voice. "Gone. Madison be dolly?"

Silence clamped on the room at the little girl's hopeful question. How could they answer? The little girl had made it clear she didn't want anyone's pity.

Running her fingers over the doll's black cotton bonnet,

Rosemary continued to look into the *kind*'s eyes. "Of course," she said, her voice as gentle as the first breeze of spring. "It can be your *mamm* or a *boppli* or—"

"*Boppli?* Like May?"

"*Ja*. Just like May." She spoke in a conspiratorial whisper, though it was loud enough for him to hear. "But I don't think any doll can wiggle as much."

Gideon smiled along with Rosemary, but Braelynn remained serious. Would the *kind* ever show joy as other kids did?

Chapter Nine

Rosemary felt eyes drilling into the back of her *kapp* the following week. She half turned away from the quilting frame where she'd been working on setting up her newest patchwork top so it could be quilted. Her quilting circle had agreed without consulting her that they'd postpone their frolic another week to give her and Braelynn more time to get used to each other. No one had said why, and she couldn't guess what had changed their minds. When they'd come for the non-*boppli* shower, she'd thought everything went as well as it could have.

Obviously, not everyone had agreed.

She forced herself to look at her quilt. Not starting on the quilt for the mud sale gave her time to finish her own. Light green diamonds were sewn between dark green diamonds with a basket design set into each one. The baskets and their triangle-shaped handles were red. The color scheme was dramatic, and she was glad she'd chosen those fabrics. She hoped Eddie would forgive her, but she was tired of working with black material.

She'd put the top onto her quilting frame along with the batting and a colorful piece of yellow-and-green-sprigged cotton for the underside, pinning it altogether with T-pins. The straight pins had been bent at the top to form a contorted T-shape, which made it easier for her to connect the layers and then remove the pins when she was done. When the top was finished for the quilt that would be going to the mud sale, she'd do the same on her other quilt frame beside the wood stove. She was eager to spend time with her friends and sisters while they sewed and chatted.

She missed seeing Iva, because she hadn't visited her elderly neighbor for almost two weeks. She'd sent food and cookies over with her sisters, but hadn't gone there herself because she wasn't sure how Braelynn would act.

The feeling of being watched seared Rosemary's shoulders. She wasn't surprised to discover Braelynn stood behind her. The little girl clutched her ragged lion and her faceless female doll while she watched as if she were seeing Rosemary for the first time.

"I'm getting this ready to quilt," Rosemary said. "Do you want to see?"

The little girl started to shake her head no, then murmured, "Okay."

Rosemary motioned the *kind* to join her.

When the little girl came to stand by her chair, Braelynn asked, "Braelynn can touch?"

"*Ja*, but be careful. There are pins in it, and they can prick."

Braelynn snatched her fingers back as if she feared the pins would pop out of the quilt and stab her. "No ouch."

"That's a *gut* idea." She bent to stick two more pins along the side to hold it to the canvas strip on the frame. Straightening, she saw the little girl still eyeing the quilt. "Would you like to have a quilt of your own?"

"Pins in it?"

"No pins."

The *kind* nodded.

Telling Braelynn to wait where she was, Rosemary went to a closet under the stairs. She stored some of her finished quilts there before taking them to Grace's shop or giving them away as gifts. She lifted out one and carried it to a table. Putting the lamp that had been on the table onto another one, she moved the table between the sofa and the rocker. She draped the quilt over the table, making sure it reached the floor on each side.

Braelynn's curiosity must have gotten the better of her because she asked, "What's that?"

"Whatever you want it to be." Rosemary smoothed the top of the quilt before bending to lift one corner. "See? This can be a door if you'd like, or you can create a door wherever you want. Inside? It can be your own buggy or your private wagon going west across the plains or a boat sailing on the ocean. Whatever you want it to be."

"A chicken coop?"

"*Ja*, but no real chickens."

The *kind*'s face fell for a moment, then she looked at the two toys she held. "It could be a home for Braelynn and Madison and Cleo."

"It could." She stepped back and gestured with a half bow. "Go in and imagine. No! Wait a moment! It's not quite right."

Again, the little girl looked baffled, then began to smile. She reverted to her normal blank expression when Rosemary yanked one of the cushions off the couch and pushed it under the table.

"Every house," Rosemary said as if she hadn't seen Braelynn hide a smile, "needs to have a comfortable bed. Do you want to try it out?"

Rosemary didn't have to ask a second time. Braelynn vanished beneath the draped table, and the quilt fluttered. The *kind* began talking to her toys about how their new home should be arranged.

"Braelynn's house," the little girl repeated several times as if trying to convince herself the space was her own.

As Rosemary turned back to her quilting frame, Braelynn peeked out and asked, "Braelynn's house now?"

"*Ja.*"

"Braelynn's house tomorrow?"

Her heart ached for the *kind* who feared she'd be moved again without warning. "*Ja.* It's your house tomorrow, too… unless we have company and we need to use the table."

Braelynn didn't answer as she considered Rosemary's words, then she asked, "Braelynn have cookies with company?"

"*Ja.*" Rosemary smiled as she had to blink away the tears clinging to her eyelashes. How she longed to hug the *kind*, but knew it would send the little girl running.

"Braelynn's home today and tomorrow and till company comes and Braelynn has cookies."

"That sums it up *gut.*"

"*Gut,*" the youngster said before ducking beneath the quilt again.

Braelynn loved her sanctuary so much Rosemary had to coax her out for both dinner and supper. Though the little girl wanted to sleep in her *house*, Rosemary reminded her it would be waiting for her in the morning, and Braelynn agreed to sleep upstairs. Rosemary half expected to find her back under the quilt-covered table in the morning.

It had been the best day since Braelynn had come to the farm. The little girl had spent the day playing with her stuffed toys and coloring. She'd stretched out on her stomach with her feet beneath the table as if she didn't dare to sever the connection with it.

Rosemary had sped through her chores and had time to make Braelynn's—and Gideon's—favorite chocolate chip cookies. The last batch was in the oven when she put down her needle on the quilt frame. She stood and rubbed her lower back.

She smiled as she looked at Braelynn's "house." Such a small thing had been so helpful to the *kind*. She wished she could think of other ways that would ease Braelynn's fears.

Home.

It was such a simple thing, but, like everything since Eddie's death, it had become complicated.

Her gaze shifted from the living room to the kitchen. How many houses had she and Eddie looked at before they'd chosen this place to be the home they planned to share for decades?

"Oh, Eddie," she whispered, not wanting her voice to echo up the stairs to the *kind*. "It wasn't supposed to be like this."

She rested her hands on the rocking chair her *grossdawdi* had made for her before he'd died. She'd mourned him, but had celebrated his long life. She couldn't do the same for Eddie because she'd buried her new husband eight months after their wedding.

Even now, the pain of that day when she'd learned of his death pierced her. Closing her eyes, she tried to force the memories aside. They wouldn't go, and she was swept back in time to the long night of wondering where her husband was.

She hadn't wanted to panic when dawn had arrived and Eddie hadn't come home. When Erma had stopped by, Rosemary had assured her younger sister she wasn't worried, that Eddie must have been delayed as he'd been before. But she'd been fooling herself because he'd never been so late. She'd kept breakfast warm as long as she could, but around three that afternoon, she had pulled the desiccated remains of the meal out of the oven and tossed it away.

As the sun had headed toward the western horizon again,

her brain and body had felt as if they were mired in a swamp. She'd found it difficult to put two words together in a row when both her sisters returned to see what they could do to help. Erma had sat with her while Alta, their middle sister, had taken the buggy and gone to alert Jonas who lived on the far side of the creek that bisected the valley and their twinned church districts.

Rosemary had sat as her sister insisted, but her stomach had churned, and she'd been afraid she was going to be sick.

"Are you okay?" Erma had asked.

She'd nodded, not sure she could trust everything to stay down if she opened her mouth. Not that there could have been much in her stomach. She hadn't eaten all day.

So they'd sat and tried to talk, every topic drifting into oblivion after a few words.

For hours, they'd sat and tried to talk.

And then a knock had come at the front door. She'd exchanged an anxious glance with her sister. Nobody came to the front door except *Englischers* and trouble.

It had been both. A police officer with the news of Eddie's hunting accident. After that, everything had been a blur of well-meaning friends and loving family who were determined to support her every moment of the visiting hours funeral in the very room where she stood. She'd let herself go numb, walking through the motions when all she'd wanted was to see her husband's smile and hear his voice.

The timer went off in the kitchen, pressing the memories into the depths of her mind. Rosemary padded, barefoot, into the kitchen where a single lamp burned. She opened the oven door and peered in as the heat slapped her cheeks. The cookies were ready. She took out the tray and slipped them onto wire racks to cool. The aromas of chocolate and brown sugar danced around her as she turned off the gas oven.

She glanced around the kitchen, her gaze alighting on the pegs by the door. One peg was empty. The one where Eddie had hung his hat whenever he was home.

"I miss you," she whispered.

She shut off the lamp and went into the living room. Putting out those lights, too, she climbed the stairs to the bed they once had shared.

The morning was white.

The fresh snow hid the gray and dirty snow that had turned into icy chunks. The ground was white, the tree branches were white along with the lingering leaves on the crab apple trees, the barns were white. Even the sky was white. When Gideon glanced out his shop's window, only the tree trunks along the edge of the snow-covered road broke the perfect expanse of white.

A closer look revealed the marks left by a rabbit that had crossed the field on the other side of the road. Narrow tracks had been left by a buggy's passing along with the wider breadth of car or truck tires. The plow hadn't come through yet so the snow's edges were stitched in a smooth seam to the farm's lane.

Nothing moved. It was as if the whole world was celebrating and wanted nothing to ruin its hushed perfection.

Then a bright red cardinal landed on a branch across the lane. Its crimson contrasted with the white world surrounding it.

Gideon smiled as he looked around his shop. It had taken him all day yesterday and most of this morning after milking to get his tools back to where they belonged. Nothing had been stolen, he'd been glad to discover. Just pulled off the hooks holding the forms and the awls and the cutters in place.

Who had vandalized his shop? And why? Those two questions had taunted him with every breath yesterday.

Braelynn? whispered a small voice in his head.

He disregarded it as he had before. The little girl couldn't have reached the uppermost tools on her own. Someone else—someone taller—had made the mess. It wouldn't have taken anyone long to yank the items off the wall or rip apart his bed. He had no idea who might have been responsible.

A motion beyond his window caught his eye, and he watched Rosemary's buggy turn into the lane. When it slowed to a stop, he was glad to put aside the piece of leather he'd started slicing into strips for more belts. Making belts was *gut*, but he longed for a customer who would ask him to do something more intricate like working on a buggy harness or a saddle or some leather gloves for working with a chain saw.

Opening the door, he called a greeting.

Rosemary leaned out and asked, "Do you have a minute to *komm* to the house?"

He nodded, as the cautious voice in the back of his mind was urging him to say he was too busy. By her taut expression, he guessed she'd learned some disquieting news.

About her husband or about her husband's daughter?

He wouldn't get any answers by staying there. Grabbing his coat and hat, he went along the lane, using the buggy tracks as his path through the snow. Rosemary and Braelynn had gone into the house by the time he reached it.

He went in and wasn't surprised to see Rosemary putting a plate and glasses of *millich* on the table. Braelynn grabbed two cookies, ignored the *millich* and vanished beneath a quilt propped up on a table in the living room.

"It's her place," Rosemary said with a strained smile. "I set it up for her yesterday, and she loves spending time there."

"I used to have a place like that," he said, taking off his hat and coat. He hung them by the door. "It was my haven from sisters who always wanted me to play dolls with them. I preferred my trucks and animals under a blanket hung between dining room chairs." He sat. "But her refuge can't be the reason you wanted to talk to me."

"No." She chose a chair facing him, then lowered her voice. "I went to see Jonas this morning. He shared what he's learned from Children's Services. He had to talk to a bunch of people, and the gist of it is that a search has to be made to discover if there is anyone who's a closer relation than I am."

"Closer than a step*mamm*?"

"A grandparent or an *aenti* or *onkel* on her *mamm*'s side." She wrapped her hands around a glass, staring into the *millich*.

"How long will that take?"

"It could be months." Her fingers shook so hard they rocked the glass against the table.

"What happens in the meantime?"

"Jonas has persuaded them to let her stay here while they're searching. I may have to be licensed as a foster parent. I'm sure Naomi will help me."

He put his hand over hers before he could halt himself. A tremble rushed through their fingers, and he realized she wasn't the only one fighting strong emotions. Touching her created an unexpected bridge between them, and he sensed her fear and grief at the idea of losing Braelynn.

"You aren't alone. You're going to have help from the whole community," he said, stopping himself before he added, *And me.*

"I know, but she's starting to open up to me. If she's taken away, I don't know what it'll do to her." A half sob burst from her.

The sound brought his gaze to her lips. They were compressed, but softened as he continued to look at them. Her fingers shook more beneath his, and he swept his other hand under hers, enveloping them. When he raised his eyes, they locked with hers.

He was overpowered by the sorrow and fearful anticipation... and wonder in them. He understood the fear and sadness. But the wonder? Was the same flicker in his eyes as he reveled in the warmth of her soft skin?

Again, his eyes dropped toward her lips. His own tingled at the idea of pressing against them. If he stretched across the table, would she pull away?

The door burst open.

Gideon jumped to his feet, hoping his face didn't show the pulse of guilt pumping through him. Not that he had anything to be guilty about. Nothing had happened.

Except in his imagination.

God, don't let me do or say anything that will harm Rosemary more.

A red-haired boy rushed into the kitchen as cold air invaded the house. Who was he? He didn't look more than ten. The boy scanned the room, then ran past Gideon to where Rosemary sat.

"Brandon!" she cried. "What's wrong?"

"It's *Aenti* Grace's shop. It's been hit!"

Before he or Rosemary could react, an elderly woman appeared in the doorway. She was tiny, not much taller than the boy. Her black bonnet was pushed back on her head, revealing her almost white hair.

Rosemary hurried to the door and put a hand under the woman's elbow. "Saretta! *Komm* in and sit." Without looking in his direction, she said, "Gideon, this is Grace's *mamm*, Saretta, and that's Grace's nephew Brandon. This is Gideon Wingard. What did you say, Brandon?"

"*Aenti* Grace's shop has been hit."

His *grossmammi* put a hand on the boy's arm. "What he means is someone broke the windows in Grace's shop. Who would do something like that?"

Gideon couldn't keep from thinking of the vandalism in his shop. It seemed minor in comparison with smashed windows, but were the two connected?

A frown threaded Rosemary's brow. Did her thoughts match his?

He had no chance to ask because she said, "We need to help Grace."

The boy grinned and waved his arm for them to follow him. His *grossmammi* said, "Go ahead."

"I can't!" She lowered her voice. "I don't want Braelynn around broken glass."

"I'll stay here with her," said Saretta as she glanced around. "Where is she?"

Rosemary pointed to the table with the quilt over it. "She's there. I'll be back as soon as I can." She grabbed her bonnet and coat and was out the door before anyone could respond.

Gideon ran out after her. She and the boy were climbing into a buggy with a horse he didn't recognize. Rushing to it, Gideon put out a hand to halt the boy from closing the door.

"I'm going with you," Gideon said.

She told him to climb in beside Brandon and close the door. He barely sat before she gave the command to the horse to hurry down the lane. She drove with care as she turned onto the snow-covered blacktop, though he could tell she wished she could fly to the shop, straight across the fields.

The boy answered their questions, but he didn't know many details. Only that the shop windows had been shattered. His hands clenched into impotent fists, and Gideon gave him a curt nod when the boy looked at him. The youngster uncurled his fingers and spread them across his black trousers. His jaw remained taut, however.

As soon as the buggy drove past the huge auction barn and

turned into the driveway leading to the parking behind the shop, Rosemary shoved the reins into Gideon's hands. "Here."

He grabbed them, calming the horse who'd sensed an abrupt change in drivers. He said nothing as Rosemary climbed out and walked to where tiny pieces of glass twinkled under the bushes. Snow hadn't gathered there, and the ground was as raw as her expression before she opened the door with its broken window and went inside.

As soon as the horse's reins were lashed to the hitching rail, Brandon followed her inside. Gideon was going to do the same, but paused when he heard hammering. He came around the far corner of the shop to find Rosemary's brother, Joel, and a man Gideon didn't know nailing a sheet of plywood over an open section of a three-window bay.

"Need help?" he called.

Joel answered, "Glad to have some extra hands, Gideon." He tilted an elbow toward the man holding the plywood in place. "That's Adam Hershberger. He's our deacon."

"Today I'm the all-around handyman," Adam replied with a nod.

"I'm Gideon Wingard. I'm renting Rosemary Mishler's shop."

"Nice to meet you." Adam shifted the piece of plywood so Rosemary's brother could hammer it into place. "I take it you and Joel have met?"

"*Ja.*"

A gasp came from through the glassless window beside them. Shock blared from Rosemary's face, and he realized he hadn't had a chance to tell her about her brother's visit. No, he'd had plenty of chances, but he'd been too focused on the vandalism at his shop, and Joel's visit had vanished from his mind.

She rushed away from the window.

Gideon sighed and was surprised to hear the sound echoed

by the other men. Adam and Joel exchanged a glance he could read easily. They were worried about Rosemary, but had no idea how to help her. Joel had admitted as much earlier.

Adam sounded like a deacon when he said, "This stalemate between you and Rosemary needs to come to an end, Joel."

"I know."

"If you sat down with her, maybe you could resolve it."

Joel shook his head. "I wish it could be that easy."

"Why can't it?" interjected Gideon, then he mentally kicked himself for being drawn into the tangle of relationships surrounding him.

"I'm not welcome in her house."

Adam said, "You don't know that for sure."

"I know her late husband didn't want me there. He thought I'd cause her more heartache."

"Would you have?" The question popped out before Gideon could halt it. A veil of secrets seemed to cling to the Mishler farm, and he was tired of having to find his way through a maze of misunderstandings because he didn't know what was going on.

He'd left his family that was determined not only to know all his personal business, but to interfere in every facet of it. Now, in Bliss Valley, everyone acted as if they wanted to hide everything behind a cloak of smiles and welcoming words.

"No," Joel said as he pulled another nail from his tool apron. Positioning it against the wood, he pounded the nail in. "That should hold even if we get strong winds."

The men moved in silent accord to the next window. Picking up the piece of plywood waiting there, Gideon helped Adam hold it in place while Joel began hammering.

Adam said in the same quiet but adamant tone, "If you know that in your heart, you need to persuade her Eddie was wrong about you."

"How can I speak against the man when he's barely cold in his grave?" Joel shook his head.

"How can you *not*?" Gideon thought of the pain in Rosemary's eyes when she'd looked out to see them working together. "She's taken in her husband's *kind* and is raising Braelynn with as much love and kindness as if she'd given birth to the girl herself. If she can forgive Eddie for failing to tell her about his daughter, don't you think she can forgive him for being wrong about you?"

The other two men didn't answer right away as they went to get another plywood sheet. Were they unwilling to answer or did they have no idea how to?

Once the board was positioned, creating a barrier between them and the interior of the shop where Rosemary was, Joel said, "Rosemary is my favorite sister." His lips twisted in a wry grin. "I know it's wrong to say I've got a favorite sister, but it's also wrong to lie. Ain't so, Adam?"

The deacon chuckled. "It takes some of us longer to learn that lesson."

"True." Both men looked at Gideon as Adam added, "We weren't the best behaved kids in the community when we were younger."

Now it was his turn not to know how to answer. There were the rumors he'd heard about Joel, but nobody had mentioned anything about Adam's past mistakes.

He was given a reprieve from responding when Joel said, "I never would do anything to make Rosemary's life more difficult than it is now."

Gideon wondered if Joel was referring to Eddie Mishler's unexpected death or Braelynn Mishler's unexpected arrival. He didn't have a chance to ask before Joel went on.

"I thought Rosemary would let me help her, but she's stubborn."

"Or she doesn't dare to risk her wounded heart again." Gideon leveled his corner of the sheet.

It shifted, and he had to tighten his grip as both men looked at him in astonishment. Joel grabbed the other side before the plywood slammed against the window's frame.

"Do you think that's what it is?" Joel asked.

"I don't know. It was a thought."

"A *gut* one," Adam said.

A trio of other men Gideon didn't know came to assist in covering the windows, and the conversation shifted. When all the broken windows were covered, Gideon went to see if Rosemary and Brandon were ready to leave.

The interior of the store was darker than he recalled. The warmth had vanished, too. Not just because of the cold seeping around the boards. When he'd entered the shop before, it'd been filled with the happy voices of customers and quilters.

A lantern had been lit and placed on the counter. As he blinked, he saw Grace and Rosemary working side by side.

"Okay," Grace said, fighting to keep her voice steady. "These quilts were displayed in the windows. They'll have to be repaired and cleaned. One of them is your latest, Rosemary." She lifted a blue, purple and green quilt off the top of the stack and tilted it one way, then the other.

Gideon wasn't surprised when he heard the tinkle of glass falling on the floor. Before Rosemary could take the quilt, he reached for it. "Let me. I'll shake it again outside."

"Danki," Rosemary said, her voice as dull as her eyes. She followed him to the door and watched while he flapped the quilt and sent glass flying across the snow.

He handed it to her once he was sure the glass was off the fabric or no longer hiding in the stitched lines. As he walked into the shop, his boot struck something that slid across the floor.

"What's that?" he asked.

"One of the rocks used to smash the windows," she answered with a sigh. "They're scattered all over the shop. I don't know why someone would do this."

"Do you have any suspicions of who did this?"

"I do."

When she didn't add more, he considered—for a single heartbeat—not pressing her. He had to think of his own business. The end of each day reminded him that it was one less he had to prove he could make his business a success in Bliss Valley. Though he didn't have as many large windows, he had plenty of valuable stock in his shop. There had been other times when Amish businesses had been a target because the vandals and thieves believed plain people didn't go to the police.

"Who do you think it was?" he asked.

"I'll tell you who it was," said a familiar voice from behind Rosemary. She turned to see her sister Erma wearing a fearsome frown. "*That woman* is trying to make trouble for Grace again."

Rosemary sighed. Erma always said *that woman* as if the very words tasted disgusting on her tongue. Because they did. Yet, she understood too well why her sister was upset.

That woman was Tiffany Spanner. The owner of the Amish Quilt Emporium on Main Street in Strasburg. When Grace Coffman had managed the shop for Tiffany, the Beachy sisters and other quilters had put their handiwork there on consignment. Almost from the beginning, Tiffany had delayed and delayed paying them and then dumped the whole problem in Grace's lap, insisting a plain woman should deal with plain quilters. The matter had come to a head after Eddie's death when Grace had, after years of putting up with Tiffany's nonsense, stood up to her boss and quit.

To say everyone had been shocked would have been an understatement. Grace had always been like a mouse, clinging to the corners and not making a squeak. But even Grace could only endure so much, and she decided she wanted a new boss. Herself. Grace opened Quilts Are Bliss, the shop where Rosemary and her sisters and several other women who once quilted for Tiffany now displayed and sold their work.

That had left Tiffany's shop with fewer quilters and fewer authentic plain quilts, and she blamed Grace for the defections rather than looking at her own record of tardy and partial payments and open disdain for plain women. As soon as the new shop opened, Tiffany had begun spreading half-truths about the shop and its wares. She didn't make it a secret her goal was to close Grace down and make the quilters come back to her, begging her to sell their quilts.

So far, she hadn't succeeded. No one doubted Tiffany wouldn't stop trying to cause trouble until she destroyed Grace's business. Everyone involved with Quilts Are Bliss looked over their shoulders, waiting for the next assault on the business and their reputations. They were determined to save Grace's shop because she appreciated their hard work.

"You need proof to back up such an accusation," Gideon said.

Erma sniffed her opinion of his comment before going to help Grace sort quilts.

Rosemary started to apologize for her sister's cold reaction, but he asked, "Are you ready to go? I need to get back to work, and Braelynn will be wondering where you've gone."

"Oh, my! If she thinks I'm abandoning her, too…" She hurried to where Grace was going through another pile of quilts. "Do you need me any longer? I should get home to Braelynn."

"We're fine." Grace smiled. "Go home to your sweet *kind.* I'll take Brandon home with me."

"If you need anything—"

"Don't worry. I'll let you know."

Rosemary picked up the quilt she needed to repair and waved a goodbye to her sister before going out with Gideon on her heels. When she saw LaVern standing on the other side of the road in front of his store, she was shocked by the loathing in his eyes that looked as hard as the stones on the floor in the shop. He noticed her looking at him, and his gaze eased as he gave her a quick smile before rushing inside his grocery store.

Had that hateful glare been aimed at Gideon or the shop or both?

"Rosemary?" Gideon asked from beside her.

"Let's go." She didn't look back as she went to the Coffman's buggy. She had a lot to think about.

Chapter Ten

Nervous energy buzzed through Rosemary that evening. Braelynn had been overjoyed—for a second—when Rosemary returned to the house. The little girl had scooted under the table to her private world as if ashamed of revealing her feelings.

Saretta had given Rosemary a sympathetic hug before leaving to return to her own home. Gideon had disappeared into his shop, and Rosemary had tried to continue on with her day.

It'd been impossible. She couldn't concentrate on anything, and she couldn't sit for more than a moment without finding herself on her feet. She wrestled the boxes and trunks from the attic and stacked them in one corner of the living room. Going through them more thoroughly had seemed like a way to focus, but even that hadn't worked. Her mind swirled in too many different directions. She'd made supper and put Braelynn to bed, and the unsettled feelings deepened until she found herself pacing from the front of the house to the back in an endless loop. Working on repairing the quilt that had been damaged in the attack on Grace's shop hadn't helped. Making another dress for Braelynn would have been as ineffectual at calming her racing thoughts. She needed to do something physical, something that required her to use her body more than her mind.

Something to help her forget the repugnance in LaVern's eyes as he'd stared across the road at Grace's shop and at Gideon. She wished she could confront him and ask if he'd thrown the stones through the windows. She must not assume he was guilty, and asking him would be hurtful if he hadn't been involved.

A knock at the kitchen door made her spin to look into the kitchen. What was Gideon doing here at this hour? And, as important, why had her heart done a cartwheel at the thought of him being at her door?

Rosemary went to the door. "You don't need to knock, you know," she said as she opened it.

"I know." Gideon stepped into the light and brushed snow off the shoulders of his coat. "But I wasn't sure if you'd want to see me."

She didn't pretend not to understand. During their ride home from Grace's shop, they'd been silent. Her thoughts had been too snarled with the sadness of seeing the damage, the shock of viewing LaVern's candid expression and Gideon's dismay when he admitted he'd previously met her brother.

"You should always feel free to come here," she said.

"Really?"

"Ja." She realized she meant it because Gideon had become a part of her daily life.

Were her thoughts displayed on her face? She feared so when Gideon said, "I'm sorry to intrude on you yet again. I saw your lights were on, and I thought I'd see how you were doing. And please don't say you're fine. I can tell you aren't."

"I wasn't going to say that," she replied, though the words had been on the tip of her tongue. "I'm not fine. I'm upset someone attacked Grace's shop. She's my friend, and I've been praying for strength for her and for the perpetrator to step forward and admit the crime."

"That's not likely." He pulled out a chair and sat at the table. She did, too, facing him. "It was the act of a coward, someone who does their dirty work cloaked in shadows. That kind of person won't come forward and admit their crime. You may be upset, but I'm angry."

"Anger solves nothing."

"I know that, but it's what I feel. I keep thinking if my shop had been attacked, I'd want everyone to be furious."

She flinched at the word *attacked*. That's what it'd been, but she'd tried to keep that thought out of her head because it led to the question of why Grace had been targeted…and the one of why LaVern had worn such a venomous expression.

To deflect from the uncomfortable train of her thoughts, she said, "There have been incidents like this before in Bliss Valley."

"It seems like such a nice place."

"It is a nice place, but even the nicest places have troublemakers." She sighed. "At least I know my brother wasn't involved."

"I can't imagine your brother doing something like that."

"Everyone else can. When he was a kid, Joel and his friends got into a lot of trouble. But that's in the past."

Her tone must have warned him she didn't want to say anything more on the subject because he pointed at the boxes she'd stacked in the living room. "What's that?"

"Stuff from the attic."

"Eddie's?"

"No, from the family who lived here before." She refrained from adding that Eddie had been in Bliss Valley only a month before he asked her to marry him. Wanting to escape from her home where nothing had been right since Joel had fled, she'd accepted Eddie's proposal. She'd longed for a life and a home without any drama.

If she'd had any idea she was running straight into more drama, would she have thought twice before agreeing to marry a man who'd kept his daughter from her?

"Do you need help bringing anything else down?"

"That's everything, even the locked one. I've been hoping I could find the key around here, so I don't have to break into it. The trunk is in *gut* shape, and I don't want to destroy it by opening it to find there isn't anything but mothballs and dust inside."

"So you don't know where the key is?"

She pointed toward a drawer by the refrigerator. "There are some old keys in there. I'll try them once I get through these things. I don't think the people who owned this house threw out anything." She smiled, happy that she could. Talking to Gideon was helping her find her calm center, the place where she went when she prayed and felt God's presence in her life.

How did Gideon make her feel like that? No, she wasn't going to examine it closely. She was going to be grateful.

Gideon smiled at her. "Whoever sold you this house must have been like my family. Nobody in my family can bear to part with a single thing. I wouldn't be surprised if *Mamm* has every drawing and paper I brought home from school. My *grossmammis* wouldn't have let her throw out a single thing, even if she wanted to."

"Your family is close, ain't so?"

"Like a boa constrictor."

Her brows shot up at his ironic tone. Was he jesting? No, she discovered when she saw the firm set of his jaw.

"Is that why you came here?" she asked.

"Ja." He pushed himself to his feet, and before she could speak, he added, "I'm glad you're doing okay. *Gut nacht.*"

By the time she'd pushed back her chair and stood, he was gone. She stared at the closed door. How had she failed to see he was as adrift in life as Braelynn was?

On Friday, exhaustion dragged every step Rosemary took after being awakened in the middle of the night by Braelynn's night terrors. It had taken almost three hours to calm the *kind*, and Rosemary doubted she'd done much to soothe Braelynn. More likely, the little girl had collapsed from fatigue.

It had taken Rosemary two more hours to find sleep because she'd been so wound up. Her arms were bruised where the *kind* had lashed out at her. A wave of nausea washed over her, and she put her hand over her stomach. Had Braelynn kicked her? It seemed as if the little girl had been determined to strike her in every possible place.

As Rosemary finished the dishes and came into the living room to work on her quilt, she told herself she couldn't blame Braelynn. The *kind* had been frightened to madness. Though Rosemary had tried to get the little girl to talk about her nightmare, Braelynn had been unable to speak. Only to shriek and fling her arms and legs in every direction as if fighting off an army of assailants.

Rosemary heard tentative footsteps and saw Braelynn coming into the living room. She huddled into herself, looking like a cornered little chick, desperate to flee but longing to be cuddled.

How much did Braelynn recall of her nightmares? *Please, God, let it be nothing. Show me how to help her realize she's safe here.*

As she offered the little girl a smile, inspiration burst into her head. She sent up a prayer of gratitude as she asked, "Would you like to learn to sew, Braelynn?"

Rosemary was shocked when the *kind* nodded. Sure the little girl would either ignore her or scowl as she did when asked a direct question, it took her a few seconds to register what her eyes had shown her.

Patting the sofa cushion beside her, she reached into her sewing basket for a couple of scraps. She frowned when she saw the fat quarters Iva had given her and urged her to make something for herself. She'd forgotten about the odd gift and the odder request.

Braelynn sat next to her and watched as Rosemary selected a needle and a spool.

"I'll thread the needle for you today, but you must learn to do it. Young eyes are better for the task than older ones." Rosemary smiled.

Braelynn shifted her gaze to the needle, her face somber. She took it with quivering fingers. Her small teeth gripped her lower lip as she tried to match the motions Rosemary showed her in a scrap.

Praising the *kind* for her attempts, Rosemary remembered her own first ones. They'd pulled the fabric in different directions and had been as rough as a dirt road. *Mamm* had been patient, and she must be the same with Braelynn.

When the thread was used up, she asked, "Would you like to try cutting a few pieces you can sew together? That would be more fun than stitching around and around, ain't so?"

The *kind* nodded. Her quick fingers dipped into Rosemary's sewing box and pulled out a pair of pinking shears with bright yellow handles.

Rosemary hid her smile. If Braelynn had waited for her to choose a pair of shears for her, it would have been those pinking shears. They were small and had a rounded tip. Getting a longer strip from her scraps box, she spread it out on the table in front of the *kind*.

"Cut whatever shapes you want," she urged. "Then I'll show you how to connect them."

Braelynn bent over her work, and Rosemary found she was holding her breath as the little girl cut two circles and then a diamond.

"Like yours," the youngster said as she pointed to the quilt.

"Like mine." Smiling, she took the scissors and put them in her sewing box. "Now you need to thread the needle."

As the little girl bent to try, her locket fell out of the front of her dress.

"That is such a pretty necklace," Rosemary said in what she hoped was an off-hand tone.

The *kind*'s head jerked up. "Braelynn's."

"*Ja*, I know it's yours. I'm not asking you for it. I'm just saying it's a very nice necklace."

Braelynn continued to frown as if she didn't trust a single word Rosemary was saying. She dropped the needle, thread and fabric on the table and stood, defiant.

Who hurt you? Rosemary wanted to cry out. Doing that would send the little girl scurrying away again.

"Does it have a picture inside it?" she asked the *kind*.

"Picture?"

"Sometimes people put pictures of someone special in a locket. Is there someone special in yours?"

Braelynn looked at the locket as if she'd never seen it before. Cradling it on her small palm, she asked, "Inside?"

"*Ja*. Do you want to look?" She held out her hand, and the *kind* snatched the locket away, turning her back on Rosemary.

"Braelynn's!"

"I know it's your very special locket. If you open it and want to share whatever might be inside, *komm* and find me. I've got a load of laundry to get on the line. It looks as if it might snow again by nightfall."

She picked up her sewing box, not wanting to leave it for the *kind* to explore. Sharp scissors and boxes of pins and needles could hurt a curious youngster.

Rosemary blinked back tears as she pulled clothes out of the washer and dropped them into the laundry basket. For a wondrous moment, she'd thought she was making progress with Braelynn, reaching past the defenses the *kind* kept raised around her. Sitting side by side had been precious, but that had vanished like a clap of thunder when Rosemary had dared to discuss the locket.

Why?

Why?

Why?

The question buffeted her harder than the winter wind as she carried the laundry outside to hang it on the line. The icy wind swirled around her, flapping her skirt and apron. Her heart was colder as she prayed for God to heal the pain within the *kind*.

She halted in the midst of her prayer. It was too much like the one she'd prayed almost every day, seeking solace for her own pain after Eddie's death.

"Help us both," she whispered, her cold-chapped lips barely able to form the words. If she wept, her tears would freeze to her cheeks, a display for the whole world to see.

After she'd hung up the final garment, she turned to hurry inside. She gasped when she saw the little girl standing behind her. Braelynn's coat wasn't buttoned. Her boots were on the wrong feet and her mittens were backward, too. The thumbs flapped on the outside of each hand. She held the locket in one hand.

"Open." She paused, then said, "Please open."

"Let's go inside. I need to get my fingers warm before I can open your locket." She rubbed her gloved hands together, watching the little girl's gaze focus on them instead of Rose-mary's face. That was *gut* because she didn't know if she could keep a smile off her lips.

Not only had Braelynn sought her help, but she'd said please. Rosemary had wondered if the little girl knew the word.

Inside, Rosemary took off her coat and knelt in front of the *kind*. She didn't speak as she examined the locket until she found the tiny latch built into the right side. Popping it open, she peered at the photo inside it.

The picture was so small that at first Rosemary couldn't discern whom it depicted. She turned the circle one way, then another. Realization struck her. The photo wasn't of Madison or Eddie. It was of a very young Braelynn.

Knowing she was unlikely to get any answer, she asked, "Did the necklace belong to your *mamm*, Braelynn?"

"Don't know. Maybe."

"I think it was hers before it was yours."

The *kind*'s forehead ruffled with bafflement.

Rosemary answered the question the little girl hadn't asked. "Do you know why I think that? Because the picture inside is of you."

"Braelynn?" She held the open locket almost to her nose.

Drawing it back enough so the *kind*'s eyes could focus on the image, she said, "When you were a tiny *boppli*. Maybe on the day you were born. See? The *boppli* looks like you."

"Braelynn big girl."

"*Ja*, now. But this picture was taken when you were a lit-tle *boppli*." She let the locket drop into the *kind*'s hand. "Your *mamm* put your picture in her locket, because you were pre-cious to her. She wanted you close to her heart."

The little girl stared at the open locket, her lower lip trem-bling.

"I'm so glad," Rosemary said, daring to reach out a hand

to stroke the *kind*'s back, "we opened it so you could see how much she loved you."

The little girl snapped the locket shut and, with a furious glare at Rosemary, ran out of the room and up the stairs. A door slammed on the second floor.

Rosemary stood with a familiar sigh of frustration. She should be accustomed to Braelynn's peculiar reactions, but she'd thought this time she was breaking through the barriers the little girl guarded zealously.

Knowing Braelynn wouldn't respond if she knocked on the bedroom door, Rosemary went into the kitchen to start their midday meal. She decided on a thick beef stew, but her stewpot wasn't where she usually kept it. Remembering Braelynn had helped with the dishes several times lately, Rosemary searched through her cupboards in the kitchen and the utility room. Pans and pots clattered, threatening to deafen her, but she didn't stop looking until she found the stewpot in the cupboard where she kept her extra laundry supplies.

Rosemary busied herself browning beef and chopping vegetables. She went into the cellar to get cans of chowchow and applesauce, which would complement the stew. As she returned to the kitchen, she heard a soft plop.

She halted, straining her ears. Nothing. She was about to tell herself she'd imagined it when she heard the sound again and saw a drop of water strike the kitchen table, splattering on an onion.

Raising her eyes, she gasped when she saw several more drops on the ceiling. Water was coming through it.

She left the jars on the counter. She ran up the stairs. She didn't stop when she passed Braelynn's room. The door was open, and the little girl was perched on her bed, sharing a book with her stuffed lion.

Rosemary threw the bathroom door open so hard it crashed

into the wall. She didn't step in when she saw water pouring from the toilet. More was pooled on the floor. Had the septic tank backed up? No! The water was coming from the toilet tank. It hung at an odd angle. What had happened?

No time for that now. Kicking off her sneakers and pulling off her socks, she held up her dress. She knew it wasn't wastewater, but she grimaced as she stepped into the bathroom. She took care not to splash the water over the edge of the door as she tiptoed to the water shutoff behind the toilet. It refused to turn.

She needed help.

Racing back to Braelynn's room, she scooped up the *kind* before the little girl could protest. She carried her down the stairs and dropped her on the sofa. She sped into the kitchen and groaned when she saw more drips oozing through the ceiling. She grabbed the cookie jar and put it in front of Braelynn.

"Don't move other than to pick out a cookie," Rosemary ordered.

"Two for Braelynn?"

She headed toward the back door. "Okay. Two."

"Three for Braelynn?"

Rosemary didn't answer. She'd played this game before. Braelynn wouldn't be satisfied until she persuaded Rosemary to let her have as much as she wanted. She stuck her bare feet into her snow boots. She threw open the door and ran toward Gideon's shop.

Gideon looked up as the door burst open. A customer? He smiled, but it disappeared when Rosemary came in, her eyes wild with dismay.

"What's wrong?" he asked.

"I can't turn off the water in the bathroom. The toilet is flooding everything."

He didn't ask another question. He grabbed his hat and pushed past her. She followed him, but his longer legs left her several paces behind by the time he reached the back door.

He went in, not waiting for her. Seeing the water falling on the kitchen table, some drops and a few steadier streams, he ran into the living room. Braelynn had chocolate on her face and a cookie in each hand. She watched him without any expression, then took a bite of one of the cookies.

Taking the steps two at a time, he heard Rosemary's lighter footfalls behind him as he reached the top.

"Third door on the left," she called.

He ran to the open door. He grimaced as he saw the water and the leaking toilet. Squatting, he grasped the water shut-off. He tried to turn it.

It wouldn't budge.

He knelt in the cold water, seized the handle with both hands and twisted it. When it moved a half inch, he gritted his teeth and tried again. This time, it moved a bit easier. He kept exerting pressure until it closed.

The water kept cascading out of the toilet tank for a few seconds and then began to slow.

Something struck his foot, and he looked back to see Rosemary dropping towels onto the floor. They instantly were soaked. She picked them up, wringing them out in the tub.

"Got more?" he asked.

"In the linen closet in the hall."

He slipped past her and into the hall. Realizing he didn't know which door it was, he took a chance and opened a narrow one. A staircase behind it led to the attic. Closing it, he went to another narrow door. Shelves inside were stacked with bedding and towels. He grabbed the towels.

He paused when he saw wet marks on the floor of the room

that must be Braelynn's because there were toys scattered in it. He frowned. Were those smaller footprints among Rosemary's?

Not taking time to look closer, he rushed to the bathroom. He tossed the towels across the floor. In less than twenty minutes, the water had been absorbed and dumped into the tub. Soon the floor was wet, not flooded.

"Danki," Rosemary said as she reached for another drenched towel.

"What happened?" he asked.

She dropped the towel on the mountain in the tub. "I saw water dripping through the kitchen ceiling and came up here. I found the toilet broken."

"Where was Braelynn?"

"Up here." She shook her head. "No, Gideon, don't even think she was involved. She's a *kind*. She wouldn't know how to break a toilet tank."

Gideon knew she was right, but he couldn't keep from thinking of the small footprints in Braelynn's room. When he told Rosemary, she went to check. He followed and sighed. The water on the floor had evaporated.

"I saw what I saw," he said.

"I'm sure you did." She wrapped her arms around herself. "It was chaotic. I grabbed Braelynn and ran. I don't remember if her feet touched the floor or not."

"But if her feet were wet—"

"She could have stepped in the spots I made."

He nodded, accepting her argument made sense. Yet, he couldn't shake his feeling that not everything was as Rosemary believed. He didn't think Braelynn could break the toilet, but she could have seen the water flooding out and not bothered to tell Rosemary.

Stop it!

Accusing Eddie's daughter—a five-year-old—of being malicious was wrong. But he couldn't get Braelynn's blank face out of his mind.

"Do you have another bathroom?" he asked, returning to the matter at hand.

"No."

"You're going to need a new toilet right away. Where can I get one?"

Relief lightened her expression. "LaVern keeps plumbing supplies at his store. He may have one."

"I'll check there first. If you need help putting it in—"

"I don't know how to replace a toilet, so *danki*, I'm grateful for your offer."

He hated to steal her smile, but he said, "Actually I was going to suggest you ask your brother. He told me he'd like to do more to help you."

She pressed her lips together and didn't reply for a long moment. Then she said, "No."

"Rosemary, you're reasonable about everything else. Why are you being stubborn about Joel?"

"I don't need to explain myself. If you don't want to get the new toilet for me, I'll go and get it myself."

He almost told her to go ahead. She was giving him the perfect out *not* to get more involved in her messy life. He should tell God *danki* and do as she asked.

But he couldn't. She needed help. He could give it. *Ye shall not afflict any widow, or fatherless child. If thou afflict them in any wise, and they cry at all unto Me, I will surely hear their cry.*

The verse filled his mind even as he prayed, *God, sometimes You make Yourself very clear.*

"I'll get a new toilet," he said. "I'll be right back with it."

She nodded, saying nothing.

He walked toward the stairs. He knew if he had a lick of sense, he'd keep going, despite the verse repeating from his heart.

Chapter Eleven

Gideon parked in front of LaVern Spaeger's store. Lashing the reins over the hitching rail, he glanced across the street at Grace's shop. The windows were still covered by plywood, but the sign out front said Open. He wondered how long it would take for the glass to be delivered and replaced.

He headed into the bulk store. It was dim inside because the light from the few propane lamps was swallowed up by the dark concrete floor and the shelves filled with cans and boxes.

At a narrow counter to the right, LaVern was checking out a woman with three toddlers, who were treating her as if she were a maypole. LaVern glanced his way, then held up a finger to ask him to be patient.

Gideon nodded, though he didn't want to be alone for a moment with his thoughts. He'd fumed during the drive to the shop, and now his frustration clamped around him again.

Why was Rosemary refusing to let her brother into her life again? Joel Beachy admitted he'd made plenty of mistakes, but so had her husband.

"How can I help you?" LaVern asked in a clipped tone.

Startled, Gideon wondered what he'd done to annoy the man. No matter. He was here on business. Rosemary's business.

"Do you have a toilet? Rosemary's tank broke."

At the mention of her name, LaVern's whole demeanor changed. "Is she okay? Did the water damage anything?"

"Too soon to tell," he replied, ignoring the first question. "Do you have toilets here?"

"Ja." He crooked a finger. "This way."

It didn't take long for Gideon to choose between the two toilets because they were identical. He hefted the tank while LaVern carried the lower part out to his wagon.

"Bad business over there, ain't so?" Gideon mused.

LaVern glanced at Grace's shop. "She shouldn't have opened up her shop here."

"Why?"

"There aren't many houses around here, and kids who like to cause trouble like an easy target."

Gideon went back inside with the glum man so he could pay for the toilet. Not wanting to let the conversation end there, he said, "Rosemary mentioned things like this have happened before."

LaVern didn't answer, but Gideon wasn't sure if it was because the storekeeper didn't want to or if he was busy figuring out the tax on the toilet. He calculated it once, then wasn't happy with the answer and tried again. Coming up with a different number, he did the whole process a third time before telling Gideon the total.

"Who's installing this?" LaVern asked.

"I am." He wasn't going to relate the discussion he'd had with Rosemary about her brother helping. "Since Eddie's death, she's had to learn lots of things, but plumbing hasn't been one of them."

"She's taken too much on herself. She needs a husband."

He looked at the total and pulled out his wallet. Handing LaVern his debit card, he said, "Her husband has been dead four months. She's still reeling with the grief from that horrific accident."

LaVern ran the card. As he handed it back, he said, "There are those who say it wasn't an accident."

Not an accident? How was that possible? Eddie Mishler had been shot in the woods, not far from the farm. Not once had Rosemary suggested there might be anything to it other than a tragic accident.

"What do you mean?" he asked with care. He needed to be cautious with inviting gossip.

The storekeeper shrugged while he held out the receipt to Gideon. "Just what I said. People aren't sure it was an accident. Nobody else was there when Eddie died. Who's to say if he shot himself accidentally or on purpose?" LaVern walked away from the cash register.

Gideon considered giving chase and demanding LaVern explain himself. He didn't. The man had disappeared through a door in the side of his store. He might as well have shouted he wasn't going to say another word.

Was LaVern right? Or was it a rumor like so many others? Based on nothing but supposition? While Gideon replaced the toilet in Rosemary's bathroom, he asked Rosemary a couple of leading questions, but she seemed puzzled at why he was asking them. Honestly puzzled. How could it be that she hadn't heard the rumor LaVern was spreading?

He declined her offer to join her and Braelynn for supper, because he didn't want to chance slipping up and mentioning LaVern's comments to them. Instead, he returned the tools he'd used to the barn where Eddie had stored them. He should go to his shop and work. Why? It wasn't like he had any deadlines in front of him.

Knowing he wouldn't sleep if he didn't get some answers, he decided there was one person he could ask. He headed across the covered bridge at the heart of Bliss Valley and up the hill on its far side. It was past dark when he reached the bishop's house. Seeing lights in the kitchen, he wondered if he'd be interrupting supper for Jonas and his family.

The door opened, and Jonas came out on the porch. "*Komm in!*" came the bishop's welcoming voice. "If you've journeyed this far, don't stop when you're steps from our warm hearth."

With a wry grin, Gideon jumped from his wagon and climbed the steps to the porch. "Do you have a moment, Jonas?"

If the bishop was surprised to see him, the man gave no sign. "Of course. We're about to have dessert. Join us."

Jonas hadn't been exaggerating when he said he had a warm hearth. A massive two-sided fireplace took up one whole wall of the house Gideon guessed had been built before the United States declared independence. Slate floors were heated by the fire that crackled a contented song to itself.

A woman was standing beside a modern stove. She was shorter and wider than her husband who resembled a pipe cleaner with his lanky form and bushy beard. Her graying hair was drawn back from her apple cheeks and kind smile.

"This is my wife," the bishop said. "Myrtle, this is Gideon Wingard. He's new in Bliss Valley."

She wiped her dimpled hands on a dishcloth. "Aren't you the leatherworker who's rented the Mishler's old dairy house?"

"*Ja.*" He instantly liked the older woman. Serenity emanated from her like the gentle heat from the fire on the hearth.

"Nice to meet you." She made shooing motions. "Go on into the living room, and I'll bring you cake and *kaffi*." She raised a finger, cutting off Gideon before he could speak. "The bishop thinks better when he's got a fork in his hand."

He laughed along with what sounded like a long-standing joke between husband and wife. Going with Jonas into the comfortable room on the other side of the chimney, he was glad to sit by the fire. The day's chill had sliced into his bones, and he needed to thaw.

They spoke of trivialities while they enjoyed chocolate cake with coconut frosting and large mugs of fragrant *kaffi* along with Myrtle. She took their plates and refilled their cups before leaving them alone to talk.

The bishop wiped his hands on a napkin and smiled. "What can I do for you? It must be important for you to be out on such a frigid night."

"I need you to help me untangle some gossip."

"That may require a better man than I am." He chuckled. "You'll have to be more specific on which gossip you're referring to. There are always a dozen or more stories circulating. The Amish grapevine is the most efficient line of communication known to mankind."

"And most accurate?"

"Now there's the rub, ain't so?" The bishop's eyes narrowed. "I've learned to double-check with some very trusted sources any rumors I hear."

"I could use some of those trusted sources now."

"About which rumor?"

"The one that Eddie Mishler's death may not have been an accident. That he might have killed himself."

The bishop leaned forward, any hint of a smile gone from his face. "Where did you hear that? From Rosemary?"

"No. As far as I know, she doesn't know about the rumor. She seemed baffled when I hinted at it."

"If she hasn't heard it yet, I'm sure she will."

"I hope not. If it's not true." He paused, then asked, "Or is it true?"

"All I know is the police haven't closed the case on Eddie's death." The bishop's voice was grim.

Gideon was stunned. He'd been so sure Jonas would chuckle at the rumor and assure him it was nothing but idle talk. Somehow, he managed to ask, "The case is still open after almost five months? Did they say why?"

"I spoke with Valerie Pfeffer." Jonas sighed so deeply it seemed to come from his marrow. "She's our local police chief, and she's as close-lipped as a horse that doesn't want to take the bit."

"She must have said something."

"*Ja.* She said to leave the investigating to the police."

Gideon sank back in his chair, frustrated. "I don't want to get in their way, but I want answers."

Jonas arched a brow as he picked up his cup and sipped. "I think I said pretty much the same thing, but Chief Pfeffer didn't budge. She does an excellent job, and she's made sure any trouble in Bliss Valley is taken care of quickly."

"Like the damage at Grace's shop?"

"She's already following possible lines of inquiry. Her words, not mine, so don't ask me what she knows and whom she suspects." Leaning forward, the bishop said, "I know you want to help Rosemary." He folded his hands between his knees. "We all do. She's suffered a great loss, and being able to know what happened to Eddie and why would bring her solace. However, we must not get caught up in chasing rumors and half-truths. That could cause more grief."

"Which is the last thing I want to do."

"I know, Gideon, and I know God has the answers to everything that has happened and will happen. This is one of those times we must wait for Him to reveal the truth to us on His schedule."

"Which doesn't jibe with mine." He didn't bother to make it a question when he already knew the answer.

"When does it? The Bible is filled with verses counseling us to be patient. God's timing is perfect for He sees the beginnings, middles and ends of our stories. Trust Him, Gideon."

"I want to, but my failings get in the way. I've never been a patient man."

"Few of us are." Jonas drained his cup. As he set it on the table beside him, he asked, "Will it help if I let you know anything else the police chief tells me about their investigation?"

"*Ja.* A lot."

"You will be second on my list, then."

"With Rosemary first."

The bishop hesitated, then said, "In return, I'd like to ask if you'll be by her side if the news I have to share is bad."

"But shouldn't it be her family?"

"They are almost as devastated as she is. Rosemary will need someone who wasn't torn apart by Eddie's death. You could fill that role. Will you?"

That voice at the back of Gideon's mind went on high alert, shrieking that agreeing to get more caught up in Rosemary's trouble would draw him in further. He'd come to Bliss Valley so he could concentrate on work.

Even as he thought that, he heard himself say, "Of course, Jonas."

As he drove back to Rosemary's farm, Gideon had time to ponder what the cost of his curiosity about Eddie Mishler's death would be. It was too late to renege on his offer, and he didn't want to. She'd need someone there with her if the news turned out as LaVern had suggested.

Would Eddie Mishler have committed suicide? Everyone

had been sidestepping the word, but suicide was what LaVern had suggested. Gideon's gut churned at the thought. What would have caused Eddie to take his life? Had Rosemary seen any clues to his despondency, or would the truth—if he'd killed himself—come as a complete shock to her?

He drove up the lane, so he could put his horse in the barn next to hers. As he came back out into the night, he started to duck his head into the collar of his work coat. He paused when he saw a motion on the lawn.

Rosemary! He frowned as he strode through the crunchy snow.

"What are you doing out here on such a cold night?" Gideon asked.

"Looking at the stars," she said, straightening.

He saw a tube beside her and realized it must be a telescope. "You've got to be freezing."

"I don't think about the cold when I'm admiring God's handiwork." She wrapped her arms around herself.

He couldn't help but wish his arms were around her instead. The thought almost knocked him to his knees. Where had that come from? He needed to build his business and prove to himself that he could make a life on his own before he considered courting a woman.

Rosemary went on, a simple joy in her voice that he'd never heard before, "I've been watching birds since I was a little girl, but one winter night when most of the birds were far from here, I turned my telescope toward the sky. I was astonished by what I saw. Astonished and in awe."

"May I look?" Better to stare at the stars than to be discovered gawping at her.

"Of course. Put one eye to the eyepiece and close the other one. It's aimed at Mars right now."

He bent, being careful not to touch the telescope. He peered through it and discovered the blurry circle he'd seen without the telescope had become ruddy with darker sections spread across it. Not a perfect circle, but much more clear than he could see with the naked eye.

"That's amazing," he said.

"It is, ain't so? I find it's comforting to know that as vast as the universe is, God loves each and every one of us. I'm awed by how He has made so many different places in the sky, but He also has kept His eye on every corner of His creation." She smiled as he straightened and turned toward her. "And every corner of our hearts and our souls."

"Many, o Lord my God, are Thy wonderful works which Thou hast done," he said in a respectful whisper, *"and Thy thoughts which are to us-ward: they cannot be reckoned up in order unto Thee: if I would declare and speak of them, they are more than can be numbered."*

"Psalm 40, the fifth verse."

"One of my teacher's favorite verses." He gave her a lopsided grin. "We said it almost every Monday at the beginning of school."

"One of my *mamm*'s favorite verses." Her smile slid off her face, and she sighed as she drew her coat close to her again. "I heard her say it when she was discouraged. Which was pretty often in the year or two before Joel jumped the fence and more after he was gone. It was her way of praying for God to keep His eye on my brother when she couldn't."

"You had no idea where he was after he left?"

She picked up her telescope and folded the tripod holding it. When she walked toward the house, he fell into step beside her. "Not until after Samuel King returned. Samuel told *Mamm* about what he and Joel had been doing until Samuel decided to come home. But after that, we had no idea where Joel was. We heard rumors he was dead."

"Which weren't true."

"No, but we didn't know that at the time."

"And now he's back home."

"*Ja.*" Before he had a chance to say anything else, she said, "*Gut nacht*, Gideon." She toted her telescope into the house, closing the icy night and him out.

He hunched into his coat like a turtle in its shell as he strode down the lane. So many questions swirled around Rosemary and her family, and if he were wise, he wouldn't try to find the answers.

He knew, in this case, he was going to be a fool.

The police officer thanked Rosemary for her cooperation, but she guessed from how quickly he stood and bid her a *gut* day that his mind was already on the next person he was going to talk to.

She shivered as she closed the door. She'd projected an aura of calm while answering his questions, but couldn't maintain it. Though she wanted to help Grace find out who had broken her shop windows, it'd been appalling to speak to a policeman who resembled the one who'd taken her brother away after church last fall.

Joel had asserted he wasn't guilty, and he hadn't been because he was released.

She looked at where Braelynn was playing under the quilt-topped table and sighed with gratitude that the interview was over. Braelynn had moved the table closer to the locked trunk, so she had a solid wall on one side of her "house." Had she heard anything the police officer had said, or had she been too intent on her toys?

Just the sight of the playhouse was a reminder—though Rosemary didn't need one—that her brother's experiences weren't what upset her while talking to the cop, but the thought that had flashed through her head when she opened the door to find the officer there.

Had he come to her door to take the little girl away?

It had been a silly reaction, because Jonas would have alerted her if Braelynn was being removed from her house.

Lord, I used to believe everything would turn out right, that You longed for the best for me even when I didn't know what that was. I need to trust You haven't changed in spite of how much I have.

The back door opened, and her heart did a pair of jumping jacks until she heard a woman's voice call her name. Disappointment opened a chasm in her, but she ignored it. Why would Gideon come to the house after she'd left him standing in the snow last night?

Rosemary hadn't expected to see Laurene Hershberger in her kitchen along with her stepdaughter Mary Beth. Laurene still showed signs of not having been plain her whole life. Her hair was growing out and didn't stay under her *kapp*, but there was an air of contentment surrounding her that Rosemary envied. Contentment and happiness in the life that she'd found among the people her own family had left behind.

"*Gute mariye,*" Rosemary said before Braelynn burst into the kitchen with a happy squeal.

The two little girls ran to each other, both talking nonstop. That neither of them could understand the other didn't slow them. In fact, it resolved the issue of waiting for one to finish before the other responded.

"Can Braelynn and Mary Beth go out to play?" Braelynn asked.

When Laurene gave an indulgent nod, Rosemary said, "*Ja.* But don't go beyond the barn." She repeated the words in *Deitsch.*

Both girls giggled. As soon as Braelynn had pulled on her coat and mittens—on the correct hands this time—and boots, the two vanished outside, chattering like a pair of excited squirrels.

"Would you like some *kaffi* or tea?" Rosemary asked after the door closed behind the *kinder.*

Laurene shook her head, then shoved her hair back under her *kapp* with the ease of habit. "We can't stay long. I…" She frowned. "You look as white as a bleached sheet. What's wrong?"

"A cop came to talk to me about the damage to Grace's windows. He asked me where I was at the time when they guess the windows were broken. He wrote down my answer, and that was that." She attempted a tremulous smile. "I know I didn't do it, but he made me nervous."

"And guilty?"

Her laugh was sincere. *"Ja."*

"Don't worry. They're asking everyone the same questions. I get the feeling they're going through the motions. Nobody was hurt, and finding the truth will be like picking out a specific stone in a gravel drive." Laurene opened her black purse. "I stopped by to give you this."

She pulled out a business card and handed it to Rosemary. In unadorned print, it stated Charles Satterfield. Beneath the name she read *attorney-at-law.*

Rosemary raised her eyes. "Why do you think I need a lawyer?"

"I'm hoping you don't, but I know there must be questions about other family Braelynn may have. Questions about who has the rights to custody of her."

"I'm her step*mamm.*"

"Family issues can get messy." Her lips twisted in the caricature of a smile. "Trust me. I know that too well. Charles is easy to talk to. He'll be able to give you some *gut* advice. I've already contacted him and explained a little bit about your situation. I didn't think you'd mind."

"Not at all." In fact, Rosemary would have been more than happy to let the deacon's wife handle the whole situation.

"Charles knows you might call. Keep the card as backup in case you need it."

"Danki." Pesky tears welled up in her eyes.

"I'm glad I can help. Now I can't stay. I told Adam I would—"

The back door crashed open, and the two little girls ran in. Braelynn was holding something small and wiggling close to her.

"What do you two have?" Rosemary asked, repeating the question in *Deitsch*.

Mary Beth grinned, her eyes twinkling. "We found a *schwatz bussli*."

Rosemary looked at the black kitten. "Where did you find it?"

"In the barn." Braelynn's grin was wide.

"Can you tell me where in the barn?" When she saw Braelynn's petulant expression, she hurried to add, "The *mamm* cat will be looking for her little ones. This one must have wandered away from her. We must make sure the *mamm* cat knows her *boppli* is all right."

"*Mamm* sad because her daughter gone?"

Had the conversation taken an abrupt turn? Were they still talking about the cat and her litter? Or was Braelynn referring to her own *mamm*?

"*Ja. Mamm* cat wants to make sure her kitten grows up big and strong, so the kitten can play with you."

Braelynn giggled. When she looked at Mary Beth, the other girl giggled, too.

"We need to go," Laurene said in an apologetic tone.

"Go ahead. Braelynn and I will make sure the kitten gets

back to the rest of the litter." She looked over the *kinder*'s head. "And *danki* for Charles's information."

"I hope you never need to use it. *Komm mol*, Mary Beth. We need to meet your *daed* before he wonders where we've gone."

Mary Beth took Laurene's hand with an ease Rosemary wished Braelynn would show with her. Thanking Laurene again, Rosemary reached for her own coat as soon as the Hershbergers left.

"Let's put the kitten back in the barn," she said.

"Kittens like bowls of cream," Braelynn argued.

"Little kittens only like the *millich* their *mamms* give them." She opened the door. "*Komm* with me, and I'll show you."

She wasn't sure if the *kind* would agree, but Braelynn, cuddling the kitten, followed.

"Mary Beth says her name is *Schwatzbussli*," Braelynn said.

Rosemary started to explain *schwatz bussli* were the *Deitsch* words for black kitten, but when she saw the happiness on the *kind*'s face as she petted the tiny creature who was nestled close to her chin, she said, "That's a nice name, but a big one."

"It's big because she's going to be a big cat." Braelynn smiled up at her. "She's going to be bigger than Cleo."

"And she's going to be your friend, too. Just like Cleo."

The little girl nodded.

"Once she's big enough to be on her own, she can be yours if you'd like."

"Braelynn's *Schwatzbussli*?"

"*Ja*, but you might want to give her a shorter name so she'll come when she hears it." She tapped her finger on her chin as if deep in thought. "How about *Schwatzi*?"

Braelynn spoke the name, and the kitten's ears perked up. "She likes her name. If…" She gasped. "She's buzzing. Do you think she swallowed a bee?"

It took every bit of Rosemary's self-control not to laugh at the innocent question. "She's purring. That's what a cat does to let you know it's happy."

Braelynn considered that for a moment, then asked, "What do people do when they're happy?"

"We smile. We laugh. We sing, ain't so?"

"Braelynn wishes we purred." She rubbed her chin against the kitten's soft fur. "Then Braelynn would know when she's happy."

Rosemary choked on her gasp that she couldn't let escape. The little girl didn't recognize happiness? That was so sad Rosemary's heart ached. So sad she wasn't sure she could face it on her own.

Iva.

The old woman's wise face filled her mind. Iva would have some *gut* advice for her.

As soon as the kitten was returned to its litter, much to the delight of Braelynn who cooed to each of the kittens and petted the *mamm*, Rosemary went into the house and filled a plate with cookies. She took Braelynn with her on a long-overdue trip to her neighbor. She considered telling the little girl whom they were visiting, but how could she explain Iva Chupp to a *kind*?

"Are you home, Iva?" Rosemary called as she did each time she came to the house.

"Where else would I be?" came back the usual answer. There was a pause to give Rosemary a chance to take off her coat and boots before Iva asked, "Did you bring me cookies?"

Motioning for Braelynn to come with her, Rosemary walked into Iva's sunny living room. The old woman was sitting in her usual chair with sewing on her lap.

"Of course, I brought you cookies."

"What flavor?"

"Molasses sugar cookies."

"My favorite!"

"And," Rosemary said with a smile, "I brought you some-one else. A new neighbor. Braelynn Mishler, this is my very dear friend, Iva Chupp."

"You're old!" the little girl exclaimed.

Rosemary tried not to cringe. Before she could chide Brae-lynn about remembering her manners, the elderly woman said, "That I am. It's wrong to be filled with *hochmut*, and I can't be proud that God has decided to let me stay on Earth so long. I've come to believe it's because He thinks I've got a few more things to do before He calls me home."

"Braelynn gots home."

Iva nodded to Rosemary's quick explanation about the place the *kind* had made her own under the table. "Would you like to see what I'm working on, Braelynn?"

The little girl nodded and edged closer.

"Bring two cookies with you," Iva ordered. "One for you and one for me. Rosemary can get her own."

That brought a big grin to Braelynn who hurried to obey. She sat in a chair beside Iva's while they enjoyed their cookies as if they'd never had one.

Rosemary chose a seat that gave her a view of both of them. Why hadn't she brought Braelynn over sooner? Iva shot her a frown, and Rosemary guessed her elderly friend was think-ing the same thing.

For the first time in almost two weeks, Rosemary was able to relax as she listened while Iva asked about Braelynn's day. The little girl told her about her kitten and her house under the quilt. Iva listened as if the *kind*'s words were the most im-portant in the world. Then the old woman described the repair work she was doing on the worn quilt. Braelynn hung on her every word, fascinated, though Rosemary guessed she had no idea what Iva was talking about.

"Want to hear something special?" Iva asked. "My *daed* was a cowboy."

The little girl's eyes lit with excitement as she selected two more cookies, giving one to Iva.

"He didn't ride the range out west, though," Iva went on. "He was a seagoing cowboy. Do you know what that is?"

Braelynn shook her head.

"Long ago, there was a big war, and the war went on for a long time. For years and years." She paused, then asked, "How old are you, Braelynn?"

She held up five fingers. Iva lifted her own gnarled hand and raised one finger next to Braelynn's hand. When the little girl's eyes widened, Iva gave her a solemn nod.

"By the time the war was over after six long years, the farmers came back to their farms and found the animals were gone. Some had run away, frightened by the noise of guns. Others had disappeared. The farmers discovered their barns and homes had been destroyed. They wanted to rebuild, but what *gut* would that hard work be if there weren't any animals? What would the people use to plow their fields or give them *millich* or eggs and meat? It seemed impossible."

Iva paused to let Braelynn respond, but the little girl remained silent. However, it was, Rosemary noted, a different sort of silence. The *kind* was sitting forward, her gaze centered on Iva's face as she awaited the rest of the story. The cookie remained uneaten in Braelynn's hand, so mesmerized was she by the tale Iva was spinning. When Iva looked over the little girl's head, Rosemary nodded a silent request for her to continue.

"So some *gut* men here in this country decided to share the largesse the *Gut* Lord had given us. They were from the Church of the Brethren, and the man who got the program underway had had the idea to send cows for *millich* for *kinder* in Spain before the war that had just ended. One big problem is Spain and the rest of the countries that had been ruined by the war were on the other side of the ocean." She paused again. "Do you know what an ocean is? It's a huge pool of water almost five thousand miles across."

Braelynn's eyes widened further, but she didn't speak.

"The men asked for animals to be donated," Iva went on, "and our people responded with open hearts. Once the men had cows and horses to share with those who needed them, they had to find a way to send them across the ocean."

"In a plane?" asked Braelynn.

Iva shook her head and smiled. "This was a long time ago. Before I was born. My *daed* went on a ship and took the animals across the ocean to a place named Greece."

"Braelynn's daddy is dead." There was less emotion in the *kind*'s voice than when she'd asked about the plane.

"Mine is, too," Iva said. "It's sad for us, but we must remember they're blessed to be close to God's glory."

The rest of what the two said was lost to Rosemary as her head spun. She must have asked Iva to watch Braelynn. The old woman must have agreed because the next thing Rosemary saw clearly was the plain cemetery in front of her.

She stepped out of her buggy and stared at the white plank fence surrounding the gravestones. Each stone was identical to the one next to it except for the name and the dates cut into it. She walked on numb legs to the stone with Eddie's name on it.

Staring at the cold surface beneath her fingers, she struggled with the things she wanted—she *needed*—to say to him. "I'm trying to understand, Eddie. I really am."

No answer came back. No peace eased the storm in her soul. No healing offered solace for her heart.

She drew her fingers back from the stone, wondering why she'd come. Her husband wasn't here in the cold snowy cemetery. Only his body was in the simple wooden casket beneath the earth. Not that she'd seen him in it, because the top had been sealed during the viewing. The shot that had taken his life had been too much for the mortician to repair.

But one question refused to be silent. "Why didn't you tell me about Braelynn?" The cry burst from her throat as she stared up at the scudding clouds. "Did you think I would despise your *kind*? We could have raised her together. Eddie, she is your *kind*! Why did you turn your back on her?"

The wind hissing around the brim of her bonnet was the only answer she got. The only answer she'd get as long as she was alive.

Chapter Twelve

Rosemary didn't try to pretend that church today was going to be the same as any other Sunday. Today was the day her brother was going to step forward and ask to be forgiven for his past mistakes.

She remembered someone doing the same years ago. The woman had been placed under the *bann*, but hadn't left Bliss Valley. She'd sought guidance for whatever she'd done wrong. Rosemary didn't remember being told why the woman was seeking forgiveness. Rosemary had been a *kind* at the time. Back then, the extra time for communion, a wedding or any other rite made her more antsy on the hard bench as church continued beyond its usual three hours.

Today, her nerves were taut for another reason. How would Braelynn act during their long service? She'd been so *gut* at Iva's house, but how would she cope with so many people she didn't know?

Braelynn looked adorable in her blue bonnet. Picking a

couple of cat hairs off the little girl's black coat, Rosemary smiled at her.

"Are you ready?" Rosemary asked as she prayed, *God, please reach into her heart and bring her joy. Help her believe that she can trust me and You.*

"For what?"

"For church?"

"What's church?"

Startled, Rosemary forced a smile. She shouldn't be surprised Braelynn had never attended church before today. Everything the *kind* said suggested there hadn't been any stability in her life.

"Church is where we gather together to thank God for everything He has given us."

"Who's God?"

She was shocked, but hid it as she said, "God is our Heavenly Father, the One who made the whole universe."

"Even Braelynn?"

"*Ja*, and He has loved you from before you were born. Though you can't see Him with your eyes, you can hear Him in your heart. The most important thing is knowing He loves you."

Rosemary was amazed when Braelynn didn't ask more questions as they went out of the house into the early morning cold. They needed to be at the Kings' house by eight, and it was a twenty-minute drive. She was glad the battery in the buggy had a full charge so the heater would keep their toes warm on the way.

When she saw Misty hooked to the buggy, her eyes widened. Gideon came around the back and said, "I'm hoping I can get a ride with you. Domino isn't a big fan of cold mornings."

"*Ja*. Of course. We're glad to have you along." She said the words to be polite, then realized how much she meant them. The upcoming church service was going to be emotional, and she was glad she didn't have to make the drive with just Braelynn to keep her company.

With a smile, he swung Braelynn onto the buggy's back seat. He offered his hand to help Rosemary in. She almost told him she got in and out of her buggy on her own many times each week, but her fingers slid onto his palm. As his closed over hers, enfolding them in warmth, he drew her a half step closer.

She gazed into his eyes, which were an enticing shade of caramel. She could imagine that sweetness whirling around her. Would it be warm and welcoming?

"Rosemary?" The soft caress of his voice urged her nearer, but the bubble around them popped when he asked if she was going to get into the buggy.

Climbing in and thanking him for his help, Rosemary gave him a fleeting smile before he asked Braelynn how she was doing. Braelynn launched into a story about the black kitten that didn't abate until they were pulling into the Kings' farm lane. They waited as the passengers in the buggies ahead of them got out and the horses were unhitched and placed out in a field where they could enjoy the warming sunshine.

Rosemary's legs were unsteady beneath her as she got out. Braelynn rushed past her and toward the other *kinder* who were gathered with the women on one side of the barn door. The men stood on the other side, talking.

"It will be all right," Gideon said from behind her.

"I pray you're right."

"Haven't you heard? I'm always right. Except when I'm wrong." A slow smile spread across his face, setting his eyes aglow. She could have lost herself again in their depths, but she shifted her own gaze across the barnyard to where Braelynn stood with Naomi's twins. After the service, she'd talk to Naomi and arrange a get-together for the youngsters.

"*Danki*, Gideon. I needed a smile today."

"Glad I could give it to you." He started to say more, but he was called to join the men.

Rosemary walked in the opposite direction. When the doors were opened to welcome them inside, she sat among the women with *kinder*. Braelynn looked around with curiosity, but after one question, nodded when Rosemary put her finger to her lips.

When it was time to sing, she put her arm around the little girl and was pleased when Braelynn didn't pull away. Instead, Braelynn tried to sing along with the words she didn't understand. Rosemary doubted she'd understand them even if they were in English, but it didn't matter because Braelynn was enjoying being with the twins and Mary Beth.

The usual pace of the service changed when Jonas stepped forward and held out his hands as if to encompass the whole gathering. From a room at one side of the barn, Joel emerged. Rosemary held her breath as he came forward.

Every eye was on Joel as he stopped where the bishop stood with the two ministers on either side of him. Adam, in his role as deacon, moved next to his friend. She saw the glance the two men shared before looking as one toward Jonas. Their expressions were somber as befit the moment, but Rosemary thought of the many times she'd seen Joel and Adam laughing along with Samuel. Since the three had been scholars, they'd been great friends, creating a bond nothing could destroy, not even their own stupid decisions.

When Joel knelt, his head bowed, Rosemary realized that, until this very moment, she hadn't been sure if her brother would set aside his pride enough to humble himself before the *Leit*.

Adam began the second verse from the fourth chapter of 2 Corinthians: *But have renounced the hidden things of dishonesty, not walking in craftiness, nor handling the word of God deceitfully;*

but by manifestation of the truth commending ourselves to every man's
conscience in the sight of God.

Silence followed his words, and nobody moved until Jonas took a step toward her brother. The bishop said, "Luke in the fifteenth chapter of his gospel reports our Lord's parable of the lost sheep. Jesus told this parable, *What man of you, having an hundred sheep, if he lose one of them, doth not leave the ninety and nine in the wilderness, and go after that which is lost, until he find it? And when he hath found it, he layeth it on his shoulders, rejoicing. And when he cometh home, he calleth together his friends and neighbors, saying unto them, Rejoice with me; for I have found my sheep which was lost. I say unto you, that likewise joy shall be in heaven over one sinner that repenteth, more than over ninety and nine just persons, which need no repentance.*" He gazed around the benches facing each other in the barn. "Let us rejoice that Joel has let himself be found and he has once again welcomed God in his heart. Let us be gladdened at how God has kept him close when he didn't realize God was beside him."

Hearing a soft intake of breath behind her, Rosemary looked over her shoulder to see Grace dabbing at her eyes with a handkerchief. Grace loved Joel with all her heart. Rosemary prayed her brother wouldn't break her friend's heart by keeping secrets as Eddie had hers.

Because Joel hadn't been baptized when he jumped the fence and spent ten miserable years in the *Englisch* world, refusing to believe he'd be welcomed back into his family, Jonas didn't ask him about repenting or have the *Leit* vote to accept him back as a member. She shuddered, realizing what *Daed* would be facing if he decided to return after failing for weeks to ask for forgiveness for lies about an affair while he was married to *Mamm*, the affair whose result had been Joel and his biological sisters. *Daed* had chosen to remain an outsider rather than admit what he'd done had been wrong.

The seat where he'd once sat was now empty. She guessed that soon the men would shift to fill the spot so any sign of Wyman Beachy's presence in the community would disappear as if he'd never been a part. She sent up a prayer for *Daed* to come to his senses, but stopped when Jonas began to speak again.

"*Let my soul live,*" the bishop said, "*and it shall praise Thee; and let Thy judgments help me. I have gone astray like a lost sheep; seek Thy servant; for I do not forget Thy commandments.*"

She heard her brother's relief. "*This gate of the Lord, into which the righteous shall enter. I will praise Thee: for Thou hast heard me, and art become my salvation.*" His voice remained strong until the final words.

With that, Joel accepted forgiveness from the *Leit*. Nobody would speak of the matter again. He had confessed to his sins and was forgiven by everyone.

Except Rosemary. She wished she could forgive him, but though she could have said the words, she would have known they weren't sincere. Her heart refused to let the wounds his leaving created heal. They were too deep, too raw.

Tears filled her eyes as she watched her brother look in Grace's direction. The love between them was so powerful it seemed to flood the room. He had needed to ask for forgiveness before he could be baptized. Once that happened, he and Grace could marry and begin their life together.

A life like the one she'd hoped she'd have with Eddie.

The thought of her late husband tore her from this special moment. If the *Leit* had known about Braelynn before Eddie's death, would he have been required to come as Joel had to ask to be forgiven for his sins? Though her husband had tried to hide his *hochmut*, he'd been a proud man. He'd believed buying the farm for them so soon after he moved to Bliss Valley was a sign of his past success. Marrying her and providing for her, he'd told her more than once, would ensure his future success.

Now he was dead.

Somehow, Rosemary got through the rest of the service, depending on habit to know when to sing and when to pray. Her prayers were aimed at allowing her to keep up her calm facade. God must have heard her, because nobody seemed to notice how quiet she was as the service ended and preparations were made for the meal they'd share.

Her *gut* spirits began to return as she watched Braelynn soar on a tire swing before switching places with Mary Beth who'd been pushing her. Braelynn babbled her excitement in English, and Mary Beth talked in *Deitsch*, but they seemed to understand each other.

"*Kinder* have their own way of communicating," Jonas said as he came to stand beside her.

"It would seem so." She couldn't help but be curious why he'd sought her out.

As if she'd asked that aloud, the bishop said, "I wanted to let you know I've heard from my contacts in western Pennsylvania."

"What did you discover?" she asked, too anxious to give him time to explain.

"Not much."

"Oh." She didn't know what else to say.

"Two had Mishler families in their districts, but none of them knew an Eddie Mishler. One of them knew a Mishler Eddie's age, but that man's still living in that district with a wife and five *kinder*. The rest had nobody with that name or that age who'd left."

"Oh."

"I've asked them to check with other bishops there and in Ohio. Some districts straddle state lines." He sighed. "They'll do their best, but they didn't give me any reason to believe that looking farther would get the answers you want."

"That doesn't make sense."

"I know. Are you sure Eddie said he was from western Pennsylvania? Maybe he meant he was from west of Lancaster County. There are a bunch of other settlements I could contact."

"It'd be like looking for a needle in straw."

He nodded. "I know, but if you'd like me to, I will contact other bishops to seek their help."

Her eyes shifted to Braelynn. The little girl deserved to know what other family she possessed. Her stomach twisted at the thought of one of those relatives wanting to lay claim to the *kind*. Which was more important? The truth or hiding from it?

The answer was obvious. "If you could contact a few more," Rosemary said, "we might find a way to discover where Eddie was from. In the meantime, I'll look around the house and see if I can find something to point us in the right direction."

"That's a *gut* idea. The slightest clue could lead us to the truth."

Patting her on the shoulder, he left her to watch the little girls playing. Jonas took his position as their bishop seriously. He saw the extra effort he was making to solve the enigma surrounding Eddie's past a part of the reason God had raised him to the task of being bishop.

"Busy?" asked another voice behind her.

She looked back to see LaVern. "Just keeping an eye on the girls."

"Braelynn seems like a *gut kind*."

"Some days." She chuckled to take the sting out of her words. "Days like today, she's a joy to be around. Other days... Well, all I can say is that she has a mind of her own."

"Being a *mamm* seems to agree with you. You're glowing with happiness."

"I'm happy," she said, glad he hadn't seen past the guise she'd kept in place all day. "*Danki* for noticing."

"I notice everything about you, Rosemary."

She lowered her eyes. Why couldn't she have a conversation with LaVern without him trying to flirt with her? It hadn't been like that when Eddie was alive. On the other hand, Calvin Hertzler hadn't seemed to care if Eddie witnessed his flirting with her or not.

"*Danki* for helping Gideon put the new toilet in his carriage," she said, hoping to move the conversation to more banal topics.

"Does it work okay for you?"

"Fine. LaVern, I should—"

He didn't let her finish. "Listen, Rosemary. I think... That is, we should..." He rubbed his hands together. "Why don't we get married? I know Eddie would have given his blessing to our marriage."

She wasn't sure which outrageous comment to respond to first. Marry LaVern Spaeger? She couldn't imagine spending the rest of her life with a man who made her feel uncomfortable. As far as Eddie blessing their marriage, LaVern was fooling himself. He must not know her late husband had spent time with him only because he was Calvin's friend. What had Eddie called LaVern? A clown. In fact, until Rosemary's brother returned to Bliss Valley and focused Eddie's bile on him, her husband had complained that every minute he spent with LaVern was a waste of time.

"*Danki*," she said, "but no."

The hope in his eyes vanished, and she wondered if there was a way she could have told him more gently.

"I don't plan to marry again," she hurried to add.

"The bishop will be on your doorstep before the year's out to remind you of your duty to the community. A widow needs someone to look after her farm and her stock." He swallowed, then said in what was an afterthought, "And herself."

"And I will listen to Jonas."

"But not to me when I ask you to marry me?"

"LaVern, it hasn't been five months since Eddie was shot."

He hunched into himself. "You don't have to remind me of that. I think about it every day."

Rosemary had to fight her normal inclination to reach and touch his arm in sympathy. Once she might have done that without thinking. Everything had changed between them when he asked her to marry him.

And kept insisting.

She'd been honest when she told him she wasn't ready to think of marrying again. A hint of guilt pinched at her. Because her daydreams had led her in the absurd direction of imagining Gideon asking her to walk out with him didn't mean anything. Daydreams were just daydreams. Whimsies that had no basis in reality.

"LaVern," she said, eager to escape her own thoughts, "we need time to heal from our grief. That's why we make time for mourning."

"A year. I know." He gave her a look like an eager puppy, if a puppy was more than six and a half feet tall and seemed to wear the same stained shirt every day. "Will you marry me if I ask you a year and a day after the anniversary of Eddie's death?"

"I can't say."

"That's not a no." He grinned. "All right, Rosemary. Mark your calendar. I'll ask you in September. It's a date."

He squeezed her hand and strode away with a lightness to his usually heavy steps.

She opened her mouth to call after him. He must come back so she could explain how he'd misunderstood what she'd said.

A cry came from where the girls were playing. Mary Beth had fallen and scraped her hand. Hurrying to them, she knew she should put LaVern and his unending proposals out of her head. She just didn't know how.

Gideon turned away as LaVern rushed back to the barn as if he had the most exciting news to share. He clenched his hands at his sides. At first, he'd thought LaVern was going to tell Rosemary the gossip about Eddie's death. When he hadn't, Gideon had been suffused with relief.

Until he heard LaVern propose.

Again, he'd almost stepped forward, but Rosemary's kind rejection halted him. Had it been a mistake not to interrupt when he saw how LaVern was upsetting her? Gideon hadn't wanted his own presence to lead LaVern into spilling the rumor.

"Everyone okay?" he asked as he walked toward her and the two little girls. He saw tears dampening Mary Beth's face. "What's happened?"

"Mary Beth hurt her hand." Rosemary was gentle with the *kind* as she led her toward the Kings' house. "Let's find something to put on it to take out the sting."

"I'll find Laurene or Adam, if you'd like."

"*Danki*, Gideon." The smile she gave him sent a shiver of anticipation through him as he thought about driving with her back to her farm.

That thought propelled Gideon's feet, and he soon located Adam and Laurene. They went to take over the care of their daughter who'd calmed enough to enjoy an extra piece of pie. Braelynn claimed she needed one, too, so Gideon waited until the little girls were done.

He breathed a quiet prayer of thanks when Rosemary said it was time to leave. He regretted his reaction when he saw her brother watching them, his smile not concealing his hurt. Rosemary didn't notice because she kept her eyes averted from Joel. Only when she was climbing into the buggy did she glance in her brother's direction and only then, Gideon suspected, because Joel's back was turned.

Braelynn talked about the kids she'd played with, sharing every little detail until she halted mid-word.

Rosemary looked into the back and murmured, "She's asleep. Wore herself out playing."

"She had a *gut* day," he replied. "Did you?"

"It was nice to see everyone as we gathered to worship."

He fought his hands that wanted to tighten on the reins. He recognized her cool tone. It meant she was trying to dampen her feelings and only show what she thought was safe for others to see.

Suddenly, she reached behind the seat and called, "Braelynn, wake up!" He didn't have time to ask what was going on before she shouted, "Look! To the left!" She turned to lift the little girl over the back of the seat and onto her lap. "That way, Braelynn! Look!"

He was about to ask what she meant when he saw great wings lifting from the remnants of last season's corn. The sun glinted off pure white feathers on the bird's head.

"A bald eagle," he breathed out as he watched the majestic bird rise against the brilliant blue sky. Drawing in the reins to slow the buggy, he exclaimed, "There's another on the ground."

"They must be young brothers who are hunting together." She shifted to let Braelynn squirm in between her and the door where she'd have a better view. Pointing to the field, then to the sky, she guided the little girl to see the beautiful birds. "I didn't know there were bald eagles around here. I thought they nested by the Susquehanna River."

"They must be spreading out in search of food. It's *gut* having them around to clear out the vermin."

Braelynn gasped as the first eagle returned, shoving against the one that had been eating whatever they'd caught or found. "Why did eagle do that?"

"Eagles don't like to share," Gideon said, smiling as he continued to watch the birds tussle. Both took the air, circling away from the buggy. "Brothers can be like that."

"Braelynn doesn't have a brother," Braelynn said.

"Me, neither," Gideon replied, looking at the little girl whose lower lip was trembling.

"No sisters, either. It was Braelynn and Mommy and then Catriona and then Tom and Cyndi." Her nose wrinkled. "Didn't like them. They didn't like Braelynn, either."

"Your *mamm* loved you," Rosemary said. "I know she did."

"How?"

"Because I can't imagine anyone not loving you, Braelynn. You're a sweet girl."

An odd expression crossed the *kind*'s face, but then she shook her head. "Catriona and Tom and Cyndi didn't like Braelynn. Heard them say so."

"Was Cyndi the lady who left you here?" asked Rosemary.

"No, that was Patsy."

"Were you with her after Tom and Cyndi?"

The *kind* shook her head as she stared out at the fields, looking for the eagles again. "That was Josh." She counted on her fingers. "Then Gloria. She smelled funny. Then Josh again. Then Catriona again. Then Andrea. Oh, I forgot Keiko. She was before Andrea and was nice, but she had to move, so Braelynn went back to Catriona." Looking at them with a triumphant grin, she said, "*Then* Patsy. Now you."

Rosemary's voice softened as she asked, "Was Patsy the one who hurt you?" She touched the *kind*'s arm. "Made the bruises that were here."

"Patsy didn't like Braelynn." Her eyes blazed with sudden fury. "Braelynn didn't like Patsy."

Gideon heard Rosemary saying something to calm the little girl, but his heart was beating too hard for him to pick up the words. Beating with fury that the *kind* had been passed from person to person like a plate of sandwiches. Had any of those people tucked her into bed, made sure she said her prayers, taught her to love God?

His gaze collided with Rosemary's, and he saw his disgust mirrored in her eyes. How could these people have treated a *kind* worse than they would have a dog? The saddest part was Braelynn seemed to think there was nothing out of the ordinary about what had happened to her. Why hadn't one of those people called the authorities? Then they could have tracked down Eddie and insisted he take care of his daughter.

Then Gideon wondered if that would have made things even worse for the *kind*. If Eddie had been unstable enough to kill himself, who knows what he might have done with the added stress of having responsibility for his daughter?

Gideon sucked in his breath. Was he accepting LaVern's gossip as the truth?

He didn't dare speak as he continued along the road toward the farm. When they reached it, all he yearned to do was find sanctuary in his shop and his work. Instead, he accepted Rosemary's offer to join them for supper.

He shouldn't stay, but LaVern had been right about one thing. A widow was granted a year to mourn, but then everyone would expect her to remarry.

And Gideon knew one other thing for certain. He wasn't going to stay in Bliss Valley to see her wed another man.

Chapter Thirteen

Rosemary lifted the last of the supper dishes off the table and smiled as Braelynn collected the silverware.

"What can I do?" Gideon asked.

"There is a coconut cream pie in the refrigerator," she said. "If you'll get it, we'll enjoy some dessert."

As they worked together, Rosemary wondered if she could have imagined her dreams of having a family would evolve into the life she was living. Her husband was dead, and another man sat in his chair at her table. The *kind* she'd prayed for had suffered too many changes in her young life and no longer trusted anyone. But Rosemary was grateful not to be alone tonight. God had answered her prayer and brought others into her home.

She served Gideon a generous slice of pie and another for Braelynn. The little girl had a bottomless pit because she ate as much food as any adult. Rosemary tried not to think about how often the *kind* might have been hungry in the past. Slicing a much smaller piece for herself, she refilled their glasses with *millich*.

When Rosemary sat, she grimaced. All day long, her dress had felt tight. She'd noticed it during church services, but figured it was because Braelynn was sitting so close. The little girl was on the other end of the bench now. Though she wished she could blame the discomfort on her dress shrinking in the wash, a cotton/polyester mix didn't lose its shape. The truth was she'd been enjoying too many sweets along with Braelynn. She pushed her pie away untouched.

"Are you okay?" asked Gideon before he lifted another bite of pie on his fork.

"Full." It wasn't a lie. Her dress felt more than full.

"The pie is *gut*."

"I'm glad you're enjoying it." She smiled at Braelynn who was eating her dessert as if she hadn't seen food in months. "At least, you're taking time to taste it."

The *kind*'s head popped up. "You said God loves Braelynn?"

Realizing she was getting accustomed to the little girl's odd segues, she said, "I did, and He does."

"You said God is Braelynn's Heavenly Father?"

"I did, and He is," she said, not sure where the little girl was going with her questions. She noticed Gideon had lowered his fork to his plate and was looking from her to the *kind*.

"Braelynn's daddy is dead."

"I know." She kept her voice steady. "Your *daed* is with God."

The little girl's eyes widened. "Braelynn's daddy is with God?"

"*Ja*. We are God's *kinder*. He calls some of us home sooner and some of us home later."

"Wish Braelynn could see Braelynn's daddy."

Rosemary pushed back her chair and held out her hand. "*Komm* with me." She motioned for Gideon to join them before she led the little girl into the living room. Opening the Bible she kept by her rocking chair, she paged through to where she'd stashed the photograph of Eddie and Madison Nesbitt.

Sitting on the sofa with her finger in the Bible to mark the page, she waited until Braelynn had crawled up beside her. She glanced once at where Gideon stood with his hands on the back of the rocking chair. He gave her the slightest nod and a gentle smile.

Her heart lurched, some of the broken pieces melding together at the warmth of his support. She hadn't been sure she'd made the correct choice, and having him offer her silent encouragement was *wunderbaar*. After months of having to make all the tough decisions on her own, she hadn't guessed how much she'd appreciate having someone by her side, urging her to do what she felt was right.

Only Braelynn nudging her as the youngster nestled against her kept Rosemary from savoring more of the comfort she hadn't realized how much she needed. Affixing a smile on her face, she opened the Bible and lifted out the photograph.

"Gideon tried to show this to you the day you came here. Remember?"

The little girl nodded.

"You didn't want to see it then, but I think you do now. It's a picture of your *mamm* and *daed*."

Braelynn stared at the image as if afraid if she took her eyes off it, the picture would disappear. Then as if she were about to caress a baby bird, she stretched out one tiny finger and brushed the faces in the photo. She patted her own cheek as if trying to find something to connect her to the people she was looking at.

"What's wrong with them?" the little girl asked.

"What do you mean?" Rosemary hoped the *kind* didn't see how her own hands were trembling.

"They're little." She pointed to them before touching her own chest. "Braelynn is big."

"It's just a picture."

When Braelynn frowned, Gideon interjected, "Like the pictures in your coloring book."

The little girl gazed at him, puzzled.

When he looked past the little girl as he came around the chair and sat facing them, Rosemary nodded her silent permission for him to go on. He did, saying, "Remember the picture you colored for me. A picture of *Schwatzbussli*, ain't so?"

"*Ja.*"

"But it wasn't the same size as *Schwatzbussli*, ain't so?"

Understanding widened her eyes. "*Schwatzbussli* little, picture littler."

"Like this picture of your *mamm* and *daed*."

More pieces of Rosemary's heart were stitched together as she listened to his kindness while he eased Braelynn through the steps to reach understanding. She thanked God for bringing Gideon into her life so he could help Braelynn.

And me.

Braelynn stared at the picture, her lower lip beginning to quiver. Big tears rolled down her cheeks, but she didn't make a sound. When one fell on the photograph, Rosemary fought her instinct to wipe it away. Instead, she put her arm around the *kind*.

"Braelynn's mommy is gone," Braelynn whispered. "Braelynn's *daed*, too."

"I know," Rosemary said as softly. "And I know they would be with you if they could."

"Braelynn wants Braelynn's mommy and daddy." She tugged on Rosemary's arm. "Rosie, let's go and find them."

Astonished by what the little girl had called her, Rosemary blinked hard to keep her own tears from falling. Years ago, her brother had called her Rosie. Ten years ago to be exact.

Since Joel had left Bliss Valley. Afterward, a few friends had used the nickname, but she'd discouraged it. She'd believed she was glad the nickname had been forgotten. Now she wasn't so sure she should have relinquished it. She liked Braelynn having a special name for her. It suggested the *kind* was beginning to trust her as Joel once had. As she'd once trusted him. The trust between her and Braelynn wasn't a lot yet, maybe not even a full step forward. More like the wiggling of a single toe at the beach, moving a few grains of sand.

How much else had Joel taken with him when he jumped the fence, leaving her behind?

Knowing she couldn't answer that now, she drew the little girl onto her lap and cradled her close. "Your *mamm* and *daed* are with God. We can't see them with our eyes or talk to them with our mouths. We have to use our hearts."

"Hearts don't talk," retorted the always literal *kind*.

"Not out loud. That's why you've got to be quiet and listen. You love them, so they'll always be deep within your heart."

Braelynn put her finger to her lips, then was silent for about five seconds. "Braelynn no hear them."

"Sometimes it takes them a while to speak to us." She leaned the *kind*'s head against her breast. "Listen. What do you hear?"

"Thump-thump-thump."

"That's my heart beating."

Braelynn's mouth became a perfect circle. "Does Braelynn's heart do that, too?"

"Everyone's heart does."

"What do hearts say?"

Rosemary faltered. How could she tell the little girl that too often Rosemary's heart hammered out thick slabs of guilt?

Gideon spoke into the silence. "It's saying you are never alone. God and everyone you love is in there. The beating is so you'll remember they never are far from you."

Biting her lower lip as if she were no older than Braelynn, Rosemary nodded at him as he had to her. She hoped he understood that his simple words had touched her own aching heart, and she prayed they had Braelynn's, too.

The *kind* curled into a ball on Rosemary's lap, but reached out when Gideon handed her the stuffed lion. Pulling it close to her face, she stroked the worn fabric with trembling fingers as she began to sob again.

Nobody spoke or moved until the *kind* had cried herself to sleep. Rosemary wondered if Gideon was praying—as she was—that God would help them find a way to ease the little girl's grief.

Holding up the small saddle he'd been working on the past week, Gideon nodded. The stitches he'd used to close the torn leather were hardly visible. It hadn't taken him long to repair the damage. He could have had it finished days ago, but his shop had been bustling with customers interested in his services. It was as if a floodgate had opened, and the work he'd despaired would come his way had arrived all at once. He had two more saddles to repair as well as a harness. He had orders for a half dozen thick collars used by draft horses and mules, which he must have ready before plowing began in four to six weeks. Other customers were looking to replace broken reins and traces. He'd sold all the pieces he'd made in advance.

He wouldn't have been so far behind if, after running some errands, he hadn't come into the shop this morning to find it trashed a second time. Why was his shop being targeted? Was it a prank or was there something more malicious in the mess?

Lowering the saddle to his worktable, he glanced at the other ripped saddle waiting for his attention. He thanked God that nobody had been hurt when it'd been torn by a teenager doing what he shouldn't have.

"When did you get to be such an old fogy?" Gideon asked himself with a chuckle. "You used to think skiing behind a buggy or racing them was the ultimate in excitement on a Saturday night. It could have been you who snagged a branch while pushing your horse to a faster pace."

At a knock, he looked across his workspace. Rosemary was silhouetted in the doorway. Though she wore the same heart-shaped *kapp* as every other plain woman in Bliss Valley, he knew it was her. It wasn't solely her height. Instead, something about the way her fingertips lingered on the door's molding as if she might flee at any moment and the tilt of her head as if she carried the whole world upon her shoulders.

He needed to tell her about the mess he'd found. He realized now wasn't the time because he noticed Braelynn was with her, half-hidden behind Rosemary's black coat. When she peeked out, he saw curiosity on her delicate face.

"Are you busy, Gideon?" Rosemary asked.

"No. *Komm* in."

She did, bringing the *kind* with her. "I heard voices, and I thought you had a customer."

"Just me talking to myself."

"My *mamm* says that's a sign you need to get out more."

He laughed. "Mine would say the same."

She froze and stared at the mess. "What happened?"

"It's pretty obvious, ain't so?"

"I'm hoping you're going to say you never had a chance to clean up because you've been so busy."

"No, I cleaned it," he said. "Someone decided to *unclean* it."

She pressed her fingers to her lips, something she did, he'd learned, when she was so upset she didn't trust her own words.

"It's okay," he said, though it wasn't. "I'll take care of it."

"The police—"

"Haven't found whoever broke Grace's windows. I don't

think they're going to have much more luck finding who did this."

"Do you think it's the same person?"

The question knocked the air out of him. Early on, he'd thought the two incidents—now three—might be related, but he'd dismissed that idea. Maybe he shouldn't have.

"I've got no idea," Gideon replied, "but I think I should mention it to Jonas or Adam the next time I see them."

"That would be wise. I'm sorry this is happening to you, Gideon."

"Me, too."

When she approached his worktable, he relished her graceful motions. No matter what Rosemary did, it was as if she wanted each move to be as beautiful as one of her quilts. He wasn't sure how she did it, and he found watching her fascinating.

Gideon made sure his face revealed none of his thoughts as she looked at the saddle he'd finished. He smiled and waved when Braelynn went back outside to play in the snowbank by the shop. Rosemary didn't warn her away from the road or to be careful. The growing trust between the two of them was a joy to behold.

"This is well-done," Rosemary said, drawing his attention back to her. "Harold will be pleased."

"How did you know this was Harold's?" he asked in surprise. Not surprised she knew Harold Coffman, who was Grace's *daed*, but that she'd recognized the saddle.

She touched the leather smoothed by years of use. "Grace mentioned her nephews are eager to get back to riding as they did when they lived in Montana. This saddle is the right size for a ten-year-old boy like Brandon."

"*Gut* guess. Harold told me his sons used it, and one of them tore it years ago."

"Trying to jump a fence?"

"Or racing." He grinned. "I got the idea his boys were competitive. Not what I would have expected from meeting Grace. She's very quiet."

"Probably wise in a family with so many loud boys."

He chuckled. "I can sympathize with older sisters. I learned young to stay away from their games, because they always wanted me to be the *boppli* when they played house."

When she didn't laugh, he came around the table to stand beside her. "Why did you stop in, Rosemary?"

"I spoke with the lawyer Laurene recommended."

"On the phone or in person?"

"On the phone for now. He wants to take some time to study the legal ramifications of our situation first." She rubbed her hands together and glanced toward the window, which showed Braelynn stomping on a chunk of snow, trying to break it into tiny pieces.

"About what could happen if Madison's family is found and wants custody of Braelynn?"

She nodded and looked as young and frightened as Braelynn had the day they'd found her in Rosemary's kitchen. "We need to know what we're facing. Or whom. Charles—that's the lawyer's name—mentioned we may need to hire a private investigator."

"You're okay with that?"

Shaking her head, she said, "I can't see Jonas agreeing to that."

"Me, neither." He thought of how he couldn't persuade the bishop to try to get some information on Eddie Mishler to share with the police.

"I can understand why he feels that way. God brought Braelynn into my life. I shouldn't question His ways or His reasons."

"But you're curious what God's reasons are."

She smiled for the first time since she'd come into the shop. "I am."

"Humans have been questioning God's reasons for as long as we've been on earth." He returned her grin. "If Adam and Eve hadn't done that, we'd be in the Garden of Eden still."

"I can't help but believe that is a lesson in why *not* to let our curiosity get the better of us." She glanced toward the window again. "If it were just about me, I'd let it go. But it's not."

"What are you going to do?"

"I thought I might try to find some of the people who knew Madison and Braelynn. I could ask a few questions myself." She fingered a piece of leather he'd pushed to one side.

He couldn't help but notice how her hands trembled. "You're shaking."

"I can't help it. When I heard her listing off those names, I wanted to shriek my anger at how she'd been treated. I keep telling myself that those same people can be the way to make sure she isn't treated like that again."

He knew Rosemary well enough to realize if she wanted to shriek, she was distraught. Even when Braelynn was at her worst, doing everything she could to irritate her, Rosemary hadn't raised her voice.

Now Rosemary wanted to go off on a quest to find the very family she hoped didn't exist. He opened his mouth to offer his help, then shut it as he sighed and ran his hand back through his hair. *Stop thinking of yourself!* the small voice from his conscience berated him, and he deserved it. God had led him here. Gideon couldn't let himself forget that for a moment. He ached to help, to ease her anxiety when she feared for the *kind*...to learn why his heart beat faster when she was near.

"Where do you want us to start?" Gideon looked straight into Rosemary's eyes.

"Us?"

He wasn't sure whether to be annoyed or delighted at her surprise. He went with delighted. "I want to make sure that little girl isn't hurt more."

Her eyes glistened with elation at his offer to help. His hands itched to sweep around her waist and pull her up against him as he sampled her lips that looked so sweet. Disappointment riveted him when she turned away.

Not from him, he realized, but to check on Braelynn before she said, "She doesn't know any surnames. If they were spoken in front of her, she wasn't much more than a *boppli*, so she wasn't listening."

"So we're right back to where we were."

"I'd hoped when I showed her the picture, it might help. All we've done is upset Braelynn. The poor *kind* didn't recognize her *mamm* or Eddie."

"Which means they didn't spend much time with her."

"I thought of that, too." Raising her gaze toward the ceiling as if she could see through it, she said, "The more I learn, the more I'm confused. Eddie was fond of *kinder*. He enjoyed playing ball with the kids after church services, and he was one of the first to volunteer when the school needed some work done."

"Though you didn't have any scholars there."

"*Ja*. He used to say it was an investment in our *kinder*'s futures." She closed her eyes and sighed as she linked her fingers together in front of her. "At the same time, he'd abandoned his own *kind*."

"Maybe he didn't have any choice."

She stared at him, aghast. "What do you mean?"

Shocked to find himself defending the man, Gideon chose his words with care. "I'm guessing, but maybe Braelynn's *mamm* didn't want him to spend time with their *kind*."

"Why?"

"I don't have the slightest idea, but some *Englischers* use their *kinder* as pawns in their anger at each other. If that's what happened, then Eddie may not have known Madison was dead." *Or discovering the truth could have been the reason he shot himself.*

Again, he chastised himself. He couldn't let rumors intrude on Rosemary's search for the truth.

"We can stand here and ask questions until the sun goes down," he said. "What we need to do is get some facts."

"I think the county children's protective office in Lancaster City might be the best place to begin. If Eddie didn't help Braelynn and her *mamm*, maybe someone there did."

He nodded, remembering the woman who'd left Braelynn at the farm. She'd had *city* written all over her. "I can't go tomorrow because I need to finish a few projects. How about on Thursday?"

"Ja." She moved toward the door. "Though I don't want to go there, we could also check the homeless shelters. Someone may remember seeing them. I'll bring the photograph to see if anyone remembers Madison or Eddie."

He stepped in front of her. "Rosemary, you need to keep one thing in mind."

"What's that?"

"You may not like what we discover."

Her face paled, but she kept her chin high. "I know. I'm prepared."

As she left, he hoped she was because he wasn't.

Chapter Fourteen

The next morning, Gideon heard the door to his shop open as he was finishing his scrambled eggs and toast, the only meal he could cook, so he often had it for supper as well as breakfast. Even occasionally in the middle of the day.

Putting down his fork, he went out to see Rosemary entering with Braelynn who was carrying a small basket. His lips pulled into a smile so wide he wondered if it'd leap right off his face.

"We thought you could use more eggs," Rosemary said.

"Could you smell my cooking up at the house?"

"*Mamm* has mentioned she often smelled eggs frying when she walked past."

He took the basket the little girl held up to him. "*Danki. Danki* to you, Braelynn, and to the chickens."

The *kind* stared at him and said nothing. He was curious what she was thinking, but before he could ask, Rosemary spoke.

"I called for a van for us tomorrow. They'll be here around ten a.m."

He shifted his eyes toward Braelynn who had moved away to examine another saddle that he was working on. It had far more damage than the one Harold Coffman had brought in. Not from hard use, but from what looked like rodent damage.

Rosemary continued, "*Mamm* is coming tomorrow to teach Braelynn how to make her special chocolate cake. It's a rite of passage for the women in our family to learn to make *Mamm*'s cake."

"And tomorrow Braelynn's going to learn?" His hope the little girl would look at him was dashed when Braelynn's shoulders stiffened. He wondered if she was distressed about Rosemary leaving her with someone else.

The same thought must have occurred to Rosemary because she smiled and said, "It should be ready when you and I get back around supper time. Wait until you taste *Mamm*'s chocolate cake, Gideon."

"Your *mamm*'s and Braelynn's special cake, ain't so?"

Again, he hoped the *kind* would react, but Braelynn continued examining the saddle as if she'd never seen anything as fascinating.

"It's going to be yummy." Rosemary's voice was strained.

Going over to the little girl, Gideon said, "I know you're going to learn to bake a special cake, but if you'd like, on another day, I could show you how to make something with leather."

Rosemary's eyes widened in dismay. "I don't think—"

"There are plenty of things a *kind* can make. Not everything requires an awl or the knife or a sewing machine." Her distrust vexed him enough so he asked more loudly than he intended, "Do you think I'm *dumm* enough to let a *kind* near those things?"

He regretted his question when she recoiled. She went to

stand next to the door as if he'd pelted her with the heavy metal tools.

Closing the distance between them, he put a hand on her shoulder. She drew it away, folding her arms in front of her.

"Don't," she whispered.

"Rosemary, I'm sor—"

"Don't!" she retorted.

He tried to see her face, which she kept averted. "I'm trying to apol—"

Again, she interrupted him. "Please don't."

"Don't apologize?"

"Don't act like *Daed*. He always shouted at us and then apologized, and his apology was supposed to make everything okay. As if he'd never yelled in the first place."

She seldom spoke of her life before she'd married Eddie. Why hadn't he noticed that before? What she'd said confirmed the suspicions that had begun to blossom when he spoke with Joel. Their *daed* had had unreasonable expectations of his *kinder*.

How different from his family! His parents, grandparents and sisters had showed him how much they loved and cared about him. Too much, he'd thought, but now he had to begin to wonder if he'd been too quick to judge. Knowing he was loved by his family was a *wunderbaar* gift he shouldn't have taken for granted.

It sounded as if Rosemary hadn't enjoyed the same cocoon of family that he had. Sorrow flooded him. He wasn't sure what to say, so he did the only thing he could think of. He put his arms around her and drew her to him. She resisted a second before softening against him. Her face pressed to his shoulder, and he rested his own on her *kapp*. The scent of her soap was fresh and yet enticing at the same time.

"I'm sorry," she murmured. "I shouldn't have said that."

"It's okay."

"No, it's not." She raised her head, and her mouth was a bare inch from his.

He could no more have stopped from kissing her than he could have stopped breathing. His hand at the back of her head brought her mouth under his. The sweet warmth of her lips filled his mind, and he discovered having her in his arms was more thrilling than any daydream. Then her arms were around his shoulders, and she was kissing him back, and all thought vanished.

Sometime—was it a second or a century?—he drew back and gazed into her eyes. Her expression looked as amazed as his must. Had it been right or wrong to kiss her? He couldn't be sure right now. All he knew was that he wanted to kiss her a second time. As he tilted her lips beneath his again, his eyes were caught by a motion across the room.

Braelynn was watching them with a scowl. When she noticed him glancing at her, she turned away, but not before her face went blank.

Pushing out of his arms, Rosemary stepped back. She looked from him to the *kind*. Dismay stripped the dreamy look from her face. Without a word, she went to the little girl, took her by the hand and went to the door.

"*Danki* for the eggs," he called in their wake, then berated himself for what had to have been the stupidest thing any man had said after kissing a woman.

Braelynn looked back at him, and he saw tears in her eyes. He took a step to follow, but she pulled away from Rosemary and raced toward the house. He wasn't sure how he could have messed up so much in such a short time.

When Rosemary and Braelynn went next door after lunch, Iva looked as if she hadn't moved from the chair where she'd been sitting the last time Rosemary had checked on her earlier in the week. She was wearing the same dark blue dress and the same black apron and the same white *kapp*. The same ancient quilt was draped over her knees as she worked to fix more of the torn seams and the ripped fabric.

"Cookies?" the old woman asked in lieu of a greeting as she did each time Rosemary visited.

"Of course." Rosemary smiled and motioned for Braelynn to set the plastic plate on the table beside Iva. Oh, how *gut* it felt to wear a smile after the strained ones she'd had for the little girl since they'd left Gideon's shop. "Braelynn helped me make applesauce nut cookies today."

"Applesauce nut cookies?" Iva grinned. "My favorite."

"Are they all her favorite?" asked the little girl.

"So far." Rosemary winked, hoping the *kind* didn't suspect that underneath her cheerful demeanor she was wracked with worry about going to Lancaster City tomorrow to begin the search for Braelynn's past.

Everything had been changed by Gideon kissing her. Though she still was grateful he was joining her to search for the truth, she wasn't sure what to say or do the next time she saw him. She had told everyone who asked she wasn't interested in finding a new husband while she mourned Eddie. Now...

She must act as if the kiss hadn't happened. Braelynn was depending on her to get to the truth. For that, she needed Gideon's help. He had a perspective that wasn't mixed up in her anger and grief aimed at Eddie.

Why had Eddie never told her about Braelynn?

How was she going to make sure the little girl was well taken care of?

The questions buffeted in her head. They were so loud she was having trouble concentrating. She couldn't chance missing a vital clue to Braelynn's past. She owed that much to Eddie's daughter.

Not just as his daughter. Braelynn was becoming a vital part of her own life. The idea of the little girl being taken away threatened the recently mended bits of her heart.

And worrying about what might wait in Lancaster kept her from thinking about Gideon's kiss. Everything went in a circle like a maddened merry-go-round, and she couldn't find a way off.

"Tell Braelynn more about the cowboys and the ocean," she heard the *kind* say and forced her attention to the conversation in front of her.

Iva smiled, the motion shifting her wrinkles. "If Rosemary has time."

"Rosie?" asked Braelynn. "Hear the story."

"All right." She smiled at the elderly woman and the youngster. Hearing more of Iva's tale would be a *gut* way to pass the time. Better than worrying about something that might not happen...or the kiss that had!

Iva hooked her needle into the quilt, then leaned her elbows on the arms of her chair. Her gaze turned inward as she said, "My *daed* was a *gut* man, and he didn't believe one man should kill another. Not even in a war. So when the war came and he was called to be a soldier, he asked to be given other work. He was sent south of here to Maryland as well as to West Virginia. In both camps, he spent his time logging along with other men who believed as he did. That we should live as Jesus preached and turn the other cheek and forgive. He labored hard and never complained, but he missed my *mamm* and he missed his herd, so when he heard about taking cows and horses and chickens across the ocean—"

"In a big boat," Braelynn piped up.

"That's right." Iva patted the little girl's head. "You remember what I told you before. My *mamm* was sad because he was going, but she believed in the job he was going to do. He was taking animals to replace the ones lost during the war."

"What if the animals had found their way home?" Braelynn asked. "Like Bo Peep's sheep?"

Rosemary smiled sadly at Iva, but was glad Braelynn had retained some innocence. The *kind* might have been passed from person to person, and who could guess what she'd seen? However, she'd been spared the horrors of a war. She hadn't had to flee from her home as bombs dropped or seen someone she loved killed by enemy soldiers. When Iva had chosen the word *lost*, the little girl had assumed the animals caught up in war had wandered away like the nursery rhyme sheep. She couldn't imagine they'd been slaughtered in battles or to fill starving stomachs.

"There would be room for all the animals," Rosemary said. "Nobody would turn away any animal that found its way home."

"*Gut!*"

At the *kind*'s easy use of *Deitsch*, Iva raised her powder white eyebrows, but continued the story. "*Mamm* didn't want *Daed* to be cold on the ocean, so she sent a quilt with him." She spread her fingers across the fabric on her lap. "This quilt. He gave it to a little girl like you, Braelynn."

"Did she tear it?"

"No, she used it and used it and used it. Then she brought the quilt back to me."

"It's ripped."

"*Ja*, but I can fix it. It goes to show that no matter where we travel, God brings us back to where we're meant to be." She patted the quilt. "Once I have it repaired, some other little girl can use it."

"Braelynn?"

Rosemary exclaimed, "Braelynn! We don't ask things of others."

"Why not? How will Iva know Braelynn likes her quilt?"

Iva wagged a finger at Rosemary. "She's got you there, my girl."

Holding up her hands in surrender, Rosemary laughed. "I can't argue with that."

"So what are you up to this week?" Iva asked, looking from Rosemary to Braelynn.

"Braelynn is going to ock-ton." The little girl jumped to her feet and twirled around the room like an out-of-control top. "Ock-ton! Ock-ton!"

"Auction," Rosemary translated in case Iva didn't understand. "There was a sign about it at LaVern's store, and Braelynn saw it. We're going to the next household auction at Calvin Hertzler's barn a week from Saturday. I thought I might get a minute to talk to him. I'd like to ask him to do a mini-auction as part of his big ones to raise money to help Grace replace her windows. Would you like to come with us?"

"Does us include that handsome young man at the end of your lane?"

Heat seeped onto Rosemary's face and her lips tingled at the memory of Gideon's against them. "I don't know if he's busy on Saturday."

"He won't be if you ask him." Iva grinned. "Going to the auction with the three of you sounds like a *gut* way to spend Saturday evening."

Rosemary knew better than to say Iva shouldn't assume Gideon was going with them. Or did she keep quiet because she found the idea of spending Saturday evening with him delightful? Such thoughts were ridiculous for a recent widow, so she tired to ignore them.

Though it was impossible as eager anticipation filled her.

She stood and motioned for Braelynn to join her. Smiling at the older woman, she asked, "Who knows, Iva? You may find the very thing you've been looking for your whole life."

"And what would that be?"

Rosemary laughed. "You may not know until you see it. Isn't that what they always say at auctions?"

"Before you go…" Iva twisted in her chair as they walked past her. "How are you coming along with those fat quarters I gave you?"

Guilt replaced her happiness. How could she tell Iva she hadn't given the fabric much thought? Then she wondered why she was acting like she'd committed a crime. All she'd done was prioritize her days.

But isn't Iva a priority for you? She paid no attention to the small voice of her conscience as she replied, "They'll be my next project. I need to finish quilting the top I pieced together around Christmas. Once I'm done with that and with the quilt for the mud sale, I'll figure out what to do with the fat quarters."

Iva nodded, a secretive smile tilting her lips. "I'm sure you'll find the perfect use for them. Sooner than you think."

Stopping in midstep, Rosemary glanced at the old woman, but Iva had picked up her needle and was working on the worn quilt. It wasn't like Iva to be mysterious. Rosemary must be letting guilt lead her into reading too much into simple words.

She kept telling herself that as she walked toward her house with Braelynn scampering along with her. The snow was thinning, and the ground was softening into mud.

"See horsey?" Braelynn pointed to a dark brown horse in a field across the road.

"It's pretty, ain't so?"

"Braelynn wants horsey, too."

Buying Braelynn a horse was out of the question, but perhaps she could find a pony to use with the cart gathering dust in the barn. Several farms in the area had miniature horses, but those were more like pets. She'd ask around and see if someone had a pony for sale.

When she said that, Braelynn gave one of her rare smiles. Then, as quickly as it had appeared, her smile disappeared. She ran toward the farmhouse, mud splattering up behind her.

Rosemary started to give chase, but paused when she realized she had a clear view of the yard and the house from the field. Whatever was bothering Braelynn might blow over like a quick summer storm if Rosemary gave her some time to think about it.

It wasn't easy to stroll through the field when she had so much on her mind. Rosemary kept her pace slow. Her gaze moved from Braelynn vanishing behind the house to Gideon's shop. A buggy was parked in front of it. Another customer? Since word had gotten around he was doing leatherwork, he'd had plenty of interest.

If he was successful, would he stay in Bliss Valley? Warmth drifted to her at the thought. There could be more sweet kisses. When he was with her, she didn't feel like she had to do everything herself. It wasn't the actual chores around the farm. He shared her concerns about Braelynn and what the *kind* had experienced and what might happen next.

But she had to think of his hopes and dreams, too. He was excited to build his business. Though he'd made time to help her with Braelynn, she knew he would have gotten more work sooner if he hadn't been so involved with her and the little girl. And he might have found the culprit behind the invasions into his workshop. If she cared about him—and she did more than she was willing to admit to herself—she needed to let him spend his time on his own pursuits.

When a small blur raced past Rosemary as she stepped into her backyard, she jumped back in shock.

One of her hens! What was it doing out of the run?

Before she could guess, another chicken sped around her. It was squawking.

She gasped when she saw her chickens in the yard. How had they gotten out? It was dangerous in the winter. Foxes would be extra eager for a chicken dinner at this time of year.

Running, she headed off one of the ruddy chickens, herding it toward the coop. Pushing it inside, she grumbled to herself when one of the hens that had been inside slipped past her.

"Braelynn!" she called. "*Komm* and help with the chickens!"

She didn't get an answer. Where was the *kind*?

Cold cramped in her center. Had Braelynn let the chickens out? Why else wouldn't the little girl help round up the flock? Braelynn adored the chickens and, despite having been pecked once, seemed set on making them into pets.

Rosemary glanced toward the house, then knew she needed to focus on getting the flock safe. She realized steering the chickens one by one back into the coop would be futile. Gripping her skirt and apron, she ran to the barn and got a scoop of corn and a short strip of wire. She hurried back to the yard and made the clicking sound to let the chickens know she'd brought a treat.

They slowed. Praying she could keep their attention, she spread the corn, a few kernels at a time, on a path toward the henhouse. She watched the chickens follow as if she were the Pied Piper, stopping to peck at the corn as they walked. Moving too fast would be stupid, so she went at their speed. She edged into the run and waited until the chickens followed her. She tossed a generous handful of corn into the far corner. As the chickens rushed to it, she went out the door, latching it behind her.

"One more," said a deep voice from behind her.

Her heart leaped before she realized it wasn't Gideon. She was amazed to see Calvin Hertzler walking toward her with a chicken under his right arm.

"Calvin, what are you doing here?" She took the hen and carefully placed her inside the coop.

"I thought I'd stop by and see how you're doing."

She wrapped the wire around both sides of the door's opening, high enough so Braelynn couldn't reach it. Giving it a final twist, she faced him. "We're doing fine."

He flinched, and she wondered if he was recalling that she no longer lived by herself.

Rushing on, she said, "Braelynn is becoming accustomed to a plain life." She glanced toward the house. "I shouldn't leave her alone for long. You know five-year-olds. They can always find something to do that they shouldn't."

"How's it going with your new tenant?" he asked in an intense tone.

"Gideon has been busy with customers," she said, keeping her own voice light and carefree. "I don't see much of him."

Not as much as I'd like. She smothered that thought, but couldn't ignore it. Not when it was the truth. However, she'd be *dumm* to share that with Calvin. He clearly was bothered by Gideon living on her farm.

Deciding it would be smart to talk about something else, Rosemary added, "I was wondering if you would consider letting us donate some quilts for your auction. I thought it would be a *gut* way to raise money to help replace Grace's broken windows."

"It's a nice idea, but I'm not selling any quilts for the next few auctions. Dean thought it might build up more eagerness at the mud sale."

Rosemary nodded. Dean Crofts was the fire chief of the

Bliss Valley Volunteer Fire Department, and he'd meshed his *Englisch* and plain firefighters into an efficient team.

"I wouldn't have thought about that."

"I'm not surprised."

For some reason, his words, though they agreed with what she'd said, annoyed her. His tone, always tinged with arrogance when he'd come to visit Eddie, hadn't changed. He made her feel as if she were as witless as one of the chickens.

Telling herself not to be too sensitive, Rosemary said, "It looks as if we may have two quilts to bring to the mud sale."

He waved aside her words. "I'm not here to talk about the mud sale."

"Let's go in. I should check on Braelynn."

As she started to move past him to go into the house, he caught her arm. She gasped and twisted it out of his grip. Emotions flickered through his eyes as his mouth tightened.

"Rosemary, I need to talk to you. It's important."

She noticed how he was shifting from one foot to the other like a scholar called to the teacher's desk. Something was upsetting him. She had no idea what he thought she might be able to do to help. Calvin and Eddie had often talked in the barn. The few times she'd gone out, they'd switched the subject before she could figure out what they were discussing. However, she couldn't fail to see their anxious expressions. She'd waited for Eddie to explain, but he never had.

Now it was too late to ask.

The familiar thud of regret hit her, but more gently than in the past. Could she have reached the place in the grief *Mamm* had assured her she would get to? A place where she missed Eddie but where each beat of her heart was no longer a separate agony? When had that happened?

When you first laid eyes on Gideon. Warning that little voice to stay silent, she said, "I have to get inside and check on Braelynn."

"Okay. I'll keep this short. Marry me, Rosemary. It's what Eddie would have wanted."

She almost fired back Calvin had no idea what her late husband would have wanted. In the month before Eddie's death, the two men had argued a lot.

"Danki," she said, "but no, Calvin."

"You don't have to give me an answer now."

"But I just did." She'd thought he'd be more reasonable than LaVern. She'd been wrong.

"Think it over, and you'll see that my offer is the best for you."

She pushed aside her irritation at his refusal to accept she didn't want to marry him. "I don't have to think it over. I've given you my answer. Please accept it."

"You can't keep running this farm on your own."

"I can."

"A woman's place is in the kitchen. It's a man's place to run the farm."

"God has brought me to this situation. Are you questioning His wisdom?"

Calvin blanched, then his face reddened. "You shouldn't put words in my mouth."

"I'm not trying to do that. I'm trying to get you to understand I am where God wishes me to be right now."

He pointed a finger at her. "You're making a big mistake."

She had to agree with him. Letting this conversation go on had been a huge mistake. She couldn't say that to him. It would make her as rude as he was.

"I'm going to check on Braelynn." She walked past him, steeling herself in case he grabbed her again.

He didn't as he said to her back, "You're going to regret this, Rosemary."

So many retorts filled her mind, but she didn't say a single one. She walked into the house and closed the door.

She leaned her head against the door's frame. Out of the corner of her eye, she saw Calvin stomp toward his buggy. She rushed through the house, stepping around Braelynn who was peeking out of her den under the quilt-covered table, and threw open the front door as he drove out of the yard at a dangerous speed. The wheels clattered against the asphalt, and the horse shied as he wielded a whip against it.

The noise must have reached into Gideon's shop, because he appeared in its doorway. The buggy barely missed him before it careened out on the road as if Calvin drove a sports car. Gideon looked from the buggy to the house, his eyes locking with hers. The distance couldn't lessen his intense gaze, but she looked away and shut the door.

Gideon would want an explanation, and she didn't want to give him one when she wasn't certain how to talk to him after their searing kiss. She'd let him get too close, and she couldn't again. If she didn't keep her private life to herself, someone might see the secrets she was hiding. Secrets of how her grief was mixed with frustration. She didn't want to be that way. She wanted to be the accepting widow everyone believed she was, though her facade was growing thin.

Too thin.

Chapter Fifteen

The wind blew down the narrow one-way Lancaster City street that was edged on both sides by cars and buildings. Gideon pulled his scarf up over his chin as he walked toward the address they were looking for. The weather had taken a turn back to winter after a few clement days.

The wind wasn't as icy as Rosemary. He'd attempted to draw her out while they waited for Keith Morris, the *Englisch* van driver, to pick them up in the early afternoon and take them into Lancaster City. It had been useless. She either deflected his questions about what had happened with Calvin Hertzler or acted as if she misunderstood him.

But was Calvin the person bothering her or was it Gideon Wingard?

What did she expect? For him to apologize for kissing her? He couldn't do that and be honest.

Maybe it was for the best that he hadn't a chance to continue the discussion while they traveled through the rolling hills to the city. Other passengers had claimed the seats around them, and when a pregnant woman boarded, Rosemary had taken the opportunity to switch seats so she no longer sat beside him.

Should he give up? He'd gotten tired of his family poking into his business. Now he was doing the same with her. Yet, it was impossible to forget the warmth in her gaze when he'd held her so briefly in his arms.

With a groan that had gained him an odd look from the woman sitting beside him, he'd stared out the window at the brick houses lining the street. Lancaster City always felt too cramped because he couldn't see wide-open fields.

Neither Gideon nor Rosemary spoke as they stepped off the van that had stopped near a glass-enclosed bus stop filled with people. Pedestrians hurried along, their heads bent into the chilly wind tunneling between the tall brick-and-stone buildings. Many were talking into a phone or what seemed to themselves until he noticed they had something stuck in their ears.

He stepped around a stroller. He jumped to the side, pulling Rosemary with him, when a bicyclist went by at a high speed.

"Okay?" Gideon asked.

"Not even close." She was pale and sweat was beaded on her forehead though the day was cold.

"Do you need to sit?"

"I'll be fine. A bit of car sickness, I think." She took a deep breath and looked at the brick-and-glass building. "Let's get this over with."

"Are you sure? We can wander around the city until it's time for the van to pick us up." He stepped between her and the door. "You don't have to do this."

"And what will I tell Braelynn when she's older and she asks me why I didn't find the truth for her?"

He reached to pull the door open, knowing she was right. He hoped her stomach would settle, and she'd be up for what they might discover in the imposing building. Letting her walk past him, he entered. The interior was somehow hushed and loud at the same time. Nobody spoke, but footfalls echoed on terrazzo floors and the sound of fingers tapping on keyboards seemed everywhere in the air.

Finding the number of the office for Children's Services, Gideon walked with Rosemary toward the door. She was silent. He clasped her hand, squeezing it. When she looked at him, he gave her what he hoped was a bolstering smile.

"God has brought us here," he said. "We need to trust He will guide us to the answers we need."

"Danki," she said, but she withdrew her hand.

Having her keep her distance might be for the best now. That would prevent her from suspecting he was also looking for answers to what had happened the day Eddie was shot. He prayed while they sought someone who had known Braelynn's *mamm*, they might get a clue to why Eddie Mishler was dead and why the police had left the case open.

After a fifteen-minute wait, a woman came forward to greet them. She was middle-aged and wore large jewelry and a bright red dress that set off her black hair with strands of silver.

"Can I help you? I'm Margaret Warren, one of the social workers here."

Rosemary introduced them.

"Come with me." She led them to an inner office, which had three large file cabinets along the wall behind the desk. The top of the desk was neat, but papers were stacked almost a foot high on one corner. Ms. Warren took the chair behind the desk and motioned for them to use the chairs facing her.

Gideon listened as Rosemary gave a quick explanation of what had happened since they'd discovered the little girl in her kitchen. Ms. Warren asked a few questions but listened with amazing patience until Rosemary was done.

"Let me check." The social worker turned to her computer and typed. "You say Braelynn's mother's name is Madison Nesbitt?"

"That's the name listed on the birth certificate."

"Father?"

"Eddie—Edward Mishler." Her voice held the emotions of a stone.

Gideon glanced at Rosemary's hands gripping her purse strap. He wanted to put his hand over them, but refrained. She was close to the end of her rope, and he didn't want to snatch the last bit from her.

Ms. Warren turned from her computer. "I don't have any record of those names in my files. I'm sorry, but I can't help you."

"Where do you suggest we look next?" Rosemary asked.

Gideon hid his smile. He should have guessed she wouldn't let this setback keep her from learning the truth.

"Here is a list of homeless shelters that take women and children. You might want to try them."

He looked at the street map the social worker handed Rosemary. There was a shelter just around the corner from where they were. When he caught Rosemary's eyes, she nodded. They thanked the social worker before leaving.

Unlike the modern government building, the address of the women's shelter was nailed to the top step of a brick row house. There wasn't a doorbell, so Rosemary knocked on the ornate Victorian door that needed paint and pieces of its decoration replaced.

It opened to reveal a woman who must have been as old as his *grossmammi*. Her short almost-white hair stuck straight up from her head like a blue jay's crest. In her lined face, her dark brown eyes weren't much more than slits, but her smile was broad.

"Come in, come in," she said. "It's not often I get to talk to Amish folks."

Gideon was startled by the effusive welcome after the professional distance they'd experienced from Ms. Warren. The old woman said her name was Carla Layden. "But you call me Carly like everyone else does. How can I help you?"

"We're looking for someone," he said.

"I'll need something a bit more specific." Carly chuckled. "You should see your faces. I'm not out of my mind. It's just that we get a lot of women coming through here. Let's get some tea and talk."

She led the way along a narrow hallway whose walls were covered with childish drawings. The kitchen at the back of the house had cabinets rising to the high ceiling. She motioned for them to sit at a long table surrounded by a dozen chairs while she put on the teakettle and got cups from a cupboard. The doors squeaked as she closed them.

"Another thing for my to-do list," Carly said with a grim smile. "It never gets any shorter. So tell me about the person you're looking for."

Rosemary repeated the condensed version of recent events. Carly sat across from them, hopping up to pour tea for them.

"Madison?" she said as she put cups in front of Rosemary and him.

"Do you know her?" Rosemary asked.

"The name is familiar, and it's not that common. Can you describe her?"

Rosemary opened her purse and pulled out the photo that had been with Braelynn's birth certificate. She held it out to the *Englisch* woman, her fingers trembling so much the piece of paper fluttered like a fan. "We think the woman in this picture is Madison."

Carly took the picture and tilted it toward the window. Sorrow washed the smile from her face. "Yes, that's Madison. She stayed here a few times about six or seven years ago. I didn't know she'd had a child. She's dead, you say?"

"That's what we were told in the letter written by the woman who left Braelynn at Rosemary's house," Gideon said.

"I'm sorry to hear that."

"You knew her?"

"I did." The old woman sighed. "She was one of the lost ones, I'm afraid."

"Lost?" asked Rosemary.

"The lost kids who live on the streets. They start as runaways and get sucked into the underbelly of the city. Lancaster is a nice place with lots of nice people, but somehow youngsters get lost. And they stay lost far too often. They're too proud or too scared to look for help. They fear they'll be sent back home, which can be worse than the streets. A few come to their senses and head home, but too many of them get swallowed by life on the streets. Drugs, prostitution, shootings. They leave home because life is tough, but they discover life on the street is even tougher. We try to help them, but we don't succeed often enough."

"And Madison was one of those?" He tried not to let appalling images fill his head, but he couldn't keep from wondering what Braelynn had seen and heard before she was left at Rosemary's house.

"Yes, though she tried to clean up her life. She really did. She spent some nights here rather than sleeping in alleys or doorways or on someone's porch. I know home wasn't easy for her. It isn't for any of our clients. Some are homeless. Some are in abusive relationships. Some are both." She looked at the photo again. "Maybe Madison stopped using because she was pregnant. She was a smart girl, so she knew drugs wouldn't be good for her baby."

"Drugs?" whispered Rosemary.

He edged his hand around hers, out of sight of the other woman. Gently he squeezed it and wished he could offer more comfort. Were her thoughts the same as his? He hoped not. He didn't want her pondering how Braelynn's odd behavior might be caused in part by her *mamm*'s drug abuse.

"She was a smart girl, like I said," Carly answered, "but drugs don't care whether you're smart or stupid. They ensnare anyone."

"Do you know where she was from?" Rosemary asked. "Did she mention her family?"

"No. Kids don't talk much about their pasts when they're with us. Most of them are running away from it, so they don't want to think about it." Tapping her finger against the photo, she asked, "Can I make a copy of this?"

Gideon started to answer, then looked at Rosemary. The photo had been given to her, so it was her decision.

"Of course," she said as she tugged at her dress. Her face had lost its rosy glow and turned a rather alarming shade of gray with each word the other woman spoke, but she was making a heroic effort to act as if nothing Carly had said wasn't something she hadn't already suspected.

"Thank you," Carly replied. "It won't take but a moment. I'll be right back. Help yourself to a piece of cake. It's in the pantry cupboard over there." She pointed to her left as she stood.

"No, *danki*. No, thank you," Rosemary corrected.

As the woman walked out of the kitchen, Gideon shifted on his chair to face Rosemary. "Are you all right?"

"I'm numb. I don't know what to think." She looked everywhere but at him.

"Rosemary, if you're waiting for me to say I'm sorry we kissed, you're going to be waiting a very, very long time."

"That's not something we should talk about now."

"Later."

Carly came back into the room and held out the photograph to her. The elderly woman didn't sit. Instead, she leaned her hands on the table.

"So Madison's child is living with you. Both of you?"

Again, Gideon waited for Rosemary to answer, but she was silent, staring at the floor as if her eyes were too heavy to lift to meet anyone else's. Heavy with tears or with grief?

"Braelynn is living with Rosemary," he said into the silence. "Her late husband was Braelynn's *daed*."

Sympathy filled Carly's eyes. "The man in the photo?"

Rosemary nodded.

"I'm sorry for your loss, Rosemary, but thank you for taking Madison's daughter into your home. Our foster care system tries its best. However, too many children come out damaged by the very structure set up to help them."

Gideon interjected, not wanting to let his chance to find out more about Eddie's life and death pass him by. "Did you know Eddie?"

"I don't remember him."

"So you don't recognize him?" He saw Rosemary's dismay.

Carly looked at the photo again, then shook her head.

His heart sank. How was he going to disprove the rumors of suicide if he couldn't find out more about Eddie? The *Leit* didn't seem to know much about him. Even Rosemary didn't know much about him.

"I'll show this photo," Carly went on, "to some of our other clients and neighbors. I'll see if I can get more information to share with you. Do you have a phone where I can contact you?"

Rosemary gave the number for the phone in the small shack in front of her house. "It's used by several families, so leave a message to call, and I'll get back to you."

Carly nodded. "There's someone else you might want to

talk to. A young woman. Around ten in the morning, you'll find her by the Central Market on Tuesdays, Fridays and Saturdays when it's open. She has a guitar with stickers on it, and she sings for tips."

"What's her name?" Gideon asked.

"I'm not sure. I saw her several times with Madison, but she refused to come in for a meal." A faint smile eased her face. "I pray that means she's making enough from her music to feed herself, and it's not pride keeping her away. But she might be able to tell you more about Madison and her child."

"Danki," Rosemary said in a strained voice as she stood. She put her hand to her stomach. "I mean, thank you."

"I understood you either way." Carly took Rosemary's hands in her gnarled ones. "I will keep your search and Madison's daughter in my prayers."

Rosemary's mouth tightened, and her jaw worked. Was she trying not to cry?

Gideon thanked Carly again. Once he and Rosemary were out in the blustery day again, he asked, "How are you doing?"

"Ask me an easier question." She gave him an unsteady smile.

He didn't reply. He hoped silence would draw her out. He'd discovered Rosemary liked to keep her emotions compressed within her. She was different from the women in his family who seldom filtered their thoughts, letting them burst out whenever and to whomever happened to be nearby. Too often, the subject of their gushing comments was his need for a wife.

Yet, now he wished Rosemary were a bit more like them. Her thoughts were tormenting her.

"I'm glad," he said, hoping she'd join in if he began a conversation, "to hear Madison went off drugs when she was pregnant."

"Me, too."

"Are you worried Eddie did drugs with her?"

Her head popped up, and he saw her shock. It had turned her face that odd gray-green again. "No. I never gave that a moment's thought. He'd suffer with a headache rather than take an aspirin." Her gaze dropped again. "I used to wonder why. Do you think it was because he witnessed Madison using drugs?"

"That's something we may never know."

She sighed. "True."

When she added nothing more, he knew he couldn't let the heavy silence fall between them again. "It looks like our next step is finding the woman Carly was talking about." He glanced at the clock on a nearby church's steeple. "The Central Market has closed by now."

She sighed, her shoulders sagging as she put one hand on the top of a trash can. When she wobbled, he put his arm around her to keep her steady. He ignored the passersby who looked at them with curiosity.

"Are you okay?" he asked as he had so many times this afternoon.

"I… I think so. I—"

She whirled away from him and vomited into the trash can, gripping the sides as if they were a life preserver. He caught her shoulders and steadied her as she retched.

What a fool he was! He'd thought she was overwhelmed with the bits of truth that had come out. Instead, she was sick. How could he have missed that?

He helped her stand straighter as she pushed away from the trash can. Tears trembled on her lashes as she wiped her mouth with the back of her hand.

"Wait here," he said, making sure she again had a *gut* grip on the trash can before he drew his arm away.

Gideon threw open the door to a nearby pizza restaurant. Buying a bottle of water and grabbing some napkins, he rushed back out. He twisted open the bottle and splashed a small amount of water on the napkins. He handed them to her.

Thanking him, she dabbed at her lips. She put her hand over her stomach as she clamped her mouth closed. He cradled her elbow while she fought for equilibrium.

"Take it easy," he said. "I know it's hard to hear what we heard today."

More tears washed into her eyes. "Especially the part about Madison being homeless and sleeping on someone's porch." Raising her head, she met his gaze. "My brother slept on someone's porch when he first came back to Bliss Valley. *Mamm* told me."

"I didn't know that."

"Nobody does beyond our family." She smiled sadly. "Nobody *did* until I told you."

"I won't speak of it to anyone else."

"It doesn't matter if you do."

"It might to your brother."

She shook her head, then swayed.

"Rosemary, you aren't well. Let's go home. I'll come back later and look for Madison's friend."

She started to shake her head, then leaned over the trash can and threw up. He wondered how there could be anything left in her stomach. She stood again.

This time when he put his arm around her and drew her close, she didn't pull away. He helped her to a nearby bench. Sitting beside her, he put his arm around her once more. When she leaned her head against his shoulder, he wished he could enjoy her nearness. He couldn't.

But he'd come back to Lancaster, as he'd told her. He'd do the best he could to get the answers they both wanted, but he was beginning to question if he'd ever find the whole truth about Eddie Mishler.

★ ★ ★

Rosemary had to wonder if rescheduling the quilt frolic had been a *gut* idea. She'd felt fine when it was supposed to be held a couple of weeks ago. Now every time she moved, her head threatened to float away. She tugged at the waist of her dress. It was too tight. Maybe it was cutting off the oxygen to her brain.

Gideon had told her during barn chores this morning that no vans were available to take him there when the Central Market was open. He'd have to wait until Tuesday. She hoped she'd feel well enough by then to go with him.

Shifting on her chair to get more comfortable, she flashed what she hoped looked like a smile to Iva who sat beside her. Iva seldom attended quilt circle meetings, but she'd asked to be part of the frolic. Her fingers darted in and out of the quilt top as if her needle was jet-propelled. Each stitch was the same size and in the feather pattern they'd decided on.

Rosemary sewed at her own pace as she tried to listen to her friends chatting. The *kinder* were gathered in the kitchen, coloring and playing with Braelynn's toys. It was a picture of domestic bliss Rosemary had longed to have. Now that she did, nothing was as it should have been.

How could she have gotten so sick during the trip to Lancaster? She hadn't eaten lunch in her eagerness to get to the truth. Instead of refusing the cake at the shelter where Carly worked, she should have accepted. Maybe she wouldn't have embarrassed herself in front of Gideon and everyone on the street.

And what had they found out? Nothing other than Madison Nesbitt had existed and was remembered by at least one person.

Everyone laughed, and Rosemary blinked, torn from her thoughts. She forced a smile again, but it wasn't necessary because Naomi was saying, "Okay, that was weird, but I've got a story from last week that's weirder. Two women were talking in the shop. One was *Englisch*, and the other was plain."

"That's nothing unusual," Grace said, not looking up from her stitching. "We get lots of different customers. Why, on Wednesday, a man came in all by himself. That's a first for the shop. He bought two quilts."

"For himself?" asked Erma.

Grace wagged her needle at Rosemary's sister. "I don't interrogate my customers. I try to help them find the quilt that works for them." She dimpled as she added, "However, he did say he was buying the quilts for his twin daughters. I got the feeling they're about Mary Beth's and Braelynn's age. He bought two of the brightest quilts we had."

"That's nice, but as I was saying before I was interrupted..." More laughter rippled around the table when Naomi looked at Grace. "Two women were talking in the shop the other day."

"An *Englisch* woman and a plain one," Laurene said in a whisper loud enough for everyone to hear.

Naomi grinned. "Do you want to hear this or not?"

"Go ahead," Grace said as she reached for her scissors to clip a thread. Setting them aside, she reached for the spool to rethread her needle. "We can't wait to hear this story after the build-up."

"I'm about ready *not* to tell you," Naomi said with a feigned glower at the women around the quilting frame.

That elicited more laughter, and Naomi waited for it to die down before she related the conversation she'd overheard. The two women had been gossiping about another woman who'd had a *boppli* without realizing she was pregnant.

"She thought she'd gained weight," Naomi said with a chuckle, "but never considered there might be a reason beyond having an extra cookie or two."

As the others laughed, Rosemary ducked her head as if focusing on the quilt top in front of her.

The woman hadn't guessed she was pregnant until labor began? Was that possible? From under her lowered lashes, she glanced around as the conversation continued. Her needle darted in and out of the layers of fabric as thoughts exploded through her head.

She'd been so sick on Thursday, and she'd been suffering the same bouts of stomachaches and nausea for the past few weeks. By midday, she'd been feeling great, except for when she was in Lancaster.

She counted back through the months. She hadn't had her courses since before Eddie died. Not that she'd been on a regular cycle like her sisters who could set their clocks by when each monthly flow began. Hers were all over the place, sometimes as short as three weeks apart, sometimes not coming for almost seven weeks.

Was that why she hadn't paid attention to how many months it'd been? No, she hadn't paid attention because she'd been caught up in her grief and her desperate need to prove to herself and the rest of the world she could keep her farm running on her own.

Putting down her needle next to the T-pin closest to her, she lowered her hands under the quilt frame. She ran them down her belly and almost gasped. There was a definite bump. A *boppli*? Delight bubbled through her for a second before reality hit with a painful thump.

Her husband was dead. She already was raising a *kind* on her own, a difficult *kind* who needed every bit of her attention. Was God sending her another in…? She counted. If she was pregnant, the *boppli* would be due in April. She must be at least five months pregnant, because Eddie had died more than four months ago.

Tears prickled against her eyes. Eddie had talked so often about how he wanted a family. She had daydreamed even more while doing her chores or quilting that they would have little ones crawling on the rag rug, which had been the first thing she'd made for their home.

She looked into the kitchen. Braelynn was coloring. How could Eddie have talked about having a family and failed to mention his daughter? He must have known about the *kind*. In the photo, Braelynn's *mamm* had been pregnant. Had something led him to believe the *boppli* hadn't survived? Had Madison lied to him?

Rosemary closed her eyes and struggled to rein in her thoughts. Had Eddie abandoned Madison when his *boppli* was born? What would have happened when he discovered Rosemary had conceived? Would he have run away from her, too?

It didn't matter. Eddie was gone, and if she was pregnant, she wouldn't be able to keep the secret much longer. Even looser clothes wouldn't help for long. As the *kind* within her got bigger, so would she.

Then everyone would know.

Then *Gideon* would know. She pushed back her chair and muttered something to excuse herself. Rushing into the bathroom, she shut the door. She leaned one hand against the wall as she fought sickness. Not from her stomach, but from her heart.

What would he think of her when he learned the truth? She'd seen how he'd looked at her as if wanting to kiss her again. And she'd wanted him to, but a *boppli* would change everything.

Would he think she'd hidden the truth from him?

On purpose?

Chapter Sixteen

Saturday morning started out wrong. Braelynn, who'd eaten oatmeal every day for breakfast, decided she couldn't stomach another bite of the hot cereal. Not ever again. She didn't want eggs or toast or anything else Rosemary offered her. She pushed everything away and complained.

Rosemary tried to have patience with the little girl. It wasn't easy when her head was reeling with the idea she was pregnant. A flutter, like a butterfly flitting by, had startled her awake last night. Had it been the *boppli* moving? Had she felt it before and ignored it?

Ignored her own *kind*?

She knew she needed to see a *doktor* or a midwife, and she couldn't put it off long. But not today. She needed to come to terms with the truth.

On top of that, as if learning she was pregnant with her late husband's *boppli* wasn't enough, she had to act normal while working with Gideon in the barn.

That morning, he'd outlined his plans to talk to Madison's

friend on Tuesday. When she'd nodded absently, she'd seen his surprise that she was taking the news with such indifference. If he only knew...

No, she didn't want to tell him, but she must make sure he didn't hear of her pregnancy from someone else. One more day wouldn't make any difference, ain't so?

Not sure why she was trying to convince herself while she finished the breakfast dishes, Rosemary flinched when her apron was tugged on. She saw Braelynn regarding her with a somber expression.

"God loves Braelynn," the little girl said.

"That's true."

"No matter what Braelynn does or thinks or says."

Rosemary didn't answer straightaway. She didn't want to give the little girl permission to do whatever she wanted. Pushing other thoughts aside, she sat at the table and brought the *kind* to stand beside her.

"God loves us," Rosemary said, "and He's a loving parent. It's important we show that we love Him back. Do you know how we do that?"

She shook her head, her hair tumbling out of the net holding it into a small bun at her nape.

Brushing the *kind*'s hair back and repinning it, Rosemary smiled. "We show God we love Him by following His rules."

"What rules?"

She considered mentioning the Ten Commandments but those might be too much for a little *kind* to comprehend all at once. She would keep it simple. "When Jesus, God's son, lived among His people, He told us to treat others as we'd like them to treat us. If we want to be treated with kindness, we must be kind. If we want to laugh, we need to do something to make others laugh first."

"If Braelynn wants to be loved, Braelynn has to love first?"

Looking away, Rosemary choked on the emotions erupting in her, conflicting and connected emotions. Some were simple like feeling blessed Braelynn was asking first about love and being loved. Others, the ones wrapping around her each time she thought of Gideon, were far more complicated.

Had he kissed her because he wanted to court her? She'd told LaVern and Calvin point-blank that she didn't want to consider a new husband until her time of mourning was past. It wasn't that easy with Gideon. He made her think she might be happy again. His kiss had seared a longing into her that she hadn't realized she possessed. Eddie's kisses had offered her an escape from home. Gideon's had opened the door to a sweet danger that shook up everything she had believed a kiss should be.

"Rosie?"

She focused on the little girl. *"Ja,"* she said with the best smile she could manage, "you have to love to be loved. You're doing a *gut* job with it, ain't so? Lots of people love you."

"Really?" Surprise widened her eyes.

"Really."

Braelynn opened her mouth to speak, then closed it. Taking a deep breath, she asked, "Can Braelynn have applesauce?"

Telling herself she should be accustomed to the youngster's abrupt changes of subject, Rosemary spooned out a generous serving for Braelynn. She left the little girl eating contentedly and went into the utility room to begin yet another load of wash.

She hadn't guessed how much extra laundry one small *kind* could create. It would be simpler when spring came, but spring was more than a month away. The clothing would freeze on the line outside and have to be brought back in to drape over airing racks. As the garments defrosted, they'd soften over the rails and dry out. She was grateful the dresses she and Braelynn wore were polyester and cotton. Heavy material like towels took so much longer to dry.

The day sped by as Rosemary did laundry and prepared Braelynn's favorite lunch of a church spread sandwich. The mixture of peanut butter and whipped marshmallow was something every kid seemed to adore. The little girl went up to her room where she played while Rosemary continued to do her chores.

Each time Rosemary passed a window that offered a view of the end of the lane, she paused. She didn't see Gideon, so he must be hard at work, too. She considered taking Braelynn to talk to him, but turned away from the window each time as she thought of the truth she was hiding from him.

Glad the sun wasn't setting as early, Rosemary went out in the late afternoon to get the frozen laundry. She arranged it on the trio of drying racks in the utility room.

Finishing, she chafed her hands together before pulling the clothespins out of her pocket. She had dropped so many into the snow while wearing gloves that she'd found it simpler and more efficient to do the chore with bare hands. Now her fingertips tingled as blood circulated through them again.

She put the clothespins in the caddy that looked like a *kind*'s bright turquoise dress and looked out the door toward the barn. It would be time for milking soon. She couldn't wait for the warmer weather when she could turn the cows out into the meadow. That would save time on cleaning the barn twice a day.

"No time like the present," she said as she pulled on her coat again. Her chores shouldn't take long because she and Gideon had done a big cleaning that morning. When she was done, she'd warm some leftover stew for her and Braelynn's supper.

The yard was littered with mounds of icy snow, but wider patches of brown grass were opening every day. As she walked toward the barn, she glanced toward where daffodils and tulips would be blooming in less than two months.

Opening the door, she went inside a single step.

Where were the cows?

She gasped when she saw the rear door was pushed open enough for them to escape. She ran to the door. She shoved it aside and scanned the pasture.

It was empty.

Where were the cows?

Her eyes widened when she saw the open gate next to the barn. How had that come unlatched? It'd been hooked closed since she brought the cows in for the winter in November.

Spinning, she raced out of the barn. Cows weren't God's smartest creatures. They could have wandered into the road and wouldn't know enough to get out of the way of a vehicle. If a car struck one, not only would the cow be killed but the driver and passengers could be hurt.

A motion caught her eye as she rushed down the lane. Braelynn was looking out her bedroom window.

Rosemary gave a quick wave, but didn't slow. She'd answer the *kind*'s questions later. For now, she had to halt a potential disaster.

She skidded to a stop, putting her hand out to grab a tree when the most extraordinary sight met her eyes at the spot where the lane intersected the main road. A buggy was following her small herd as they walked toward her.

Gideon burst out of his shop and stared at the odd parade going by. Tossing something inside, he trailed along until the cows reached where Rosemary stood.

She stepped aside to let the herd pass her by. The buggy stopped as it drew even with her.

An old man slid open the door. "Are you looking for these

ladies?" asked Adam's great-*grossdawdi* whom everyone, young and old, called *Grossdawdi* Ephraim.

"*Ja!*"

She and Gideon herded the cows into the barn and made sure both the door and the gate were latched. When they came out, *Grossdawdi* Ephraim was waiting by his buggy. She invited both men in for something hot to drink. They accepted with equal enthusiasm.

Rosemary poured *kaffi* and brought them a heaping plate of chocolate chip cookies. Sitting, she called to Braelynn. The little girl appeared in the doorway. She stared at the elderly man, but didn't come closer even when Rosemary explained *Grossdawdi* Ephraim was her friend Mary Beth's *daed*'s great-*grossdawdi*.

"He found our cows," Rosemary said, motioning for the *kind* to come closer.

The little girl edged a single step into the kitchen, then paused, her gaze going from one adult to the next.

"Did you see how our cows got out?" Rosemary made sure there was no accusation in her voice. "The gate was open."

"Braelynn doesn't know." She inched closer to the table, her gaze focused on the cookies.

"It'd be okay if you did know." She smiled, though she didn't feel like it. "We want to make sure it doesn't happen again."

"Braelynn doesn't know." She stomped her foot. "Braelynn doesn't know!" She snatched a pair of cookies and then dashed into her tent under the table.

Rosemary sighed as she saw sympathy in the men's eyes. With a sigh, she picked up the *millich* jug.

"*Danki* for bringing the cows back, *Grossdawdi* Ephraim," she said as she poured *millich* into her *kaffi*.

The old man stroked his long gray beard. "I've got to say it's the first time I used a buggy to herd cows."

"I wish I knew how they got out."

A faint sound, too muffled for her to tell if it was a giggle or a sob, came from the living room. A quick blur rushed up the stairs.

Braelynn! Had the little girl, despite her protests, opened both the door and the gate? Just as Braelynn may have opened the door to the chicken coop?

Rosemary hadn't thought the *kind* was tall enough to reach the gate's latch, but she'd underestimated what the little girl was capable of in the past. A determined Braelynn could have let the cows out.

She wanted to sigh. If Braelynn was behind the prank, her tricks were becoming more dangerous. Putting salt in the sugar bowl was one thing. Releasing the cows was something else entirely.

Yet, one thing bothered her. When she'd confronted the *kind* about the sugar bowl or the chickens, Braelynn had refused to answer. Today, she'd answered, denying she'd set the cows free. That was different. Did it mean anything?

Rosemary was still musing about what to do when *Grossdawdi* Ephraim finished his *kaffi* and cookies, thanked her and went out to his buggy. Gideon repeated the old man's words as he stood. She was shocked when he left, too.

She grabbed her coat and followed Gideon outside. He stood on the back porch, waving to the elderly man who was driving away.

As soon as the buggy was far down the lane, Gideon faced her. "What do you think happened?"

"I think Braelynn let the cows out."

"You really think that?"

"How else would they have gotten out?"

He rubbed his fingers under his chin and frowned. "You've seen her in the barn and around the coop. You'd think each of the animals was her special pet. Why would she endanger them?"

"She might not know it's dangerous for them to be out."

"After all the times you've warned her not to go near the road? She knows."

"I know I didn't open the gate," she said. "Did you?"

"No."

"And there were the chickens. She wouldn't talk about those."

His scowl deepened. "I've been thinking about that, too. I'm bothered by one thing."

"What's that?" Had he seen something she'd missed? Something that would help heal the wounds both she and Braelynn had endured.

"Don't you think it's coincidental Calvin was loitering around your backyard the day the chickens got out?"

His question threatened to knock her back on her heels. She hadn't given that any thought. In fact, she'd tried to wipe away every memory of that uncomfortable discussion from her mind. Could Calvin have let her chickens out?

"Why would he do that?" she asked.

"To play the hero for you. I bet you were grateful for his help."

"I was." Something icky, something like a dusty cobweb that held on and wouldn't let go, clung to her at the thought of being manipulated by another man.

No! She wasn't going to think of how sometimes Eddie had pouted until she gave in to whatever it was he wanted. That had been manipulation. She'd known it at the time, but she'd given in because she'd been so eager to keep peace in their house. She hadn't wanted to be caught up in the troubling undercurrents she'd despised at her parents' house.

To think of another man trying the same heartless game…

"Gideon," she asked in a cool tone that belied the furious heat of her thoughts, "did you see Calvin around here today?"

He shook his head. "No."

"So he didn't let the cows out. Just as he probably didn't release the chickens from their run." She glanced into the house and saw Braelynn reaching for another cookie. The little girl quickly ran out of the kitchen and hid under her tent. "I'm going to have to keep a closer eye on her. I wish I knew what triggers her to do something naughty."

"You can't watch her every minute of every day and every night."

"What choice do I have?"

She was shocked to see regret in his eyes. What did he have to feel bad about? She almost asked, but he halted her by saying, "I can help, you know."

"You've got a business to run."

"And you've got a house to run as well as a business." He put his hands on her shoulders and held her gaze. "Let me help. I can give you some time to catch your breath a couple of times each week."

"How?"

"She can spend that time in my shop."

"With your tools?"

"I'll watch her, Rosie." He flushed as he jerked his hands back. "Sorry. I'm picking up Braelynn's habits."

"It's okay."

"You don't mind if I call you Rosie, too?"

"No, I don't." The words came from her heart, amazing her with their sincerity. She liked the sound of the name she'd had when life was filled with delight and promise. Taking that name back now might be the first step on the path she could follow to happiness again. She wanted to be Rosie again and reclaim the joy she'd lost. "But I'm sure you don't want me to call you Giddy."

He laughed. "Please don't." He grew serious again as his eyes shifted toward the back door. "Will you be all right?"

"We'll be fine." She put her hand on the doorknob.

"Rosie?"

Oh, how she liked to hear him use that nickname! She glanced over her shoulder as she reminded herself she didn't have any right to flirt with him. Not when she was carrying her late husband's *kind*. *"Ja?"*

"I was wondering if you were planning to go to the auction on Saturday?"

"Iva wants to go, so I thought I'd take her. Are you going?"

"Been thinking about it." He leaned his shoulder against the post holding up the porch roof. "I wasn't sure if you'd feel comfortable going to Calvin's auction barn after turning down his proposal."

"How did you know he proposed?" She stared at him in disbelief.

"LaVern mentioned it to me when I was at his store earlier."

"How did *he* hear about it?"

Gideon shrugged, but a smile played around his lips. "I got the feeling Calvin had been complaining about his best friend's widow not having a lick of sense."

"If I didn't have a lick of sense, I would have told him *ja*." How dare the men gossip about her! Cold speared her. What would they say when the word got out she was expecting a *boppli*?

"That's what I said." He chuckled. "Some men like speculating more than they like work. I got the feeling LaVern was pleased with your decision."

Rosie wasn't going to tell Gideon that LaVern had shown his interest, too. "I'm not worried about Calvin at the auction.

He'll be too busy to pay attention to anyone except those who are bidding on what he's got for sale."

Was she trying to convince him or herself?

When he nodded, he said, "All right. Why don't we go together? That would be fun, ain't so?"

"*Ja*," she said as she opened the door and slipped inside before she said something stupid like how much more fun it would be if she and Gideon could be in her buggy alone.

She touched her belly, feeling the slightest flutter. The *boppli*! It was real, and she knew that for her and Gideon, it would never be just the two of them.

Around ten in the morning, you'll find her by the Central Market.
Carly had been right, Gideon learned when he went into Lancaster alone on Tuesday. Braelynn had woken with a cough and had been fussing, so Rosie hadn't wanted to leave her.

Rosie!

The name fit her perfectly. In spite of all the blows life had thrown at her, she was imbued with a sense of joy that drew him like iron to a magnet.

He'd offered to come to the city another day, so Rosie could come, too. She'd urged him to go and get the answers they both were eager to find. So he had, and now he was approaching the brick building on North Market Street.

It didn't take him long to find the young woman Carly thought might have information about Madison Nesbitt. She stood near where the words *Central Market* were set into the bricks over the arches atop a pair of double doors. Blond hair hung in her eyes. Those blue eyes were outlined by thick black lines that reached almost to her ears. The front of her guitar was covered with so many stickers with bizarre images he shifted his eyes away. She was talking to another person dressed in black as she was.

Noticing the open guitar case with a few coins and a single dollar bill in it, he reached into his pocket and pulled out his wallet. He dropped in five dollars while she was immersed in her conversation. At the same time, he prayed the young woman wouldn't waste the money on alcohol or drugs.

"Do you have a minute to talk...?" he asked when the other woman in black walked into the market building.

She hesitated, then said, "Adele. My name is Adele, and yeah, I've got a little time before I need to get started."

From the way she hesitated on the name, he guessed it wasn't hers. He didn't press. "I'm Gideon, and I'm looking for some information on Madison Nesbitt."

"Are you a cop?"

"No." He glanced at his plain clothes and chuckled. "Does this look like something a police officer would wear?"

"You could be undercover. I heard about one cop who dressed up as an Amish woman to catch some crooks."

He laughed again. "That must have been quite a sight."

A faint smile tugged at her lips, and he realized she was younger than he'd first guessed. Barely twenty. When he asked her when she'd last seen Madison, she told him it'd been almost four years before.

"So you knew about her daughter?"

"Braelynn was a cute little thing." She toyed with the tuning knobs on her guitar. "Why do you want to know about Madison?"

"Her daughter was left with my neighbor, and we hoped to learn what happened to Madison."

"We didn't hang out much once she had her kid." She pulled her coat to her chin and looked both ways along the crowded city street as if she were a rabbit watching for a lurking wolf. Sunlight glinted off a small jewel in one side of her nose. "Sometimes the kid's father would babysit for a couple of hours, and then Madison and me could find something fun to do. That didn't happen much."

"So Eddie spent time with Madison and Braelynn?"

"At first, he visited once a week, but later on, he didn't come often. I think the last time he was around was Braelynn's first birthday."

Over four years before. No wonder the little girl didn't have the faintest memories of her *daed*.

Curious what might have made Eddie stop visiting his *kind*, he asked.

Adele continued to tune her guitar, and he wondered if she'd answer him. When he was about to give up and pose a different question, she said, "That's around the time he started hitting her."

"He hit her? On purpose?"

Adele sighed. "He could be a nice guy, but he had a bad temper. She always had an excuse for the bruises he left on her. He convinced her it was her fault when he slapped her around. I tried to get her to report him to the cops, but she didn't."

"Why didn't you?"

"I did." She raised her chin to meet his eyes steadily. "I reported him, but Madison wouldn't press charges. There wasn't anything else any of us could do. Eddie got on her about every single little thing, complaining about how she was seeing other men."

Gideon tried to swallow past the horror clogging his throat. If Eddie had abused his girlfriend, had he abused his wife, too? He wanted to rush home *right now* and ask Rosie. The thought of her suffering the same abuse infuriated him. He took a breath to calm himself. He needed to get every bit of information he could from Adele, and there wasn't anything he could do to change the past.

And if Rosie wanted you to know, she would have told you. How he hated that voice of reason! Having it whisper in his mind was one of the reasons he'd wanted to keep his distance from everyone in Bliss Valley. He hadn't, and now it was taunting him again.

"They weren't married, were they?" Gideon asked to cover up his thoughts.

"No!" Adele laughed. "Good thing, too. Madison had enough troubles without having to raise *two* kids."

"Two? She had another besides Braelynn?"

She gave him a look that suggested he was dim-witted. "I mean her baby *and* Eddie. He always acted like a kid who'd snuck out of the house and wanted to par-tay. Y'know what I mean?"

He hoped he did. There were plain teens who took the idea of a "running around" time to extremes. Like Rosie's brother and his friends had, according to the tales he'd heard. Why would she have married a man like that when she'd been so hurt by Joel?

The answer to that was simple. She must have had no idea about Eddie's real past. What else had her late husband hidden from her?

Hoping he wasn't pushing too hard, he asked, "What about the last time you and Madison spent time together?"

She shrugged. "The usual. We had a pizza and some beers over at the place she liked on Market Street."

"When was that?"

"About six months or so before she died."

"Do you know how she died?"

Again, she shrugged. "I've heard stories, but I don't know what's true and what's not."

"What did you hear?"

She lowered her head, but not before he saw the glitter of tears. "That Madison died from an opioid overdose. Opioids are—"

"I know what they are," he said. "Our community isn't immune."

"I'm sorry to hear that."

Gideon didn't doubt Adele's words were sincere. In her voice, he heard the regrets of a woman who'd seen too many give in to the drug's powerful allure and lose everything.

"She died less than a month before her kid turned two." She rubbed her knuckles against her eyes.

Grief threatened to consume him as he thought of a little *kind* having her *mamm* vanish just before her birthday. All she would have understood was that her *mamm* had left and hadn't returned.

Or had Madison dumped her *kind* long before then? He thought of the many names Braelynn had listed as her caretakers. She might have been separated from Madison long before the young woman died.

"What about Braelynn's *daed*...her father?" he asked. "Did Eddie take care of her after Madison was gone?"

"No, he was long gone by then." Her nose wrinkled.

Gideon hesitated, then asked the question that had been gnawing at him. "Was he Amish?"

"No!" She snorted a derisive laugh. "He was a musician in several different metal bands that played around the city whenever they could get a gig."

Eddie Mishler had been a musician? Was he one of those kids who broke every rule before returning to his community to be baptized? Who *had* Eddie Mishler been before he came to Bliss Valley?

"Anything else you can tell me about Madison or Eddie?"

She glanced at the people coming out the Central Market's doors. "Look, I've got to get to work. I've told you everything I remember. I've spent the last few years trying to forget it."

"*Danki*. I mean, thanks."

"Sure." She looked at him and tried to grin, but her eyes were filled with deep pain. "Got any requests? I saw the money you dropped in my case."

"Just that you have a *gut* day...and a *gut* life."

She stared at him for a long minute, then nodded. Without another word, she turned away and began to sing an old folk song about saying goodbye to a dear friend for the last time.

The heartrending melody followed Gideon as he walked away.

Chapter Seventeen

The auction barn was filled to capacity and beyond. The noise and the air of anticipation eased the grief Rosie couldn't dislodge from her heart. When Gideon had returned from Lancaster and told her how Braelynn hadn't seen Eddie since she was a little *boppli* and she'd lost her *mamm* before she was two, the pain she'd tried to shove aside after Eddie's death flooded back. She mourned for her late husband and a young woman she knew only through Braelynn.

Had Madison been stubborn, too? No, the little girl had gotten that from Eddie. Had Madison been fearful of the world and what might lurk in it as Braelynn was? Was she resistant to kindness, too? How many people had tried to help Madison escape the hold of opioids? Or had her problem been passed from person to uncaring person as her daughter had been?

Too many questions about Braelynn's *mamm* never would be answered. Just as many about her *daed*. Eddie had asserted he couldn't carry a note when they sang during church. He'd laughed when he was approached to take a turn as *vorsinger,* the man who began each line of a hymn to keep the *Leit* on pace and on key. She remembered him suggesting they find a crow because its caw would be better than he was.

It had been nothing but an act. An act to cover up his past, but why? Singing in a band wasn't typical plain behavior, but kids were given leniency during their *rumspringa*. A few took it too far...as her brother and his friends had. Those mistakes had been forgiven when the trio stepped forward for baptism so they could walk with God.

So why haven't you forgiven Joel?

The question jarred her, and she refused to consider it a moment longer as she focused on the auction. That was what she needed to do. Enjoy the present moment while she could rather than wallow in her grief and shame.

But how?

There was another question she couldn't answer, but she was going to try.

She'd contacted the lawyer Laurene had recommended again, sharing the information they'd gathered in the city. Charles Satterfield had listened and taken notes before asking her permission to do a bit of looking himself into Madison Nesbitt's past. He had resources through his law practice and the internet she couldn't access.

"Only agree if you're ready for all possible consequences," he'd said.

"What consequences?" She hadn't been sure if she'd shivered from the cold of sitting in the unheated phone shack or the portent in his words.

"First of all, we may not find anything ever."

"I realize that."

"Or it may take months, possibly years, to track down her family."

"I understand that."

"Do you understand as well," he asked, his voice becoming compassionate, "that if her family is found, they may have a better claim of custody of the child than you do?"

It hadn't been easy, but she'd said, *"Ja."* To both that question and to having him search. Her heart stuttered while she calmly agreed for him to find out what he could about whatever family Braelynn might have. At the same time, she prayed for God to guide her to do what was best for the *kind*, even if it wasn't the best thing for herself.

Taking a deep breath, Rosie looked at where Calvin stood behind a podium. He held a gavel while his gaze swept the barn, seeking new bidders for the ugly painting two of his assistants were holding up.

From where Rosie sat a few rows from the back, she had an excellent view of the hands and paddles going up. A row of telephones and computers were set on tables to the right side of the room, and more bids were shouted from the people sitting behind them.

When had Calvin added phone and online bidding? She hadn't been to his auctions since one she had attended with Eddie last summer. Back then, the bidding had been only for those present. She was agog at how Calvin handled bids from every direction.

Beside her, Iva listened with a big grin on her face as her nimble fingers worked on piecing together the top for a small lap quilt. Braelynn knelt on the floor on the other side, using the chair to hold her coloring book and crayons. The little girl had gotten bored, not understanding what was happening around her. Braelynn had recovered quickly from whatever had been bothering her earlier in the week. Could it have been allergies that caused her coughing and nose running? She hadn't had a fever. Whatever it had been, the *kind* seemed to be over it.

The hammer came down on yet another item. Rosie sat back on the bench, releasing the breath she hadn't realized she was holding. A bidding war was always fun to watch, but she hadn't guessed a dusty old painting of a scowling man in a cracked and chipped frame would bring more than a thousand dollars.

When she saw the two bidders exchanging a glance, she was startled anew. She understood why the winner was smiling. But why did the man who'd stopped bidding as the price reached fifteen hundred dollars grin back as he shrugged? He was acting as if he didn't care someone else was taking home the painting he must have coveted.

"You look puzzled," Gideon said as he sat beside her and stretched past her to give a steaming cup of *kaffi* to Iva.

"I am." She explained what she'd observed.

"That's odd." He shrugged. "But *Englischers* do plenty of odd things."

"As we do," Iva said with a chuckle. "I've learned trying to guess why people do what they do is a *gut* way to make sure I don't sleep at night." She winked at Braelynn. "And I like to sleep at night."

"Braelynn, too!" chirped the little girl as she hopped up and sat on her chair. "Braelynn is glad Rosie doesn't snore like Patsy does."

Iva glanced at Rosie in astonishment. With a slight shake of her head, Rosie hoped she was conveying to the elderly woman that asking another question might not be a *gut* idea. Not in front of Braelynn.

"I snore." Iva's eyes twinkled.

"How do you know?" Braelynn asked.

"My husband used to tell me I was so loud I could wake a groundhog hiding in its burrow in the middle of winter." She chuckled. "Said my snoring would throw off predictions for spring because I woke the groundhogs early."

"Braelynn's mommy snored loud, but then she stopped."

Rosie heard Gideon's sharp intake of breath as her own caught in her throat. As Braelynn chattered on, she forced herself to relax. The little girl wasn't talking about the night her *mamm* had died. Or if she was, Braelynn wasn't bothered by it.

Looking over the *kind*'s head, she saw the sympathy in Gideon's eyes. He'd hated having to share what he'd learned. Her assurances that nothing he said about Madison had surprised her hadn't been able to lessen the impact of the truth. Since that conversation earlier in the week, he hadn't spoken to her about anything other than about barn chores or the weather. She hadn't been sure if he would join them for the auction, but he had.

At the auction, he kept the conversation light, as if he wanted to forget the mess he'd let himself get dragged into by renting her old dairy shed. If she had half a brain, she'd let him stay distant. If he wasn't nearby, she didn't have to worry about letting slip the truth about her pregnancy. Between that and Braelynn and the farm and having another quilting frolic at her house in a few days, she had enough to concern herself without worrying about when or if he would kiss her again.

One year of mourning, she reminded herself as she had so often during the past week. What had been her haven from the world had become the fortress she'd raised in the battle with her own heart.

Rosie heard a roar of applause followed by Calvin knocking his gavel on the podium. She blinked and stared at the front of the barn again. Her eyes widened. Most auctions in Lancaster County—at least the ones she'd attended—had offered farming equipment and household goods. Calvin's auctions used to be focused on those items, too.

The item for offer was a necklace that looked like it was made out of silver and diamonds. She couldn't imagine how much it was worth, but the bids Calvin was taking told her the final bid might outpace her imagination.

When had he started selling artwork and jewelry? She didn't remember seeing any in the preview.

Maybe because it was too valuable to leave unattended, she told herself. That made sense, but uneasiness roiled inside her as she watched the items go for absurd prices.

She scanned the room. Nobody else seemed to be bothered by the odd items.

Don't look for trouble where there isn't any. She almost smiled at the testy sound of her thoughts. She didn't need to look for trouble. Her life was awash with it.

As if to prove that, she noticed Calvin's sister Lori Ann huddled with LaVern and his sister Teresa near the door facing the telephone bank table. Lori Ann patted her stomach and leaned forward to whisper something to her companions. They glanced in Rosie's direction, their eyes wide with shock, and she looked away, hoping they hadn't seen her watching them.

What had that meant? She could think of one answer. How had Lori Ann discovered Rosie was pregnant? She cringed at the thought of those notorious gossips spreading the news before she was ready to share it herself.

When Braelynn's head dropped onto her lap as the little girl gave into sleep, Rosie knew she had the perfect excuse to escape. Coming to the auction had been a mistake.

Suddenly, she was tired. Tired physically and mentally... and in spirit. *God, I need Your strength to keep going.* The prayer seemed to sap the last of her energy, and she wasn't sure how much longer she could stay awake. A yawn escaped, despite her efforts to hold it in.

"Ready to go?" asked Gideon.

"*Ja.*"

Scooping up Braelynn, she edged to the end of the bench.

Gideon helped Iva up and then held out his arms to Rosie. She almost stepped into them, yearning for the comfort of someone who would understand how overwhelmed she was.

She was halted when he said, "I can take that little one from you if you'd like."

"No, I'm fine." Her smile was as false as her reassurance. "I'm sorry we're leaving early."

"Don't be. I don't have any need for a diamond necklace."

She smiled feebly. It was the best she could do, and she sensed he knew that. The thought should have offered her comfort. Instead, it made her realize how much her life had become linked to his. She needed a way to make sure it was disconnected as soon as possible because she didn't want him to feel obligated to keep helping her and her growing family.

Gideon knocked mud off his boots four days later before he walked into his shop as the setting sun touched the tips of the trees at the western horizon. Delivering several repaired pieces of tack to his customers had made for a *gut* day. It was rewarding to see the pleasure on people's faces when he presented them with what he'd brought back to a useful life.

What was that on his worktable? Hanging his hat by the door, he went to the table. He picked up the pink envelope and opened it, astonished how his fingers quivered when he realized it was a Valentine's Day card. Why had it been left in his shop on February 13?

No name was on the envelope, but he opened it. Inside was a handmade card. Stamps of chickens and kittens had been placed in a heart shape on the front of the folded piece of paper. Opening it, he stared at the words inside.

You are loved. More than you know.

Beneath those words was Rosie's name. His heart skipped a beat. How many times had he heard people talking about a heart doing that? He hadn't believed it actually happened. Not until now.

He was holding his breath. He let it out with a quick gasp as he looked at the front and the interior of the card again. A Valentine's Day card from Rosie? He thought how she'd kept him at a distance since last weekend's auction. She'd decided, he'd assumed, that their kiss had been a big mistake and should be forgotten as they went back to being tenant and landlady.

As he glanced at the card again, he realized he'd made another mistake. Not about Rosie's feelings for him, but about the card.

She'd signed it with large block letters and a hand-drawn chicken. It hadn't been meant for him. No one liked chickens as much as Braelynn. If he hadn't been dumbfounded at the idea Rosie had left him a Valentine's Day card, he would have seen that.

But why was a card she'd intended to give to Braelynn in his shop? Had the *kind* brought the card herself?

He frowned. Braelynn had told him she wouldn't enter the shop unless he was there. When he'd tried to impress upon her the danger of the tools he used, she'd nodded and said she understood.

Had she?

Really?

Gideon scanned the space, noting every tool was in place. He opened a few drawers. Nothing had been disturbed. His knives were in their slots. His sewing machine was as he'd left it. His rivet machine as well.

He thought about yesterday when the *kind* had come to his shop. She'd been alone, and one look had told him she had something important on her mind.

"Gideon, stop them!" she'd exclaimed without a greeting.

"Stop who?" He had gotten used to Braelynn starting in the middle of a conversation.

"Nasty guys."

"Do you know their names?"

She'd screwed up her face in concentration, looking so cute he'd almost smiled. If he had, she would have been too annoyed to continue talking. She spoke to him so seldom.

"Kevin... No, something like that. The other guy's name is a lady's name."

"Are you talking about Calvin and LaVern?"

"Yeah." Her head had bobbed, making her braids bounce on her shoulders. Her nose wrinkled. "Don't like them."

He'd wanted to agree, but asked, "Why not?"

"They tell me what to say to Rosie."

"About what?"

Gideon had to submerge his growing annoyance while Braelynn related how both men had pestered her to convince Rosie to marry one of them. The *kind* wasn't naive, and she'd ascertained the men were being kind to her to make her do as they asked. Her instincts of self-preservation, honed by the tough life she'd lived, had warned what they wanted wasn't right. Not that Braelynn had understood the ramifications of the men's interest in Rosie. She'd been irritated by them bothering her.

He'd advised her not to listen to the men and, if they bothered her again, to let Rosie know. Braelynn hadn't acted as if she liked those suggestions. Had she decided to take matters into her tiny hands by bringing him the Valentine's Day card? Had she thought Rosie had planned to give it to him?

No matter. Gideon slid the card in its envelope, folded the flap in and reached for his hat. Setting it on his head, he went along the lane toward the farmhouse. It was odd to realize he hadn't been inside in over a week. Not since he'd told Rosie what he'd learned in Lancaster.

He hesitated at the back door, then knocked, feeling almost as much like a stranger as he had the first time he came to the house.

It opened, and Rosie frowned. How could she be so pretty when she was scowling?

"Why are you knocking?" she asked.

"You know why."

She faltered, then stepped back. "*Komm* in."

Gideon glanced around the kitchen, but saw no sign of Braelynn.

"She's in her den," Rosie said. "She went in earlier, and she's spent most of the morning there."

"I think this is yours."

She took the pink envelope with a bemused expression. "Where did you get this? I had it hidden in a drawer to give to Braelynn tomorrow with breakfast."

"Not hidden well enough." He explained how he'd discovered the card in his shop. "It looks as if she found it and delivered it to me."

"I'll speak with her, Gideon. I know you don't want her in your shop when she's not supervised."

"Nothing was touched."

"*Gut.* She's behaving better, and I'm trying to have more patience. We're taking it one day at a time."

"More than some people do."

Her forehead furrowed. "What do you mean?"

"I saw your visitors yesterday."

A blush rushed up her cheeks. Though he was glad to see the color that had been missing the past week, he wasn't proud of the way he'd brought it forth. Why couldn't he halt himself from sniping at Calvin and LaVern? The two men hovered around her like mosquitoes during a summer twilight, as irritating and persistent.

Gideon wondered now if he'd been wrong not to walk over to the house when he saw first Calvin and then LaVern stop by. Neither had stayed long, so he knew they hadn't found a warm welcome.

Or had it been something else? Rosie appeared devastated. His fingers closed into fists at his sides, though he forced them to open as he envisioned those gossips eager to share the rumors he'd heard about Eddie's death. Fool that he was, he should have told her as soon as he'd heard himself rather than leave her to their unkind words.

But what are kind words to tell a woman her husband committed suicide? Haven't you been unable to find the right ones, too?

"Did LaVern and Calvin say anything to you about the rumors going around?" he asked.

"Which ones?" Again, her face became gray.

"The one about—"

A wail interrupted Gideon, and he looked toward the living room. Rosie rushed into the other room and bent to pull back the quilt over the table. Squatting, she stretched her hand toward the little girl he could see huddled beneath it.

Rosie gathered up the *kind* and lifted her into her arms. "She's as hot as a stove," she said as she stood. "Will you go to the phone shack? *Doktor* Simon's phone number is on a slip pinned to the wall. Call the office and ask if he can see Braelynn straightaway."

"Symptoms?" he asked, pleased how calm he sounded.

"High fever and lethargic." She paused when the little girl let out another cry. "And in obvious pain."

The next few hours were a blur of getting through to the *doktor*'s office, a hurried drive to where it was located west of downtown Strasburg, an examination and tests, and waiting for the results. Braelynn moaned and whined the whole time. Through it all, Rosie maintained a calm he envied. Even when the *doktor* assured her Braelynn's tests were normal and to take her home and keep her warm and push fluids, Rosie's demeanor remained serene.

"I'm sorry," she said to the short balding *doktor*. "I panicked."

"Compared to some mothers I've encountered, you didn't come close to panic." He chuckled and winked in Gideon's direction. "You're a first-time mother, and every first-time mother worries with every virus. Stop at the desk and set up an appointment for her to have a visit once she's feeling better, so we can have some baseline information going forward." He went out of the room.

"I feel silly," Rosie said.

Gideon started to remind her she couldn't be faulted for doing what she thought was best for the *kind*. Braelynn's mewl, complaining of an aching head, interrupted him. Scooping up the little girl, he helped her get into her coat while Rosie went to the desk. He carried Braelynn to the buggy and placed her in the back seat while they waited for Rosie to come out.

"Mommy," the youngster whispered. "I want my mommy."

"She wants me and Rosie to take care of you right now." He prayed it wasn't a lie. Wouldn't Madison have wanted someone to tend to her *kind* when she wasn't able?

He couldn't imagine anyone who would be more loving and caring than the woman walking toward the buggy. He gave Rosie a smile as she climbed in. The little girl was asleep before he gave Domino the command to go.

"I'm glad it's just one of those twenty-four-hour bugs," Gideon said in a hushed voice as he drove back toward the farm. "My nieces and nephews get them all the time. They're sick for a day and then running around the next as if nothing ever happened."

"I've been thanking God it was nothing more." She bowed her head, but he could see a hint of her crimson cheeks beneath her bonnet. "I'm sorry I went right to the worst possibility."

He smiled. "You love that little rapscallion, ain't so?"

"She's my responsibility."

"It's okay to love someone who doesn't know how to love you back."

"But it's not easy."

"And it's okay to admit you love someone. Doing so won't mean that person will be taken from you."

She stared at him as if she couldn't believe what she'd heard. "Why are you saying something like that?"

"Because it's true, ain't so? You've lost others you loved. You think if you say you love her, she'll be taken away from you."

"God's plans don't work like that!"

"You're right." He rested his elbows on his knees and looked at her, trusting the horse knew the way back. "They don't. So why are you acting as if they do?"

"Because you're right. I'm scared of what could happen if someone comes to claim her." She looked at her clasped hands on her lap. "Maybe I shouldn't have called the attorney and agreed to let him search for any family Braelynn might have."

"Do you really believe that?"

"I don't want to lose her."

"Put your faith in God."

"It is, but—"

"No buts, Rosie." He curved his hand around her nape and tilted her face toward him. "I don't know why God has placed so many challenges in your way, but you must never falter—not for a moment—in knowing He wants what is best for you. All you need to do is reach out and grasp it."

"Is that what you did when you came to Bliss Valley?"

"Ja," he said, not hesitating on his answer. "My life needed to change, and He put the inspiration for a shop into my mind when I heard you had a place to rent. His timing is perfect. We need only accept the invitation to follow Him when He calls us to move in a new direction." He leaned toward her, his gaze on her soft lips.

"Rosie!" came a cry from the back seat.

She jerked away and turned to the *kind*.

He turned his eyes back to the road before either Rosie or Braelynn saw his frustration. But, as he'd just told Rosie, they needed to accept God's timing. No matter how tough it was.

Chapter Eighteen

At the knock on her door shortly after midday, Rosie looked up, astonished. Nobody had come to her front door since Eddie's funeral. And, other than Gideon when he'd first arrived, nobody knocked on either door.

Maybe it was someone looking for Gideon. Or an *Englischer* who'd taken the wrong turn on the twisting roads and was looking for directions to Strasburg or Willow Street or Gap.

"Just a moment!" she called as she slipped her needle in the fabric to hold her place on the mud sale quilt stretched on the frame. She'd decided to work on the feather pattern so the project would be done sooner. It'd given her quiet time to sit while Braelynn played on the floor beside her.

Smoothing her apron over her wrinkled dress, she glanced toward where the *kind* was immersed in building a whole settlement out of Lincoln Logs. The little girl didn't look up as she placed green boards on one of the buildings.

Rosie went to the door. When she opened it, savoring the

clement breeze dancing across the porch, her greeting dried up in her throat.

"Gideon! Why are you coming to the front door?" she asked, confused.

"We need to talk to you," he replied without his usual smile.

"We?"

He stepped aside to reveal another man on the porch. Joel! Torn between wanting to hug her brother and telling him to go away and never return, she couldn't do anything but stare at him.

Joel was the epitome of an Amish man, the very type he'd once loathed. From his straw hat to his black coat that was unbuttoned to reveal the suspenders holding up his broadfall trousers and down to his work boots, there was no sign he'd spent almost a decade living as an *Englischer.*

She had no idea how long they might have stood there in silence if Gideon hadn't asked, "May we *komm* in?"

Her voice refused to work, so she stepped back and motioned for them to enter. She closed the door, then leaned against it. Her fingers itched to fling it open again; yet her heart teased her to let her brother stay so they could talk.

Really talk. Not a conversation in passing. Not about the weather or news from their community.

Really talk. About how the past decade had changed them and how it hadn't. Was Joel still ticklish on his left side? Had he gotten over his obsession with red velvet cake and Lapp's coconut ice cream? Could he still wink with both eyes? She could only wink her right eye, and she'd always admired his ability to do it with both eyes.

But not a single word would pass her lips.

Gideon's hand on her arm sent a bolt of electricity racing through her. It snapped her out of her shock as if he'd held a defibrillator to her chest. Her heart thudded, but she was no longer sure if that was because of his touch or her brother standing in her living room.

"It's okay," he said.

She wanted to believe him as Joel regarded her with a regretful gaze that threatened to reopen the wounds she'd believed were scarred over.

Her brother turned to the *kind* playing in the middle of the room and spoke in English. "Braelynn, how nice to see you."

"You are Braelynn's *onkel*, ain't so?" the little girl replied.

He arched his brows as Rosie remembered him doing so many times when she wasn't any older than Braelynn. "You're already learning to speak *Deitsch*. You're a smart little girl."

"*Ja*. Braelynn smart."

"That's no surprise. Anyone who can build such nice log houses must be smart."

"Pretty houses, ain't so?"

"Almost as pretty as the person building them."

"Rosie made Braelynn a new dress." Standing, she grabbed the hem of her skirt and pirouetted. She put her hand over her mouth and giggled.

Rosie watched the exchange with astonishment. Braelynn had been so hesitant to talk to her and Gideon when she first met them. With Joel, she was a chatterbox.

Stepping away from the door, Rosie said, "Let's go out on the side porch to talk." She saw hurt flash through her brother's eyes, and she guessed he was thinking she was trying to give him the bum's rush from her home. She almost told him that there wasn't any door off the porch other than the one to the house. If he didn't trust her...

Why should he trust her when she hadn't decided if she could trust him?

"That sounds like a *gut* idea." Gideon glanced at Braelynn, and Joel nodded, understanding Rosie thought it was better not to talk where the *kind* could hear.

"*Ja.*" She wanted to take Gideon's hand so the connection between them wasn't broken. Instead, she locked her fingers together in front of her as she led the way to the side porch.

Overgrown bushes shaded the porch, which needed repainting. She hoped to bring a couple of comfortable chairs out when spring arrived, but for now the space was empty. Even so, it felt overcrowded when the three of them stood there.

Joel turned around. "Last time I was out here," he mused as if to himself, "these bushes were thick with leaves."

"At Eddie's funeral?"

He faced her. "I'm sorry, Rosie. I shouldn't have reminded you of that day."

"It's not as if I'll ever forget it." She sighed. "Everyone avoids talking about it, as if they think that will erase Eddie from my mind."

As soon as she spoke those words, she realized they weren't true.

They weren't true because of Gideon. He didn't expect her to forget Eddie. He'd encouraged her to learn more about the man she'd loved, the man she'd married, without realizing how little she knew about him.

She looked at where he was resting one shoulder against the wall by the door. His expression was closed, but she could see powerful emotions in his eyes. Gideon's eyes always revealed his thoughts, even when he was trying to protect her from the truth that always hung between them like the malevolent finger of a tornado. As she watched, his face fell into dismay. Not for himself, but for her. From the moment they'd met, she'd known he was a man who felt things strongly. Now, as she spoke from her heart, she was warmed by his compassion.

It was as if God Himself had reached down and wrapped her in His arms, letting her know she wasn't alone and she was loved.

Loved? Could Gideon love her? How? She'd done everything she could to keep him away. Even when she'd needed someone by her side in the tough days after Braelynn's arrival, she'd made sure he knew she was welcoming him in because desperate times called for desperate measures. Not because she appreciated his kindness, his generosity, his patience with her and the little girl. He could have walked away. He should have because he'd made it clear he'd come to Bliss Valley to get away from messy family situations.

And then he dove into hers to help her and Braelynn.

Something soared in her heart, something from the most damaged parts where hope had been banished. Its flight faltered when she saw Gideon's grim face.

"What's wrong?" she asked.

The two men exchanged an anxious glance before Joel said, "Gideon and I need to talk to you. We thought it'd be best for the two of us to be here for this."

"This what?"

"A rumor."

"What rumor?" Her roiling anxiety dropped to a slow simmer. "There are always rumors zooming along the Amish grapevine. New *bopplin* and old romances rekindling."

"This one is different," Gideon said.

Her gaze flicked to her brother. "Is the rumor about you?" There had been so many chasing Joel after he returned to Bliss Valley that it got to the point she had no idea which were true and which pure conjecture.

"No."

"Then are you talking about the one where the police are about to arrest the person who put stones through Grace's shop windows?"

Gideon's eyes widened. "I hadn't heard that. Is it true?"

"Who knows?" She shrugged.

"So who do they say did it?"

"That's also a question the rumors aren't answering, though there's a bunch of speculation." She thought of what Iva had said earlier that morning about a runaround group causing trouble near Quarryville and the elderly woman's curiosity if they'd been the perpetrators.

Rosie didn't believe the rumor was true. The attack seemed more personal. Why break the windows in Grace's store but none in LaVern's right across the road? That didn't make sense.

"There's always a lot of speculation," Gideon said.

"True. But if the rumors weren't about the broken windows—"

"They're about you."

"The rumors are about me?" Shock weakened her knees, and she sat on the porch railing. She stared at him and then looked at her brother who nodded as if he were reluctant to discuss this with her. Sorrow hit her anew. Once upon a time, they'd talked about everything under the sun. She couldn't pinpoint when that had stopped, but she knew how much she regretted having lost that.

"Are you all right?" Gideon asked.

"I will be once you tell me what's being said about me."

He moved to stand beside her, leaving a hand's breadth between them. His shoulder was so close she could have rested her cheek on it. She'd learned his shoulders were strong enough to hold the weight of any burdens she might place there. The other thing she'd learned was she shouldn't get used to depending on his support. He was her tenant, and he shouldn't be more.

Tell that to your heart. The little voice in her head was becoming snarky. *It's not listening.*

"The rumors are more about Eddie than you," Joel said.

At the reminder she and Gideon weren't alone, she stood. "Eddie? Five months after his funeral? That doesn't make sense."

"Rumors seldom do." Joel sighed.

She glanced at Gideon. Realizing he was having a tough time finding the words, she put her hand on his arm.

"Go ahead," she said. "Just say it."

"I don't want to hurt you."

"I know you don't."

He put his hand over hers, not to capture it but to provide a tacit acknowledgment of what her heart was already telling her. That the guise of being no more than landlady and tenant was worthless. They'd grown beyond that to become friends...and her heart hoped for more.

"We've got to ask you a tough question," Joel said.

"Go ahead."

Gideon cleared his throat. "Was there anything unusual about how or where your husband was found after his death?"

She shook her head. "No, he was found by LaVern. He'd joined the authorities looking for Eddie. They found him in a place where he often went hunting. It wasn't far from his favorite fishing hole." She caught his gaze and tried to hold it. When he looked away, she asked, "What's wrong, Gideon? What have you heard?"

"I don't know of any way to cushion this."

"Then don't. I'm a grown woman. Tell me what's being said."

"It's being said that what happened wasn't an accident."

She tried to digest his words. "Are you saying someone killed Eddie?"

"I'm not saying anything, but others are."

She looked from Gideon to her brother. "No! That's impossible. He was a *gut* man, fair and honest and faithful. Everyone believed he would be the next one chosen by lot to be ordained."

"Maybe so," Joel said, "but I've heard the rumors, too."

"You're both wrong! Nobody disliked Eddie. Nobody would have killed him."

"Nobody is saying that." Gideon's voice was hushed, but pain slashed through it.

"But you said—"

Gideon put his hands on her shoulders as if she were a *kind*. "They're saying, Rosie, that he killed himself."

She opened her mouth to respond, but no sound came out. Or maybe it did, but she couldn't tell because every other noise around her was skewed, rising and falling in a chaotic melody. Was she screaming a denial or frozen in place as her heart roared its disbelief?

Eddie killing himself? No! He'd said so many times how much he had to live for. Though she hadn't known then about his daughter, she'd been sure of his love for her. He'd been overly protective at times, as he had when he'd told her brother to stay away from their farm, but she couldn't fault him for that.

Could she?

Nothing made any sense any longer. The husband whom she'd been certain had kept no secrets from her and to whom she'd poured out the contents of her heart hadn't told her about his little girl. She'd thought she knew Eddie Mishler.

She hadn't.

So how could she know if he'd do something as appalling as taking his life, the life God had blessed him with, the life he was supposed to spend with her?

Had her husband been so unhappy he couldn't face life any longer? She thought of how cheerful he'd always appeared.

Appeared!

What had he really been thinking? Had he regretted marrying her? Or had the secrets he carried in his heart been too much for him to live with?

She was shocked when she realized how much she hoped it was the latter. She should have sensed his pain and helped him. Wasn't that what a *gut* spouse did?

Rosie looked at Gideon and away, unable to bear the grief on his face. Not grief at Eddie's death, but sorrow that they were having this discussion. He hurt at the thought of hurting her.

How, Lord, she cried silently, *can I know what Gideon's thinking but I was so deaf to what was in Eddie's heart and mind?*

Now the rumor was spreading that her husband had killed himself. Why hadn't she heard it? Her family and her friends must have worked to protect her from the rumors. She thought of the many times when someone had started to speak and then halted themselves. What a *dummkopf* she'd been! She'd believed they'd guessed she was going to have a *boppli*, but they hadn't wanted to say anything until she told them the *gut* news. Instead, they'd been whispering about Eddie's death.

She couldn't believe he'd killed himself. Eddie had been talking about their future on their farm and with the family they'd have.

But he'd never mentioned his daughter.

Why not?

It was another question she couldn't answer. The only one who knew the truth was Eddie, and he couldn't tell her.

If she'd been able to tell him about the *boppli* inside her, he would have deemed it the very best of news. Wouldn't he have been thrilled?

She wasn't sure about anything now.

Gideon said, "Eddie killing himself is just a rumor, Rosie."

Holding up her head, she said, "And plenty of rumors aren't true."

"That's right," her brother replied. "You shouldn't believe everything you hear people saying, especially people who don't know better. You know your husband, Rosemary."

Tears welled into her eyes as she heard his kindness. "I'm Rosie again."

He smiled. "The name I gave you when you weren't much more than a *boppli*? Rosemary was too much of a mouthful for a little kid."

Gideon went to the door into the house. "I'm going to check on Braelynn. Take all the time you need."

As the door closed behind Gideon, Joel smiled sadly. "He's a decent man, Rosie."

"Braelynn is very fond of him."

"And you?"

"I've been a widow only a few months." She hated giving her brother the trite answer, but to say more… She couldn't do it.

He leaned against the porch rail and sighed. She hadn't intended to wound him with her attempts to protect her ravaged heart.

"I've missed you, Rosie." Her brother's voice shattered the ice holding her heart in its cruel grip.

"You see me around."

"*Ja*, but not often. Truth be told, I miss the real you. The laughing, joy-filled girl I used to know."

"That girl has grown up."

"But growing up doesn't mean we have to give up our happiness and be smothered by our burdens. God accepts our burdens to carry Himself."

She looked at her clasped hands. "Happiness is a gift, Joel, and I treasure it, but right now, it's not easy."

"I'd like to help. I'd like to be here when you need someone to talk to. Like you used to talk to me when we were *kinder*."

"I'd like that."

"Does that mean you've forgiven me?"

He'd been so blunt she couldn't be anything else. "I'm trying to." She wasn't ready to admit she had no idea how to get past the mountain of pain that had grown layer by layer for a decade.

"What must I do to earn your forgiveness?"

"I don't know."

"Are you angry with me?"

"*Ja.*" Her quick answer startled her as much as it did him. She hastened to add, "I don't want to be angry with you, Joel. You're my brother, and I love you."

"I'm glad to hear that."

"What?"

"That you still love me."

She blinked back fiery tears. "Joel, don't you understand? It's because I love you so much that I've been so angry. You left without telling me goodbye."

"I know." He reached across the space between them and took her hand in his much wider one. "Do you want to know why?"

"*Ja.*"

"It's because I was too much of a coward to face you."

"Coward? You stood up to *Daed* all the time."

"I did, but *Daed* and I are too much alike. Both of us found a refuge in anger. All you ever offered me was a little sister's adoration."

"I did *not* adore you!" She rolled her eyes. "You were a smelly teenager who filled our house with drama."

"And you were a pest who followed me around, getting underfoot."

She stuck her tongue out at him as she would have done years ago. When he mirrored her action, she couldn't keep from smiling. He'd smiled all the time when they were kids. Even when *Daed* was making his life miserable, Joel had been her beloved playmate. He'd taught her to ride a horse and a scooter and how to drive a buggy. The last had been just before he jumped the fence, and she'd pretended when *Daed* offered to teach her that she'd never taken lessons with Joel. By that time, *Daed* had decreed her older brother's name must never be spoken.

With the void in the house and the empty chair at their table, she'd clung to the hope that Joel would return, so their family could be whole once more.

God, danki *for bringing my brother back to me. And* danki *for opening my eyes to see the man he's become instead of letting myself wallow in pain.*

"I prayed night after night for God to bring you home," she said as if he'd heard each of her thoughts.

He blinked, startled by the abrupt change of subject. "You did?"

"*Ja.*"

"I thought you weren't happy I was back."

"Eddie decided—"

"Eddie isn't here any longer." He sighed. "I'm sorry, Rosie. I didn't mean that as cold as it sounded."

"I know you didn't. And I didn't mean for it to sound heartless when I told you I'm having a hard time trying to forgive you."

"But you are trying?"

"*Ja.*" Tears trickled into her eyes, and she stepped into his embrace when he held his arms out to her.

His hug was recognizable, her haven when their *daed* was on a rampage, striking out at anyone nearby. He'd protected her for the first years of her life, and when he was at his worst in the weeks before he vanished from Bliss Valley, that hadn't changed.

And then he was gone, and she'd been left with the job of protecting her younger sisters from *Daed*'s rage. Only then had she realized how much Joel had endured to keep her safe. Instead of being grateful and understanding, she'd turned her grief and pain to anger.

"I'm sorry, Rosie," he said as she stepped out of his hug.

"I am, too. Please forgive me. I understand why you had to leave home, and I should have told you that as soon as you came back."

"I'll forgive you if you forgive me."

Blinking on her tears, she nodded. "Always."

"Always," Joel repeated, and his smile returned. "So when are you going to tell everyone?"

Rosie frowned. "Tell everyone what? That we've forgiven each other?"

"No." He pointed at her middle. "That you're pregnant."

Her eyes widened so much she thought they'd pop right out of her head. "How did you know?"

"I wasn't one hundred percent sure."

"So you tricked me!"

"No, I wanted to congratulate you. From everything I've heard, you're a *wunderbaar mamm* for Braelynn, so I know you'll be amazing with this *boppli*." His easy grin soothed her annoyance again until he asked, "So when are you going to tell everyone?"

"Not yet."

"*Englisch* women can't wait to share the news with the world and show off their baby bump to everybody."

"Plain women don't announce a *boppli* as *Englisch* women do. We wait until it's obvious and then nobody talks about it much until the birth."

"Does Gideon know?"

"No." She dashed her tears away as she lifted her chin.

"Why not?"

"It's none of his business."

Joel made a rude snort. "Can't you see the man has you on his mind all the time?"

"I need time to mourn Eddie." Her voice caught. "And to deal with what you and Gideon have told me."

Her brother's face softened. "You're right. I'm sorry. I don't want you to make the same mistake I almost made when I realized I was in love with Grace. You can either reject that love and spend the rest of your life coddling your broken heart."

"Or?"

"You can take another chance on letting love into your life. It can heal your heart." He held up his hand as she opened her mouth to speak. "Don't say it, Rosie. I know your arguments. Every one of them, because I had them with myself. I felt I wasn't worthy of love. Not giving it or receiving it. I kept pushing it and Grace away. I thank the Lord every day that Grace was patient and persistent enough to wait until I finished coming to terms with my past. Don't make the same mistake I did, Rosie. If you love Gideon, don't push him away."

"You forgot one important thing. What happens if I let myself love someone and they leave me and my heart is broken all over again?"

"What happens if you love someone and never tell them? Do you think that will break your heart less if they leave?"

She didn't have an answer. At least, not one he'd want to hear. He and Grace were happy together. They were planning a future together with Grace's parents and nephews. Rosie had once been where they were now. Talking about a wedding with the man she loved.

A man who, if rumor was to believed, had killed himself.

How was she going to come to terms with that truth? How was she going to believe Eddie's death wasn't because of something she hadn't done or had done? There must have been signs of depression; yet she'd missed them. She'd promised to love him through sickness and through health…and she'd failed.

Gideon couldn't concentrate the rest of the day. He'd ruined several pieces of leather because his mind had been on Rosie rather than his work. He shoved aside another belt he'd cut in the wrong place, making the whole length unusable.

He had considered remaining at the house after she and Joel came back inside. In fact, he'd assumed Rosie would ask him to stay when her brother left after getting a "tour" of Braelynn's village of log cabins. Instead, she'd stood by the door and waited for him to go, too. She wouldn't meet his eyes or even look in his direction.

Going to the window that gave him a view of the farmhouse, he wondered how many times he'd stood there as he pondered what to do next. Had he made a huge mistake coming to Bliss Valley and renting the building from Rosie? He'd thought when he kissed her, she'd know he wanted more than friendship with her, but she now acted as if they were the strangers they'd been the day he first came to her door.

Her grief when he and Joel had told her about the rumors of Eddie committing suicide had been heart-wrenching. She was blaming herself for not seeing Eddie slip into self-destruction.

And Gideon was blaming himself for telling her about the rumor.

His eyes widened when he saw Rosie walking along the lane alone. Was she going to get the mail? She didn't leave Braelynn by herself in the house very long.

Grabbing his coat, he shrugged it on and pulled on his hat as he stepped out into the afternoon that had grown chillier and damper. The minute he emerged from the building, she halted.

Before she could flee back to the house, Gideon asked, "Do you have a moment?"

"For what?"

She wasn't going to make it easy. Walking to where she stood between two puddles of melted snow, he asked, "How are you doing?"

"About as you'd expect."

"I'm sorry to hear that."

She nodded, but didn't reply. She seemed fascinated with the button in the middle of his coat.

"About the rumors—"

"How long have you known about them?"

The question he'd hoped she wouldn't ask, but now that she had, he wasn't going to prevaricate. "Several weeks."

"And you never told me until today?" Her eyes rose to meet his, and he saw pain and betrayal in them.

"I didn't want to say anything until I had some facts."

"You could have told me so I would have been prepared when I heard them."

"I did. We did." His words tumbled over themselves as he tried to explain everything at once. "When Joel came here today, asking if I'd heard the rumor about Eddie, I knew I couldn't keep the truth from you any longer. We decided together to tell you."

"The rumor may not be true!"

He longed to step forward and take her in his arms, but she was too encased in hurt and grief for him to reach her. Or worse, she'd push his arms away. How was he going to convince her he'd kept the rumor to himself because he'd wanted to avoid this conversation?

"Rosie, I don't know what to believe. One thing I know is Eddie Mishler wasn't the man he pretended to be."

"You never met him! How can you say that?"

"Because I know he beat Madison Nesbitt." He gasped at his own words that had escaped as he struggled to deal with the pain coming off Rosie in heated waves like air above a summer pavement.

"What?" She gawped at him.

"Madison's friend Adele told me about Eddie hitting Madison."

"Adele?"

"The girl who plays the guitar by the Central Market in Lancaster."

Rosie looked at the ground, then past him before her gaze aimed at him with laser precision. "Why haven't you told me before now?"

"I wanted to. Rosie, you've got no idea how much I've wanted to tell you, but it never seemed to be the right time."

"I can understand that."

Relieved she comprehended how difficult it had been for him to have this information and not be able to share it, he began to reply, *"Dan—"*

"What is the right time," she demanded icily, "to tell a widow her late husband was accused of hitting the *mamm* of his *kind*?"

"Rosie, I didn't want you hurt."

She wasn't listening to him, he realized, when she snapped, "Who else knows about this?"

"Nobody."

"You didn't share this with Jonas?"

"I saw no reason to." He cut her off by saying, "I've been wondering one thing."

"What's that?" She looked away, and he guessed she was trying to prepare herself for what she expected him to say next.

He'd thought about this conversation so many times, playing and replaying in his mind what he wanted to say, how he could soften his questions. But every word had vanished from his head.

So he blurted, "Did Eddie ever hit you, Rosie?"

When she didn't give him a quick no, sickness clawed at his gut. Eddie Mishler had vowed to love her as a wondrous and cherished gift from God. Yet, Eddie's past had tainted everything, even the life of the wife who hadn't known a thing about it.

"Rosie?" he asked again.

"Not on purpose," she said at last.

He frowned. "What's that supposed to mean?"

Her head rose, and she met his gaze with her tear-filled one. "It means just what I said. He didn't intend to hit me. He was upset at how long it took to milk the cows one morning, and he was about to slap his hand on the wall. I got in the way. It was my fault."

"Or he convinced you it was your fault."

"Don't say that, Gideon! You didn't know him."

"But others did. He hurt Braelynn's *mamm* enough that her friend called the cops."

Shaking her head, she shut her eyes and took an unsteady breath. "I'm tired of having the past draped over me so I've got to fight my way out from its grip, day after day." She whirled on her heel and walked toward the house.

He caught up with her before she reached it. She might have continued as if he weren't there, but he stepped in front of her, blocking her way unless she wanted to wade through two huge puddles.

She motioned for him to move aside. When he didn't, she

cried, "No more secrets!" She shocked him with her vehemence. "I'm tired of secrets. Everywhere I turn, I'm surrounded by secrets."

"Or you're surrounding yourself with secrets."

She stared at him, her mouth agape. She recovered herself before he could ask what *she* was hiding. "Maybe you should look at your life before you tell me how to live mine!"

"I'm not—"

"Your rent is paid until the end of the month. After that..." She didn't continue. She didn't need to. Her words were crystal clear. She wanted him off her farm.

This time, when she pushed past him and strode toward the house, he didn't give chase. He lifted his foot out of the puddle and shook the muddy water off it. He almost called her name, but didn't. If she turned around, what was he going to do?

Tell her she was right? She already knew what he'd tried to conceal from everyone, including himself. He'd hidden the truth to protect her.

But he'd ended up hurting her worse.

Chapter Nineteen

"Where are you going?"

Gideon looked up and saw Braelynn standing in the doorway between his shop and his private room. Her eyes were focused on the bag on his bed. He'd been stuffing socks into it.

"Nowhere," he said, though it was a lie as well as the truth.

The little girl stepped closer to him. "That's what they did when they didn't want Braelynn."

"Packed your things?"

"Most of them." She looked at the stuffed lion she held. "Teddy is gone. Braelynn gots Cleo."

"I'm glad you do." He went to the kitchen table. When the little girl followed, he asked, "Does Rosie know you're here?"

"Rosie working on her muddy quilt. Braelynn wants to see Gideon."

He smiled, though he hadn't thought he would be able to after the harsh words he and Rosie had exchanged earlier. The *muddy* quilt must be Braelynn's description for the quilt being made for the mud sale. "I'm glad you dropped by."

"Braelynn didn't drop anything." She crushed her lion to her.

"I mean that you came to see me."

"You should say what you mean." She tilted her head to appraise him with an expression very much like Rosie's. "Braelynn says what she means."

"That's *gut*." He sat at the table and motioned for her to take a chair. "Are you hungry?"

"No. Had church spread sandwiches."

He was astonished. Rosie always served the *kind*—and often him, too—a hot meal at noon. Telling himself not to be absurd, because Rosie had been beyond upset when she stormed away, he swallowed his sigh. Everything had imploded in a single day. He should have told Rosie everything Adele had said as soon as he returned from the Central Market. Maybe then, when she hadn't been so distraught about the idea of her late husband being suicidal, he might have found a better way to ask her if her husband had ever struck her.

His hand clenched on the table as he thought of Eddie hitting Rosie. Lowering it to his lap before the *kind* noticed, he prayed for God to take the rage from his heart.

"So where are you going?" Braelynn asked.

He should have known he couldn't distract her, especially as he didn't have a cookie jar. Propping his elbow on the table, he said, "Home."

"This is Gideon's home."

Her simple assertion threatened to undo him. One thought had been racing through his head after Rosie left him standing alone on the lane. He'd made the biggest mistake of his life leaving Smoketown because he'd just changed one set of complications for another.

Standing, he went to look in his shop. Projects waited to be finished, projects he'd agreed to do. How could he walk away from people who'd trusted him to do as he said?

People like Rosie.

He shook his head, but said, "*Ja*, this has been where I'm living. I lived with my family before I came here."

"Like Braelynn lived with Mommy?"

Regret for not choosing his words with more care hit him like a fist. How could he answer the little girl? It had to be with the truth, no matter how difficult it was.

Just as Rosie had been honest when she last spoke with him. *I'm tired of secrets. Everywhere I turn, I'm surrounded by secrets.*

"I lived with my *mamm*, my *grossmammis* and my sisters as well as a few *aentis*," he said.

"You gots lots."

"That's true."

"Braelynn gots little." She looked at her stuffed lion.

He reached across the table and patted her shoulder. It was an awkward motion, but it was the best he could manage. "A little can be *gut*, but you've got lots, Braelynn. Rosie loves you lots."

The *kind*'s head jerked up as if tugged by an unseen hand. She stared at him for a long minute before she said, "Rosie loves Braelynn and Gideon. Gideon loves Braelynn and Rosie. Braelynn heard you and Rosie. You were angry. Now you're going."

"I must."

"Why?"

Again, he chose the truth. "I don't know, other than I must go."

"You don't love Braelynn?"

"You know I do. Just like Rosie loves you." He softened his voice as he added, "But I've got to go."

Horror filled her eyes. She slid off the chair and backed away.

He took a single step toward her, but she turned and ran away as Rosie had earlier. Just like Rosie, she didn't look back.

And again, he knew he'd hurt someone he hadn't wanted

to. He stuffed more things into the bag. What wouldn't fit, he'd get later when he came back for his tools.

Was he a coward—or worse, a fool—for running away? Maybe, but he couldn't stay and inflict more misery on the two he loved most in the world.

Rosie clutched the plate of cookies in one hand and held on to Braelynn's hand with the other. Her face felt frozen in what had to look like a macabre smile, an expression she'd worn since Braelynn burst into tears halfway between their home and Iva's. It hadn't taken much prodding to get the little girl to reveal what had upset her.

Gideon went away. Goodbye, Gideon.

Such simple words that packed a painful wallop. Wanting to believe she'd misunderstood the *kind*, Rosie had asked a couple of questions until she realized she was upsetting Braelynn more. The facts were simple. Gideon had packed up his clothing and had told Braelynn he was leaving.

Without saying goodbye to Rosie.

Just as Joel had.

As Eddie had.

If rumor was to be believed—and she prayed it wasn't— Eddie had left her that day with no intention of coming home. He'd left without a single word to offer her comfort or to let her know how tormented he was. If she'd known...

God, why didn't You open my eyes to what was right in front of me? Why didn't You push me to tell Eddie how much I loved him before he left that day?

No answers.

There weren't any answers about why Gideon had decided to give up his dream of his shop in Bliss Valley after her outburst. She'd told him to leave, but had she meant it? She had at the moment, but now... Now she wasn't sure. Not about anything. Why hadn't he come and told her about his plans before he left? He'd just left.

As Eddie had.

Dearest Father, how can I bear this grief again? I thought Gideon cared about me. Cared a lot. As I care so much for him. He kissed me, and I dared to believe You'd blessed me with a new love.

She couldn't blame God for her own foolishness. Listening to her heart had been her first mistake…and her second one.

No! Falling in love with Eddie hadn't been a mistake. She touched her curved abdomen as she looked at the *kind* by her side. Eddie's love had brought her two phenomenal gifts.

And falling for Gideon hadn't been a mistake, either. He'd helped her with Braelynn. He'd annoyed her and delighted her, and he'd reminded her she was still alive.

Taking a deep breath, Rosie opened Iva's back door. She squeezed Braelynn's hand and tried to smile, but the little girl didn't look in her direction. They walked into Iva's living room.

"Cookies?" the old woman asked.

"Of course." Rosie's smile felt like a garment with too much starch. She placed the plate on the table "I thought you'd like some chocolate pinwheels."

"Chocolate pinwheels?" Iva stuck her needle in her pincushion and ran her hand along the old quilt on her lap. She didn't add anything else.

"You don't like chocolate pinwheels?" Rosie asked.

"I don't like your expressions."

Braelynn sobbed and threw herself onto the quilt, clinging to it as she clung to her toy lion.

Iva stroked her head with her gnarled fingers, but raised her eyes to Rosie. A slight motion with her head was an order to sit.

Rosie did, too distraught to think of a reason to make her

excuse and escape. Iva's eyes might be old and weak from years of focusing on her tiny stitches, but they saw clearly.

"He's gone?" the old woman asked, further proof she might be confined to her house most days but hadn't lost her ability to discern the state of the hearts around her.

"That's what Braelynn told me."

"He said nothing to you?"

"No."

"He's not Eddie Mishler."

She flinched. "I know that, Iva."

"Then you should know he would be honest with you if he was leaving and not coming back." Iva sighed. "I was impressed with Gideon when we went to the auction. He is kind, and he thinks a great deal of you and the *kind*." Her gaze dropped to Rosie's abdomen, and she corrected herself. "The *kinder*."

Rosie didn't bother to ask how Iva had guessed about the pregnancy. Joel had, too. Had Gideon? Was that the real reason he'd left? Because he didn't want to see Eddie's *boppli* in her arms? That didn't make sense. Gideon and Braelynn adored each other, and she was Eddie's daughter.

No, she wasn't. Not really. Eddie had relinquished any rights he had to Braelynn when he abandoned her and Madison. Worse, when he'd hit Madison. Rosie raised her fingers to her cheek. The bruise was long gone along with the echo of Eddie's abject apologies for striking her, but the memory, now tainted, remained.

"But he's gone," Rosie said, more to herself than to Iva.

"No, he's gone away. He's not gone." She grasped one of Rosie's hands. "He's still in your heart, and I'm sure from what I saw that you're in his. Some men need time to come to their senses. Give him time."

Rosie pulled in a ragged breath as Braelynn crawled up to

sit beside her. Putting her arm around the little girl, she asked, "How long?"

"Only God knows that, my *kind*," Iva said, "but you know as well as I do that He knows the beginning, the middle and the end of your story. Just as He knows mine and Braelynn's and the sparrow's and the stars in the sky. You are a new widow, and you've asked for a full year of mourning before committing your heart again. Have you considered that God is offering you an answer to your prayers?"

"By having Gideon go?"

"He's gone away. Not gone," she said as she had before. "He's a *gut* man from a *gut* family, and I know he's had to deal with a lot of pressure from his *grossmammis*."

"You know his family?"

"*Ja*." Her eyes twinkled as she released Rosie's hand and reached for a cookie. "In fact, one of his *grossmammis* wanted to marry my Perry. Before he was my husband, of course."

"But you stole his heart."

"No, Perry gave his heart to me willingly, as I gave him mine. That's what love is. I knew what sort of marriage I wanted after watching my parents'. My *daed* never went out the door without giving my *mamm* a kiss. Not even when he left to become a seagoing cowboy." She sighed. "It took my *mamm* a long time to understand why *Daed* decided he needed to escort a shipload of livestock across the ocean."

"I thought he was doing his alternative service as a conscientious objector."

"He was, but there were a lot of other things he could have done closer to home. *Mamm* had expected him to come home to us once the war was over."

"Instead, he went to Europe with a ship filled with cows and horses."

"And chickens," Braelynn interjected. "Lots of chickens."

A Hope for Healing

"That's right." Iva smiled at the little girl. "My *daed* said chickens were a special gift to those who needed animals because each hen would have a bunch of chicks. Unlike cows that usually have a single calf." Her face became somber again as she looked at Rosie. "But don't you see? No matter how long he was away, no matter how far he traveled, he always kissed my *mamm* before he left. It was an unspoken understanding between them that a kiss lingered until the next kiss."

"What if there hadn't ever been another kiss?"

"I can't answer that, and neither can you. All I can tell you is no matter where we travel, God brings us back to where we're meant to be." Without a pause, Iva reached for another cookie. "You know something? I think these are my favorite."

Rosie laughed, even as tears filled her eyes. She thanked God for Iva and her kindness and wisdom and the faith she shared. She had to accept the truth in Iva's words. Gideon would come back if it was where he was meant to be.

She had to believe that.

She had to.

Otherwise... She didn't want to think about otherwise.

Rosie wandered through her darkened living room and into the kitchen. She lit a single lamp before going to collect her coat and bonnet. With Gideon gone, the barn chores, twice a day, were solely her responsibility again. She opened the door, taking a deep breath before the evening's cold stole the last of the warmth from her.

She gasped when she saw a light on in the barn. Ignoring the patches of ice, she ran toward the barn and threw open the door. She scanned inside. Gideon! Where was he?

Her breath exploded out of her when she saw her brother bending to wash a cow before he milked her. The door slammed behind Rosie, and he glanced up. His smile was a sad one.

He put his hand on the cow's back as Rosie walked toward him. "I thought you could use some help this evening, Rosie."

"*Ja*, I do." She dampened her dry lips. "So Gideon told you he was leaving?"

"He stopped by and asked me to take over the chores for you."

"For how long?" Hope started to rise in her heart.

"He said he'd let me know."

She turned away, not wanting to cry in front of her brother. When his hands settled on her shoulders, she raised her chin to keep her tears from falling. She longed to throw herself into his arms as she had when she was a *kind* and had tumbled, scraping her knee. He'd always been there to offer her comfort.

Until he wasn't any longer.

Just like Eddie.

Just like Gideon.

Wrenching herself away from him, she said, "This is kind of you, Joel, but I can handle the chores myself."

"Don't be stupid, Rosie!"

She faced him, not daunted by his stony expression. She guessed her own was identical. "Don't call me stupid! I may have been, but I'm learning the only one I can depend on is myself. I don't lie to myself."

"You don't? Even about the *kind* growing under your heart? It seems to me you've been doing everything you can to keep that a secret. I don't know why."

"You don't?" She fired his own words back at him. "Can't you see there are already too many rumors about me and Eddie? I don't want to cause more."

"This wouldn't be a rumor. It would be glad tidings you and Eddie have been given the family you wanted."

She shook her head. "You know that won't be all that's said."

"What do you care if someone speculates there must be

a reason you haven't told anyone?" He put his hands on her shoulders again. "Remember the rumors going around in the fall that I was a drug dealer? I never sold drugs. Never. That was a rumor started by Lewis Philbrick." Rosie's shock at the name must have been on her face because he said, "I guess Grace has mentioned him to you."

"She has, and so have other people. Everyone was talking about the man who hung around the school last fall and tried to involve Grace's nephews in his schemes."

"Schemes sounds like fun and games, Rosie. Philbrick isn't either. He's an evil man. More evil than you can imagine. Stalking a couple of kids is the least of his crimes."

She marveled at her brother's self-restraint. He was furious Lewis Philbrick had frightened Grace's nephews. Years ago, when Joel had been a teenager, he would have flown off in a fury to get vengeance on anyone who threatened his sisters or his friends. A life of turning the other cheek hadn't been for him. Now, though he intended to live a plain life, he had to fight his own instincts to protect those he loved.

Why hadn't she seen the battle waging inside him? It wasn't so different from the one she fought each day. He was grappling with his past and grasping for his future while he walked a tightrope of expectations in his present. She was trying to escape the tentacles of her past, the questions that could only be answered by her dead husband. They wove around her like a smothering vine, keeping her from envisioning any future as she struggled against those invisible bonds to get through each day.

"But they are safe now," she whispered.

"No one is safe. Philbrick hasn't left the area. I'm sure of it. I don't know what he's up to, but he doesn't care whose life he destroys. That's where he's different from me." His voice deepened with grief. "My goal when I was on the other side of the fence was to destroy my life, not others'."

"I didn't know."

"I know you didn't, but you do now. You know you're strong enough to stand up to whatever fools gossip about. You've got your family and your friends and God. That's a powerful army safeguarding the truth, Rosie, and safeguarding you."

She ached to believe him, as she wanted to believe Iva. Her heart whispered she could never find healing for it until she did. She hoped she was brave enough to try.

Chapter Twenty

"He's home! Our boy is home!"

Instead of stiffening as he usually did when he walked into the front door of the stone farmhouse, Gideon threw his arms around the women surging toward him. He planted his feet, knowing they could knock him to the floor with their exuberance. Hands grasped his, pulling him in different directions.

"Don't tear me apart," he said with a laugh. It was a tired laugh because he'd dragged his problems with him every step of the way from Bliss Valley. Now he was home.

Or what had been home. He wasn't sure where home was any longer.

He looked across the room to where his *mamm* stood, watching the enthusiastic greetings of the rest of the women in the household. Her face was impassive. Why was she remaining apart when everyone else was greeting him? He'd thought she'd be the most excited for him to return home.

Gideon took a step toward her but halted when two of his *aentis* linked their arms through his. At the same time, *Gross-*

mammi Wingard, the taller of his two *grossmammis* who both lived under the family's roof, announced, "Sit down, boy." When he moved toward a chair by the wood stove, she banged her cane on the wood floor like a queen about to make a decree. "No, no, not there. In the kitchen. We're about to have our supper."

How could he have forgotten in such a short time away how early his *grossmammis* insisted on them eating their evening meal? It was weird returning to the house where he'd grown up. On one hand, it felt as if he'd never left, but on the other, things that had been commonplace before now left him feeling disoriented.

He'd been changed by his time in Bliss Valley, but life had continued on here in its unchanging pattern. Looking around, he wondered how what was once so familiar could have been overlaid in his mind by the comfort of Rosie's house. It was strange not to have to step between her two quilt frames, which claimed most of the living room.

But things *had* changed in the farmhouse. He let the conversation flow around him as he looked at the kitchen. He didn't remember the second row of pegs by the back door. Low ones that would be just the right height for his nieces and nephews. The tablecloth was different, too. *Grossmammi* Bawell had been reluctant to get rid of the yellow-and-white-checkered cloth that she asserted made the kitchen always look as if it were filled with sunshine while *Grossmammi* Wingard had complained about how it was impossible to clean. And the old cast-iron teakettle had been replaced by a steel one with a copper bottom.

Small changes he might not have noticed right away if he'd been living in the house were like slaps across the face, each one a reminder of how foolish he'd been to expect everything to remain the same.

One thing hadn't changed, though. The women took seats along the sides of the table and left the chair at its end to him. It had pleased him at first to lead grace, then it had riled him because they'd assumed he was ready to be the man of the household. He'd gotten tired of being told he needed to do a man's job when he was a boy trying to figure out what God wanted him to become.

Looking back, he could see the women in his life had been trying to prepare him for what would be expected of him for the rest of his life. Exactly as Rosie was with Braelynn, guiding her.

Learning with love.

It was just that simple.

"You lead us in grace, Gideon." *Grossmammi* Wingard frowned at the others as if daring them to countermand her command.

"It would be my honor, *Grossmammi*," he said, bowing his head.

He had a long list of things to be grateful for, most especially having Rosie and Braelynn in his life. Were they still part of his life? He'd left without saying anything to Rosie. Only Braelynn's intrusion had led to him saying goodbye to her.

Had he been wisely cautious or a stupid coward while driving his horse out of the lane as fast as possible? If he'd faced Rosie, she could have told him she was serious about wanting him off her farm. He couldn't have risked that.

Well, there was his answer. He was a coward.

Clearing his throat when he realized he might have let the silent prayer go on longer than the others expected, Gideon raised his head to see *Grossmammi* Bawell reaching for the biscuits before *Grossmammi* Wingard could. Neither woman would admit she was competitive with the other, but everyone in the house had witnessed the contest for years. *Grossmammi*

Wingard picked up the applesauce beside the biscuit platter, smiling as if she'd been going for that.

The meal was like every other one he'd had under the family's roof. The women, except for *Mamm* who seemed focused on her meal, tried to bring him up to date on the latest gossip in the plain community and among their *Englisch* neighbors. Smiling upon hearing about new *bopplin* and looking somber when told about how the construction along Old Philadelphia Pike was causing trouble for everyone, he was amazed when he heard that the bishop who'd been trying to force baptism on young people had announced he was moving.

"Nobody is sorry to see him go," *Grossmammi* Wingard said.

For once, his *mamm* didn't look horrified at her *mamm-in-law's* plainspoken pronouncements. *Mamm* nodded and so did the others around the table. The conversation turned to which of their ordained men might be chosen by the lot to replace the bishop.

Gideon listened as he tried to clean his plate. More food appeared on it as soon as he'd eaten half of what was already there. *Grossmammi* Bawell acted as if he hadn't had a single decent meal since he'd left.

"I've sampled your cooking skills," she said in a chiding tone. "You put the plain in plain food."

He smiled and patted her vein-lined hand. Neither of his *grossmammis* would stop trying to run his life, but he now realized that was part of the price one paid for being loved. Rosie had taught him that, along with so many other things. "I'll never be the cook you are, *Grossmammi*, but I've managed."

She shook her head. "A growing boy like you needs more than a simple soup or stew. *Ach*, I wish you'd have let us know you were coming home. I would have made some of your favorite cookies. I know you don't bake."

"No, I don't, but Rosie does."

Oh-oh! He saw his *grossmammis* and *aentis* sit a little straighter as their eyes zoomed in on him as if they were using Rosie's telescope. He didn't have to read their minds or have them speak their thoughts to know they were wondering about Rosie and his relationship with her. He almost told them that any inquisition would be a waste of time. He knew his feelings for Rosie, but wasn't sure of hers for him. She'd kissed him, and she'd kicked him out of her life. If he'd told her how his heart longed to belong to her...

He halted that thought. He didn't want to be like Calvin and LaVern, pushing her into a corner so soon after her husband's death.

Digging into the noodles as if he had nothing else on his mind but filling his stomach, Gideon gave one-word answers until the women realized he wasn't going to say anything else. He knew they'd get together after the meal to discuss how to get every tidbit of information out of him.

"Gideon," *Mamm* said as she rose from the table. She didn't add anything else, but he stood, too.

Neither of them spoke as *Mamm* led the way upstairs to the small sewing room that was her retreat from her extended family. She'd opened the door to him often when he was a little boy, welcoming him in after school so he could tell her about his day. It had been a special place that they shared as their family grew and grew to fill every other corner of the house.

Mamm's sewing room had shelves to hold fabric and a sewing machine that resembled the one Rosie used to make clothes for Braelynn. His own clothing had come from this one, made by *Mamm*'s skilled and loving hands.

Pulling out the chair near the sewing machine's table, *Mamm* motioned for him to bring another in. He found one in the bedroom that had been his. It still was his, he realized, as he looked around. Though his two cantankerous *grossmammis* disliked sharing a room, neither had moved into his.

"Were you so sure I'd be back?" he asked as he set the chair next to where *Mamm* sat.

"Back? *Ja.* Back to stay? No." She put her hand on his arm and patted it as she had when he was no older than Braelynn. "I saw your joy when you left to open your business, Gideon. Where is that joy now?"

Trust *Mamm* to cut right to the source of his pain! She saw parts of him nobody else did, looking at him with love's eyes. Nobody else but Rosie, who hadn't been fooled by the walls he'd raised to hide his feelings.

"My joy is back in Bliss Valley," he replied, knowing it was senseless to be anything but honest.

"Tell me."

He did, the words falling from his lips and his heart faster and faster until he could barely keep up with his own story. *Mamm* listened, her hands folded on her lap.

When he'd finished, he felt drained as if relating his experiences had torn down every defense he had and washed him free of pretense. What was left was the realization that he'd returned to Smoketown because he didn't want to cause Rosie more pain. If making her happy meant he had to leave her, that was what he had to do.

"It sounds as if you've been a blessing to her, Gideon," *Mamm* said with quiet compassion.

"She's been a blessing for me."

"I heard that." She smiled as she put her hand to the center of her chest. "I heard it in my heart. So what are your plans now?"

"Plans?" He'd made a lot of different plans for Rosie and him. Most had been dashed by reality.

"I know you, son. I know how you like to have everything

planned out. I can't believe you don't have plans for you and Rosie."

"I did."

"So…?"

I'm tired of secrets. Everywhere I turn, I'm surrounded by secrets. The agony in Rosie's voice reverberated in his mind, and he knew he'd never forget it, no matter how far he tried to run.

"Each one has fallen apart."

"Why?"

"You don't ask simple questions."

Mamm shrugged. "What's so complicated? Isn't it as simple as if you love her or you don't?"

"It might be if she weren't so newly a widow and had the responsibility for an abused *kind*."

"The timing may not seem right to you, but it must seem right to God because He brought you into her life now. God has plans for us we can't see. Those plans may not make any sense to us, but they do to Him."

"Is that how you felt when He brought your *mamm* and *Daed's mamm* to live with you?"

Mamm smiled. "I see that decision as proof God has a *gut* sense of humor, and He wishes me to have one as well." Her voice grew serious. "Now I can also see how lonely it must have been for them after your *grossdawdis* died. I was blessed to have your *grossmammis* here when it was my turn to become a widow. They've shown me there is a life to be had after you lose the love of your life."

"But you never remarried."

"I never met a man who was willing to take on me, your *grossmammis* and your *aentis*."

"And my sisters and me."

She chuckled. "*Ja.* We came as a package deal. But, son,

God has opened a door for you, and all you need to do is step through it."

"You're right." From the moment he'd left Smoketown, he'd believed he'd find a better life in Bliss Valley. He had, but not in the way he'd anticipated. He'd thought he was going there to build a business, and God had given him the chance to build a life with Rosie and Braelynn. Instead of telling Rosie the truth, he'd kept his love for her a secret. He laughed at his own foolishness.

"What's funny?"

"*Mamm*, you're right, God has a sense of humor. How else do you explain I had to come back to this house of matchmakers to realize they've been right all along when they told me what I need is a family of my own?"

Rosie poured cold cereal into Braelynn's favorite bowl. She hadn't slept much last night. Each time she closed her eyes, she saw the betrayal on Gideon's face when she told him to leave.

She was here, and Gideon was...not. Was that what God had planned for them?

Pushing aside the disturbing thoughts, Rosie listened for Braelynn. When Rosie had come into the house from the barn where Joel had again helped with the chores, she'd been sure she'd heard the little girl walking around upstairs. Now silence.

The *kind* had had a tough day yesterday with Gideon's leaving. Rosie gave a terse laugh. It had been a tough day for both of them. Though tempted to let Braelynn sleep in, Rosie knew if she did, the little girl wouldn't go to bed at a reasonable time tonight.

Wiping her hands on her apron, she went toward the living room. She got as far as the doorway before she stopped and stared, not wanting to believe what was right in front of her eyes.

Destruction. Wanton destruction.

She'd intended to finish her quilt later this week. That wouldn't happen because the outer edges of the quilt were in shreds. Every stitch she had sewn was ripped, leaving the pattern no longer discernable.

Who?

Why?

The questions battered her skull as she took one tentative step forward, then another. She froze when her gaze shifted to the other quilt, the one she'd worked on along with the other Bliss Valley quilters. The one scheduled to be delivered to the fire department in time for the mud sale in two weeks. The eight-pointed star in the center had been incised in a ragged circle that left only tiny bits of the points remaining. Everything between the outer circle of the biggest star with its sixteen points and the inner square border of dark blue had been sliced away. It looked as if a sharp knife had been taken to the rest of the quilt, tearing away every bit of its beauty.

Putting her hands over her mouth to keep her gasp from escaping, she stared at the ruined quilts. Looking at them sent a piercing pain deep within her.

She knelt on the floor and picked up some torn pieces from the star quilt. Beneath them was the pinking shears with the yellow handle, which Braelynn had claimed for her own. Her shoulders slumped as she remembered the day she'd first let the *kind* use them. Their first real connection had been made while Braelynn selected scraps and made her first stitches. From there, the *kind* had begun to open up to her like a beautiful flower.

Now everything had taken an appalling U-turn.

Footsteps on the stairs brought Rosie's head around to see Braelynn coming down. The little girl held a paper bag, the bottom banging against each tread. Tight against her side was Cleo, her ragged mane draped across her elbow, and the plain girl doll.

Her gaze locked with Rosie's, and her face went as blank as the doll's. It was as if Rosie was looking at the unresponsive *kind* who'd eaten cookie after cookie the day she'd been abandoned in the kitchen.

No! Rosie wanted to cry. *I don't want us to go back to that day.*

Braelynn stepped off the lowest riser and didn't come any closer. Her eyes shifted once toward the quilting frame, but focused again on Rosie.

It was enough for Rosie to understand what the *kind* wasn't saying. "Did you do this, Braelynn?"

"*Ja.*" No emotion filled the little girl's voice.

Rosie stared, shocked. She hadn't expected Braelynn to reply in *Deitsch*, though the little girl used it more and more often. Nor had she guessed the *kind* would admit to destroying the quilts.

"You cut out the star in the middle?"

"*Ja.*" The *kind* was defiant, but it was a weak defiance.

"Why?" Rosie asked.

Braelynn shrugged, and her lower lip wobbled. She stared at the floor as she walked toward the kitchen.

Rosie jumped to her feet, steadying herself on the quilt frame before giving chase. Now wasn't the time for queasiness. Now was the time for helping Braelynn.

The little girl was reaching for the knob on the back door by the time Rosie entered the kitchen.

"Stop!" Rosie cried.

"Why? So you can yell at Braelynn?"

"You know what you did was wrong, ain't so?"

Braelynn lifted her chin, but was blinking to keep from crying. "This is it. Say it."

"This is what?" She grew more confused with each word the *kind* spoke.

"This is it. That's what Patsy said. She looked at the cat and his short whiskers, and she said, *this is it.* Then she brought Braelynn here."

"The cat had short whiskers?" she asked, confused what a cat had to do with Braelynn being left at her house.

"*Ja.*"

"Why?"

"Because Braelynn cut them." Pride sifted into the little girl's voice. "Braelynn didn't get scratched."

Rosie bit her lower lip to keep herself from smiling as she thought how furious the cat must have been and how quick Braelynn had to have been to evade its claws.

"You know cutting a cat's whiskers is wrong, ain't so? The poor cat needs its whiskers to let it know if it can get through a tight space. Without them, the cat might not be able to escape a dog chasing it."

"Really?" Braelynn looked uncertain.

"Patsy never explained to you why she was angry?"

Braelynn gave a shrug, but her lips quivered more. "Patsy was always angry. She didn't want Braelynn, and Braelynn didn't want her. Now it's your turn. Tell Braelynn to leave as you did Gideon."

She flinched. She couldn't halt herself. She'd lost her temper with Gideon, and now she was reaping the rewards of hiding behind anger. She hadn't wanted him to see how deep she hurt at the thought of Eddie killing himself and how horrifying it was to know that the time he'd struck her might not have been an accident.

Gideon was gone, and she didn't have any idea how to bring him back. She couldn't make the same mistake with Braelynn.

Stepping forward as cautiously as she would have approached

a frightened bunny, she resisted her yearning to put her arms around the *kind*. That might send the little girl fleeing out the door.

"You really believe I'm going to send you away?" she asked.

She nodded, gnawing on her lower lip.

"You're wrong." She knelt in front of Eddie's daughter. No, Braelynn wasn't Eddie's daughter any longer. She was Rosie's. Her precious daughter, who was loving and exasperating, often at the same time. "I'm never going to send you away."

"Even when Braelynn does something awful?"

"If *kinder* were sent away each time they did something wrong, there wouldn't be any in this whole county. Nor adults. Everyone makes mistakes. We forgive the mistakes. Remember? We did that for your *onkel* Joel."

"Not mistakes. On purpose."

Rosie sat on her heels, but didn't let her gaze shift from the little girl's. "Like putting salt in the sugar bowl and letting the chickens free?"

Again, Braelynn nodded. Her eyes filled with large tears. "*Ja.*"

"And the cows?"

"Braelynn didn't do that. You think Braelynn did, but Braelynn didn't. A bad man did."

Bad man? Rosie wanted to ask the *kind* to describe the man she was talking about, but it wasn't important right now.

"I believe you," Rosie said.

"You do?" Two large tears rolled down the *kind*'s cheeks.

"*Ja*, I do."

"Braelynn broke the toilet by yanking on the top. It made a mess in the bathroom."

Rosie nodded, realizing she'd forgotten about that.

"And Braelynn cut up the quilts."

The quilts! The thought of that made Rosie's heart lurch,

but not as much as she thought of the anger and frustration and pain the little girl must have been suffering.

"Now," Braelynn whispered, "you send Braelynn away like everyone else does."

Tears slammed into Rosie's eyes, falling before she could halt them. No wonder sweet Braelynn had tried to shut herself off from the world. The little girl believed, with *gut* reason, she'd only be with Rosie a short time, and then she'd be dumped on another stranger.

It all was suddenly clear. The steps forward when Rosie began to believe that Braelynn felt at home, and then the way Braelynn had retreated within herself, hiding under the quilt and keeping everyone away. The mischief that had become more than childish pranks. The longing in the little girl's eyes that had cut deep into Rosie's soul. How many times since Braelynn was a tiny infant had she been shunted aside, left with someone whose voice and touch were unfamiliar?

Framing the *kind*'s face with her hands, Rosie didn't want Braelynn to miss a single word she said. "Braelynn Mishler, if you never believe anything I say to you, believe this. There is nothing—*nothing*—you can do that would make me leave you. We are family. You and me."

"And Iva?"

"Most definitely, Iva is part of our family. Along with Alta and Erma and Joel. *Grossmammi* Beachy—"

"And Laurene and Naomi and Adam and Samuel and Mary Beth and Jared and Jesse and May and *Grossdawdi* Ephraim and Grace and Jonas and *Aenti*—"

Rosie drew the *kind* closer to hug before the little girl recited the names of everyone in the community. "We're blessed to have such a large and *wunderbaar* family."

"And Gideon, too?"

It took every bit of her willpower to keep her smile from

slipping. How was she going to explain to a *kind* what she didn't understand herself?

A shadow crossed Rosie, and she saw someone coming onto the back porch. Her heart shouted Gideon's name, but the sound never reached her lips as Calvin Hertzler shoved the door open. It bumped into Braelynn who stumbled forward with a cry. Catching the little girl, Rosie scowled.

"Be careful, Calvin!" she snapped as she stood, steadying the *kind*.

"Advice you need to take for yourself, Rosemary."

Only then did she notice he was sweating, though it was chilly outside. He glanced over his shoulder, then pushed farther into the house and closed the door.

"What are you doing?" she asked, pulling Braelynn to her.

He asked a question of his own. "Where's Gideon?"

"He's not here."

"I've heard he's tucked his tail between his legs and headed back to his *mamm*."

She didn't dignify his snide remark with an answer. Instead, she folded her arms in front of her and looked at him without blinking.

His eyes shifted first. "We need to talk. It's time you gave me an answer to my question."

"What question is that?"

He wiped sweat off his upper lip. "I've asked you to marry me, and you need to tell me you will. I'm tired of waiting around while you babysit Gideon Wingard. He's gone, and I'm here, and you're going to marry me."

"Have you been drinking?" She couldn't imagine any other reason for his outrageous behavior.

"We have."

"We?" She glanced back at the door. "You and LaVern?"

"Don't worry. He's not coming. He's too busy with the police."

Every word he said baffled her more. "Why is LaVern busy with the police?"

"Because someone tipped off the cops that he broke the quilt shop windows."

"No!"

"*Ja.*" He chuckled, the sound like a rasp grating on rusty steel. "He's confessed. He'd intended to buy the property but she beat him to it."

"So he thought he'd drive her away with vandalism?" She rolled her eyes. LaVern seldom thought about the consequences of his actions before he plunged in. Eddie had told her stories about saving his friend from his own foolishness more than once. But Eddie wasn't around to guide LaVern any longer. It shocked her to realize how many holes Eddie had left in their lives when he died.

Calvin said, bringing her attention back to him, "What a mess! I expect my house to be kept much neater than this."

She frowned at him as she led Braelynn by the hand out of the kitchen. She didn't want the *kind* hearing Calvin's presumptuous comments. After kissing Braelynn on the head and sending her upstairs to unpack, she waited until the little girl was out of earshot before she said, "I think you need to leave."

"I want an answer to my proposal before I do." Not giving her a chance to reply, he went on, "But I also came over because I wanted to give you a heads-up. The cops are asking questions again about Eddie's death."

"I know." She was relieved he'd changed the subject, but wished he'd leave. "They're still investigating Eddie's death. They don't believe it was an accident."

Calvin's shoulders slumped. "It wasn't."

"I know. I heard—"

"A rumor that Eddie committed suicide."

"You heard it, too?"

"I started it."

She reeled back a couple of steps, bumping into Braelynn's table. "Why?" she whispered, glad the little girl was upstairs, too far away to hear what was said by a man Eddie had considered a trusted friend.

"You wouldn't understand."

"What do you think I won't understand?" she retorted. "That you turned in one friend to the police while you lied about another one? That sums it up pretty well, ain't so? Get out of my house, and don't come back!"

He reached for her, but froze when a fist hammered on the front door. Before Rosie could react, it crashed open. An *Englischer*, dressed in a bright blue golf shirt and khakis beneath his black coat, strode in as if he owned the house. Looking at the torn quilts, he gave a humorless smile. His eyes narrowed when they focused on Calvin.

"You should have known there was no place you could hide, Hertzler," the *Englischer* growled.

Calvin's face became a strange greenish shade. "I'm not hiding. I'm visiting a friend."

"Who else is here?"

"Just her kid."

The man turned to Rosie. "Get her."

"Now, see here—"

Calvin seized her arm and twisted her to face him. "Do as he says! Now!"

Drawing her arm out of his grip, she said, "She's upstairs."

The *Englischer* motioned with his head for her to get Braelynn.

She was about to ask a question, but the unadulterated fear on Calvin's face dried her words in her throat. Going to the stairs, she put her hand on the newel post. She started up, then saw Braelynn at the top. The little girl ran down and clutched her hand, leaning against Rosie's skirt. Putting her other arm around the *kind*, Rosie stepped back to the table with the quilt draped over it. Her foot struck the trunk, and she stiffened. The *Englischer* wasn't paying attention to her or Braelynn.

Rosie glanced over her shoulder. The front door was ajar, and it wasn't far away. Could she get Braelynn out without the *Englischer* noticing? He was intent on Calvin who was cringing.

"Braelynn," she whispered, bending to the *kind*. "I've got a new game for you. I want you to run out the door and to the barn. Find *Schwatzi* and the rest of the litter. Hide with them until I come for you." Braelynn nodded, but before she could take a single step, Calvin let out a frightened gasp as the *Englischer* jabbed a finger against his chest.

The little girl held more tightly to Rosie's hand and hid her face when the man snarled, "Where's my money, Hertzler?"

"I—I—I—"

The man focused his snakelike eyes on Rosie. "Is this your family?" He didn't give Calvin a chance to answer. "What a pretty wife and daughter you've got! Wouldn't it be a pity if something bad happened to them if you don't pay me what you owe me?"

"She's not my wife. The kid's not mine, either, Mr. Philbrick."

Philbrick? Where had she heard that name before? Her mind was too frozen with fear to function.

"Then what are they doing at your house?" Mr. Philbrick asked in the same oily tone. "I thought you knew I like my private business to be private."

"It's not his house," Rosie said, surprising herself with her own bravado. "It's—"

"I asked him the question," snarled Mr. Philbrick. "Not you. I thought your women knew how to hold their tongues."

Calvin shot her a frantic glance.

Ach! Rosie bit her lip as she remembered when she'd heard the name Philbrick before. She and Joel had talked out on the side porch about Grace's nephews being stalked...by Lewis Philbrick.

A terror more powerful than any she'd ever experienced surged through her. *Dear Lord, keep us safe.* The prayer repeated over and over, coming from her heart that was crying out to God.

And to Gideon. Would her final words to him have been in anger? No, that wasn't how she wanted it to be. She needed to apologize, to tell him she blamed him for the very thing she was doing herself. Keeping secrets. Secrets she couldn't speak of.

Because she wasn't sure if she should be happy or sad when she thought of her *boppli.*

Because she feared Gideon, who'd made no secret of his determination to live his life free of obligations to others, would desert her and the *kinder.*

So she'd pushed him out of their lives before he could walk away on his own. She hadn't known she would regret every single second she'd lost with him.

A phone rang.

Rosie's head turned to the *Englischer* who was pulling a cell phone out of his pocket.

Calvin spun to face her again. "You've got to help me, Rosemary." His whisper cracked on every word. He glanced at the other man who seemed to be ignoring them as he did something on his phone.

"Help you?" she asked. "How?"

He ran a finger over his upper lip, which was again beaded with sweat. "You heard him, Rosemary. I need to pay him

off. Then I won't do business with him again. It's not worth
it. He's ruthless."

"He wants money. I don't have much, Calvin. Maybe twenty
dollars. That's all I've got in the house."

"Eddie had plenty, and he told me it was here. I know you
know where it is."

"You're right. It's right here."

"Where?"

"In my house and in my herd and in my fields. That's where
everything Eddie had went. He invested in our future together."

"You're wrong. Where have you hidden it?" He grasped the
quilt hanging over Braelynn's table and yanked it off. Coloring books went flying across the room like dying butterflies.

Rosie was shocked when Calvin cursed as he rammed his
foot against the trunk. It moved an inch, but no more. She'd
never heard a plain man speak so. Looking past him to the
Englischer, she shivered. That man was driving Calvin into
hysterics.

Forcing her voice to remain calm, she said, "Calvin, argu-
ing is silly. If there had been more money, Eddie would have
told me."

He gestured toward Braelynn who scowled at him. "You've
got proof right there that he wasn't as honest as you thought
he was."

"He told me he'd always take care of me and I'd never have
to worry about not having food to put on the table."

"Aha! There you go. He had money. I asked Eddie, and he
refused to help me, even with his last breath."

A horrible sickness bubbled into her stomach. "You were
with him as he was dying?"

"*Ja.*"

"LaVern, too?"

He shrugged or tried to. His shoulders looked as stiff as if he carried the whole auction house on them. "We started the day together, but LaVern wandered off."

"Giving you the opportunity to ask Eddie for a loan."

"*Ja.*" His mouth tightened. "You see whom I'm dealing with, Rosemary. I knew Eddie had enough money to pay off Philbrick."

"Eddie left me the farm. Nothing else." She glanced at the *Englischer* who was still on the phone. "Why do you owe him money?"

"A business arrangement that hasn't gone the way I'd hoped. I—"

Philbrick barked an order, and Calvin backed away from Rosie and Braelynn.

Rosie looked from one man to the other as Philbrick said, "Hertzler, you've had your chance. Give me my money. I don't want to make you watch your little lady friend and her kid pay for your incompetence."

"Don't hurt my Rosie!" Braelynn yelled, raising her fisted hands.

Rosie lowered the *kind*'s arms, wondering how many other times Braelynn had had to defend herself. Such a task was too much for a five-year-old. She wanted to hug the little girl, but didn't dare to take her eyes off Calvin and the *Englischer* who was walking toward them as if he owned them.

With a flash of horror, she realized Philbrick did own Calvin. The *Englischer* had sucked him into his scheme, whatever it was, never showing his vicious side until Calvin was enmeshed in his snare.

Beside her, Braelynn whispered, "I'm scared, Rosie."

"I'm scared, too." She tried to give the *kind* a smile, but failed. "But let me listen to them now."

"Braelynn help?"

"*Ja.* You can help by praying, *liebling.* Pray with all your might."

The little girl didn't ask what she should pray for, and Rosie didn't explain. She wasn't sure she could. It was clear from what the two men were talking about that they were involved in some illegal business together, and that business centered around the auctions at Calvin's barn. What had Calvin gotten himself into?

As if she'd asked that question, Calvin rushed over to her. She backed away, bumping up against the front door. She considered pushing it aside and running out, but halted when her gaze was caught by Philbrick's reptilian one.

Calvin grabbed her shoulders and gave her a sharp shake. "You've got to marry me."

"Calvin..."

"You've got to marry me, or—"

"Or what?" called a dear voice from behind her.

Gideon's voice!

She was torn between crying out to him to free them and telling him to get out before he was hurt. She didn't have a chance. The door slammed against the wall. She jerked Braelynn out of the way. Forms in dark uniforms pushed past her.

Philbrick ran toward the kitchen. More police officers raced into the house, trying to cut him off. One advanced on Calvin.

Scooping up Braelynn, she edged away one careful step at a time. When she bumped into a hard chest, she glanced over her shoulder.

"Gideon!"

His name came out in a rush of gratitude.

He took Braelynn from her, holding the *kind* in one arm and, as the little girl flung her arms around his neck, he held out his other hand to Rosie. She took it, knowing she never wanted to let it go.

Chapter Twenty-One

Gideon pulled Rosie out onto the porch. Not caring who saw, he wrapped his arms around her and Braelynn. He held them as he fought to take a steady breath. Had he inhaled since he'd driven toward the farm, determined to apologize to Rosie, and seen the police vehicles gathered just out of sight of the house? He doubted he had after he heard they were after someone in Rosie's house, someone who had hostages.

Gut sense had fled from his head. He'd left his wagon and Domino by the side of the road. Sneaking through the meadow, he'd reached the house. He'd never imagined he'd lead a dozen police officers inside, their guns drawn.

Something crashed in the house as he pressed his face into Rosie's disheveled hair. Something else shattered. Rosie winced against him, and he tightened his embrace.

"It's all right," he whispered against her *kapp*.

"I know." Another thud came through the open door. "It's just stuff. Nobody I care about is in there."

Braelynn looked back and whispered, "Cleo."

"She'll be okay," Gideon assured her as he set Braelynn on her feet. "She's a brave lion. Like you're a brave little girl."

Braelynn grinned. "Braelynn brave." Puzzlement ruffled her brow. "What's brave?"

Gideon grinned, something he hadn't thought he'd be able to do a moment ago. When Rosie chuckled, she stepped away to hug Braelynn. They froze when a gun fired.

He didn't think. He grabbed Rosie and Braelynn, yanking them off the porch. He pressed them into the dirt and snow by the steps, covering them with his own body as he prayed none of them would be hit.

More shots.

He heard Braelynn sobbing. He ached to comfort the *kind*. He didn't move. He didn't let Rosie or Braelynn move.

Shouts came from the house. Feet pounded on the stairs beside them. He didn't move. He didn't let the others move.

"It's safe," said a deep voice. "They're both in custody."

Gideon pushed himself up to sit in the snow. He helped Rosie sit, too, and they looked up as one at a man wearing a state trooper's uniform. Then her gaze turned to meet his own, and everything and everyone else vanished.

"You came back," she whispered.

"*Ja.*"

"Why?"

He started to answer, but paused when the trooper shifted his feet and cleared his throat.

"That's something," Gideon said, "I'll have to explain later."

He got to his feet. Rosie took Braelynn's hand and stood as gracefully as if nothing more exciting had happened than they'd invited the police to join them for a snack.

The trooper opened the door and motioned for them to come back inside. Gideon put his hand against Rosie's back as she and Braelynn led the way into the house. He was too aware of how the situation could have turned out differently.

He gasped when he saw the destruction in the living room. Two quilts lay in pieces on the floor amid their collapsed frames. Another quilt was thrown into a corner, and the table it'd been covering was tipped over on its side. The trunk beside it was at an odd angle, and gaping holes were visible on two sides. Had bullets hit it?

Two windows had broken panes, and he knew they'd been hit by whoever had been shooting. A hole in the wall between them was the focus of attention for two police officers.

"It's good," the trooper who'd brought them inside said, "that Philbrick is a lousy shot."

As Braelynn rushed forward to scoop up her stuffed lion and sat on the floor to make sure Cleo was unhurt, Gideon asked, "Calvin and Philbrick did this?"

"Not all of it," Rosie replied. "That's something *I* will have to explain later."

He would have asked another question, but a state trooper came over and introduced himself as Eric Knox. Rosie took a step back.

"It's okay, Mrs. Mishler," the trooper said.

"You're the one who took my brother away after church, accusing him of selling drugs."

He nodded. "Your brother helped our investigation of Philbrick and his web of dealers in the county. Now we've got Philbrick, and he's claiming we don't have a crime to pin on him. I don't know why some criminals talk like they're in a cut-rate gangster movie. He knows we've got plenty to charge him with. It'll be up to the district attorney which charges she wants to bring first. When I mentioned that to Philbrick, he shut his mouth other than to say he wants his lawyer."

"What about Calvin?" she asked.

Gideon's head swiveled to where Calvin was sitting at the kitchen table. "What's he doing here?"

"Another long story." Rosie looked at the trooper. "What will happen to him?"

"He's a friend of yours?" Trooper Knox asked.

"Not exactly, but he is part of our community."

He nodded. "His situation seems a little less cut-and-dry. I've already talked to your bishop about our suspicions of Hertzler's auctions being used to fence stolen goods and laundering cash."

"You knew?"

"We *suspected*. We need to go through the books and see what we can find. I've let Jonas know that. We'll be working with him and your other church leaders to keep them informed as the case goes forward."

"Excuse me," she said, walking into the kitchen.

Gideon ran after her. He didn't know what she planned to say to Calvin, but he didn't want her saying it alone.

"Tell me what happened to my husband," she said as she stopped in front of Calvin.

He raised his head, revealing a haunted expression. Glancing past her to the trooper, he said, "I asked Eddie for help. He told me I'd made my own trouble, and all he could do was give me advice. Advice that had worked for him when he got into trouble. Leave and not come back. Change my name. Change my life. Become someone else. Find a woman to marry to give you respectability and forget about everything and everyone in the past." He stared at the floor. "When he realized he'd said too much, he warned me not to repeat it to anyone. I said you deserved to know, and he told me I'd be sorry if I said a single word to you. Then I saw his hands shift on the gun. I thought he was going to shoot me. We fought for the gun. It went off. I think he pulled the trigger by accident, but he was struck. I panicked and fled." He looked at Rosie, his gaze imploring. "He was my friend. I knew his advice was *gut*, especially about finding a woman to marry. I chose you, Rosie."

"Then tried to intimidate me into marrying you so you could get your hands on the money you believed Eddie had."

"He did have it!" He sighed. "*Ja*, I tried to convince you to marry me. When you didn't agree, I decided to show you how much you needed a man around here."

"So you let my cows out?"

"They didn't get hurt." He frowned at Braelynn. "I got the idea from your brat."

"She's not a brat. She's a dear *kind*. My *kind*."

"Whatever. I wanted to get Philbrick off my back so I could forget about the past."

Gideon said, "Forgetting the past isn't any way to look to the future. Were you looking for the money you thought Eddie had when you trashed my shop twice?"

"I didn't do any damage." He glanced at the state trooper. "I thought Eddie might have stashed his money in that old shed." His lips twisted. "He didn't."

Trooper Knox put his hand under Calvin's elbow and brought him to his feet. "Come with us, Mr. Hertzler."

Braelynn wove a path among the police officers who were finishing their work. Holding up her toy, she announced, "Cleo is okay."

"*Ja.*" Rosie drew Braelynn into an embrace. "We're okay."

"Not Braelynn's tent," announced the little girl, wiggling free. "The table is tipped over. There's a big hole in the trunk. Sparkly thing on the floor, too. That mean man was mean to Braelynn and Rosie." She put her hands on her hips and glowered past them.

"Don't worry. The police have him in custody." Rosie ran her hand across the *kind*'s hair, trying to soothe her. "He won't hurt us now. Or ever. The police officers have taken him away."

Braelynn shook her head. "No, not that mean man. *That* one." She pointed to Calvin who was standing by the back door while the trooper checked something on his phone. Calvin hung his head as another trooper led him out the back door. "He made Rosie scared." She hesitated for a moment, then whispered, "Braelynn was scared, too."

Rosie hugged the *kind.* "I'm sorry you were scared, Braelynn."

"He wants to take Rosie away." She looked up at Gideon. "Don't let him do that!"

"I won't."

"Rosie says Braelynn never needs to go away."

His heart reinflated as he heard the certainty and delight in the *kind*'s voice. "I'm glad you're staying, Braelynn."

"Braelynn is happy, too." A sob burst from her. "Braelynn stays. Rosie stays. Don't let anyone take her away."

"I won't," he repeated. "I promise you, Braelynn, I won't let anyone take Rosie away from you."

"Amish people don't make promises," Braelynn said with a lopsided grin.

"Sometimes we do." He shifted his eyes toward Rosie. The ravages of fear lined her face, and he couldn't miss how her fingers trembled. "We make promises to God that we hold deep within our hearts. Promises about love."

"Braelynn loves Rosie."

Putting her hands over her mouth, Rosie whispered in amazement, "You do?"

"*Ja.*" The little girl grinned. "Rosie loves Braelynn, and Braelynn loves Rosie."

Gideon waited for one of them to say those same words to him, but they didn't. Rosie was called away to answer questions, and Braelynn went back to her table, setting it upright again. He was going to help her, but there were questions for him, too, as well as sharp words about being so *dumm* and potentially ruining the best chance the police had had in months to capture Philbrick. He knew they were right and accepted the dressing down without comment.

It was more than two hours later before one of the troopers came over to them to let Rosie know that they were leaving with their prisoners, and to inform her that she should plan to come to the station to give a written statement tomorrow.

"Me, too?" asked Gideon.

"That would be a good idea." He nodded to both of them, then walked out, closing the door and leaving them with the disaster in Rosie's living room.

The door reopened, and a different state trooper stuck his head past it. "Mrs. Mishler, there's a man out here who says he urgently needs to talk to you. Says he's your attorney. His name is Charles Satterfield, and he's saying he's got the information you've been looking for."

Rosie wasn't sure if she gasped or if Gideon did…or maybe it was both of them. The last time she'd talked to the lawyer they'd agreed he would search for any living members of Braelynn's *mamm*'s family. What had he discovered?

"I'll talk with him," Rosie said.

"Now?" Amazement filled Gideon's voice.

She glanced at Braelynn, then said, "Take Cleo upstairs and make sure…" She wasn't sure what else to say.

"Braelynn make sure Cleo is happy to be here," the little girl supplied.

"*Ja*. Do that." She smiled until the *kind* was out of sight up the stairs. "All right. I'll talk to Mr. Satterfield now."

The police officer nodded.

Gideon didn't say anything, but stepped closer to her as the door opened and an *Englischer* stepped into the house.

His dark hair was streaked with gray at his temples. He wore a navy suit with a bright red tie, and he carried a slim briefcase. His eyes focused on Rosie as if she were the only person in the room. "Mrs. Mishler?"

"*Ja.*"

"Are you able to speak with me now?"

"I can leave," Gideon said, "if you need to talk privately."

"Don't go, Gideon." Rosie grasped his sleeve, hoping the motion said what words couldn't at that moment. She resisted putting her hand against her side to make sure the *boppli* was safe after the morning's horrific events. If she did, the motion might pull her dress snugly across her belly, revealing the fact she hadn't shared with anyone other than her brother and Iva. "I can talk with you now, Mr. Satterfield. This is Gideon Wingard."

Mr. Satterfield nodded at Gideon, then looked past them. "Who is that?"

Rosie turned to see the little girl creeping down the stairs. Holding out her hand to the *kind*, she said, "This is my step-daughter, Braelynn Mishler."

The attorney smiled warmly at Braelynn. "You are a well-loved little girl."

Rosie's heart threatened to stop beating as fear stiffened every muscle. Beside her, Gideon's face grew taut. Did he fear as she did that the attorney's words meant that members of Braelynn's family had been found?

"Perhaps," the *Englischer* said, "you might want to read this, Mrs. Mishler, before we go any further." He set his briefcase on Braelynn's table and opened it. Pulling out a file folder, he handed it to her.

She should have thanked him for his kindness, but words had jammed in her throat. A *gut* thing, because her stomach was threatening to spew everything in it onto the floor.

She groped for the rocking chair. Gideon's hand on her arm steered her to it. When he started to step away, she said, "No! I want you to read this, too."

"If you're sure…"

"I am." She held his gaze, praying he understood she was talking about so many things other than what might be lying in wait in the folder.

He stepped behind her to read over her shoulder at the same time Mr. Satterfield walked into the kitchen to give them privacy to read what he already had. Not wanting to think why else he might have left, she opened the folder. A single page was inside the file. It contained a neatly typed note. Picking it up so Gideon could see the words, too, she read:

Dear Mrs. Mishler,

Thank you for having your attorney start the search that brought him to us. Your search is the answer to a prayer we've been praying for more than seven years because it was that long ago that our granddaughter, Madison, ran away.

Let us introduce ourselves. We are Gavin and Lee Nesbitt, and we raised Madison from the time she was twelve. Her parents couldn't care for her any longer because of their drug addictions. She saw too much and learned too many of the wrong things. We'd hoped we could help her see her life didn't have to be ruined as her parents' were. We thought she'd listened because she was a good teenager, never giving us a moment's worry.

Until she ran away two weeks before her high school graduation. We didn't hear anything from or about her until Mr. Satterfield contacted us. The news of her death is, as you must know, more painful than we can express. We'd always prayed she'd come to her senses and come home to us. Now we know that won't ever happen, though we plan to have her reinterred in our church's cemetery, so she can be with her parents again.

Rosie had to stop reading as tears blinded her. The anguish in the simple words was heartrending. Gideon's hand stroked her shoulder, and his fingers quivered, sharing that he was as moved by the letter as she was. Smaller fingers settled on her arm, and she looked at Braelynn.

"Rosie sad?" she asked.

"*Ja.*"

"Braelynn make better?"

She put the note on her lap and put her arm around the little girl. "You always make everything better."

The *kind*'s smile warmed the cold spot in her heart, and Rosie kissed the little girl's cheek. That seemed to satisfy Braelynn because she went back to the table and resumed gathering up the scattered toys.

Though she didn't want to, because she feared what the rest of the letter might say, Rosie picked up the letter and continued to read:

> *Mr. Satterfield tells us as well that our granddaughter has a daughter and that your late husband is her father. He let us know that Braelynn is living with you in your home, that you took her in when she was abandoned by one of our granddaughter's feckless friends. We know you are Amish, and we hope you will be willing to do as we must ask.*

Rosie gulped as she reached the bottom of the page, unable to turn it over to see what the Nesbitts wanted. What else could Braelynn's great-grandparents be asking for other than to have custody of her?

"Don't fear the worst until you have to face it," Gideon said from behind her.

She reached up and put her hand over his on her shoulder.

Giving it a gentle squeeze, she took a deep breath before she flipped the page over.

> *We want to be part of our great-granddaughter's life, but our health problems prevent us from being good parents to such a young child. If you are agreeable, we would like to be able to come and visit Braelynn for an afternoon each month. She's all we have left of our granddaughter, and we pray that getting to know Braelynn will offer us some solace.*
>
> *No matter how you respond, we want you to know we are grateful that you have welcomed Braelynn into your home and into your heart. We hope we can thank you in person, but the decision is yours. You know better than we do what would be best for Braelynn.*

It was signed with the Nesbitts' names.

As she lowered it to her lap, she glanced at where Braelynn was stacking her coloring books next to her plain dolls. The little girl's hair had escaped almost completely from the net that was supposed to hold it in place, and a bit of dirt was on the tip of her nose. She looked like a happy, content *kind*, and Rosie knew she couldn't ever ask for more for Braelynn.

Coming to her feet, she held out her hand to Gideon. He took it as they turned to see Mr. Satterfield come back into the living room.

"Do you have any questions?" the attorney asked.

"No," she said, "but I do have an answer for the Nesbitts. Please let them know that we'd be happy to have them visit Braelynn whenever they wish."

"I will let them know, and I'll keep you apprised of any formal custody agreements that may be needed." He smiled at them. "I like days when I can deliver happy news. If you have any questions—any at all—let me know." He bid them a *gut* day before going out the front door.

Gideon said nothing as Rosie went to close the door behind the attorney. He was thrilled for her and for Braelynn. But what of him? How did he fit into this new family? Did he fit at all?

When she turned and faced him, she rubbed her hands together. He noticed they were shaking. The rage he'd felt when he heard Calvin relate what had happened the day Eddie died welled up in him again, but he pushed it aside. Being angry wouldn't change anything. Neither Calvin nor Eddie would be bothering Rosie any longer. The tale of what had happened at the auction barn would soon be spread far and wide by LaVern, who must be furious that his erstwhile friend had sent the police after him. Could the auction business survive if Calvin didn't have to repay what he owed Philbrick?

"It's going to be a real mess," he said more to himself than to Rosie. "The people who have been robbed will want their items back or, at least, the money that was paid for them."

She pushed away from the door and bent to pick up some pieces of the torn quilts. "The police will have to find the people who were robbed and the people who bought the items."

"How?"

"From what Eddie said, Calvin has always kept very *gut* records."

"Even for his crimes?"

"We can pray so."

Again, he was overwhelmed by her amazing faith that God would make everything right. And why shouldn't she? Hadn't God brought Braelynn into Rosie's life at what was, in retrospect, the perfect moment?

"So what happened to the quilts?" he asked.

"Nothing that can't be repaired." She smiled at Braelynn. "Ain't so?"

"Is so!" The little girl grinned and jumped to her feet. She hugged her toy and Rosie at the same time.

"I don't understand," Rosie said, as she dropped the torn fabric onto the sofa, "why Calvin believed Eddie had any money to lend him. What little Eddie had when he died was set aside to pay our property taxes. If you hadn't come along and rented from me, there might be an upcoming real estate auction sign by the road now."

"Eddie must have led him to believe there was money or at least something valuable. Somewhere."

"Like this?" asked Braelynn, holding up her hand.

Gideon stared at the diamond ring on the *kind*'s small palm. It was a small stone in a simple setting. He'd seen similar ones on *Englisch* women's left hands and knew they were given as a gift when a man asked a woman to marry him.

"Where did you find *that*?" he asked.

Braelynn pointed at the old trunk that had been part of her quilt-covered den. The two bullet holes were about the size of the *kind*'s palm, large enough for a ring to fall out.

"It must have been inside the trunk!" Rosie exclaimed.

"We need to get it open," he said as he took the ring and balanced it on his own palm, "and see what else is there."

"Not Braelynn," the little girl announced. "There might be spiders and rats and dinosaurs in it."

"I'm sure there aren't." Rosie smiled.

Braelynn picked up her box of crayons. "Be careful." She held out a bright red crayon. "Use this if a dinosaur gets too close. Dinosaurs don't like red."

"*Danki.*" Rosie kissed the top of the little girl's head and sent her to get some cookies for a snack. The *kind* raced into the kitchen.

Gideon didn't bother to ask how or why Braelynn thought that as he knelt beside the trunk. "The whole thing is askew, but it's still locked. I'm going to have to pry it open."

"Go ahead."

He motioned her away as he picked up a section of her quilt frame. "Stay back. In case something pops and flies through the air."

He threaded the length of wood through the loosened lock. He pressed hard. The lock flew open. Something struck the ceiling and ricocheted into a corner.

"It missed me," she said when he glanced over his shoulder with concern.

"*Gut.*" He lifted the top of the trunk and pulled out the tray that concealed the larger area below. Stepping back, he gave her room to reach into the trunk, which was filled with *Englisch* clothing. An elegant watch was on top. She lifted the steel watch out and read the name on its dial.

"'TAG Heuer Aquaracer.'" She looked at Gideon. "Do you know that brand?"

"No, but it looks like a fine and expensive watch."

Putting it on the table, she moved aside the clothing. He saw a dark suit and some ties as well as ripped T-shirts with appalling images of demons and other creatures on them.

He picked up one of the latter. "This goes along with what Adele told me when I talked to her at the Central Market. She said Eddie was in a heavy metal band. They wear stuff like this."

"I think I'd be foolish to ask how you know that."

He gave her a strained smile. "Some of my *Englisch* friends during our teens liked that kind of music and thought I would, too."

She reached past the clothing. Something crackled, and she drew out a large manila envelope. It bulged in several spots. She stared at it. He guessed she wanted to look inside at the same time she wanted to toss it in the trunk and pretend she'd never seen it, because whatever was inside could change her life.

Again.

"Let me." Gideon took the bulging envelope from her. He drew in a sharp breath after he'd opened it and looked inside.

A hundred dollar bill sat on top of a stack of money too thick for him to hold with one hand. As he riffled through, he discovered every single bill was the same denomination. He handed the envelope back to her and searched in the trunk.

Raising his head, he said, "There are six more envelopes in there along with legal papers that look like deeds for properties in Delaware and New York." He tapped the envelope she held. "*This* must be the reason Calvin thought he had a chance to borrow money from Eddie."

"But how would Calvin know about it when I didn't?"

Rosie stared at Gideon, hoping he had a *gut* answer to her question. Her head throbbed as she tried to take in the astounding sight in front of her. She'd wondered how many more secrets Eddie had kept from her, and now she was learning. She put her hand over her *boppli*. Would Eddie ever have been honest with her?

Gideon smiled without humor. "You're asking me something I can't answer, Rosie. You'll need to ask Calvin that."

"No, *danki*. If I never speak to him again, that will be a blessing."

"You need to mention what we've found to the police when you give your official statement, so they can include it in their questioning. However, I suspect it won't make any difference. They're going to be more interested in Calvin's and Philbrick's accounts than what Eddie had. They'll have people going through both his and Philbrick's books with a fine-tooth comb, and I wouldn't be surprised if they find a lot of lice and fleas popping out in every direction."

"What a horrible image!" She laughed, surprising him.

And pleasing him, she realized.

Why did you come back? she wanted to ask. *Are you back to stay?*

She restrained from speaking as he held up another envelope. This one was padded. When he handed it to her, she opened it and found what looked like paychecks. A dozen of them. The dates were a year ago, and the checks had been issued by a construction company near Watertown, New York.

"Did you notice the name on the checks?" he asked. "They were made out to Edward Michelin."

"Michelin sounds like Mishler."

"And he did tell Calvin to go somewhere and change his name."

She handed him the checks to examine as she pulled a small box out of the envelope. Flipping it open, she said, "It's another diamond ring."

He whistled as he tilted the box so it caught the light. "A ring with a much bigger diamond. It must be worth a lot of money." Handing it back to her, he asked, "You've never seen it before?"

She shook her head. "I thought all of Eddie's money had gone into buying this farm." She closed the box and reached into the envelope again. She pulled out a smaller envelope. When she opened it, a gold necklace fell out.

It resembled the locket Braelynn wore. Like the little girl's, it was heart-shaped, but instead of a cross on it, there was the image of what looked like interlocking rings.

"Wedding bands," she breathed. "Like the *Englisch* wear."

Gideon put the jewelry box next to the watch on the floor. "If you want to hear my guess—"

"I would because my brain seems to be stuck in neutral."

"I suspect Eddie was born and raised Amish. Watertown is

in northern New York. There are Amish in that area. Maybe he was born among them. Or maybe he did what he told Calvin to do and fled from his home to somewhere far away. From what you've told me, he knew how to speak *Deitsch* and was familiar with our ways of worshiping."

"He was."

"But this jewelry doesn't belong to a plain man. It didn't belong, either, to a man who played in a rock band. This belongs to a woman."

She opened the locket. It contained two pictures set side by side. One was Eddie, and the other photo looked like Braelynn's *mamm*.

"How did Eddie come to have it?" she asked herself as much as Gideon.

"Maybe he'd intended to ask her to marry him, and he didn't get a chance." His face grew long. "Or she might not have wanted to marry him if he was abusive." He entwined his fingers with hers. "I'm sorry, Rosie. I shouldn't have said that."

"Whether you say it or not, it doesn't change what happened to Madison or to me." She set the necklace next to the jewelry box and the envelopes. Coming to her feet, she looked at them. "There's enough money to keep the farm going for a while. As for the jewelry and the deeds, I'll have to figure out what to do with them. It's Braelynn's legacy."

"You could always sell them and put the money away for her to have a home of her own when she's ready for it." He picked up the necklace. "Everything but this. I know it sounds sappy and sentimental, but if she were my *kind*, I would want her to have some sort of physical legacy from me."

She took the necklace and slipped it into her apron pocket. "I agree." Putting the rest of the items back in their envelopes, she laid them on top of the clothing. "I hope Eddie can rest in peace now."

Gideon stood, too. "What about you? Can you be at peace now?"

She looked at where Braelynn was stretched out on the kitchen floor, surrounded by crumbs and coloring a picture of a large rooster. Delight filled her heart as she imagined so many days and years ahead when the little girl would be part of her daily life. Her fingers settled on her abdomen. Of *their* lives. She lowered her hand away as her gaze moved to Gideon.

"Why did you come back?" she asked, unable to keep the question silent.

"Because I couldn't stay away. When you told me to go, did you really mean it?"

"I was angry." She couldn't hide behind half-truths any longer. "Not at you, but at me. I should have admitted that, but lashed out at you instead."

"You had *gut* reason to be upset. I was like a paddleball, bouncing here and there. I was telling myself I wanted nothing to do with anyone until I found out what God wanted for me. Yet, I kept interfering in your life."

"You never interfered."

"No? I remember you mentioning that more than once."

She gave him a sheepish grin. "You're right. I was overwhelmed, too, but I wanted to prove to everyone that, no matter what, I could handle everything on my own. I was so proud and relieved when I rented you the building, because I believed that would solve my problems with money so I could concentrate on making the farm a success."

He edged closer and curved his hand along her face. She let him tilt it toward his as he said, "I've admired your persistence in the face of astounding odds from the first time I met you. That admiration has deepened to much more. Now, all I want is for you to be happy, and I need to know if you are happier when I'm here or when I'm gone."

She didn't hesitate. "I'm happier when you're here. I've been miserable since you left."

He glanced around the room and gave her a cock-eyed grin. "That's pretty obvious."

"I'm being serious."

"I know you are." He took her hands and sandwiched them between his. "And I'll be just as serious. I'm in love with you, Rosie. I came here to escape my family's matchmaking, because I thought the only thing that was important to me was building my business. I was wrong. The only things important to me are you and Braelynn."

"Braelynn?" chirped the little girl as she jumped to her feet and raced to them.

Rosie smiled when Gideon picked up Braelynn and swung her around until they both were giggling.

"What do you think?" Gideon asked as he set the *kind* down.

"About what?" Braelynn asked.

"About letting me be part of your family."

The little girl's eyes widened. "Braelynn has a family?"

"*Ja.*" He winked at the little girl as he said, "You and Rosie are a family." His gaze softened as it met Rosie's, and she knew he was letting her choose when to tell Braelynn about her great-grandparents. Not today when so many horrible things had happened. That wasn't how she wanted Braelynn to remember learning about them. He took her hands and brought them to his lips, kissing first one, then the other. "Let me be a part of it. The three of us."

"The *four* of us," she said, steeling herself for his response.

His brows rose. "Four?"

"I'm pregnant." She drew her hands out of his and smoothed her apron over the bump in her abdomen. "If you don't want the obligations of raising another of Eddie's *kinder*, I understand."

"Clearly you don't." He smiled at Braelynn who was listening, watching their faces with her intense gaze. "Why would you think I would love one of Eddie's *kinder* and not another?" He brushed the back of his fingers against her cheek. "How soon will the *boppli* be joining us?"

"Probably April."

"So, Rosemary Beachy Mishler, will you do me the honor of becoming Rosemary Beachy Mishler Wingard? We can arrange a quiet wedding in a few weeks."

She shook her head. "I can't."

"What?" Dismay blossomed in his eyes.

"I need to mourn Eddie for the full year before I can think of remarrying. It's what I said I would do, and I'm not going back on my word."

"You still love him that much?"

She closed her eyes, unable to bear the pain on his face. "I love the man I believed him to be. I always will." She opened her eyes again and gazed upon the face she loved more than any other. "But he's the one who broke my heart into so many pieces I didn't think it could be put back together. I was wrong. You are the most exasperating man I've ever met, but you are also the kindest and the funniest and the dearest." She took his hand and pressed it over her heart. "You have healed my heart, Gideon, when I didn't think that would be possible. Just keep asking me to marry you in a few weeks."

"I will until the day you say *ja*." He wrapped her in his arms and lowered his mouth toward hers. In the moment before he claimed her lips, he whispered, *"Ich liebe dich."*

She wasn't surprised when Braelynn flung her arms around them and said, "Braelynn loves you, too."

Gideon gave Rosie a quick kiss before he placed another one on the top of the *kind*'s head. He laughed as the little girl danced around them. There would be time for much more delicious kisses. Plenty of them.

And she couldn't wait to savor each and every one.

Epilogue

Rosie edged the step stool closer to the wall set between two windows that offered a view of the blooming crab tree in the yard. The clumps of blossoms were pink-and-white balls of springtime color. "Try that."

Clambering up it, Braelynn held the wall hanging they'd quilted together against the fresh light yellow paint. "How's this?"

"Maybe a bit higher." Gideon took the top of the rectangle pieced together from the fat quarters Iva had given Rosie. He adjusted the left side an inch. "There. Perfect."

"I agree," Rosie said as she looked at the wall hanging and the matching quilt waiting to be put into the crib for her *boppli*. Iva had been right when she'd said Rosie would find the perfect use for the fat quarters. The bunches had given her the right amount of material to make the two pieces. She and Braelynn had used torn strips from Rosie's ruined quilt to bind them.

The quilt made by the quilting circle had been pieced back together. Instead of quilting the outline of the stars, Rosie and her friends had created a pattern of concentric circles that hid the damage. The quilt had been a big hit at the mud sale and brought one of the highest final bids.

Since then, no foods had been switched or animals released or quilts destroyed. Braelynn had begun to believe the assurances Rosie and Gideon offered her daily. Her home was on the farm, and she wouldn't have to leave until she was grown and ready to make a home of her own.

Rosie, with Gideon's and Joel's help, had arranged for the sale of the diamond rings and the properties that Eddie had purchased. The resulting funds were far more than she expected, so she donated half of the money to Carly Layden's shelter for homeless and abused women. It was enough to be able to add four additional rooms onto the old house. The new wing would be known as the Madison Nesbitt Annex. Rosie planned to take Braelynn to visit once she was old enough to understand how hard her *mamm* had tried to protect her from the worst parts of her life.

The little girl giggled as she helped hold the quilt hanger in place while Gideon hammered nails into each end of it. "Braelynn—I like the quilt, too."

In the past couple of weeks, Braelynn had begun to stop referring to herself by name. It was, Rosie prayed, a sign the little girl understood she was home to stay, that she didn't need to use her name each time she spoke because she wasn't among strangers any longer.

"When *Grossdawdi* and *Grossmammi* Nesbitt get here this afternoon, they'll see the hard work you've done, Rosie," Gideon said as he stepped back and admired their handiwork.

"I couldn't have done it without Braelynn." Rosie held out her hand as the little girl jumped from the stool.

Braelynn grasped it. "Isn't it pretty, *Mamm*?"

Would she ever not smile each time Braelynn called her that? Rosie squeezed Braelynn in a big hug.

"Almost as pretty as my lovely girls," Gideon said with a wink.

"If you think a tugboat is pretty." Rosie clasped her hands over her distended belly. Warm days had arrived as they turned the calendar over to April, and everything around her was blooming. The *boppli* was scheduled to be born in two weeks, but Rosie wondered if either she or her *kind* could wait that long.

Just as she wondered how she was going to wait until September to become Gideon's wife. They planned to be married during the same service as Joel and Grace. The three *mamms* along with Gideon's *grossmammis* and Iva had taken over the details, discussing how many cakes should be made and if apple pie or peach pie should be served for the evening meal. Rosie had been so busy making clothes for the *boppli* and a rapidly growing Braelynn that she'd let her sisters pick out the fabric for her light blue wedding dress.

"Or one of those super cargo vessels." He laughed and ducked as she tossed an unfolded diaper at him.

"Do you say such nice things to all the women?"

"No," he said, locking his hands behind her back, "only to the one woman who holds my heart." He brushed his lips against hers, and she softened against him.

A sharp kick from within made Gideon chuckle as he released her. "I get the message. Leave *Mamm* alone!"

She put her hand on the small of her back and grimaced. "I think this one is trying to kick his or her way out."

"His," Braelynn said at the same time Gideon said, "Her."

For the past three months since Gideon had returned to the farm, the little girl and the man Braelynn now called *Daed* had debated whether Rosie was having a girl or a boy. The little girl hadn't given up her mischievousness, but she helped Gideon around the house when Rosie needed to rest. They'd chosen names together.

"Be *gut*, little one," she said. "I don't know whether you're a boy or a girl, but you need to learn some manners."

"Be *gut*, Saul," Braelynn said.

Gideon shook his head. "Be *gut*, Hope."

"Will you two stop?" Rosie asked in mock dismay. "Whether it's Hope or Saul, we'll treasure this *boppli*. I want this *boppli* to know we must never give up on God and His blessings."

"Saul doesn't mean hope, ain't so?" Gideon asked as he put away his tools.

"No, Iva told me the name means the one who was prayed for." She ran her hand over her dress that stretched across her belly. "And that fits this one."

"What if it's one of each?" Gideon winked at Braelynn who dimpled in delight. "They say multiples run in families."

"Who knows?" She smiled. She started to add more, but the sound of a car door closing in the yard halted her.

Braelynn ran to the window and waved to her great-grandparents before yelling, "They're here!" She ran out.

Gideon put his arms around Rosie as they walked out of the room so they could greet the Nesbitts together. In the past three months, all of them had become closer as the Nesbitts were invited to be a part of Rosie's family and Gideon's.

He pretended he couldn't reach around her, making Braelynn giggle. "Are you sure-sure you're not having twins?"

"I'm sure-sure… I think."

As the most beloved people in her world laughed along with her, she knew Iva had been right when she said, "All I can tell you is no matter where we travel, God brings us back to where we're meant to be."

As she welcomed her soon-to-be-husband's lips on hers, Rosie knew she was right where she wanted to be.

Forever.

★ ★ ★ ★ ★

If you liked this story from Jo Ann Brown, check out her previous books in the Secrets of Bliss Valley series:

A Wish for Home
A Promise of Forgiveness
A Search for Redemption

Available from Love Inspired!
Find more great reads at
www.LoveInspired.com.

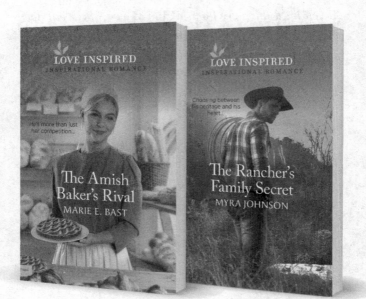